THE WOLF
OF OLD TOWN

HENRY T LARSEN

Cover design: Luke Harris, WorkingType Studio
Typesetting: WorkingType Studio
Editing by: Manuscript Assessment Agency and Susan Lawson

Website: www.writecreativepress.com
Facebook page: facebook.com/Henrytlarsen1
Instagram: @henry.t.larsen

CONTENTS

Contents

The breezes at dawn have secrets to tell you
Don't go back to sleep!
You must ask for what you really want.
Don't go back to sleep!
People are going back and forth
across the doorsill where the two worlds touch.
The door is round and open
Don't go back to sleep!

Jalāl ad-Dīn Muhammad Rūmī

PART 1

INGRID

CHAPTER ONE

INGRID
NOVEMBER 1987

'You're not to go to any of the servos in town. Do you hear? They mark up. You're to fill up at the Caltex on the highway near Sea Drive Road. They're selling for thirty-six cents a litre this week.'

'Righty-ho!'

'But don't buy any of the groceries from there. After you fill up, I want you to come back into town and buy from the Coles opposite the station. I've written down the specials.'

'Righty-ho.'

'What is it with this *righty-ho,* Haywood? Are you one of Snow White's dwarves?'

'No Mr Symes. It's an expression.'

'Well stop saying it. You sound like an idiot.'

'Righty ... I mean, yes Mr Symes.'

'You're only to buy home brands. Nothing fancy. I don't want you sending me to the poor house.'

'Yeah, I understand. You want your shopping done as normal,' said Doug Haywood, putting on his high-vis jacket and turning to leave.

'You drive to the service station and the supermarket and nowhere else! Do you hear?' demanded Arthur Symes, rising stiffly from his stool and flourishing his cane at his departing employee. 'Or there will be hell to pay.'

'Righty ... I mean, yes Mr Symes.'

'Haven't you forgotten something, Haywood?'

With his hand on the doorknob, Doug froze and inhaled sharply. He turned around slowly, dreading the smirk waiting for him.

'You forgot the money and the shopping list,' Arthur Symes said with an imperceptible upturn of his lips.

Feeling stupid, Doug held out his upturned palm. He wanted to give the old man a clip around the ears; rain down on his wizened head all manner of obscenities. Instead, he forced a crooked smile.

Arthur Symes, with a quivering hand and a fretful eye, doled out the money. Six tens, six one-dollar notes, followed by three twenty-cents pieces, a five-cent piece, followed by two one-cent pieces. Placing each banknote and coin into the sweaty palm of his hulk of an employee made Arthur Symes feel sick, as if he had torn off his own fingers.

'That should cover the fuel and all items on the grocery list, but I want change this time!' Arthur said, flourishing his cane. 'Or I will take it out of your pay. Only home brands, do you hear?' he shouted at the slamming kitchen door.

Doug made his way down the weed-strewn path and rolled up the garage door. He gently tugged away the covers, and for several minutes stood ogling his employer's cherry-red 1969 Holden HT Monaro.

Doug put up with a lot from his employer: being talked to like a stupid schoolboy, the humiliation of doing his weekly shopping, and vacuuming his rooms. But he realised he would crawl across broken glass so long as the old man gave him these few hours on a Thursday to drive one of the first Australian muscle cars built: a piece of motoring history. Looking at it gave him an erection.

Doug slid into the driver's seat, the groan of upholstery against his frame was like the sounds of satisfying sex. He put the key into the ignition, and opening the choke a little, started it up. His body shivered as the V8 5.7 litre engine throbbed into life beneath him.

Some Thursdays, Doug let it idle in the garage for ten minutes, just so he could close his eyes and meditate on the smell of its leathery upholstery, rub his fingers across the dashboard, feel the engine pulsating beneath his body, and imagine he owned the car.

After letting it idle for a time, he inched it slowly out the garage, along the crunching gravel driveway, before easing it slowly onto the road, careful not to let the bumper bar scrape the asphalt.

He turned right and had gone only twenty metres when a flash of yellow on the road revealed Toby Zachariah coming out of Symes on his yellow bike and pedalling home.

Doug gripped the wheel tighter, and coming close behind him, revved the engine and beeped the horn three times. Toby jumped in his saddle, and losing control ploughed into a parked car before falling onto the nature strip.

Doug braked and leaned over to the passenger seat window. 'You need training wheels for your bike, Toby.'

Toby said nothing. He rose from the grass and checked his bike before dusting down his jeans and white T-shirt with a print of a caterpillar cocoon.

What a stupid T-shirt, thought Doug.

'I want you in nice and early Toby,' said Doug. 'The old man has an important shipment coming from Sydney and I want you to help clean up the back room before its arrival.'

Toby didn't answer or look him in the eye. Doug inhaled sharply and frowned. Of all his crew, Toby annoyed Doug the most. Especially since Toby returned from extended sick leave. The new Toby, calmly examining his bike, left Doug irrational with anger. He respected the old Toby, who was willing to stick up for himself, even give a little lip. This new Toby out of the hospital, he wanted to punch to the ground, shake him by the collar and tell him to *grow a pair.*

Toby mounted his bike.

Doug revved the engine and Toby jumped off his bike again. Doug roared with laughter and drove away.

As he descended Symes Street to the turn off into town, the crest of the waves from the Pacific Ocean, like the heads on a million beers, came into view. Looking at all the water made him thirsty.

He reached the bottom of the hill and turned left into Old Town Road, smiling at the image of Toby sprawled on the nature strip. At the second intersection, he turned left into Pauls Road, and after passing the railway line soon joined the highway, doing one hundred. The Angels' 'Am I Ever Gonna See Your Face Again?' played on the radio. He sang the chorus, imagining he spat it at Toby, at the old man, at half the people in Old Town.

He filled up at the specified Caltex. One week he had driven all the way to the Shell servo in Whalers Point, the next town fifty kilometres down the coast. The old man had docked three dollars from his next pay. Two dollars fifty for fuel and fifty cents for wear and tear. He didn't dare do that again. The old man always checked the speedometer on his return.

He drove slowly back into town, conscious to enjoy every bump in the suspension, every subtle adjustment he made on the steering wheel, the massaging feel of the engine throbbing through his feet and up his torso, the smell of leather upholstery filling his nostrils.

In town, he slowed to forty kilometres. Outside the Railway Hotel, he cocked his right arm on the open window and revved the engine three times, hoping one of the boys from the footy club would see him from a window seat. He drove into the Coles carpark, pulling off the perfect parallel park. *If only it could be an Olympic sport*, he thought, *I would be an undisputed gold medallist.*

Pulling a black cap low over his face, he did the old man's shopping, quickly and without thought. All tasteless home brands. He managed to sneak the ice cream and the tinned soup past the check-out chick. He would use the saved money to buy two schooners.

Throwing the groceries in the boot, Doug headed to the Railway Hotel. He made it as close as the door when he heard his name called from across the street.

'I thought I saw you drive into town,' shouted Alan Marshall, the station master, as he ran across the street. 'Arthur's niece has arrived from Sydney and is looking for directions to his house. Can you give her a lift?'

Doug vaguely recalled the old man mentioning the arrival of a relative, though he thought it would not be for another month. He had only remembered because the old man made him vacuum the spare bedroom and fix up the blinds.

Doug sighed. He looked at the door of the Railway Hotel and all the bragging he would do. He looked at Alan and thought of the consequences if he failed to drive *the niece* to the house. She would have to catch a taxi. The old man would no doubt dock the fare from his pay.

'I'll get the car,' he growled, dismissing Alan Marshall with a wave of the hand.

He expected to find a mean-tempered woman, like the old man, waiting for him as he drove into the pick-up zone. Yet no one greeted him.

He waited a few minutes before jumping out of the car, cursing the Syme name under his breath as he stomped into the station waiting room.

A few paces inside, Doug came to an abrupt halt.

Instead of the hag of his mind's eye, a young woman with coffee-coloured eyes and long dark hair greeted him with a radiant smile. *Nothing like a Syme at all*, he thought.

He stared at her open-mouthed for some time until she looked down at the bags, which bulged with odd hard shapes.

'Oh yeah, right,' he said. 'Hi! I'm Doug Haywood.'

'Ingrid Symes,' she said.

Thank God the suitcases have wheels, he thought. *They weigh a tonne!*

He managed, after several goes, to stuff both bags into the boot with a heave, crushing one or two shopping bags in the process. It didn't matter about the groceries. He had crushed several bags before. The old man never cared. Doug would tell him he had selected his crushed items from the no-frills remainder bin. *That would make the old boy happy, thinking he received something on the cheap.*

Doug felt confused as he drove through the town towards Symes multipurpose store with this beautiful woman in the passenger seat. He felt as if he mixed his two favourite things–top-shelf bourbon and ice cream. Apart they made sense. Together they created sensory confusion. He wanted to enjoy the weekly ritual of the car. The knowledge he drove an Australian classic. That others in the town would be watching him in the driver's seat. That he was important enough to drive Arthur Syme's car, the richest man in town. One of the richest in regional New South Wales. But the waft of her perfume, the thought she sat only centimetres from him, ruined this simple pleasure.

'Nice car,' she said, surveying Doug from the corner of her eye. 'Is it yours?'

Doug puffed out his chest. If any other girl sat in the car, he would say yes. But this was the boss's niece, so she would soon find out.

'It's your uncle's,' he said. The dashboard hummed. 'However, I'm the only one he lets drive it.'

'You work for my uncle?'

'Yeah, I'm his right-hand man. Number two.'

It wasn't true, but wasn't wrong either.

'I see,' Ingrid said, not believing him. From his scuffed steel-cap boots, his stained khaki pants, his unironed white shirt with Symes logo, his high-vis jacket, and the scent of Old Spice aftershave mixed with petrol fumes, she guessed him to be no higher than the foreman. Given certain privileges for his services no doubt, but nothing more than a tool, a dogsbody, kept on hand to run errands.

Ingrid turned from him and gazed out the window at the run-down stores, the poorly dressed people coming in and out of shops: men in shorts or tracksuit pants, the women in cheap skirts and tops, some pushing prams, a couple of brats in tow. She wondered if she had made the right choice leaving Sydney and coming here.

A flash of yellow came into view on the road ahead. Doug saw Toby and the impulse to make him fall off his bike again flared, but he remembered this beautiful girl next to him, so put the urge from his mind.

Ingrid meanwhile, noticed they passed a rather good-looking, blond-headed boy on a yellow bike. She watched him from the side-vision mirror until he pulled out in front of the library, and she too put him from her mind.

They entered an industrial zone, the square-metre value of land diminishing with each revolution of the wheel.

'My uncle lives out of town?' she asked, trying to keep the rising dread from her voice.

'He lives next to the shop.'

'The shop?' Ingrid repeated, her heart sinking at the word, *shop*. It sounded so small, so cheap. She imagined living in a dank, polluted street with graffiti-strewn walls, and rusted and decrepit factories, surrounded by wire fences and weed-infested demolished blocks. Symes would be some poky little shop among these, selling trinkets for the vast machinery of commerce. She would rather leave than be reduced to living like that. This would not be her. Greatness beckoned, not the toil of a shopkeeper.

Maybe I could ask this foreman to drive me back to the station? Then she remembered her bank balance, crossed her arms and sighed.

They left Old Town Road with its car yards selling utes, four-wheel drives and tractors, and ascended a steep hill. In the rear-vision mirror she saw the Pacific Ocean sparkling, as if encrusted with a million eighteen-carat diamonds.

The neon Symes sign came into view first, then the building. Ingrid's eyes widened. It wasn't a little hardware shop at all, but a large multipurpose store. She tried to calculate its dimension: three thousand, four, possibly five thousand metres; *the land value over two million for sure*, she thought. *If he owned the land, it would mean my uncle was rich!*

They passed the carpark and the car slowed. Doug reversed into the driveway. It gave him a chance to put his hand on the back of her seat and show off his driving skills.

All Ingrid's fears vanished. From the rear-vision mirror she gazed on a beautiful two-storey house with a lush green lawn and a pebbled path ambling past rose bushes to a rustic porch. Even from an initial look, she knew it stood on a quarter-acre block.

Doug parked in the garage, unsure what to do next. The old man hated him coming in through the front door and messing up the front rooms. However today, he brought his niece, and he was reluctant to come via the back door like a no one. Besides, he did not want her to see him unload and put away the shopping like a some lackey.

He decided to risk the old man's wrath and take her through the front door, and while uncle and niece exchange pleasantries, he would sneak back to the car and quickly take the shopping bags via the back door and deposit them on the kitchen bench as if they had been there all along.

He took out her bags and led her up the crunching pebbled path to the front door. Ingrid admired the neatly cut lawn, inhaled the scent of the red roses, and noted the machine gun rat-tat-tat of the sprinkler as Doug opened the front door with a rattle of keys.

'Mr Symes,' Doug called out into the gloom of the hallway. 'Mr Symes, I have someone here for you.'

Ingrid followed Doug through a hallway and into a large room. After the brilliance of the late afternoon sunshine, it took time for her eyes to adjust to the darkness of the room.

A long, imposing oak dining table set for twelve solidified in the dim light. On the other side of the room lay a full-sized pool table set for a game. A bar stocked with spirits and sporting memorabilia sat along one wall, and next to this a large chess board was ready for the opening move, with two armchairs either side waiting for opposing players.

An enormous room, thought Ingrid, as she took in the leather sofas and numerous armchairs facing each other. She noticed a dividing wall pushed back and realised she looked at not one room, but two. It reminded Ingrid of the lobby of the four-star hotel where she worked in Sydney before travelling through Europe — spacious and clean. Before she could think of another word to describe the room, she saw a figure hunched over a walking stick silhouetted against the wall at the far end.

The moment of truth had arrived. She took a deep breath and readied herself.

'You're several months early,' Arthur Symes said. 'I expected you in January.'

'A change of plans, Uncle. I ran low on cash and returned early.'

In the hallway, the cuckoo clock announced 5pm.

'I did leave a message by phone several weeks back,' she added. 'A man took the message and said he would pass it onto you.'

Both Ingrid and Arthur glared at Doug struggling with Ingrid's bags on the stairs.

'I suppose I can do with more labour for the Christmas rush,' Arthur said, looking her up and down and trying to reconcile this tall, bosomy woman pulsating with youth and beauty, with the sickly one-year-old creature he remembered twenty years ago. *Had the feud over my father's estate been that long?* he thought. It was twenty years since he had last spoken to his fraternal twin brother Marcus and his sister-in-law Debbie. They had moved to Sydney, while he remained in Old Town to continue their father's legacy.

Ingrid saw his reticence and growing cynicism, and decided to take the initiative.

'Uncle Arthur, I would like to thank you for inviting me into your home. After the death of both my parents, I've had no family to turn to. You're so generous taking me in. I know there has been a great gulf between our families. It was my mother's greatest wish to reconcile the two brothers. It may surprise you to know, as he grew older, my father realised he had made a great error, and only pride prevented him from reaching out. Before he died, he confided in me that it was he who was in the wrong. I believe it killed him in the end... the knowledge he'd wronged you and couldn't bring himself to acknowledge it.'

Ingrid's eyes filled with tears. 'Let me say now, as his only child Uncle Arthur, my father's sorry.'

Arthur's eyes moistened, his throat clogged. *Of course, I was right to keep Marcus out of the business*, he thought. *I was the brains. Not stupid, timid Marcus. If I had listened to him, Symes would still be a small general store in town. Besides, what had Marcus ever done with his life? Become a lowly accountant for an obscure manufacturing firm in Sydney. No doubt living the high life off the dividends I sent him annually.*

'I accept your apology on his behalf,' he said, unable to hold back the tears any longer. He embraced his niece. She was warm and soft; her perfume reminded him of Debbie.

He knew he would lose all control and turn into a blubbery mess if he kept this up. Luckily, he caught sight of muddy footprints on the carpet below.

'Doug!' he cried out, pointing at the offending stain.

Doug, so amazed to see tears in his boss's eyes, a sight he had never seen in the fourteen years at Symes, had forgotten his plan to move the shopping quickly and surreptitiously into the kitchen. Instead, stunned, he had stopped in the doorway, observing this touching scene. He even felt himself softening towards his employer. That is, until he heard his name hissed.

'Clean this up now, Doug! How many times have I told you not to come in through the front door and the entertainment rooms with your filthy shoes?'

Doug blushed as Arthur screamed, 'Get the vacuum cleaner now, or I'll dock you for the steam cleaning.'

Doug's frustration and pent-up rage at his employer returned. *The humiliation of vacuuming in front of this beautiful girl!* How he wanted to knock his employer to the ground. Stand over him and tell him he wouldn't put up with his crap anymore. But Doug went to the cupboard and took out the vacuum cleaner, cursing his employer under his breath.

Arthur turned to face his niece, who was settling into a leather armchair. He shooed at her as if she was a dirty pigeon resting on his favourite statue. She jumped up in fright as her uncle poked her with his cane, his voice booming, 'Out! Out! This isn't Friday. Out of this room!'

Arthur corralled her through a door with a few pokes of his cane into a kitchen as the vacuum wheezed into life.

The kitchen was dingy with a lived-in feel. A battered TV sat on top of a small dented fridge. Opposite this sat a small rickety table with the remnants of a half-eaten pie. Along one wall hummed an industrial fridge and freezer with a big chain and lock wound round its handles. Tattered and stained grey curtains fell limply in front of cobweb-coated windows. They looked as if they had not been cleaned in ten years. Ingrid winced at a strange odour hanging in the air.

'Sit, sit,' commanded her uncle.

Ingrid sat gingerly on a banged-up sofa next to the table. It squeaked, and she readjusted her posture due to a hard lump. Arthur took a stool, and moving it close, sat next to her.

'Now let me tell you the rules of the house,' he said. 'Firstly, you're not to enter the main rooms outside of Friday and Saturday nights. They're for entertaining and I'm not paying for additional cleaning. On that point, you're to clean up after yourself. Dinner is at six sharp. You're not to bring friends home or play loud music. This is a quiet house. You start work at 8am and finish at 4pm Monday to Friday. I will be setting your pay. You will be on three months' probation and you're not to keep any pets.'

'That's a long list,' smiled Ingrid, half bemused, half alarmed. 'Is there any rule around breathing?'

To Ingrid's dismay, her uncle scratched his chin and looked absently past her, as if considering what rules to establish around this most basic human function.

Luckily, a chastised Doug entered the kitchen back door, lumbering under the weight of his employer's weekly shopping.

'Did I get change this time?' asked Arthur, rising to his feet and rounding on his employee.

'Four dollars and twenty cents,' said Doug, slamming the money on the table.

Snatching the money, Arthur counted it greedily before committing it to his pocket. He limped over to the bench, picked up the shopping docket and rummaged through the plastic bags.

'This ice cream and tinned soup ... I don't see it on the list.'

'Take it up with the cashier,' said Doug.

'I will. I will!'

Ingrid rose and examined the shopping. 'Not a single piece of fruit or vegetable in any of the bags. All tinned foods and frozen meals with the cheapest and nastiest cuts of meat.'

'I want to know why these biscuits are crushed,' Arthur said, holding a packet of home-brand teddy bear biscuits.

'The shop assistant picked it from the remainder bin at a better price.'

'The shop assistant?'

Doug wanted it to sound like it was the shop assistant who saw to the old man's groceries, not himself. He just happened to pick them up from the supermarket.

The old man checked the docket against the supermarket specials page in the local paper.

Fuck, I'm done, thought Doug.

Luckily, the excitement of the weekly groceries and his niece's arrival proved too much for the old man. He put down the docket and placed his hands on the table to steady himself and take several deep breaths.

He looked up at his niece then Doug irritably.

'Show my niece to her room, then you can come down here and put this lot away.'

A red-faced Doug led Ingrid up a smelly and creaky back staircase to the second floor.

'Well, this is your room,' said Doug, opening a door.

Doug lingered for some time until Ingrid smiled, and he realised he should leave.

Once alone, Ingrid locked the door and sat on her rickety, lumpy bed. She took one deep breath after another trying to control her galloping heart.

After settling her nerves, Ingrid contemplated her new surroundings miserably. Her bedroom was a disaster. Apart from a hideous print of a laughing clown, the walls were bare and yellowing. The writing table and chair before her looked as if it had been sourced from the cheapest and meanest disposal store in town. She began to weep at the sight of the plastic sunflower on her bedside table, her uncle's idea of a decorative touch. *What have I gotten myself into? What have I gotten myself into?*

She cried for a few minutes more. She wanted to grab her bags and head back to Sydney. Yet again, the thought of her bank balance tempered any impulse of flight. She took several deep breaths and dried her eyes. Rising to her feet, she walked over to the window and, peeling aside the tattered drapes, gazed through the cobwebs to the monolithic Symes store across the wire fence.

She closed her eyes and visualised her uncle's wealth, like water from a burst fire hydrant pouring into her bank account. She sat rigid, mentally holding this image in her mind.

After five minutes of affirming her intention, she opened her eyes and, leaning against the window, looked at the Symes store ... *money in the land, the building and the stock. Why was a rich man like Arthur Symes living liking a pauper in this beautiful old house?*

She would make it her job to find out.

Chapter Two

Symes Multipurpose Store

'Okay you lot. We have a new starter at Symes. Her name's Ingrid, and she's Mr Symes' niece,' said Doug, prowling before the assembled employees like a caged and hungry lion eyeing a dazzle of zebras.

It was Friday afternoon. The store was closed, and Arthur Symes was about to pay the staff. They were all there, even those rostered off, waiting patiently in the main office for their money.

'I want her treated well,' Doug said after a pause, watching his boys at the back of the room. He gave a cursory glance at the girls, but remembered bitterly that he had no jurisdiction over them.

Pat said I made them feel uncomfortable. I'm too touchy-feely.

He had told Pat, 'So what if I put my arms around several of the girls and called them *darl*. All I am doing is trying to be friendly.'

This bitter memory flared, and as compensation, he wagged his finger at his boys.

'I want you all to be on your best behaviour!'

Doug eyed Toby sneaking in late through the office door and moving to the back of the assembled staff.

'We have a new person at Symes,' he shouted, pointing exclusively at Toby. 'Her name is Ingrid, and she's the boss's niece.' Toby turned white, his mouth falling open.

Ingrid blushed. She wanted Doug to shut up. The newly arrived boy stared at her, and Doug's shouting made him pale and frightened.

The others in the room also wanted Doug to shut up. They wanted to sample the food laid out behind him before Mr Symes called their pay. Usually Pat, Mr Symes' personal assistant and notional 2ic, made all the important announcements on Fridays. She would have been brief and polite, but with her laid-up in hospital, the duty fell to Doug. He made happy announcements sound ominous. In his voice, news of a staff engagement reverberated as a divorce, every birthday notice, a death sentence, every announcement of a new starter, the beginnings of mass sackings.

'We're a good crew here at Symes,' Doug said.

At the back of the room, Toby tottered on his feet.

'Are you okay Toby?' one of the ladies asked. Toby clutched at two people for support before straightening.

'I'm fine. I'm fine,' he said, looking up at Ingrid, who noted his look of surprise, even alarm. She made a step towards him, but he turned and scampered from the office.

Startled by the young man's reaction, and struggling to remember if she had seen him before, Ingrid failed to notice that Doug had stopped speaking and the room waited silently for her to speak.

'I'm so glad to be here. I hope to get to know all of you over the next few weeks ...'

She noticed that no one in the room looked at her, their gaze extending towards the strong room, the door of which opened as she started speaking. Her uncle's voice thundered out: 'Anderson E!'

Edna Anderson, the cashier, shuffled in to receive her pay.

* * *

Arthur Symes considered Friday afternoon the best and the worst part of his week. After lunch, he locked himself in the strong room, and for a few hours he could enjoy his wealth undisturbed before the wages and expenses took some of his babies away. He loved to look and touch his notes and coins, the physical manifestation of his wealth. He loved how the twenty-cent pieces glistened in the light. He loved to drink in the coppery one-cent pieces; loved to count and sometimes recount the takings for the week from several of his businesses across town. He loved how the armed guards brought his children to him, and how he hated sending them away. He loved the scrunching sound the notes made as he counted them, their smooth feel caressing his palm. Occasionally, he put a one-cent piece in his mouth and enjoyed its tangy taste. Some Fridays, he closed his eyes and inhaled the smell of his money. Often, he kept some of his children back. He could not send them all away to some impersonal institution. The shelves bulged with money.

After the counting came the pays, his heart aching as he put each note into the yellow payslips. He liked to eye each staff member as he handed over the money. It grieved him to think of his money wasted at the pubs and on the pokies; and on other frivolous pastimes, such as fishing or fashion. He believed money, like people, should be productively employed in investments, and begetting other money.

'Spend it wisely,' he would say. Occasionally, he tempted them. 'Why don't you leave some here and I will invest it for you?'

None took his offer. Most of his workers, he sighed, were a lazy, unimaginative lot, content with their petty lives of drinking beer, gambling, cricket, football, and gossip.

Ingrid watched each employee troop through the strong room door to emerge several seconds later counting their money. The administration room gradually diminished in number until she remained the only person in the room.

She didn't expect 'Symes I' to be called out after only one day. 'Saunders J' was followed by 'Zachariah T'. She looked about the empty room. No one. Her uncle called again: 'Zachariah T'.

Through the office door, the boy who had turned pale and fainted, appeared. He gave Ingrid a quick, worried glance before walking into the strong room. She recalled where she had seen him before: the good-looking, blond-headed boy on the yellow bike, the day she arrived in Old Town.

Arthur buried his head in his hands and rubbed his eyes. He had the last pay to give away. His money leaving always drained him. He looked up and jumped in his seat.

'Toby,' he said, clutching his chest, 'you should put bells on your shoes.'

Toby said nothing.

Arthur prided himself in understanding his people, knowing their interests, their loves, and most of all their weaknesses. That's what made him so successful. How he made his money.

If you know what buttons to press you could control a person. But not Toby. An odd fish, Arthur thought. *So quiet, so self-contained. So out of place in my business.* He didn't know what Toby did outside of work. He knew the others did not like him. But he didn't care. Toby did his work and didn't complain, and that was all Arthur cared about.

'Here's your money, spend it wisely,' Arthur said. Toby took his pay but lingered in the room. Arthur dropped his head but sensed him still standing there.

'Why are you staring at me?' Arthur demanded, banging the table with his open palm.

'Mr Symes,' Toby began in a shaky voice.

Silence followed.

'What is it boy? You look nervous. Spit it out.'

'You need to be careful.'

'What do you mean?'

'It's happening'

'What's happening?'

'You need to keep your money safe. Put it all in the bank.'

'What are you talking about?'

'I've seen things.'

'What things? Stop taking in riddles.'

'I ... I ...'

'Get to the point,' snapped Arthur Symes, looking at his watch. 'I have a dinner party to organise.'

Toby trembled and gulped.

'Uncle,' Ingrid appeared at the door, 'Mrs Sárosy rang from the house. She said she will be cooking goulash tonight and not the roast.'

'I gave strict instructions for a lamb roast,' Arthur said, slapping the table again. He made a mental note, as he did every second week, to sack his weekend cook.

'Enjoy your dinner party, Mr Symes,' Toby said, and he marched out of the room. Ingrid tried to engage Toby with a smile, but Toby cast his eyes down and fled the office.

'That's one strange boy,' Arthur said, shrugging his shoulders. Ingrid thought him strange too, and interesting. There was something about him. Something she couldn't put her finger on.

CHAPTER THREE

THE DINNER PARTY

'It must have been a shock having your mother pass on so soon after your father,' said Doris Hannell, the mayor's wife.

'It was a terrible time for me,' Ingrid said. 'After Mum's funeral I felt so lost. I headed to Europe for a year.' Ingrid wiped a stray tear from her eye.

'Where did you go in Europe, dear?' asked Lara Ludlow, the wife of the state member for Oldham, changing the subject, as she didn't want to pry too early in her relationship with the niece of such an important man.

'Oh, the usual places. Paris, Rome, Amsterdam, Zurich.'

Ingrid was glad of the change of topic. Trying to be sad and teary blurred her peripheral vision, making it difficult to keep her eyes on her uncle at the bar.

The dividing wall was spread most of the way across the middle of the room, except for a small opening. On the other side of the dividing wall, the men played billiards and drank, while their women remained at the dinner table to sip coffee, eat dessert, and interrogate the newest member of their social circle.

'I stayed mainly in youth hostels, moving from city to city,' continued Ingrid, dividing her attention between the women at the table and furtive glances at her uncle, visible from where she sat.

She had noticed how over the course of the last ten minutes, each of the men, one at a time, left the game to sit at the bar. Her uncle fixed them a drink and passed it to them on a long, fat yellow envelope.

She had noticed this odd phenomenon while answering the ladies' questions.

'Talking of Europe, did anyone see that terrible news story?' asked Mrs. O'Shea, the wife of the Trades Hall leader in Old Town.

'Yes,' said Janine Tabberat, the leading realtor in Old Town, 'of the body of the girl they found at the bottom of a ravine in Austria. They believe she slipped and fell while out hiking and remained buried under five metres of snow all winter, only finding her body after the snows melted away.'

'And no one knew she was missing,' said Doris.

'I'm so thankful I have my uncle. For if I slipped and fell when overseas no one would know I was missing too,' Ingrid said, dabbing at her eyes with a napkin.

'Excuse me,' she said, rising to her feet. 'I need to freshen up.'

'Of course, dear,' the women murmured in unison as Ingrid with her eyes downcast marched from the room.

Out in the hallway, she smoked a cigarette and waited a discreet few minutes before surreptitiously tiptoeing back to sit on the men's side of the room. She placed herself in the armchair in the shadows close to the bar and eyed her uncle with the young detective. She strained to listen into their whispered conversation.

'Thanks for your effort in the …' she heard, before the rest of the sentence was swallowed by the breaking of snooker balls. 'Here's a little something for your efforts.'

She watched as her uncle passed across a glass of scotch on top of a thick yellow DL envelope. The young detective placed the envelope in the breast pocket of his coat before taking a sip of his scotch and smacking the glass back down on the bar. He used the bar room mirror to smooth his hair, catching sight of Ingrid watching him. Smiling, he swivelled on the barstool and, noticing her all alone, came and plonked himself down in the armchair opposite.

'Your uncle is a generous man and a good host.' He smiled again, showing his bleached white teeth.

'Yes, I agree,' Ingrid said, spying the yellow envelope in his breast pocket as his suit coat flapped open.

'He also has a beautiful niece. It will make coming to Friday night dinners even more appealing.'

He reeked of aftershave and stale alcohol. At dinner, she had the misfortune of sitting next to him and found his manner conceited and his conversation full of bravado. Occasionally, she had to move her chair a little way from him to avoid his foot, which often strayed to touch hers. Ingrid shared a raised eyebrow with Janine Tabberat across the table.

'Where is your wife this evening?' Ingrid asked, glancing at the gold wedding band on his finger.

'Mrs C is at home with the kids. Besides,' he said, leaning forward, 'we have an arrangement.'

Arthur Symes came up behind the detective and placed a hand on his shoulder.

'You see this man here, Ingrid? He's the future police commissioner of New South Wales. No criminal can rest easy when this man is around.'

Rob puffed out his chest.

With pool cue in hand, Paddy O'Shea, leader of the Old Town Trades Hall Council, overheard the boast. 'Yes, but at what cost?'

'At what cost?' spat Rob. 'I get the scumbags off the streets. The ones selling drugs to your kids. The ones that are breaking into your houses when you're on holidays. The little pricks stealing your flashy new cars.'

'But your methods ...' began John Smith, District Court judge and Janine Tabberat's partner.

'I arrest them and put them before your court. Why don't you do the right thing and put them away where they belong?'

The men had stopped playing snooker and wandered over to the conversation. With the partition now pushed back by Arthur, the women were hushed as they listened too.

'If you followed the correct procedures they would be convicted. If I convict them, a higher court will overturn the decision.'

Rob shot to his feet. 'Dimitri is a drug-dealing, lowlife scum who would be behind bars and not selling to kids, if it wasn't for the judiciary.'

'Now, now gentlemen, remember we have Chatham House rules in this house.' Arthur stepped between the men like a referee at a boxing match, not wanting his carefully cultivated Friday nights to descend into violence, which he hated, and shrank from.

'Rob here only wants to keep this town safe,' said Arthur. Turning to John, he added. 'I also understand we must follow rules.'

Ingrid smiled at this inference to the rules.

'Why so sore on criminals, Detective Sergeant?' asked the mayor, sipping his glass of Grange Hermitage. It was why he loved coming to Arthur's house each week. Arthur always laid on the best wines for him to sample.

'It's drug dealers Rob doesn't like,' explained Arthur.

'When your parents receive a call in the middle of the night to tell you your fifteen-year-old kid brother has overdosed in a park, it puts what they do into perspective,' said Rob. 'I joined the force so I could ensure what happened to my family would not happen to another. But I sometimes wonder what the point is when I see blokes like Dimitri walk free.'

Rob stopped speaking and downed the rest of his scotch in one gulp.

The cuckoo clock pronounced the hour.

'That is a lovely broach, Deidre,' said Janine to the local federal member's wife, an obvious and deliberate change of topic.

'Thank you, Janine,' said Deidre, pawing her broach. 'I bought it in Paris last year. It's a sapphire set in an Art Deco platinum star design.'

The women eyed it closely and enviously.

'You've always had wonderful style,' said Sinead. 'A style one doesn't find in Old Town.'

'Don't get me started on the people of Old Town,' said Janine. 'Style is a foreign word for many of them.'

'I refuse to live here,' said Deidre out loud, looking at her husband with his cue stick in hand. 'After the election I have demanded that Charles relocates us to Mona Vale. I want to send my children to good schools.'

'If you will excuse me, Arthur,' said the young detective, shooting the women at the table a quick, dirty look, 'this Sydney westie better go home to his westie wife.'

Rob walked unsteadily to the door.

'Do you want me to call a taxi?' Arthur asked as the room silently watched the detective leaving.

'Booze buses aren't on around here tonight,' said Rob. 'Besides, I'm perfectly capable of driving myself the short distance home.'

After the detective left the house, Ingrid mediated on the scene she had just witnessed. She spied the women at the table leaning forward and whispering about the detective. *What had the detective done for Arthur*, she thought, *and what were in in the envelopes?*

She would make it her job to find out.

Chapter Four

Cocktails with Cheryl

'Pick me up at eleven,' Ingrid said.

'How about I join you and Cheryl for a drink?' said Doug, leaning over.

'What don't you understand about the concept of girls' night?'

Doug's forehead creased in thought, easing back to his side of his panel van and answering rather dejectedly, 'No boys.'

'Right, now pick me up from here at eleven o'clock,' snapped Ingrid, opening the passenger door.

'What? Am I supposed to wait around while you're having a good time?'

'Yes,' Ingrid said, 'and your reward will be driving a tipsy girl home.'

Doug looked puzzled. Then, as if his mind finally digested her meaning, a smile broke across his face. A drunk girl in his car. *Sweet*, he thought.

Ingrid slammed the door of Doug's panel van and entered the Lagoon cocktail lounge. It was her second Thursday night in Old Town, and she had her lift sorted back home. She would deal with a randy Doug later. For now, she needed to learn more about Symes and the mystery of the envelopes.

She was meeting Cheryl, the main administration officer at Symes, and the notional assistant to her uncle. Cheryl was a stumpy girl who knew everyone's business and was the font of all gossip at Symes. Ingrid sensed her usefulness and set out to befriend her.

During their working days together, Ingrid paid Cheryl many compliments, feeding her little bits of knowledge about herself she knew would be passed around the office. In the tearoom, Cheryl told her brief stories, including the love lives of all the people working at Symes.

Ingrid hoped that over several drinks, and without the constraint of whispering in the kitchen, Cheryl would open-up about Arthur Symes' business dealings. Her uncle was proving unforthcoming on the subject.

Ingrid insisted on buying the first round. She ordered a virgin daiquiri for herself, and with a wink at the barman, ordered Cheryl a tequila sunrise with a double shot of tequila.

The barman, a tall, bony boy called Brad, shouted her the first round. Ingrid passed him Cheryl's phone number as his reward.

Cheryl took a sip of her tequila sunrise and winced.

'Wow, that's strong. Anyway, Jason the new handyman, came to the office again. I saw him staring at me.'

Ingrid smiled and mouthed surprise. Cheryl believed every man who entered the office fell in love with her instantly, and the entire male population of Symes secretly adored her, and would, if given the chance, throw off their wives and girlfriends to marry her.

'Wasn't he working on the lock for the strong room?' Ingrid asked. This wasn't true, but Ingrid wanted to angle the conversation to her uncle and his wealth.

'Oh no, he would never work on the strong room lock. Your uncle hires a special locksmith for that.'

'How much does he keep there?' Ingrid asked casually.

'Half-a-million dollars at any one time.'

'Half-a-million!' gasped Ingrid.

'Yes,' said Cheryl.

Ingrid shook her head. 'That's far too much to store on the premises.'

'It's true,' insisted Cheryl, 'I've seen the dockets.'

'But why keep it in there? Why not a bank?'

'Your uncle's a miser who likes to keep money about him.'

'Isn't he scared someone will steal it?'

'Steal it? Oh, that's funny.' Cheryl broke into giggles.

Ingrid forced herself to laugh too, before saying, 'Why so funny?'

Cheryl slurped the last of her drink before leaning forward and whispering, 'You will soon find out.'

Cheryl hesitated and looked at the empty tables on either side of them before leaning closer and whispering, 'Your uncle controls the town.'

'Controls the town? What do you mean?'

'He pays off the council and the police. Who would dare steal from him?' laughed Cheryl.

'He pays bribes?'

'Yes,' said Cheryl. 'There are stories ... how as soon as your uncle buys property, the land is rezoned, or they find coal beneath it. Also, whenever a competitor sets up in town, the poor guy's building burns to the ground or the unions refuse to work there. It's an open secret in Old Town.'

'He has built a little empire,' Ingrid said, more to herself than Cheryl.

'Symes is only the tip of his wealth,' continued Cheryl. 'He has other interests in town providing the bulk of his money. He owns several construction companies doing work around town. His firms always win council business. He owns several big retail stores in town and has an extensive real estate portfolio worth millions. I don't know why he bothers with the shop these days.'

Cheryl slurped her cocktail, frowning into the now-empty glass.

Ingrid wanted to keep Cheryl talking about her uncle, but Cheryl's conversation, like her drink, had dried up.

Ingrid jumped to her feet, took ten dollars from Cheryl, and purchased another double shot of tequila sunrise while she asked for water to be put in her cocktail glass. She winked at Brad and pocketed the ten dollars.

Cheryl took two long sips of her second tequila sunrise and gossiped about all the people working at Symes.

'You better be careful around Doug,' said Cheryl, changing the subject. 'He has wandering hands.'

Cheryl went on to discuss Tiny, the big Samoan storeman, and his knee problems stopping him from his football career; Tom's alcoholism; and one or two gossipy stories about the girls. There was nothing in these stories Ingrid did not already know. As for the girls, their petty issues were of no interest or relevance to Ingrid. She wanted to know more about the bribes and the money.

Ingrid gave up listening to Cheryl after her third cocktail. Cheryl slurred incoherently on the topic of her imaginary love life, no matter how much Ingrid tried leading her back to her uncle and his business interests.

After another half an hour, Ingrid couldn't take Cheryl's incessant chatter any longer, so she leant over the table and whispered, 'The barman has been making eyes at you all night. Why don't we go over and sit at the bar?'

At the bar, Ingrid winked at Brad and whispered in his ear, 'My friend is easy. If you make her smile tonight you can make her smile next week.'

With Cheryl absorbed in the barman, Ingrid used the bar phone to call Doug at the Railway Hotel.

* * *

'That was quick,' said Doug as she buckled herself in. 'Did Cheryl drink too much as usual?'

'Something like that.'

'Well, seeing the night is young, why don't I take you to the beach? There's a full moon over the water tonight.'

'If you put one hand on me, Douglas Haywood, I swear I will tell my uncle, and you won't drive his car ever again.'

Doug reddened, stiffened, and started the engine. Ingrid sensed she had gone a little far. Even though she needed space to think, she also needed Doug onside. She smiled, placed a hand on his on the gear stick, and in a low voice said, 'I'm sorry, I'm not feeling well. A headache.'

'Yeah right.'

'What I want most of all right now is for you tell me more about how you won the grand final last year for the Stingrays.'

Momentarily deflated at having his advances knocked back so savagely, Doug brightened. *Even if she wouldn't consent to driving to the beach, she at least wanted to hear about my exploits on the footy field.*

Winning the competition with the Stingrays was the best thing he had done in his twenty-nine years of existence, and he never tired of reliving it. How he went over for two tries and stopped at least three, all with a cracked rib and his right forefinger popped out.

He recounted the story, this time embellishing how far down they were at half time. As he drove, he felt her hanging on his every word.

Ingrid settled back in her seat and closed her eyes. If she nodded occasionally, Doug would continue to drone on, leaving her free to meditate on Cheryl's gossip.

So, my uncle keeps a small fortune in the strong room, she thought. As for the envelopes as coasters, they made sense to Ingrid now. Bribes. Everything made sense. *Five hundred thousand dollars in the strong room! Could my uncle be so enamoured with his money to hold so much?*

Doug was relating how he had made a surprise play out of a dummy half and only a napping marker separated him from the try line, when Ingrid opened her eyes and asked: 'How much does my uncle keep in the strong room at any one time?'

What a strange question to ask, thought Doug, just as he was about to go over for the winning try. Doug slowed the car to a crawl.

'Your uncle keeps a lot.'

'How much?' Ingrid asked.

Doug sighed. *Maybe she hadn't been listening to me at all.* In his pocket, the keys for Symes cut into his leg. It was one of his greatest boasts, that he was one of the few people at Symes granted access to the building.

'Your uncle can hold anywhere up to three hundred K at any one time.'

So, the fat blather-mouth is telling the truth, thought Ingrid. *I will need to make Thursday night, cocktail night. Though I'll need to go easy on the nips.* She smiled and closed her eyes, feeling a surge of excitement at the thought of all that money within easy reach. Ingrid opened her eyes and noted Doug's long face.

'I'm sorry,' she said, placing her hand on his shoulder and leaving it there for a time. 'You had the ball and were about to go over for the winning try. How could you do it with a finger popped out and two cracked ribs?'

Doug beamed, and straightening, he continued, 'It was pure adrenalin...'

Ingrid closed her eyes and let Doug's boasting wash over her as she thought of all that money.

CHAPTER FIVE

DOCTOR JACK HARRIS

Ingrid arrived home to find her uncle seated on a kitchen stool with a velcro blood pressure cuff attached to his arm and a well-dressed man in a suit and red bowtie standing next to him reading his pulse from the monitor.

'You need to slow down and eat better, Arthur. A man of your age should not be working so hard.'

'Prescribe me some more of those pills, Jack. I'm perfectly fine the way I live.'

'Any more chest pains like the one you had tonight, and I want you to call the ambulance.'

'I don't need hospitals,' said Arthur.

'If you keep living the way you do, you won't have any choice,' said Dr Harris, ripping the velcro cuff from Arthur's arm and packing the monitor into his case.

'Why don't you come over for dinner one Friday night?' asked Arthur, rolling down his sleeve as Dr Harris took out his prescription pad and dashed off two scripts.

'You can stay for chess. I know you like chess and I can't find anyone decent to play in this town.'

'I will come with my sister Beata.'

'Beata!' frowned Arthur. 'I thought your crazy sister lived on a commune in Byron Bay.'

'Not anymore. The commune dissolved. Trouble in paradise.'

'She can come to dinner but only if she keeps her mouth shut,' Arthur said. 'I don't want her upsetting my guest with any of her mumbo jumbo.'

'I know my sister gets on your nerves, but she's also sweet, and loyal. You would like her if you spent time with her.'

'I can't see how you can be siblings. Your sister believing in all this new age rubbish and you, Jack the rationalist.'

'It's one the mysteries of life.'

'Jack here,' said Arthur, finally addressing Ingrid, who had stood at the door the whole time, 'is an atheist. That is why he's the best doctor in Old Town. He doesn't believe in any transcendental divine being dispensing cures, only facts, facts and verified facts. Isn't that right Jack?'

'Life is bedevilled by people foisting on the gullible public untested cures. A belief in an almighty Creator has caused humanity greater harm than good,' declared Jack, peering over the rim of his glasses and addressing Ingrid in a stern voice. It was a topic that Ingrid sensed he was passionate about and had given lectures on.

'One should listen to doctors over spiritualists,' chuckled Arthur.

'Correct. And as your doctor,' began Dr Harris, addressing Arthur with a scolding tone, 'if you keep working at your rate and eating as badly as you do, you will be dead in twelve months. As your one and only friend, I implore you to change your lifestyle.'

'Your pills will do the trick,' Arthur assured him.

'Now, if you will excuse me Arthur,' said Jack, 'your niece can show me to the front door.'

The doctor handed Ingrid two scripts on the front porch. 'Your uncle is a stubborn man. I want you to take good care of him. See he eats better and ensure he takes these. One is for sleeping tablets, the other is for his high blood pressure. Ensure he takes them regularly and not too much of either.'

'Yes, Doctor Harris.'

'I don't blame you if you do walk out on him,' Jack continued. 'He isn't an easy man to live with.'

'I have found that out,' Ingrid said.

'His wife Rachel left him before she died, and he threw his only son out on the street. He was only sixteen.'

'Rather harsh thing to do.'

'Arthur thought it would toughen Richard up. Teach him a lesson. Probably what broke him in the end. Richard Symes was too much like his mother. Not one to thrive on Arthur's tough love regime.'

'Throwing your only son out on the street is harsh.'

'I suppose, but being his niece, you should already know the story of how your grandfather threw both your father and Arthur out on the street to fend for themselves when they too were only sixteen.'

'Of course. Yes, oh that story. Well, it's harsh to think he would inflict it on his own son.'

'There isn't much love in Arthur's heart, I'm afraid. So be careful he does not turn on you too.'

Doctor Harris turned to go.

'What happened to my cousin?' Ingrid asked.

'I thought you knew,' he said, stopping on the porch step and turning.

'I've been overseas many years and my parents never talked about Arthur and his family.'

Jack nodded. 'Yes, I can understand, not much love lost between either brother. Your cousin, Richard, moved all over Australia. He started a family, I hear. About three years ago he died from cancer. And if you're wondering, your uncle never went to the funeral.'

'Thank you, Doctor Harris,' Ingrid said, holding up the scripts. 'I will make sure he takes them.'

Ingrid closed the front door and, standing in the shadows of the hallway, spent a long time studying the scripts and thinking.

CHAPTER SIX

PAY DAY

Ingrid sat patiently in the empty office the next day waiting for her uncle to call from the strong room: 'Symes I'.

But after Anne Sanderson the cashier departed with her money, Arthur Symes' bass voice boomed out: 'Zachariah T'.

Arthur took off his glasses and rubbed his eyes, exhausted, wanting only to go home and rest before the dinner party. He placed his glasses back on and looking up wearily, gasped. Toby Zachariah had silently entered, and now stood before him.

'My god, you gave me a fright. Here's your money.' Arthur sighed, passing across the pay envelope. 'You will find it all there.'

Arthur dropped his head and, burying it in his hands, rubbed his eyes again. But he could sense this strange boy standing before him, looking down at him.

Toby cleared his throat.

'What is it, Toby?' asked Arthur, looking up and glaring. 'Why are you staring at me?'

"I want to warn you, Mr Symes,'

'Warn me about what? What?'

'I wanted to warn you last week about ... about ...'

'About what Toby? Why the dickens are you shaking? Just say what's on your mind. I'm tired and have a dinner party to organise.'

'Last week I warned you to put your money in the bank. I want to warn you about your niece, sir.'

'What do you mean, my *niece*?'

'Um, you see. It's difficult to explain. Um, this will sound strange.'

'Say it,' Arthur said, slapping the table and rising to his feet. 'Say it now or hold your peace.'

'You're a secretive man,' Toby said, taking a step back. 'Sometimes it's best not to confide in others all your plans.'

Toby turned and walked out the door. Arthur sank into his chair and sighed audibly.

What the dickens was that all about? thought Arthur before deciding to put it from his mind. He didn't have time to mull on it, he had a dinner party to host.

Ingrid, who listened to her uncle's raised voice, watched Toby pass from the room, but not before he gave her a worried glance. Ingrid was too angry to care.

'Where's my pay?' she snapped, jumping to her feet and marching over to Arthur as he locked the strong room door.

'You receive free board and pocket money,' said Arthur. 'What more could you want?'

'It's illegal not to pay someone.'

'And what will you do with your money? Spend it on cigarettes and trashy magazines? I'm investing your money. You will thank me in a few years.'

'You can't do that. I have rights.'

'Why don't you take it up with the unions? You can mention it tonight.' Arthur laughed. In his pocket he felt the fat envelope for Paddy.

Arthur headed for the office door. Ingrid followed, fuming.

'You cheat your own flesh and blood out of money.'

Arthur swung around on the office stairs.

'I have no family. None. It is only out of weakness I let you stay in my house. At any moment I can throw you back out onto the street.'

Arthur turned and continued descending. Ingrid glared at him.

* * *

A subdued Ingrid remained watchful throughout the evening. After dinner, she sat at the table with the ladies. Her seat gave her the best view of the bar. With one eye, she watched the choreographed ritual of the men. They congregated at the billiard table smoking and laughing, each in turn peeling from the group to sit at the bar. Arthur, stationed as barman, poured each man his favourite drink, and placing it on a yellow DL envelope, passed it across the counter. A few low whispered words followed before each man downed his drink in one scull, scooped the envelope into his pocket and returned to the snooker game.

With one eye on this social phenomenon, Ingrid kept her other eye and ears on the conversation of the women.

'Well, the Gilberts want to sell up and move to Sydney,' said Janine. 'They want me to sell their property.'

'That beautiful two-storey house on the cliffs near Lighthouse Point?' said Lara.

'It's a beautiful spot but with a sealed road two kilometres away, it's not an attractive buy,' said Janine. 'I will have a devil of time attracting a buyer.'

'If there was a road leading to it, I'm sure it would sell for a pretty penny,' said Doris. 'It looks out over the water.'

'Why do they want to sell?'

'Hetty wants to move closer the grandchildren and Bill is becoming more and more incapacitated. They want to take a trip around the world first before settling on the North Shore.'

'That is what Charles and I are doing,' whispered Deidre Gibbs, the federal member for Oldham's wife, leaning forward. The women leant forward too, creating a confidential circle. Ingrid forgot her uncle for a moment, and leaning forward, she also listened.

'Charles hasn't told the party yet, but he isn't contesting the next election. We're both heading overseas. Spend time in Paris, Rome ...'

Ingrid leant back, closed her eyes, and considered this piece of news carefully. She butted out her cigarette, and turning in her seat, eyed her uncle pouring a drink for MP Richard Gibbs, a smile breaking across her face.

* * *

Arthur Symes sighed. Everyone had gone for the night and he felt tired and hollow. He cleaned the bar with a rag, then, going over to the chess board, considered his solo game. Playing black, he deployed the queen to the middle of the board. He yawned, and too tired to continue, headed towards the kitchen. He'd only walked a few steps when Ingrid, seated in an armchair smoking, startled him.

'So that's how you do it?' She took a drag on her menthol cigarette.

'You shouldn't be in this room after the guests have left,' barked Arthur.

'You bribe all the important people in the town. Council employees, federal and state government politicians, police and union officials.'

'You shouldn't be smoking in this room. It's a filthy, disgusting habit. Put it out now!'

Ingrid took a long drag on her cigarette and blew it up towards her uncle's face. Arthur coughed.

'You're not a businessman. You're a crook.'

'How dare you say that!'

Arthur had the urge to bend down and slap her.

'You sell crap products at highly inflated prices and you can get away with it because you use your contacts to shut down competition.'

'You don't know what you're talking about,' said a furious Arthur Symes as he walked away.

'I watched you tonight. You invited each of the men one by one to the bar and passed their drink on top of a yellow envelope. How much do you pay them?'

'How dare you,' said Arthur stopping.

'How much did you pay the detective to fire-bomb your competitor's store three weeks ago? What about the mayor to rezone the land you own favourably? I hear you and the two politicians have already bought a sizeable chunk of land on a large coal deposit. How did you manage that?'

'You're living under my roof. Eating the food from my fridge,' hissed Arthur, coming close to her and pointing his finger in her face. 'I can have you thrown out on the street. I've done it before. Don't think ...'

'I won't do it again. Yada. Yada. Yada,' said Ingrid, mimicking her uncle's croaky voice, and making a quack-quack motion with her hand. 'Like you did with your son, Richard?'

Ingrid butted out her cigarette and, taking another one from a packet, lit it, blowing her first drag into her uncle's face. Arthur wanted to slap it from her mouth.

'You can pack up your bags and leave tomorrow,' Arthur said, stunned at her insubordination. Usually, he could terrify anyone into submission, but Ingrid looked at him coolly, blowing more smoke in his direction. He coughed.

'You're not my niece. You're dead to me.' He started to walk away.

'You throw me out on the street, Uncle Arthur dear, and I will tell everyone in town what a rotten bastard you are.'

Arthur stopped and scoffed. 'My wife tried that. It didn't work. Everyone knows I'm a rotten bastard.'

'Oh, but you haven't seen me cry,' Ingrid said, and she burst into fake tears.

'Oh, he's a monster,' she sniffled to her imaginary audience. *'He struck me! He struck me across the face with his fists. Oh my god! The man is evil.'*

Arthur froze. Her tone was convincing.

Ingrid stopped crying and glared at her uncle.

'People would tolerate much from a man like you, but mistreating a young girl. What do you think your political cronies would do when the scandal hits the newspapers?'

Arthur opened his mouth and tried to say something, but nothing came out. No one had ever dared defy him. Not his employees, not his business associates, not his competitors, nor his family. Especially his family. *My soppy and weak son left without a murmur.* His wife, too terrified to raise her voice in dissent, walked out rather than put up with his controlling ways. *But this girl is different. She's made of sterner stuff.*

'Don't misunderstand me. I don't condemn you,' Ingrid said, butting out her cigarette and rising to her feet. 'I admire your initiative and drive. How you have built an empire in a god-forsaken town like this.' She placed a hand on his shoulder. 'I want to help you. I want you to teach me your ways. One day I want to say, I was Arthur Symes' niece.'

Arthur said nothing. He considered her words carefully. If he was to be truthful, they touched him. Her hand lingering on his shoulder was also a new experience.

'How can you possibly help me?' he snorted, but did not throw off her hand.

Ingrid smiled, and leaning forward, whispered, 'The large house at Lighthouse Point is up for sale.'

'So?'

'Well, if a man like you bought it, and used your contacts in the council to create a sealed road between it and the freeway ... why, you would quadruple your money overnight. Also, Richard Gibbs is retiring at the next election.'

'Richard's retiring?' gasped Arthur, unable to contain his shock. This meant he needed to consider his replacement. *What would it mean for my current business opportunities?*

Ingrid saw his surprise and continued. 'While you have been concentrating on keeping the important men on side, you have forgotten their wives and girlfriends are also an important source of inside information.'

She leaned close to his ear and whispered, 'I can help you become the richest man, not just in Old Town, but in all of Australia. Imagine all the money you and I can amass. See all that money piled high in the strong room. How much fun it would be to count it, to look at it, to taste it.'

She took a step back and smiled. 'You and I are more alike than you realise.'

'I need to think this through,' Arthur said, looking down at the carpet.

Ingrid watched him walk away perplexed. She hadn't expected this. She expected either complete failure or modest success. But not this indecision.

* * *

A strange feeling came over Arthur as he eased slowly up the stairs. A dreamy whimsical sentiment expressing itself as a snatch of music stole over him. Arthur did not care for music, but it came to him as a brassy trumpet sound. He felt his arthritic limbs begin to sway to the beat inside his head. *What was the name of the song?* He addressed this question to the moon, smiling at him through the window of his room.

As he put on his pyjamas for bed, the image of Ingrid came to mind. His shoulder was still tingling from where she had touched him.

Usually, when he threatened people, they gulped, sweated and shook before their demeanour sagged. But not Ingrid. She had met his attack, first with silence, then haughty insubordination. He could still smell her cigarette smoke. Her demeanour reminded him of his younger self.

He closed his eyes and sat on the bed feeling the breeze from the open window caressing his face.

Inhaling sharply, he remembered the name of the song. 'What is This Thing Called Love'. He played the tune in his head. *How many years has it been since I last heard it? Since I danced with Ingrid's mother, Debbie on the porch of this house before Marcus took her away from me.*

He closed his eyes and saw Ingrid's face before him, unflinching, unemotional, not a flicker of fear. Those beautiful chocolate-coloured eyes, the softness of her checks. He fell onto the bed and felt a warm glow sweep through his body. He opened his eyes and the moon, so big, stared down at him. *How beautiful it looks*, he thought. He tried to not think of her, but it wasn't possible.

Ingrid locked her bedroom door and collapsed onto the bed taking one deep breath after another, trying to contain her heart from galloping out of her chest. Only now in the privacy of her room did she realise how terrified she had been. How she had buried her fear and played the ballsy niece. *But what have I achieved?* she asked the moon.

Ingrid heard Arthur's shuffling steps in the hallway. They came close and stopped outside her door.

He knocked. Ingrid sprang upright.

'Ingrid? Ingrid?' he whispered. 'What do you want from me?'

Ingrid smiled.

CHAPTER SEVEN

THE SHOPPING

It took Doug almost a minute to recognise his gruff employer's tone on the phone requesting his immediate presence early the next morning.

What could the old boy want? thought Doug as he slammed down the phone.

He was looking forward to spending the morning placing bets at the TAB and nursing his Friday night hangover. Yet he knew better than to defy his employer's request.

His mood brightened when the old boy barked out his instructions.

'I want you drive my niece into town. She needs to do some shopping. She will tell you what to do.'

His boss handed over the car keys. Doug watched open-mouthed as the old man, with shaking hands, placed five one-hundred-dollar bills onto his niece's palm. Ingrid planted a kiss on his forehead.

'Be gone with you,' sniffled Arthur. 'As for you,' he said, pointing at Doug, 'I want you to take her into town and nowhere else.'

Doug, stupefied by this scene, stood stock-still until Ingrid tapped him on the shoulder.

As way of distraction, Doug absorbed himself in the task of starting Arthur's car and easing it slowly into the street, feeling the engine pulsating beneath his body, smelling the dashboard, feeling the steering wheel in his hand, and how the slightest pressure on the accelerator made the engine throb faster. Anything rather than think of Ingrid next to him. In this car she made him feel so self-conscious, especially as he noticed from the corner of his eye, her watching his every move, studying his every feature.

'You like this car, don't you?'

'Yeah, she's something special,' he grinned. To impress her, he rattled off all the facts he knew on the car. 'It's a GTS 350 and has a V8 5.7 litre Chevrolet engine with 300 bhp ...'

Ingrid's eyes glazed over as Doug recited a blizzard of numbers, dates and facts. To perk her interest, she interrupted. 'How much does she cost?'

'This beauty is a collectable. North of ten thousand.'

'How fast does she go?' she asked as they stopped at the intersection of Paul and Old Town roads. To the left, Paul Road led to the highway, while straight ahead, Old Town Road led to the town centre.

'Over one-hundred-and-ten kilometres per hour.'

'Why don't you take her to the highway and open her up?'

'But your uncle only wants me to take you into town.'

'Do you see him here?'

'But he always checks the odometer after I take it out.'

'You're scared of my uncle?'

'I'm not afraid of anyone,' said Doug, gripping the steering wheel tightly.

'Then take it to the highway.'

Doug hesitated. The V8 horsepower throbbed through his body, the scent of this beautiful woman next to him filling his nostrils. The old man's contorted face appeared in his head. In the rear-vision mirror, he spied a car approaching.

Ingrid, who had not taken her eyes off his face, squinted. She saw the flutter of uncertainty and said, 'If you're worried about my uncle, you can tell him I told you to do it.'

Doug looked at Ingrid. The car behind slowed, stopped then beeped. Doug put on the left indicator and they travelled along the highway with the windows down, the needle on the speedometer trembling on one hundred, and the radio blaring.

Doug tried to remember a better Saturday morning. He drove the car all the way to Ingarel, a small town fifty kilometres further down the coast. They stopped for cappuccinos before motoring back to Old Town. At the Old Town Road turn off, The Angels' 'Am I Ever Gonna See Your Face Again?' came on the radio, and Ingrid and Doug sang the mock chorus all the way into town. People on the main street stopped to stare.

While Ingrid shopped, Doug hung out at the TAB in the Railway Hotel. Two hours later, he met her in the supermarket and helped her load the groceries into the car. He noted more packages in the back seat.

This is how it should be, he thought. *The woman shopped. The man to provide the muscle.*

As they drove slowly back to the house, Doug daydreamed.

They were driving to their house, not to her uncle's. Her uncle was dead and they were married. Doug was no longer the head storeman, but the bloke running the show. The man who sat in the strong room on Fridays sorting the pays. The man who hosted Friday night dinners with all the town big wigs.

He wondered whether this would be their story in a few years' time. Spending the Saturday morning driving down the coast in the Monaro GTS. His car. Stopping for a cappuccino before returning to Old Town. Ingrid shopping while he spent the time placing bets or on the pokies; later coming back into town for a feed and a few drinks at the Royal or the Railway Hotel. Once a month driving her into Sydney to see a band, staying the night at the Coogee Bay Hotel or an apartment near Circular Quay. It would be her treat. On Sunday they would go watch the Stingrays in action at home at the Surf Coast Oval, or away at some sleepy little town.

Later in the day, he would plop on the couch and watch the footy on TV, while Ingrid pottered in the kitchen, the sound of pots and pans put into action, the smell of an emerging roast wafting through the house.

Occasionally he would call out, 'I could do with another beer, love!'

He saw himself with the boys at the Railway Hotel on Friday nights referring to Ingrid as the missus. He wouldn't have too many drinks now he was a married man. He saw Ingrid in her apron coming up to him, planting a kiss on his forehead and saying, 'You've been so good to me Doug. Why don't you and the boys go for a weekend fishing trip?'

These musings kept Doug occupied all the way back to the old man's house. He didn't mind lugging the shopping out of the car and up the back steps, revelling in his strength as he plopped the bags on the kitchen table.

Arthur began pawing at the plastic bags as soon as Doug set the shopping down, holding up each item, assessing its value, mentally subtracting it from the money given to his niece.

He felt faint as he saw the premium mince and sirloin cuts, instead of the cheapest chuck beef. He mentally shook his head at the Chocolate Royal biscuits, instead of the home-brand teddy bear biscuits.

'What took you so long?' snapped Arthur.

'Women,' said Doug, shrugging his shoulders.

'I gave you instructions to be back before noon.'

He had not given any such instructions, but it didn't stop him from berating Doug for the sin of being perfectly useless and spending his money on so many frivolous items.

'Did you drive down the coast?'

Doug was debating whether to lie or take the verbal abuse when Ingrid said, 'I told him to drive me down the highway. I wanted to see how your car performed.'

Doug's and Arthur's chins dropped. Ingrid stood in the doorway wearing her two new purchases: a black knee-length dress and fire-engine-red stilettos.

Their gaze followed Ingrid as she walked over to the shopping and took out a packet of menthol cigarettes.

'Where's the change?' asked Arthur.

'There's none,' Ingrid said, stripping the plastic wrapping from her packet.

'How can there be no change? And what are all these items? They aren't the ones we agreed on. You were to buy in bulk. And what's with the dress?'

'Firstly, I refuse to live like a pig,' Ingrid said, applying her new rouge lipstick using the small mirror tacked onto the fridge. 'Secondly, do you want me looking like a bag lady to your Friday night guests?'

'Look ... now ...' Arthur tried to think of a counter argument. But he saw her point. He couldn't have her looking poor. He wanted to show her off to the others. The reflected glory in having a beautiful niece.

'Yet the cost. All this expense.' He snatched his car keys from Doug. 'I'm going out,' he said, heading for the back door.

'Where?' Ingrid asked.

'None of your business!' he snapped, slamming the door behind him.

* * *

Arthur drove to Lighthouse Point and gingerly took the unsealed road to the house.

Perfect location, he thought. *I'll put in an offer on Monday for the house and all the land around the point, then see the mayor about a road.*

He returned through Old Town central, stopping at the corner of Old Town and Symes roads to look at his latest acquisition. Here, Old Town Road abruptly stopped, and twenty kilometres of mangrove swamp began. From the sea it ran all the way up the hill to the bottom carpark of Symes.

The deal had only been finalised on Friday. Arthur, along with Richard the MP and several of his Friday night cronies, had used their contacts in the state government to purchase all this Crown land at peppercorn rates. Arthur had a vision for it. He would have the land rezoned and bulldoze the vegetation before building a gated community for wealthy retirees from Sydney looking to spend their final days playing golf and sailing their seven-metre ocean boats on the open sea. He would ask the council to build an overpass over the railway line, then extend Symes Road all the way to the highway. Symes Road would then be the main connector between Old Town and the highway.

It would be his crowning glory. If he worked the deal well, he could double, triple his wealth. But he needed to be careful. He would have much of his capital tied up in the venture. He needed to make it work.

I'll be glad to have Pat back on Monday, he thought, as he eased the car up Symes Road to his house. With each passing year Symes had become a bigger burden. *All the Symes people with their mundane concerns, petty jealousies, and back biting. All the cashiers with their personal problems, sick children and no-good husbands. The men with their alcoholism and divorces.* He wanted to hand it over to Pat, his 2ic, freeing him to concentrate full time on the new project.

As he stiffly eased himself out of the car in the driveway, he realised he had outgrown Symes. It had become too big, too much to manage on his own. He no longer possessed the energy to run it. He had outsourced the running of his car to Doug, now he would outsource the running of Symes to Pat.

Arthur stopped as he put the key in the front door. *I could also outsource the management of Ingrid to Pat. Put some distance between myself and this troubling new development in my life. Yes, I will be happy to see Pat's face tomorrow.*

He didn't recognise the change in the house until he made it halfway up the stairs. A small stain on the wall of the stairs that always caught his eye whenever he came up this way to his room was gone. When he reached the first landing he stopped and sniffed. A new fragrance pervaded the air.

In his room he found Maria, his Saturday morning cleaner, busy vacuuming.

'What is the meaning of this?' he cried out over the wheeze of the machine. 'You're only to clean the main rooms, no others. I will not pay you! Do you hear?' he bellowed, flourishing his cane at Maria's face.

'But Mr Symes,' said Maria, clicking off the vacuum cleaner and lowering her eyes. It was always *Mr Symes.* 'Your niece has asked me to clean every room.'

Arthur felt dizzy and gripped a bedhead for support. He felt as if his money gushed from his bank account like water from a burst water main.

'Where is she? Where is she?' screamed Arthur.

He marched out of his room and down the back stairs with the firm intention of putting an end to this nonsense. He would throw her out on the street this instant. He would not have his money wasted like this. He noted on his march down the backstairs, the old and familiar smudges on the walls that greeted his eyes each morning were gone. Also, the stale odours pervading the back stairs were gone and replaced with a rosy antiseptic fragrance. *This is too much! She has to go.* His mind was made up. His simple living arrangements, which had served him well for so many years, were being upended. *She had to go tonight!*

But when Arthur reached the bottom step, he stopped and grabbed hold of the banister. His stomach was rolling and growling. His nose was overwhelmed by the sweet and unfamiliar smell of a roast sizzling into edible form.

He locked eyes on his niece at the stove.

'I did not give you permission to increase the cleaning in this house,' shouted Arthur.

'The house is a pigsty. It needed a clean,' Ingrid said, not even turning to look at her uncle.

'It was fine the way it was,' Arthur said, feeling his resolve begin to crumble with the scent of the food. He had skipped lunch and was famished.

'I can't live in a dirty house,' Ingrid said, taking two plates of steaming, delicious-smelling food to the table.

'Why didn't you clean it yourself? You're wasting my money.'

'I can't clean the house and cook at the same time. Now sit. I've cooked us a roast.'

She still had her black dress on but had added perfume and an apron. He sat obediently at the rickety table covered with a ruby-red tablecloth.

Ingrid had wanted to eat in the main room at the long table like a wealthy person, but she surmised this as a step too far for her uncle at present. Instead, she settled for a table she found in the garage, which she had Doug lug in. She asked Martin the gardener to pick out a white rose from the front yard and she put it in a chipped vase she found in a cupboard as a decorative flourish for the dinner table. She poured Arthur a glass of Barossa Valley shiraz.

The food is wonderful, thought Arthur. He coated his potatoes thickly with gravy and ate quickly and ravenously. Ingrid was revolted watching Arthur scoff his food like a pig, masticating loudly. Pieces of half-chewed food stuck to his whiskers.

He could never enjoy the meals on Friday night as he was too obsessed with the bribes and discussing deals with his cronies. He hardly touched his food, content to dine alone eating tinned beef stew after everyone had gone.

But this meal tasted so nice. He sculled his glass of shiraz and winced at the strange taste. He didn't like it and examined the label, wondering how much it cost.

'I will be ruined with all this extra expense. You will have me in the poorhouse.'

'It's only a little extra. Besides, once you purchase the property at Lighthouse Point and you organise the council to build a road there, it will pay for these expenses a thousand times over.'

'That's several years away. I must pay for the house and the bribes to the council for the road. There's all that upfront capital with no return until many years later.'

'I was thinking Uncle, you should buy all the property around the house then subdivide it.'

Arthur put down his fork and looked at his niece carefully. *She's rather shrewd.*

'I suppose that's where you went this afternoon in the car. To look at the property at Lighthouse Point?'

Ingrid prided herself on her knowing other people. Ever since childhood she had the ability to read people's intentions.

'You went somewhere else, didn't you?' she said, an image coming to mind of him stopping his car.

He wanted to brag about his latest purchase. He wanted to tell her about his plans for the waterfront development. He lifted his eyes to his niece and opened his mouth to speak but as he did so, the image of Toby drifted into his mind, and his warning.

'Sometimes it's good to be secretive,' he remembered Toby saying. He checked himself. He wondered whether he could trust her.

'Lighthouse Point only.' He scowled, dropping his eyes and devouring his Tiramisu cake. His cheeks burned. He sensed her watching him.

Ingrid had the funny feeling that Arthur held something back. Something important.

He downed his black coffee in two gulps, grimacing at the taste. He was in a rush to be gone. *One should not surrender to pleasure or idleness*, he reminded himself. Also, he felt weak in the presence of his niece.

'Thank God Pat will be back tomorrow,' he said, plonking down his coffee cup and wiping his mouth with the back of his hand. 'She will keep you in line,' he said. *And I don't have to deal with you anymore*, he thought privately.

'Pat?'

'Yes, Pat.' Arthur rose to his feet. 'She's my 2ic.' He turned and wandered upstairs. He undressed in his clean room and crawled into the soft and newly laundered sheets.

He slept easily and deeply, knowing Pat would be back tomorrow and he could put distance between himself and his niece.

In the kitchen, Ingrid took out a notepad and Dr Harris's script for sleeping tablets. She continued to practise imitating his handwriting.

Yet she couldn't help wonder who Pat was. *What does he mean about her keeping me in line?*

CHAPTER EIGHT

PATRICIA MARTIN

Ingrid detected a new fragrance in the main office early on Monday morning. The door of the room next to her uncle's poky office, which had remained locked since her arrival, was open, and a large middle-aged woman with cropped hair was tapping away on a computer.

'You must be Pat,' Ingrid said with a toothy smile.

'And you must be Ingrid, Mr Symes' niece,' said Pat in a restrained, even voice, eyeing Ingrid over the spectacles perched on the edge of her nose. 'Your uncle wasn't clear when you would be coming to us.'

'I wasn't certain myself,' Ingrid said.

'I hope everyone has shown you the appropriate courtesy.'

'Everyone has been so nice,' smiled Ingrid.

'I assume someone has shown you the ropes and your list of duties.'

'Oh yes, Cheryl spent the first week with me showing me my tasks.'

'Cheryl ... I see. Well, we better catch up this afternoon to discuss what Cheryl has shown you and set you straight.'

'That would be great.' Ingrid forced an even wider smile. Pat dropped her gaze to the computer screen. Ingrid lingered at the door.

'Well, I won't keep you from your work Ms Symes,' said Pat, peering at her over the rim of her glasses again.

Dismissed, Ingrid returned to her desk.

So that is Pat. Officious and hardworking, not one given to idle chit chat. Not one to be taken lightly either, she thought. *Judging by her remarks Pat didn't think too highly of Cheryl.*

Ingrid was beginning to take stock of the more interesting duties performed by Cheryl, and how she could steal these away, when Toby appeared in the deserted office.

Toby stopped as soon as he saw Ingrid. The two eyed each other. Toby like a startled deer, Ingrid like an amused observer. Toby continued his march past her and knocked on Pat's office.

'Can I see you a moment, Pat?'

'Why of course Toby.'

Toby shut the door.

Ingrid went to the printer. Not with the intention of photocopying. The machine backed onto Pat's office. She closed her eyes and threw her awareness past the wall into Pat's office. Nothing, only indistinct voices. Looking about, she noted the office was deserted; the first shift not starting until 8am, fifteen minutes away. She tiptoed close to the door and, placing her ear on the wall and with her back to the main office door, closed her eyes and listened with all her might.

'I'm glad you're back,' Toby said.

'I'm glad ...' was all Ingrid could hear. Pat's voice was low and wispy.

'I want to warn you,' Toby said.

'Warn me about what?'

'I know you said it was nothing. I should forget all about it. But I've seen something. No, not seen something. I'm beginning to remember, and it involves you.'

'Oh Toby, you must see someone about this.'

'And have Dr Harris put me back in ...?'

'What ya doin'?'

Ingrid felt a poke in her back and jumped in fright, spinning around to see Cheryl's pudgy face.

'Sorry to frighten you,' said Cheryl. 'I didn't mean to. It's ...'

Ingrid took in a sharp breath. *I could kill the bitch.* This thought must have been etched across her face, for Cheryl took a step back, looking alarmed.

'I was daydreaming,' smiled Ingrid, as if Cheryl was the one person she wanted to see, even though she would make her pay for interrupting her at the most interesting part. *I don't want Cheryl offside. Not yet at least.*

'I bet you wanted to know where I was on Friday,' said Cheryl, her alarm turning to a smile, no doubt misunderstanding the look on her new best friend's face.

Ingrid, who had not given Cheryl a moment's thought since Thursday night, tried to look interested.

'I've been with Brad,' said Cheryl.

Ingrid lifted an eyebrow.

'Brad the barman from the cocktail lounge,' said Cheryl. 'Remember? The one who gave me the eye on Thursday.'

'Oh,' Ingrid said, trying to sound suitably impressed. She couldn't believe Brad, if that was his name, would be interested in Cheryl.

'It was strange. Out of the blue he called me next morning. I don't know how he obtained my number, but Friday was his day off and he invited me to the beach. For some reason he thought he was calling you.'

The door of Pat's office opened, and Ingrid stood face to face with Toby. Any thoughts of Cheryl vanished.

Toby eyed her defiantly.

'You need to see me Miss Symes,' said Pat, peering over Toby's shoulder. Ingrid realised she blocked the door.

She took a step back and Toby marched past her and out of the office, Ingrid's eyes following him as he went.

'Oh Pat, you're back,' said Cheryl.

'Yes, I am Miss Donaldson.' But Pat's gaze extended no further than Ingrid.

* * *

A steady stream of visitors came to Pat's office that morning. Pat greeted them all cordially with a shy smile, overwhelmed by everyone's concern for her health.

At nine, Arthur Symes appeared in the office. He looked like he wanted to hug Pat. He and Pat locked themselves away in his room until midday. Ingrid wondered what they were talking about, but with the office packed, listening at the door wasn't an option.

The girls threw a lunch for Pat in the administration office. Each girl brought a plate of food and a small welcome present. Ingrid noted an affection for this large masculine woman from their exchange,

Ingrid also noted a new tone in the office. Before Pat, it was relaxed and jolly. Ingrid could move here and there, talking to the girls, opening desk drawers and exploring her environment with impunity, letting the phones run unanswered. But with Pat's return, a business-like quality came over Symes. The girls' voices were quieter, people tiptoed about, conversations were now carried in whispers. Pat watched everything closely from her office, and after Toby's conversation, Ingrid thought, she watched her carefully as well.

Her afternoon meeting with Pat wasn't successful.

Pat lengthened her list of duties, and unlike Arthur, who never took much interest in what the office girls did, expected her to fulfill these.

What irked Ingrid the most was having to remain in her seat, except for lunch and morning and afternoon tea. No more wanderings through Symes.

* * *

On Tuesday, they farewelled Zhou, the finance officer in the administration office. Pat officiated. Zhou's position was posted on the notice board in the afternoon. Ingrid decided the job would be hers by the end of the week.

'Uncle, I would like to do Zhou's job,' Ingrid asked on his first mouthful of ice cream.

She had prepared a scotch fillet with mushroom sauce served with green beans, followed by ice cream with lashings of chocolate topping.

'Financial accountant?' scoffed Arthur. 'You have only been at the shop two weeks and you want a transfer?'

'I'm bored with being an administrative assistant.'

'What's the matter with your generation? Never satisfied.'

'I'm not cut out to answer the phones. I want to work with money.'

'What qualifications do you have?'

'I have a head for numbers.'

'A head for numbers!' scoffed Arthur again.

'I can do the job easily.'

'See Pat. She looks after all store business. I'm far too busy with other matters.'

'But you're the owner. You make all the decisions.'

'See Pat. That is my final word.'

Arthur continued eating.

'I thought you ran Symes. It is your name on the building, not Pat's.'

'I said see Pat!' Arthur's dessert spoon rang as he smacked it into the table.

They ate in silence, the only sound being Arthur slurping his ice cream. After licking his spoon clean, he said without looking at his niece, 'I want you to organise three lots of catering for all the staff tomorrow. I have an important announcement to make at the main breaks.'

'Oh, what is it?' Ingrid said, putting down her spoon and leaning forward.

'You will hear it tomorrow with the rest of the staff,' Arthur said gruffly, focussing his eyes on her nose and nothing else.

'Why not tell me now?'

'Because I'm not ready to tell it.'

'No concession for family?' smiled Ingrid.

'Definitely no concession for family. In my business you're an employee like everyone else.'

'How many am I to cater for?'

'I don't know! Why don't you count the staff, divide by three, then deduct ten percent?' snapped Arthur, rising stiffly to his feet.

'You don't give much detail.'

'You said you have a head for figures. Why don't you work it out?'

Arthur turned and walked away, not wanting to stay and gaze into his niece's large dark eyes, or feel her warm presence. Yet her voice followed him to the stairs.

'Do I have money for this?'

'See Pat,' he said, not turning around. 'She knows what it's about.'

'See Pat. See Pat,' grumbled Ingrid.

Arthur grinned, glad at the annoyance of his niece, but also irritated at having to concentrate on petty details when big property deals beckoned.

Only one more sleep and she would be Pat's problem not mine.

Chapter Nine

The Promotion

Ingrid wanted Doug to drive her into town so she could do the shopping at Coles for the catering. It would give her an excuse to sit down for a skinny latte and croissant at a coffee shop. But Pat, on learning of her task, intervened.

'One of Doug's men will pick up a spread from Raffles, Miss Symes. I want you to remain here and answer the phones.'

'Yes Pat,' Ingrid said with her falsest smile.

'This is Symes, how can I help you?' she spat into the phones until morning tea and the big announcement.

'I will keep this short,' Arthur said, standing next to Pat with a third of his employees crowding around expectantly. 'As you may or may not know, my business interests beyond this store over the last few years have grown substantially and now absorb increasingly large amounts of my time. To ensure the continued success of this business, I would like to announce that Patricia Martin will become general manager of Symes Multipurpose Hardware store effective immediately. All issues relating to the daily operations of the store are to be directed to Pat. I will still be around if you need to speak to me. As you know, my door is always open.'

Arthur stopped speaking and surveyed the faces of his employees. *A miserable and unattractive lot*, he thought. He hoped never to speak to any of them ever again. Yet their faces waited expectantly for more. He extended both hands towards the spread of food. 'Now, eat.'

Arthur retreated to his office, locking it behind him.

A moment of bewildered silence followed. Toby, standing at the back of the room closest to the door, burst into enthusiastic applause. The others joined in.

The applause for Pat was long, and too loud for Ingrid's liking. She shared a raised eyebrow with Doug, who shook his head and retreated with downcast eyes out the door.

A crowd gathered around Pat to give their personal congratulations. Ingrid watched the glacial stare of Pat giving way to a flicker of emotion before Ingrid lost sight of her in the crush of people.

The scene from the morning tea was repeated at lunch, then afternoon tea. Her uncle gave the same quick speech, before leaving bemused staff to clap, cheer, and gather around a shy but emotional Pat.

'A nice speech you gave today,' Ingrid said, eyeing her uncle ravenously wolf down the beef stew she spent the last two hours preparing. She had learnt the recipe from Mrs Sárosy and used it to butter up her uncle.

Arthur did not look up. Instead, he grunted.

'You must have lot of faith in Pat to give her such an important job.'

Arthur grunted again.

'I hope it all turns out well,' sighed Ingrid. 'I hope it doesn't end in tears.'

Arthur grunted again.

Ingrid pushed away her half-eaten plate of food.

'I'm sure the rumours aren't true.'

Arthur stopped eating and looked up sharply, some of the stew sticking to his chin stubble.

'What rumours?'

'Oh, nothing at all. Have you finished with your food?' Ingrid asked, rising from her seat and taking their plates to the sink.

'I said what rumours?'

'They're probably nothing,' Ingrid said, scraping leftover food into the bin.

'Tell me. You live under my roof and work in my store. You're my eyes and ears.'

Ingrid sighed. 'Okay, but promise not to tell.' She turned to face her uncle.

'Tell me now!'

'Well,' Ingrid sighed, 'I heard from Cheryl that Pat's cancer is back and she's drinking at work to cope.'

Arthur looked at his niece incredulously. 'Pat doesn't drink.'

'As I said, I don't believe it, that's why I didn't want to repeat it.'

Arthur looked at his niece shrewdly. 'You don't like her, do you?'

'What?' Ingrid put both plates in the sink.

'You don't like Pat.'

'Pat's adorable,' Ingrid said, not looking up.

Arthur threw his head back and laughed and laughed. 'I've heard Pat called many things, but adorable isn't one of them.' He wiped the tears from his eyes.

'All I'm saying is ... there are rumours,' said Ingrid, turning on the tap.

Arthur watched his niece closely for a time, then said, 'I know your game, Princess. I know what you're up to.'

Taking up his cane, Arthur flourished it at his niece. 'You're trying to drive a wedge between Pat and me. Well don't. I'm glad you don't like her. I'm glad you're miserable. It serves you right for making me live like a lavish bohemian with all this fancy food and extra cleaning.'

He did not add out loud how she also made him feel helpless and unsure of himself; instead, he added, pointing his cane at her, 'You're trouble with a capital T.'

'Me? I'm a pussy cat.'

'Not all your colleagues think so.'

'Oh?' She turned off the tap.

'But I won't talk out of school,' Arthur said. He rose to his feet, and shuffling close to her, studied her expression. He noted the flicker of interest.

'You're a piece of work,' jeered Ingrid.

Arthur chuckled. He liked seeing her disconcerted. *If she could try to plant discord, so could I. I'm not stupid. I've played the same game. Now I'll show her who is the master of discord.*

'One person warned me about you.'

'Well, I don't care who it is,' Ingrid said, turning on the tap again and adding detergent.

'Did you know Toby Zachariah before coming here?'

'No, I've never seen him before in my life.'

Ingrid scrubbed a plate.

'He warned me not trust you. Now why would he say that?'

'I don't know, and I don't care,' Ingrid said, scrubbing the plate vigorously. 'I've never laid eyes on him before. Maybe he has me mixed up with someone else.'

Arthur beamed with pleasure. Finally, he had one up on her. He laughed loudly as he climbed up the backstairs to his room.

* * *

Ingrid spent half the night staring at her bedroom ceiling trying to understand why Toby didn't like her. *What have I ever done to make him hate me so?* She had never met him before coming to Old Town, Ingrid was certain. She had a memory for faces. It baffled her.

The conversation in Pat's office with Toby. He wanted to warn Pat about something. He wanted to warn Pat about me. Ingrid's heart quickened.

Her mind flicked between Toby and Pat all night.

Pat would see reason. She would give me the job. Ingrid closed her eyes and visualised Pat saying, 'Congratulations Ingrid, you have the job.'

From down the hall, her uncle's snoring rose to a crescendo. *How I would love to put a pillow over his face and smother the noise.* She put her hands to her ears and continued the visualisation.

She saw the office table spread with food and all of Symes' employees packed into the office as Pat stood next to her and said, 'I would like to announce that Ingrid Symes will be our new financial accountant.'

* * *

The next day, Ingrid waited expectantly as Pat, on the other side of the desk, eyed her resumé with a cold, meticulous stare. 'I'm sorry Miss Symes, but I cannot transfer you into accounts,' she said, handing back her two-page resumé. 'You must complete your three months' probation before I will consider you for any other role in the organisation.'

'What about after probation?'

'First, you must pass probation.'

'Yes, and after probation?'

'I wouldn't consider you for the role of finance officer, even if you passed your probation.'

'But why?' Ingrid was shocked and perplexed.

'Ms Symes. Firstly, you don't have the skills or the qualifications to undertake the role. The person filling Zhou's position needs at least three years' experience in a similar role and must be tertiary qualified.'

'But I can do the job better than half the candidates. I have a head for figures.'

'You may have *a head for figures*,' said Pat, 'but that isn't a prerequisite for such an important role. Also, as I said Ms Symes, you will need to fulfill your probation before we will consider you for any position in Symes.'

It took all of Ingrid's self-control not to slam the door behind her as she left, even though she wanted to spit out obscenities at Pat. *How could she deny me the role? Why couldn't the bitch see my greatness?* She took a deep breath and forced a smile on her face, just like she had learned from drama class.

Instead of returning to her workstation, she found herself marching out of the office.

'How did you go?' asked Cheryl.

'Can't talk ... need to see someone,' she said, brushing past Cheryl.

She clomped her way down the steel stairs to the busy aisles, fantasising how she would grab Pat by the hair and dash her brains against the steel railing of the stairs.

On the shop floor, a customer holding a garden hose reel turned to her and asked, "Excuse me, but do you work here?'

'No!' she spat, before marching through the staff door and into the back warehouse. She brushed past Tom and flung open the back door. It was 3pm and Toby, wearing in a yellow raincoat, was unchaining his bike from the back wire fence.

She ran down the wet steps into the pouring rain and in two strides grabbed the handles of his bike as the chain came away from the fence pole.

Toby jumped in fright. His look reminded her of a startled hare she once saw on a nature show as the eagle swooped down and sunk its claws into its head. A shiver of sexual excitement ran through her body at the image.

'What's your problem with me?' she cried out, the water beating down on her hair.

'I don't know what you mean,' he said.

'Don't play dumb with me. I'm not stupid. You're talking about me behind my back to my uncle and Pat.'

Toby blushed.

'Bullseye!' she shouted.

Toby lunged for his bike, but she anticipated this move. She lifted the front wheel off the ground, and as he reached out, she spun the bike away from his grasp like a matador twirling away a cape from a bull.

Toby stumbled forward. Rebalancing, he straightened. They stood only inches apart, their eyes locking. The rain tumbled down in a roar. A curious feeling stole over her as she stared into his blue eyes.

'I don't like what you're about to do,' he whispered.

'What?' she asked, mystified.

'You should leave this town now.'

'Leave? Oh no, I can't leave. There's so much potential here,' she said automatically, as if another voice spoke through her.

'You must leave,' said Toby.

Ingrid threw back her head and laughed. She laughed long and hard, the pouring rain entering her open mouth, washing over her cheeks.

He's like a scared hare and I'm a predatory eagle. He looks dazed and pathetic.

She threw his bike aside and rushed at Toby, digging her nails into his chest. He fell back against the wire mesh fence, her face inches from his.

'If I find you've spoken about me behind my back again,' she seethed, 'I will retaliate so hard you will regret the day you were born. Do you understand?'

She looked into his blue eyes, struck by how familiar they appeared. As if she had stared into them countless times before. He looked confused, but not scared now.

She picked up his bike and with a heave threw it at Toby. She did not look him in the eye again. Instead, she turned and walked back into Symes.

CHAPTER TEN

TOBY

'Why did you have a go at Toby?' asked Cheryl the next night at the Lagoon cocktail lounge.

Ingrid took a sip of her virgin daiquiri for dramatic effect. It also gave her time to construct a story.

'I found him rifling through my bag.'

'What?' Cheryl put down her tequila sunrise.

Ingrid guessed that if the lie backfired, she could always deny it and blame it all on big-mouth Cheryl.

'I had placed my bag on the table in the tearoom while I went to make myself a cup of tea. When I turned, I found him rifling through it. He had my purse in his hand.'

'Unbelievable,' gasped Cheryl.

'He also tried to touch me.'

'What?' Cheryl's mouth widened, like one of those wooden clowns at a carnival.

'On my breast,' nodded Ingrid. 'He was so brazen about it. When he put the purse back, he reached out and touched my left breast and said he would love a feel. I was so angry I chased him out of the tearoom and confronted him at the back entrance.'

'I can hardly believe it,' said Cheryl.

Ingrid took a sip of her cocktail. She wondered whether the breast touching was an unnecessary embellishment.

'I consider you a close friend,' Ingrid said, leaning over to Cheryl and touching her arm. 'You must promise not to tell anyone. I will deny it.'

'Of course. Of course,' gasped Cheryl.

Ingrid took another sip of her cocktail, the glass hiding a growing smile. She already saw this piece of news travelling like a wildfire through Symes.

Cheryl took a sip of her cocktail before putting down her glass and saying, 'You should report him.'

'To whom? My uncle would tell me to go and see Pat, and Pat and Toby are as thick as thieves.'

'True,' said Cheryl. 'She's always sticking up for him whenever someone has an issue with him. She was the one who forced your uncle to pay him award wages.'

'What do you mean?' asked Ingrid, putting down her glass.

'I suppose you haven't heard the story yet,' said Cheryl. 'It's why most people at work don't like him. They think he's a scab.'

'A scab?'

'In a union town, scab is the worst thing to be called. It means you work for nothing.'

'What happened?'

'Well,' said Cheryl, leaning across the table, 'the rumour went around that the only reason your uncle hired Toby was because he was willing to work below award rates.'

'Toby must have been desperate for work.'

'He had only been in Old Town a day,' said Cheryl.

'Oh,' murmured Ingrid.

'He had come by bus from Adelaide that day. He told me all this on our first date.'

'You went out with Toby?'

'Yeah, for two dates.'

'Tell me more,' Ingrid said, leaning in closer.

'There isn't much to tell. He was in love with me as soon as he saw me. He was always hanging around the office. Always making a nuisance of himself. So much so he came to blows several times with Doug for leaving his post. Finally, he plucked up the courage to ask me out. We came here on both dates.'

'What happened?'

'Nothing. We just talked. Or more like, I talked. All I found out about him was he was from Adelaide and rented a place near a gym in Old Town.'

'What did you talk about?'

'Work and your uncle. He kept asking questions about the strong room and your uncle's business affairs.'

'Interesting topic,' Ingrid said.

'I even teased him about wanting to rob the place,' laughed Cheryl.

'What did he say to that?'

'He laughed and blushed.'

'And after that?'

'Nothing. I found him boring. Although I don't like a man who talks nonstop and big notes himself, Toby was the complete opposite. Getting information out of him was like getting blood out of a stone. Though he did tell me he had dropped out of studying medicine. I know he's a voracious reader. Every time I see him, he has some big book in his hands. But I lost interest in Toby after our second date. I had another two men interested in me then. After the second date he never called me, and three months later he fell ill and was rushed to hospital. I heard he died in hospital. Whatever the truth, when he came out, he didn't care about anything anymore. He didn't call me again. But I didn't care. Besides, I have Brad now.'

She smiled, and Ingrid turned to see Brad the barman approach and give Cheryl a kiss on the lips.

After a brief interlude of hellos and small talk, Brad and Cheryl began whispering to each other.

Ingrid, glad to be ignored, mulled over Cheryl's story.

Why would someone come all the way from Adelaide to this god-forsaken town? Had he the same idea as me? To befriend the best source of gossip in Symes?

It was time for her to find out a bit more about this Toby Zachariah.

CHAPTER ELEVEN

A STRANGE TALE

The next night, Ingrid stood on the porch in her new black dress and red high heels and greeted her uncle's Friday night guests.

She escorted each person to one of the leather armchairs or sofas, and engaged in pleasant chit chat with the wives while ensuring each man received their drink of choice. She put to memory their selections. *Next week I'll have their drinks ready for them without them having to ask.*

Relieved at not having to perform these tiresome social chores, Arthur admired the beauty and grace of his niece from behind the bar.

Ingrid was especially attentive to Dr Harris.

'You didn't bring your sister tonight,' she said as he walked up the path solo.

'Unfortunately, she has a migraine.'

'How sad, I was so looking forward to meeting her,' lied Ingrid.

'I want you to meet her too,' he said.

'Well, no matter,' Ingrid touched his arm in the shadows of the porch, 'tonight you can tell me all about your practice here in Old Town. Let's go inside and I will fix your drink. It's a Glenfiddich whiskey, I believe.'

Dr Harris, rather taken aback with this attention, smiled.

The young detective appeared on the front porch and grinned.

'Excuse me Rob, I will be with you shortly,' Ingrid said.

She escorted Dr Harris to the bar.

'Uncle, can you see the detective to a seat?'

Arthur, happy not having to participate in all the pre-dinner chit chat, obliged.

As soon as all the guests had arrived, Ingrid called them to sit at the long table, Arthur at one end and Ingrid at the other, with Dr Harris seated at her right. Ingrid ensured the detective sat furthest from her, closest to her uncle.

Mrs. Sarsovy served dinner: beef goulash with a side of damper bread.

Arthur, who hated ethnic food, merely shrugged his shoulders, his gaze fully absorbed in his niece at the other end of the table talking to Dr Harris.

'I hear you're seeking a transfer to Sydney,' said the mayor to the detective.

'I've applied for the drug squad.'

'I bet your wife will be happy to return to Sydney. She's from Bankstown, I believe?' said Doris.

'She likes it here,' said Rob.

'Old Town is good for young children,' said Lara. 'You have two young boys, don't you?'

'Yeah,' said Rob. 'It will be hard leaving Old Town. There are certain parts of the place I do find attractive.'

Rob glanced down the table at Ingrid, who did not look at Rob, but instead took a sip of her wine and continued her private conversation with Dr Harris.

'When do you find out?' asked the mayor.

'Next week. I've already started packing.'

'Confident.'

'I have it in the bag.'

'I hear they're going to renovate St Michael's in town,' said Sinead O'Shea, wanting to shift the conversation away from the young detective's tiresome bragging.

'What are they doing to it?' Doris asked.

'Restoring the bell tower, which was destroyed in the fire of '75.'

'As a member of the congregation David, I'm sure you will be glad of that?'

'To tell you the truth, my wife and I have stopped going to church after the incident with the young lad last year,' said David Ludlow, the state member for Old Town.

'Incident?' asked Rob.

Harris broke off his conversation with Ingrid mid-sentence to listen.

'It was one of the strangest Sunday services we have ever attended,' said Lara, David Ludlow's wife. 'The young man caused quite a scene.'

'I was never a regular member of the congregation,' continued David. 'I only went for political appearances, unlike Lara, who went every Sunday. Anyway, this Sunday, Lara pointed him out first. We were in the second row and the young lad was across the aisle in the front row looking up at the ceiling and mumbling to himself.'

'Tears were streaming down his face,' added Lara. 'It was as if he was seeing something incredible above.'

'I looked up and could see nothing remarkable, only a poorly painted ceiling,' said David. 'Anyway, we sang the first hymn, our attention drawn to the order of service. When the hymn ended, instead of Reverend John Smith being in the pulpit to deliver his Sunday service, it was the young man, with a startled Reverend Smith standing below.'

'The boy was sobbing uncontrollably,' added Lara. 'And he kept repeating, "Life is so beautiful. It's so, so beautiful".'

'He kept saying it over and over,' said David, 'before announcing he had spoken to Jesus and his message for the earth was to love one another.'

'He also raved about a girl falling through snow and mist,' said Lara. 'Clearly the boy was disturbed.'

'As security led him away, he shouted, "Daughters, if you have a red box, your father implores you to look inside. Please look inside it".'

'He also said something about an orphan. Do you remember, David?' asked Lara.

'Do you know who he was?' interrupted Sinead.

'I didn't catch his name. Lara, do you recall?' asked David.

'It was a Terry or Tony or ...'

'Toby Zachariah.'

Everyone seated at the table turned to look at Dr Harris.

'You know him?' asked Janine.

'He was a patient of mine. That is all I will say. I believe he's one of Arthur's employees.'

Arthur, who had listened with a mixture of incredulity and fascination, scoffed at the idiocy of the younger generation, stiffened in his seat, and blushed as the eyes around the table fell on him, as if wanting an explanation for his unusual behaviour.

'I don't know anything about it. Besides, what my employees do in their own time is a matter for them.'

'I'm not surprised,' said Rob. 'These new synthetic drugs hitting the streets are pretty potent. There was a stark-naked, knife-wielding addict we took into custody last week in the local park, who raved about being the King of Antarctica. It took him three days to come down from his high. These new drugs mess with the mind.'

Harris looked up from his food, and Arthur had the impression he was about to say something, when Doris said, 'Excuse me Ingrid, can you please pass the salt? Dear ... can you pass the salt? Excuse me, dear.'

Ingrid looked at Doris absently.

'Dear, can you pass the salt?' Doris repeated.

It took several seconds for Ingrid to realise that she had been holding onto the saltshaker tightly all through the story of the church service.

'I'm sorry Doris, forgive me,' blushed Ingrid.

The table progressed to a new conversational thread. Ingrid, uninterested in the new topic, turned to Dr Harris who told her and Doris a story of a patient's dog. She soon lost interest in this tale and found herself listening without interest to the discussion about the up-coming local election.

After dinner, Ingrid sat by herself in an armchair and moodily smoked one menthol cigarette after the other. She had forgotten the doctor and her guests. She was on her third cigarette when Rob sat in the armchair opposite.

'I won't miss much about this town, but the sight of you will be one of them.'

'Shouldn't you be playing snooker?' suggested Ingrid, not bothering to look at him.

'Snooker isn't the type of game I like to play.'

Ingrid took a drag on her cigarette.

'I much prefer to talk to pretty young ladies,' he said.

'There's a whole table of them over there. Why don't you take your pick?' Ingrid said, glancing at the women at the dinner table talking.

'Oh, you make me laugh.' Rob put down his glass, and leaning forward, whispered, 'I want to invite you to a little farewell do. A few select people at Lighthouse Point. I'm having a barbeque at sunset.'

'No!' Ingrid said, holding her breath. He reeked of stale whiskey.

'But you don't know what day it is.'

'The answer is no. My uncle won't allow me to go out. It's one of his little rules.'

'Keep a good-looking girl like you under lock and key? I don't believe it.'

'Believe it.'

'Rob! Rob!' Arthur was beckoning from the bar.

'My uncle is calling you.'

Rob turned and looked over his shoulder.

'I have your drink, Rob,' announced Arthur from behind the bar. He had placed a glass of whiskey onto a fat yellow envelope.

Rob sculled the rest of his drink, and winking at Ingrid, rose unsteadily to his feet and walked to the bar.

As soon as Rob left Ingrid, Harris took his seat as Ingrid tried to light another cigarette. Her hand shook. The doctor leant forward, and taking the lighter from her grasp, lit the cigarette.

'Normally I don't encourage smoking,' he said, putting the lighter down. 'But I see you're a little on edge. I hope it wasn't anything to do with the story about the young man.'

Ingrid took a drag on her cigarette, exhaling smoke towards Harris, who usually hated cigarette smoke. But he let it wash over him.

'What we had with the boy was the product of a dying brain. Hallucinations caused by the brain shutting down. Nothing to it at all. Mere delusion.'

Ingrid leant forward and listened intently. Dr Harris noted her interest, and realising he had spoken far too freely, stopped.

'You were Toby's doctor, weren't you? You treated him in hospital?'

'I'm sorry, but I have said too much already tonight,' apologised the doctor.

'What did he say to you?'

'I'm sorry, I can't speak about patients,' he stammered.

Ingrid sighed and leant back. *The doctor's right, there was nothing to it. Besides, I need to put it from my mind.*

'If you must know, Doctor Harris,' she said, changing the subject.

'Call me Jack.'

'Jack,' smiled Ingrid. 'I'm worried about my uncle.'

Ingrid glanced at her uncle at the bar, who was in a whispered tête-à-tête with the young detective.

'He isn't looking after himself. I worry about him so much. It's beginning to make me feel so depressed. I haven't had a good night sleep since coming to Old Town. I keep fearing something will happen to my uncle and I will be all alone again.'

Ingrid buried her head in her hands and sobbed a little.

Jack leaned forward and placed his hand in her free hand. She squeezed it gently for several seconds before letting it go.

'Thank you, Doctor Harris, I mean Jack, you're so kind.'

'Look, why don't I come round on Monday afternoon for a consultation.'

Ingrid, who had taken a tissue from her bag and dabbed her eyes, smiled. 'Oh Jack. You're wonderful.'

'I understand how hard a man like Arthur Symes must be to live with.'

'Thank you, Jack, thank you so much. You don't know how much this means to me.'

She smiled and her gaze lingered on the doctor for a long time.

A Moonlight Serenade

After the last guests left, Ingrid took off her shoes and climbed wearily up the stairs. As it was a warm December evening, she threw open the bedroom window and considered the full moon smiling down. She closed her eyes, and taking a deep breath, let the sea breeze caress her cheeks, her neck, and play with her hair.

The breeze carried the sounds of a distant party. The riotous cacophony of loud drunken voices, the deep throb of drum and bass, the shrill laughter of drunken women, the deep baritone of male voices arguing. The music changed stride and a familiar melody began ... 'Smooth Operator'.

She looked up at the moon and drank in its luminous form, closing her eyes and letting herself be carried away by the sensuous tune. The image of Toby floated into her mind. She saw him on his yellow bike. She saw him scared and terrified the first time their eyes locked in the office, and the eerie stare he gave her when she seized his bike.

She recalled Cheryl's story of their two dates. *And that story tonight. What did it all mean? What was he up to? He couldn't, could he?'*

She closed the window, and taking ear plugs, jammed out the distraction of the music. Sitting at the table, she took out her notebook and opened to the page listing all the people at Symes. Next to each name, she read their main drivers: Arthur Symes, money. Pat lives for work. Cheryl craves being desired. Delores the head cashier, her two boys. Doug craves status and her uncle's car. Tiny, the big Maori boy, loves his family and faith. The twins, Darryl and Dean, fishing and the high seas. Alcoholic Tom, freedom from responsibility.

If you study people long enough, you could work out their basic drivers, distilling them into a headline, which announced the key to their manipulation. But she didn't like the word *manipulation*. *Guided* was how she liked to put it. Led. Shaped. Moulded. Made useful. She decided to buy each person on her list a well-chosen gift. One aimed at ensuring their devotion.

Through observation, she wrote a headline sentence for each of the new people in her world and a possible present. All, except one. Under the name Toby Z she had wrote: ?????

Ingrid re-examined all her previous interactions since coming to Old Town. While most at Symes had gone out of their way to greet and incorporate her into the social system of the store, Toby had avoided her at all costs.

She recalled how he never came near her, and if in proximity to her, he would bypass her altogether. If she hung around the entrances at the change of shift, speaking to someone, he scurried past her, not daring to lift his eyes to meet hers. Whenever she wandered down an aisle Toby might be working in, he would quickly disappear before she had a chance to say hello.

She had put it down to him being shy and anti-social as Cheryl had stated. But she wondered if there was something more to his avoidance.

From the corner of her eye, she sometimes caught him throwing worried, furtive glances in her directions during staff briefings.

What was his issue? What drove this odd behaviour towards me? And this story tonight. My god, could he? No. It wasn't possible.

She stiffened with a resolve to immediately stop thinking about him. Push the thought of Toby and the story from her mind.

She rose from the table and, falling onto the bed, closed her eyes. Yet the image of Toby lingered, and her unanswered questions gnawed at her.

She heard a persistent rapping. She took out her ear plugs.

'Ingrid, petal.' Arthur tapped on her door again. 'Are you awake?' he whispered through the door.

Ingrid rubbed her face and sighed. She made a vow to learn the truth about Toby. She was determined to find out where he lived, and his big secret.

CHAPTER THIRTEEN

A LUCKY FIND

Ingrid tiptoed into Arthur's bedroom around 2am. Noiselessly, she crept to the bedside table, and with his snoring bellowing out, opened his top drawer. She hoped the extra two sleeping tablets crushed into his warm milk and given with a tender kiss would hold him in a deep stupor until morning.

She took his master keys, freezing as he turned towards her suddenly, his hand reaching out and grabbing her arm.

'Ingrid! Ingrid!' he slurred, before snoring once more. Ingrid, refusing to even breathe, unclasped his hand and gently put it back on his chest as he turned on his side, nearly taking her hand with him.

Ingrid crept down the stairs. To her surprise his study door remained unlocked.

Putting on dishwashing gloves, she set about looking for an employee record sheet or a master file with addresses. She began with his desk, reading over odd memos and slips of paper. She found several statements from the bank. *My god! I could learn his handwriting and take his cheque book.*

Next, she tried to open the filing cabinet with one of the keys from the master key set, but none fit.

'Shit!' she said, then, remembering the importance of silence ran to the back staircase. Arthur's rhythmic snoring came down loud and clear. She returned to her snooping, this time she rifled through the bookcase stacked with manilla folders, stock market reports, and company prospectuses. She stepped onto a milkcrate and found a little tin box on the top of the bookcase. Inside, she found a set of keys. After several goes, she opened the bottom desk drawer where she found a glass jar filled with several fat wads of one-hundred-dollar notes. She untied one wad and pocketed three one-hundred-dollar bills. *This would help with the present buying*, she thought.

She was about to close the desk drawer when she noticed an old, battered exercise book at the back of the drawer.

Settling in his chair, she flicked through the pages.

On each page was a series of numbers. On closer inspection, she saw the numbers began with a date then a series of seven digits separated by a comma.

On the first line of the first page, it read:

1/1/1973 - 4 t right 82, three t left 46, 2 t right 53, 1 t left 19.

On the line below this:

8/1/1973 –1 t left 19, 4t right 82, 3 t left 46, 2 t right 53.

She noted the same series of numbers but in a new order for each row.

She flicked through the pages until the last entry:

30/11/1987 - 19 t right 82, three t left 46, 2 t right 53, 1 t left 19.

Ingrid looked at this entry closely, re-examining the rows of numbers again.

What could this mean?

Then it hit her. *The safe. The combination to the safe!*

She took a scrap of paper and wrote with a trembling hand the last entry. He changed it every week in the same predictable manner.

She put back the notebook and locked the drawer, careful to ensure nothing was out of place before closing the study door.

She would need another way of finding Toby's address, but she went to bed happy. She had discovered something just as important.

CHAPTER FOURTEEN

FRANKIE'S GYM

The next day, Doug drove her into town in the old man's car to do the weekly shopping. 'Listen Ingrid, a few of the lads from footy are taking their missuses to Sydney next weekend to see Hunters & Collectors play at Selinas in Coogee. I thought you might want to come,' said Doug. 'I mean, we go up as friends if that is what you're thinking. Separate rooms of course. I thought you might want to leave town for a while.'

'The gym,' Ingrid said, remembering what Cheryl said about Toby. 'He lives near a gym.'

'Who lives near a gym?' asked Doug, incredulous his proposal could be countered by such a weird segue.

'Oh, a friend in Sydney.' All morning, the thought of tracking Toby consumed her every conscious thought.

'Well, what do you think about next week?' Doug pulled into the Coles carpark.

'Where's the local gym?'

'The local gym?' Doug wasn't certain whether Ingrid had a hearing problem, or she was avoiding the question.

'There's only one gym in Old Town. Frankie's. Everyone I know goes there. All the boys from footy, even bloody Toby works out there. Now what about next week?'

Doug could never understand women, and Ingrid in particular. *One day you're asking them to go to Sydney with you, the next you're taking them to the gym.*

But at least it gave him another reason to talk about himself.

All the way in the car and up the flight of stairs to the gym, Doug regaled her about his promising boxing career.

'Frank Buzzo was a famous boxer from the 60s. He was the New South Wales welterweight champion four years running. He trained my old man and me. Said I was the best young boxer he had ever seen. It was touch and go for a while, either League or boxing. Mate, if I didn't do me knee early in me twenties, I could have gone professional in either sport.'

Ingrid nodded as she cast her eyes around her surroundings.

The gym was a miserable affair. Upstairs was the reception, with two banks of treadmills, weight machines on one side, and on the other, assorted equipment with semi-naked sweaty men leering at her from the mirrored walls. Downstairs was the boxing studio. Here, men worked on punching bags and shadow balls, with two boxers in the boxing ring dominating the middle of the room. One boxer was curled up against ropes, while the other smaller boxer threw a series of jabs at his midriff.

What a great Sunday, thought Doug as they came to the ropes. *First getting to drive the old man's car on a Sunday, then showing off Ingrid to all the boys at the gym.* He even wore his tracksuit and gym gear. He hoped to spar with Frankie. Show her how good he was.

'Frankie!' he called out.

The smaller boxer broke off and Ingrid noticed that Toby was the boxer on the ropes.

'I know today isn't my usual day, but I thought we could spar.'

'Okay,' said Frankie. 'I've finished with Toby.'

Frankie turned to Toby.

'You should practise something other than rope-a-dope. You're good at it.'

'I would still like to practise it,' Toby said.

'Alrighty Toby,' said Frankie. 'I will see you at four on Tuesday. Okay, hop into the ring, Dougy.'

'So, you like to box?' Ingrid said to Toby as he climbed through the ropes and jumped down.

'No,' he said, not looking at her as he put his gloves in a Puma gym bag and took out a towel.

'You're a real mystery,' Ingrid said.

'All I'm doing is learning to defend myself,' he said, rubbing the sweat from his face.

'Are the streets of Old Town that bad?'

'One could say they have become more dangerous over the last month,' said Toby, putting his towel in his bag.

'Hey Ingrid. Watch me box,' said Doug. His track suit was off, and his hands taped and gloved.

'Your boyfriend is calling you,' smirked Toby.

'Very funny.'

Toby slung his bag on his shoulder, and with his hands still taped, began walking away.

'Talking of boyfriends. I hear you and Cheryl were once an item. You took her out on two dates.'

Toby stopped, but did not turn.

Ingrid walked up to him.

'She said you were interested in my uncle and the strong room.'

Toby did not turn.

Ingrid came closer and whispered, 'I've found out my uncle holds anywhere up to five hundred thousand in the strong room on any one day. That would buy a lot of boxing lessons.'

Toby did not move.

Ingrid came a little closer, her face centimetres from his ear. Turning her head each way, and noticing no one close by, she whispered, 'I've also discovered the combination to my uncle's safe.'

Toby turned and stared stony-faced at Ingrid.

'I don't know why you're telling me this.'

Ingrid felt a leathery paw on her shoulder.

She turned to see Doug.

'Hey, are you going to watch me box or what?'

Ingrid spun round, but Toby had disappeared as if by magic, and all that remained was the impression of his final stare.

CHAPTER FIFTEEN

CONSULTATION

'I feel so lethargic, so weak. Jack, I worry constantly about my uncle,' Ingrid said as she slumped on the bed.

'Well, your vital signs are good, but I understand how hard a man like your uncle can be for a young woman like you. I will write you out a prescription for sedatives.'

'Thank you, Jack.' Ingrid rose from her bed and placed a hand on the doctor's arm momentarily.

Jack Harris took out his prescription pad and wrote a script for a mild sedative.

'Take one of these if you feel anxious. They will relax you.'

'Thank you, Jack. You should stay and have dinner with us to tonight. I am reheating leftovers from last Friday.'

'I should be getting along,' he said, clicking closed his consulting bag.

'Jack, I insist you stay.' She placed a hand on his. 'I will not take no for an answer. I have organised the chess board for you and my uncle to play.'

'Well thank you, but first I must call my sister.'

Ingrid led him down the back stairs to the kitchen phone.

'Let me take your bag,' she said, and turning to address her uncle watching TV at the kitchen table, added, 'Uncle, Doctor Harris is going to play chess with you while I make dinner.'

She took the doctor's bag to the office, and closing the door, pressed her back to it and rifled through the bag. Finding the prescription pad, she ripped off several pages.

She jumped as the door handle turned and she felt someone push on the door. Putting the bag down, she stuffed the pages into her jean pocket, her body trembling.

Her uncle stood looking at her closely in the open door.

'Doctor Harris and I want to see you in the living room. Now!'

Ingrid walked into the living room holding her breath.

'Ingrid, you have set the board up all wrong,' Arthur said, sitting before the black pieces. 'Look, the queen should go here, and the knights do not sit at the corners, but here.'

'Apologies,' sighed Ingrid. 'Now if you will excuse me, I will prepare the dinner.'

She poured Jack a Glenfiddich whiskey before reheating last Friday's food.

They ate at the large dining table, Ingrid sitting opposite Dr Harris. She did not eat, instead she smoked and watched her uncle scoff his food. The doctor slowly and methodically ate soundlessly, one spoonful, then another, putting down his spoon occasionally to dab his chin and mouth with the napkin.

'I was wondering, Jack, about some of the patients you have treated over the last few years.'

'I don't speak about my patients' consultations,' Jack put down his spoon.

'As a doctor, I bet you have some interesting stories to tell.'

'Well of course.' He went on to tell one about a patient losing her false teeth, only for them to reappear in a biscuit tin.

Ingrid laughed at the stupid story. She hoped to lead him on to an interesting fact or even a story about someone she knew.

'I suppose people have told you crazy stories after coming back from the dead?'

Jack, who had only picked up his spoon, dropped it. A jarring note of stainless steel on china rang out. He inhaled sharply, then roughly dabbed his lips again with his napkin.

'I never take much interest in after-death stories or believe it's wise to repeat them. They are mere fantasies, and a way for some people to ease themselves through the dying process. Letting these stories out only encourages people to believe in such foolish things.'

He picked up his spoon and continued to eat.

Ingrid took a drag on her cigarette, and leaning back in her seat watched the doctor eating.

A series of images flooded Ingrid's mind. She saw a crying boy as he watched his screaming mother being led away to a waiting ambulance. She saw the boy with his sister visiting their unresponsive mother in a padded hospital room. 'Mum. Mum, when are you coming home?' She saw an image of the same boy kneeling, 'Please God, make my mum better. Please make my mum better.' She saw the same boy, older and taller, putting the Bible in the rubbish bin. She could sense his thoughts. 'I will not be like my mother. I will not be like my mother.'

'Agreed,' Arthur said, pushing away his plate and wiping his mouth with the back of his hand. 'It's nonsense.'

Ingrid, jumping at her uncle's sudden words, lost the train of images.

'Enough of all this hocus pocus,' Arthur said, pointing his knife at Ingrid. 'I want you, Jack, to warn my niece about the dangers of cigarette smoking.'

'I think she's a big enough girl to understand that it is a filthy and disgusting habit,' said the doctor, tilting his head down and looking at Ingrid over the rim of his glasses. 'Do you go out drinking in town?'

'She goes to that cocktail lounge in town,' said Arthur.

'I see,' said Dr Harris. 'Well, let me warn you. Never leave your drink unguarded, Ingrid. There have been several cases of young ladies' drinks being spiked with Rohypnol.'

'What does it do?' Ingrid asked.

'It's a tranquiliser, about ten times more potent than Valium. It is used to treat severe insomnia and assist with anaesthesia, and is freely available with a prescription. Because it's tasteless, it's known to be poured into the drinks of unsuspecting girls.'

'It is available with a prescription, you say?' asked Ingrid.

'Yes.'

'I see. Well, I will be careful with all my drinks from now on,' Ingrid said, leaning back in her seat.

She did not attempt to steer Jack to discussions on any near-death experience. She knew the response she would receive from the good doctor. Besides, she had something else to ponder.

CHAPTER SIXTEEN

A SICKIE

The next day Ingrid called in sick. She put on a performance for her uncle over breakfast, coughing and sighing.

She kept to her room in the morning, her uncle tapping on her door several times. With each knock she pretended to snore. She heard him bustling in the kitchen, walking up and down the stairs before the kitchen back door slammed. She emerged after midday to find burnt toast and cold coffee outside her bedroom door.

She took the backstreets on the bike she bought from alcoholic Tom for two bottles of whiskey she stole from her uncle's bar. She waited at the coffee shop opposite the gym for Toby to appear for his four o'clock appointment. The plan was to follow him from there.

She waited and waited, but he did not show. She walked into the gym several times, but to no avail. She cycled home to a furious uncle.

'Where have you been? I thought you were sick?'

'I was feeling better, so I went for a bike ride.'

* * *

She returned to work the next day, not daring to rouse her uncle's suspicions.

Her luck held, Pat had gone to Sydney for a training course and would not be back until Monday.

Ingrid told Cheryl she was meeting some guy in town at 3pm every day and needed her to cover the phones. Cheryl was thrilled to have a new titbit of gossip to pass around, so she didn't question the story.

Her plan was to wait halfway into town in a side street off Old Town Road. When Toby passed, she would follow. Yet Toby was an elusive customer. As soon as she saw a flash of yellow, she was off following behind. Yet he weaved in and out of traffic, turning down one side street then another. She couldn't keep up and soon lost him in the maze of streets. There was no sense as to the path he took. Each day he turned down a different side street and she was left to ride up and down Old Town Road, stopping at each intersection and looking each way for a flash of yellow. She kept re-entering the gym, trying unsuccessfully to sight her quarry.

By Friday, exhausted and frustrated, she sat outside the café opposite the gym with a cup of skinny latte, debating her next move. She finally caught sight of him pedalling down Old Town Road. He stopped outside the gym and to her surprise he looked directly at her.

The gym was on the corner of Old Town Road and Legerdemain Street. Toby looked towards her again and crossed Legerdemain Street. He stopped on the other corner and looked right at her. He tilted his head as if wanting her to follow him. Ingrid rose and, taking her bike, walked across the road.

Toby opened the squeaky gate of the decrepit blue house opposite the gym, and walking up several steps, threw the front wheel of his bike into a ring dangling on the porch roof. Toby's keys rattled as he opened the creaking door and went inside, leaving the door wide open.

CHAPTER SEVENTEEN

TWO PHILOSOPHIES

After a time debating whether to follow Toby inside, Ingrid opened the squeaky gate and walked up the concrete steps into the house.

She stood in a dank stairwell with empty boxes and plastic bags strewn at her feet.

'Toby!' she called out.

'I'm upstairs.'

She ascended the creaking stairs towards the sound of clomping footsteps and large objects being hastily moved. The stairs ended in a large musty room.

'Would you like tea or coffee?' Toby called out from behind a red velvet curtain.

'Coffee. Black no sugar,' Ingrid said, frowning at a battered armchair, the only inviting piece of furniture in the room. She placed her hand on its surface and wiped away the dust before gingerly sitting. It creaked and sagged beneath her. She took off her scarf and placed it at her feet.

She scanned the room as a kettle bubbled into life. From behind the curtain, she heard mugs and teaspoons being arranged and tins being opened.

Her surroundings, like its inhabitant, were a complete mystery. The walls were bare of any defining features. In the middle of the room sat a small battered coffee table made from stacked bricks and a plate of glass. Several Reader's Digests were scattered over its surface. An old battered couch sat on one side of the coffee table against the wall.

A red curtain served as the door to the kitchen; and to the bedroom and bathroom, she assumed. In one corner was a shabby bookcase, empty except for several random books. She saw one she knew and liked, *Past Imperfect* by Jackie Collins.

If she hoped to read Toby into these surroundings, she was disappointed. Nothing in the room hinted at any personality traits. The kettle whistled to a crescendo then died.

Ingrid was about to sneak over and part the red velvet curtain in search of more clues, when Toby came from behind it with two steaming beverages. He passed her a chipped cup before settling on the sofa opposite, the coffee table serving as their barrier.

'I see you like Jackie Collins,' Ingrid said, eyeing the dusty book on the nearly empty bookcase.

Toby took a sip of his tea before saying, 'You followed me.'

'I was only having coffee across the street.'

Toby took another sip of tea and eyed her closely.

'You've been following me for some time.'

Ingrid took a sip of her coffee.

'Okay you've got me. I confess. Observant of you. Remarkable.'

'I'm surprised you didn't use your chauffer to do the grunt work.'

She smiled at this reference to Doug.

'If you must know,' Ingrid said, 'you're a difficult person to get to know and I've wanted to become acquainted with you for some time.'

'Why?'

'Well, everyone in Symes has been so welcoming, except for you. You have been standoffish, and I was curious to understand why.'

'Don't take it as an offence, but I don't do social.'

'Why?'

'Does there need to be a reason? We're all born different. Me, I like to be alone.'

'We're two peas in a pod then.'

'We're not alike.' Toby shook his head. 'Not alike at all.'

'Why?'

'I keep to myself. While you're trying to wrap half the town round your finger for your own purposes.'

'How?'

'All the presents you intend to buy for people.'

'It's called being a good member of my community. You should try it.'

'I'm genuine with people. I don't think you do anything for the right motives.'

'My, you don't think very highly of me. What have I done to you?'

'Nothing. Yet.'

'Yet?'

'You see, I can see things. Ever since ...' He stopped.

Outside, a car turned a corner and sped up a side street.

'Ever since?' Ingrid said, putting her cup down and leaning forward.

'Ever since I saw you,' he said, taking a hurried sip of his tea.

'When you first saw me, you fainted. Why?'

Toby blushed. She liked how she made him feel uncomfortable. How he kept changing his posture in his seat.

'You saw something in me that day. What was it? A past girlfriend perhaps?'

'Yes. You remind me of someone I once knew,' he said hurriedly.

Another car turned into the street and zoomed past. Outside, a magpie warbled.

'No, that isn't it,' Ingrid said, studying Toby closely.

'You're mistaken.' He shifted on the couch.

'Tell me why,' she said. 'I'm not a bad person once you know me better. I sense we're more alike than you think. Consider me your friend.'

'I'm being honest,' he said, shaking his head.

'I heard an interesting story about you the other night.'

'Oh?' Toby hid his face behind his cup.

'You were thrown out of a church. You told people you had ...'

'I was sick. Delusional,' interjected Toby, putting down his cup on the glass coffee table top with a *crack*. The noise caught them both by surprise.

Ingrid coolly noted his agitated look. She hid a thin smile behind her cup.

'Something happened to you in hospital, didn't it?'

'I was sick.'

'What was the matter?'

'I had trouble with my pancreas.'

'Did you die in hospital?'

Toby didn't answer, he looked pale and haunted. He took a sip of his tea before repeating, 'I was sick.'

'Yes, you said that. But you didn't say whether you died.'

'You ask a lot of personal questions.'

'I'm interested. I hear so many conflicting stories about you. Like how intelligent you are. How you studied medicine in Adelaide. How you like to read, yet your nearly empty bookcase is filled with several trashy novels.'

'They're not mine,' Toby said, following her gaze to the Jackie Collins' books. 'I gave all my books away. I borrow from the library.'

'What type of books do you read?'

'Lots and lots of questions.'

'As I said, I'm curious.'

Toby looked down at his cup, as if marshalling his words carefully.

'I study philosophy and religion.'

'An intellectual?'

'No, curious, like you,' he smiled.

'I admire people who read. It shows an ambition, more than I can say for half the people in this town.'

'I can see how you would like ambition,' Toby said.

The silence returned as they both eyed each other from their seats.

'You're secretive,' Ingrid said, putting down her cup. 'I like that.'

'You see something of yourself in me?'

'There you go again,' Ingrid said. 'Always switching the conversation to me. Clever of you.'

'I'm not that smart,' Toby said.

'Very modest of you, but a *lie*!' She spat the last word, determined to shock him into openness.

'It's the truth,' he said, remaining even-tempered, but watchful.

They took a sip of their beverages in unison, eyeing each other over the rims of their chipped cups.

'What do you want out of life?' sighed Ingrid after a time, exasperated at the many dead ends and false trails in their conversation, and his muteness to her overtures. 'What do you want out of this one and only life? Do you want to be a doctor? Do you want to travel? What are you up to? Why are you so secretive? I know you're up to something. When I look at you, I see ... I see ...'

She stopped and looked at Toby wide-eyed, struck by an insight. More than an insight, but a series of images, as if she watched Toby in the third person above him and to one side.

'You travelled all the way to Old Town from Adelaide by bus. Yes, by bus. How many hours would that have been? Fifteen, twenty hours? And for what? You stepped off the bus and you walked straight to the store. All the way up the hill. You were hot, thirsty and hungry. How long did it take you to walk up? Two hours? And for what purpose? To work at Arthur Symes' multipurpose store. You could find a job anywhere in this town. Anywhere in this state. A bright boy like you should be back in Adelaide studying medicine, or trying your luck in Sydney or Melbourne, yet you chose to come to Old Town, to work at Symes as a storeman. It was as if you did it deliberately. Cheryl said you dated her and all you talked about was my uncle and his money. Is that your game Toby Zachariah? You heard about the money in the strong room and thought you would try your luck?'

Outside, two boys on a bike passed, laughing and screaming. Overhead a Cessna droned to the local airport.

'You're projecting,' Toby said.

'Pardon?'

'You're concluding from my talk with Cheryl a sinister intention. But maybe you're projecting onto me your own dark motives? You're low on money and you've come from Sydney hoping to lever a small fortune from a corrupt and mean old man.'

A motorbike whizzed past.

Ingrid burst into laughter.

'Oh, you're observant,' she said after a time, her smile draining from her face. 'Now let's stop the pretence, the games, the euphemisms.' She put down her cup and leant forward in her seat. 'I think we understand each other. I think we both want the same thing. Together we could be a great team. Together we could do it.'

'We're not the same,' Toby said, shaking his head. 'Not the same at all.'

'So, you're going to spend the rest of your life working at Symes, working as a storeman, living in a dusty rundown building like this?' She looked about her contemptuously.

Toby frowned. Ingrid could feel herself becoming exasperated. Toby was like granite. He was opposed to her, but she couldn't understand why. She didn't want to spend time wearing him down. She wanted to win him over and win him over quickly.

She noticed a thin smile come to his lips. His eyes brightened as his nervousness dissipated.

'You're the ambitious one,' he said.

She couldn't decide whether he praised or mocked her.

'I could tell from the first time I saw you. I recognised your ambition. Your desire to get ahead no matter what the cost. It is your great strength, but the reason why I avoid you.'

Ingrid jumped to her feet and paced with nervous energy.

'I promise you Toby, I won't be stuck in this town for long. I will be in Sydney, London, or LA.'

If he won't reveal himself, why shouldn't I?

She felt irresistibly drawn to revelation. As if, even with his hostility, an understanding existed between the two, as if she spoke to a comrade, a fellow compatriot. Kin. Someone who shared her language, her understanding, if not her view of the world. Unlike the others in this town, she felt no hesitancy in relating the greatness in store for her.

'One day I'm going to be famous. The greatest actress this world has ever known.'

'I believe you.'

'You can see it, can't you?'

'Yes, I can. You're a great actress. You play your character flawlessly.'

'I'm glad someone can see it,' she blushed. 'It takes effort to act, to ...' She stopped and eyed Toby closely. He looked at her intently. Something about him was familiar, as if he had been present in her most secret moments, yet she had never laid eyes on him before. She smiled and wagged her finger at him. She would not be drawn out so easily.

'Unlike some, I intend to make something of my life,' she said. 'Life is there to be taken. Can't you see it all about you Toby? Opportunities. Life is filled with them.'

Ingrid looked abstractly about her, as if she saw these *opportunities* as ripened fruit before her. Fruit she could stretch out her hand and snatch handfuls of and devour.

'Does it mean, if given the opportunity, you would steal from a rich old man?' Toby said. 'Or ...'

'Or what?'

'Kill?'

'Do you think it does?'.

'I'm saying, with your philosophy, stealing, along with any other transgression, becomes possible.'

'Are you some type of old-fashioned moralist?'

Toby smiled as Ingrid sat down again and leant forward.

'I agree with you,' Toby said. 'There's more to the world than this town. But there is also more to the world than the cities of Sydney, Melbourne and London, and all the other big cities combined.'

'So, you're a country boy at heart,' smiled Ingrid, thinking she had finally broken through his circumspection to a warm rustic centre. A young man with a sentimental yearning for a country town, a farm ... maybe a sweet country girl.

'No, I mean this physical plane.'

'Sorry? What?' Ingrid scrunched her face.

'This physical world you see around you isn't the real world. It's nothing more than a dream. It's only when we die that we truly come alive.'

'What are you saying?'

'Have you thought there's more to the world than what you see around you?'

'I don't follow.'

'This physical world is only a small part of the total universe. All around us there are other worlds, other realities, other modes of being, so real they make this world seem like the reflection in a muddy pool in comparison.'

'You're religious?'

'I don't like labels,' Toby said. 'They obstruct true understanding.'

'Look Toby. We could be surrounded by all manner of unseen worlds, but I have a simple philosophy. I believe only in things I can see and touch and taste. The world is big enough and strange enough without having to worry about things one cannot see, hear, touch or taste. A lot of hocus pocus.'

'What if it isn't hocus pocus? What if it was more real and tangible than the stuff you see and touch?'

'If it's more real than this world, why can't I see it? Why am I left to imagine it?'

'The deeper reality is there. You just need to open your mind to it, Ingrid.'

'Why should I? I want to succeed in the here and now and not contemplate something I cannot imagine.'

'What if your materialist philosophy is the wrong game?' said Toby, rising to his feet and gesticulating with his hands. 'What if you're operating in a much bigger and more important game, and the tactics you use in your materialistic game spoil your chances in the bigger one? A game where God is ever present in everything we do and think.'

'I don't believe in God!' Ingrid snapped. Toby looked startled. Her exclamation surprised her too. Toby sat and eyed her curiously. Ingrid felt a wave of revulsion for Toby Zachariah. She'd overestimated him, she finally realised. *He was right. I've projected my own beliefs, my own fantasy of what I imagined him to be, onto this sad, pathetic God botherer.*

'This is a touchy subject for you, I know,' Toby said. 'But you must stop and look at what you're doing before it's too late. You think you're in control of your destiny, but you're not.'

Ingrid jumped to her feet.

'Don't talk to me about God. I had sixteen years of the nuns teaching me about God and Heaven and all the Hell shit. If God is real, where is He? Go on, tell me Toby? It's always a HE! And like most men, He's useless. If He is so omnipotent, why does He allow wars? Or what about all the pain and suffering in the world? If He was so powerful, so good and just, why does He allow evil to thrive? Why does He allow his priests to abuse children? Why Toby, why? Or why does He allow his nuns to be so cruel? And if God exists, why does He allow so-called *Christian men*, the pillars of the Church, to abuse innocent young girls who can't defend themselves? Where is He? Why is it when you pray to make the bastard stop, God doesn't answer? Why? Why? I'll tell you why, because He doesn't exist. He's like Father Christmas and the Easter Bunny, and all the other fairy stories ... a fucken lie used to control people!'

Ingrid stopped shouting and stood for a time, breathing rapidly in the silence of the room.

Outside, a lone magpie warbled. A car turned into the street then droned away.

'I'm sorry Ingrid, truly I am,' Toby said after a time.

'Sorry. Why be sorry? I'm the one who should be sorry for people like you, with your belief in the afterlife rubbish.'

'Your vehemence tells me you do believe.'

'Don't tell me what I believe,' she hissed, pacing once more. 'I'm fed up with people like you telling me what to think and what to believe.'

'I understand your anger. Truly, I can relate to you. I was once like you. But you have God all wrong. He isn't a He or a She, but a force far greater than anything you can imagine. A being of pure love. God doesn't let evil happen. Evil happens when humans turn their back on God, or don't recognise the eternity and immensity of love all around them. There's a reason why evil happens. Without the darkness, how can we know the light?'

'And you believe that? You would rationalise all the evil in the world? Is this what bastards like you do? Well, here is a memo for people like you. God doesn't exist. What you see is what you get. The only things of consequence are my actions. My actions create my world.'

'Only to a degree,' Toby said. 'There are parts you don't control. You live in a reality far more complicated than you realise, Ingrid, with forces far greater and stronger than your individual will, moulding and shaping your every action.'

'Are you saying I have no control over my life?'

'I'm saying you need to be careful about the way you live your life. None of us are truly free. All of us are at the mercy of forces greater than us.'

'What gives you the right to sit in judgement of me?'

'I don't.'

'I spent my childhood listening to the nuns talk about fiery hell. About what would happen to sinners. I spent a lifetime getting away from them and I'm not going to have a nobody like you tell me what to think or believe.'

Hyperventilating, Ingrid stormed from the room.

She was halfway down the stairs when Toby called her name, loudly and urgently.

She stopped and looked up.

'Do you have a red box?' he asked, looking at her wide-eyed.

'What?'

'A red box?'

'No, I don't!' she said, shaking her head and continuing her march down the stairs. After a few steps, she stopped, turned, and looking up, said, 'I know why everyone hates you, Zachariah. You have a knack of getting under a person's skin.'

Ingrid turned and stomped down the stairs into the heat of the late afternoon. She took her bike and crossed the road blindly. A car screeched to a stop in front of her, its horn blaring. She gave the driver the finger before pedalling back towards Symes.

Ingrid had cycled only a metre when she slammed on the brakes and shouted, 'How the hell does he know I'm going to buy presents for everyone?'

CHAPTER EIGHTEEN

PROBATION

'Where have you been?' asked Arthur as soon as she entered through the kitchen backdoor. 'I called the store and they didn't know where you were.'

'I was shopping.'

Realising she had nothing in her hand, she corrected, 'Window shopping.'

'We have guests arriving any minute and you're not ready. Don't you have a watch?'

'I cannot work without the proper equipment!' shouted Mrs. Sarsovy, slamming down an empty pot on the stove.

Ingrid's stomach was rolling with the smell of garlic, black peppers, and tomatoes.

'My utensils are adequate for the task,' shouted Arthur, turning to berate his cook.

'Look at this knife,' Mrs. Sarsovy said, brandishing a dull blade.

Ingrid took the opportunity of the distraction to tiptoe upstairs. She spent a long time in the shower letting the water rush over her neck and down her body, and an even longer time to dress, admiring her new purchases in the mirror — a knee-length pink dress with matching high-heel shoes.

What takes this girl so long? thought Arthur, looking at his watch. He was forced to delay the dinner and carry on with small talk with his guests, which he detested. It was her job to greet their guests and deal with Mrs. Sarsovy.

Arthur was about to order everyone to leave and storm upstairs to rap on her door and demand she leave his house at once, when she finally appeared. His heart missed a beat.

The room fell quiet as she entered. Arthur noticed how every man watched her walk, and how every woman coveted her look. She passed from one group to the next.

My god she is so stylish, thought Arthur, *and she's my niece. Mine.*

'It's time to eat,' Ingrid said to the room. 'Mrs Sarsovy, please serve the main course.'

Ingrid sat at the end of the table, Dr Harris on her right as usual, and the mayor's wife, Doris, on her left.

She vowed in the shower that she would enjoy every moment of her life, relish every smell, savour every morsel of food, covet every finery, fall in love again and again and again; waste not one breath. It would begin tonight. She was determined to become rich. Rich beyond her wildest dreams; and here around this table sat the means to this end: the small-minded and self-satisfied elite of a provisional town, ripened fruit ready to be plucked and sucked dry.

During lapses in her conversation with her neighbours, she took an inventory of each person at the table. Big fishes in a little pond, laughing and happy except for one.

All through dinner Detective Sergeant Rob Charles was unusually quiet. Instead of the crude cross-table flirting he enjoyed with her on previous Friday nights, he remained mute. She noted that his eyes did not follow her about the room before dinner, or, like the other men, gaze at her at the dinner table during pauses in the conversation. Instead, he drank steadily, and by dessert was morosely looking down at his half-eaten bowl of pudding.

Arthur couldn't keep his eyes off his niece. His end of the table was quiet in comparison to hers. He had the mayor on his right and the young detective on his left. Both men were content to eat, leaving him the solitude and time to admire his niece's beauty. He marvelled at the way the candlelight played in her eyes; how she chatted easily and naturally with her neighbours; how the guests gravitated towards her, freeing Arthur of the need to always be alert, and allowing him the pleasure of relaxing and enjoying his food.

'So how did the transfer go?' Arthur asked Rob over coffee. He thought it time to make some chit chat, and remembered the detective's boast from last week.

'I'm stuck in Old Town for the foreseeable future,' said Rob, not lifting his eyes from his coffee. 'Now if you will excuse me,' he added, pushing away his cup, 'I'll grab my drink at the bar and be off. I have an early start tomorrow.'

Arthur gave him his bribe, the detective seeing himself to the door. The table watched him depart in silence. Once gone, John Smith spoke. 'Our hot-shot detective didn't win his promotion. The end does not always justify the means.'

Arthur was glad the young detective would remain in town. Contacts in the force were difficult to cultivate.

* * *

All weekend, Ingrid kept her mind busy. On Saturday, she nicked a corkboard from her uncle's study and developed her visualisation board using cut-outs from fashion magazines.

She would drive a cherry-coloured Ferrari to a wedding-cake-themed mansion by an emerald sea with an azure sky untouched by any wisp of cloud. She would be decked in emeralds and diamonds with a Gucci handbag slung over her shoulder.

On Sunday, she took an inventory of all the people she had met and their usefulness. For the men on Friday night, she registered their favourite drinks, their likes and dislikes. Next to this was her plan for each man, narrowing it down to a select few targets — Dr Harris being her number one project.

By Sunday evening, she had determined to make a new start at work. Clearly Pat had the wrong impression of her, obviously from Toby. She would deal with him in time, but for now she would need to get on the right side of Pat. Ingrid wondered what Christmas gift would be suitable. She intended to buy them during the week and hand them out individually. She closed her eyes and saw Pat smiling at her.

On Monday, she arrived thirty minutes early, hoping to impress Pat.

She found the administration area empty as expected, but voices were coming from Pat's office, the door of which was slightly ajar.

She stiffened as she recognised Toby speaking.

'My whole world has been turned upside down. I don't know what to believe anymore. I'm no longer the person I was six months ago.'

'You need to take a holiday.'

'I can't. You don't know the danger, Pat.'

'Toby, this is nothing more than your imagination. When was the last time you had a proper holiday?'

'Pat, I've confided in you. Please take it seriously.'

'I'm filling in this holiday form, Toby. I want you on leave as of today and I don't want you back here until after Australia Day.'

'I'm handing in my resignation. I'm done. I've had it. I warn people but they don't listen.'

'I'm signing this form. Go home to Adelaide. See your family.'

'I resign, Pat.'

'I've told you I have the situation under control. By the time you come back everything will be different. You'll see.'

'You're like the rest, Pat. Can't see beyond what is in front of your eyes.'

The door of Pat's office swung open. Ingrid ducked beneath her desk as Toby marched past and down the stairs.

Ingrid rose to her feet and jumped in fright as Pat loomed before her.

'I was looking for a bracelet I dropped.'

'You're early, Miss Symes.'

'I thought I would come in and get a few things done before people arrived.'

'Yes, well, I would like to see you this afternoon in my office. One o'clock.'

'Ms Symes, as you know, you need to complete a three-month probationary period,' began Pat at their meeting. 'With your uncle busy with other matters, it is left to me to review your progress. After careful consideration of your performance and standard of work, I will not be extending your employment beyond the three months, which ends on the thirtieth of January.'

The air conditioning unit hummed.

'Are you dismissing me?'

'You have a three-month probation period. I'm giving you ample notice that I will not be extending your employment beyond that time.'

'You're firing me?'

'I'm letting you stay on until the end of January.'

'But why?' Ingrid said, shaking her head. 'I can't see how you can dismiss me when I have only been here under two months.'

'Let us take last week as an example,' said Pat. 'You took every afternoon off while I was away. You left Cheryl to mind the phones. You failed to put in a leave notice for this time. It is a policy of the business that employees are to lodge a form prior to taking time off. Also, you're continually leaving your desk and wandering through the store. *Also*, I've had several complaints from customers about your rude behaviour. I don't think you're a good fit for this business. You lack the necessary customer service orientation. I know this may be harsh, but I believe this is a blessing in disguise for a girl like you. You will find work quickly in Old Town. However, may I suggest you return to Sydney. A girl like you is too talented for a place like Symes or for Old Town.'

Ingrid listened incredulously as Pat prattled on about how wonderful she was, and how wasted her talents were at Symes. She had been fired from other jobs before. Usually for similar reasons as Pat had outlined. Her continual wandering from her station. Her constant snooping and putting her nose into business unrelated to her job. Her inattention to her assigned tasks. She had left each job without a qualm or second thought. She believed she was above most petty jobs. *Pat's right. I'm far too talented for my current role, for this dump of a business.*

Yet the thought of being dismissed from Symes left her horror struck. The thought of starting again, of catching the bus into town and walking to a dead-end retail job left her cold.

Why should I care about this job? I hate it. Answering phones, filing, assisting in menial clerical tasks. Unemployment had more dignity. Yet in a blinding flash of insight, she realised why she wanted to stay. She wanted to remain close to the strong room with all its crisp notes and sparkling coins, all its wealth within easy reach. She wanted to stand on top of the office landing and look down at the shelves groaning with stock. This was the family business. She had spent weeks investing time into her uncle and these petty employees at Symes: the book on public speaking she would give to Tiny; the esky she had bought the twins; all the little gifts she would give the girls. She was about to invest in these people, and she intended to see her investment was repaid, doubled, tripled. The image of Toby floated into her mind. *He was behind this. I'll make him pay for this. He'll rue the day he was born.*

"I understand your decision Pat, but if I could stay on until the end of January.'

'Of course,' said Pat, smiling and leaning back in her chair.

'Also, please don't mention it to my uncle or the others until then.'

'I'm sorry it had to come to this Ingrid.'

'No Pat,' Ingrid said, 'I'm the one who's sorry.'

An Unfortunate Accident

Ingrid had never worked as hard as she did the week leading up to Christmas. For the first time since arriving at Symes, she decided to work diligently. Between answering the phones, she helped downstairs on the tills and restocking the shelves with Doug's crew. She even assisted several customers with a smile. On breaks she sought out each staff member and doled out their presents, watching their reception as each person unwrapped his or her gift. The harder the hug, the bigger the smile, the more she knew she had hit the mark.

Tiny's present touched her the most. He opened his book on public speaking and looked at it a long time before a tear ran down his face. She received such a bear hug she thought her ribs might crack.

The twins' present of the esky brought Ingrid a fishing invitation. She refused. After a second request, however, she said, 'Why not Dean? But you and Darryl must teach me how to tie knots with a fishing line.'

'Not a problem, love.'

* * *

She spent a night on the water, cold and seasick. Daryl and Dean marvelled at her determination to learn everything about fishing, especially how to knot fishing lines.

Christmas came, and the tempo slowed. To her surprise, she found a wrapped gift on the breakfast table with her name on it. She opened it to find a crystal bangle watch. After examining it closely under the light, she guessed it to be worth more than two hundred dollars.

'There's no need to be late now,' Arthur said, sporting the present she gave him, a dressing gown with his initials AS emblazoned on the pocket.

'If you spend your money on frivolous gifts like this you will be poor,' snapped Arthur before shuffling out of the kitchen. Yet she noticed he wore it every night after that.

Between Christmas and New Year Ingrid kept to her room and continued to practise her fishing line knots, rehearsing all possible scenarios.

Finally, New Year's Eve arrived. The store shut early at 3pm, and the staff not on holiday, and eager for extra money, assembled in the office for the briefing on the half-year stocktake. Pairs would be assigned, one to count the stock, the other person to write down the count on the stocktake sheets. Once three quarters of the stock was counted, Pat, Cheryl and Ingrid went upstairs to begin putting the figures into the computers.

Ingrid was only added to this contingency after Barb, the new financial accountant, fell suddenly ill after lunch.

Pat had softened to Ingrid since the interview. Since then, Ingrid had been a pleasant and conscientious worker. When Ingrid offered to stay behind, Pat had no hesitation in accepting. She thought it was the least she could do in the circumstance.

Ingrid was to prepare the stocktake sheets and look for errors before passing them to Cheryl for entry into the computer in Arthur's office. Meanwhile, Pat would prepare revenue results and other accounts for a definitive position in her office.

Once all the sheets were checked, Ingrid would go home.

It was after seven when the last stock-takers handed in their sheets. Ingrid gave the papers a cursory glance before knocking on Pat's door and offering to make a coffee.

'Black with three sugars,' said Pat, not looking up.

Ingrid gathered Cheryl's order and brought Pat's coffee first. Pat thanked her, took a sip, and winced. She didn't like the way Ingrid made coffee but thought it rude to complain. Besides, she was far too busy to worry.

Next, Ingrid took Cheryl's tea and shut the door quietly behind her.

'I was meaning to give you your present,' Ingrid said.

'But you've already given me a bottle of perfume.'

'I know, but you've been such a great friend and I saw this, and I couldn't resist buying it for you.'

Ingrid handed her the present.

'OMG! A Walkman!' gasped Cheryl, unwrapping it.

Ingrid motioned Cheryl to be quiet.

'I don't want the old biddy finding out,' Ingrid whispered, pointing to the wall backing onto Pat's office.

'Of course,' whispered Cheryl.

Ingrid didn't tell her she had stolen it from under the nose of a distracted store clerk.

'I've put batteries in it and here is a tape of AC/DC. You can listen to it as you plug in the figures.'

'Oh my god,' said Cheryl, barely able to supress her shock and amazement at this lavish gift, squealed and hugged her newest and greatest friend.

'Put them on and see if it works.'

Cheryl didn't need to be asked twice. She put on the headset and pressed play. Ingrid immediately heard the tinny strain of 'It's a Long Way to the Top'.

'How is it? HOW IS IT?'

What?' said Cheryl, taking off the headset.

'Nothing,' smiled Ingrid. 'I better leave. Happy New Year.'

Ingrid walked to the door

'Ingrid,' said Cheryl.

Ingrid stopped.

'You're a great mate.'

'I know.' Ingrid smiled, before closing the door.

Ingrid stood momentarily in the administration office listening to the rat tat of the keyboard, the tinny sound of music, and Cheryl's monotone singing.

She then grabbed the small step ladder by her desk and positioned it beneath the light on the stair landing. Taking several steps down the stairs, she took a tiny roll of fishing wire from her pocket. Leaning down, she made a knot around the stair railing at ankle height before tying it to a small hook she had asked maintenance to drill into the wall opposite, ensuring the line was as taut as guitar wire.

Calmly, she walked back to the landing. Turning the light switch off, she climbed the ladder and changed the light bulb for a dead one. Packing up the ladder, she moved back into the office, placing the step ladder behind the door. The music and Cheryl's tuneless voice were the only sounds. She tapped gently on Pat's office door, and without waiting for a reply entered.

'Pat.'

'I thought you had gone home.'

'I did, but I noticed something downstairs. I think there's a dead body.'

'A dead body?'

Pat looked incredulously at Ingrid.

'You need to come quick.'

Pat jumped to her feet. Although she felt extremely tired, as if she wanted to fall on the ground and sleep, this news roused her.

'Where?'

'In kitchenware.'

'Tell Cheryl to call the police!'

'I will call from your phone.'

Pat marched out of her office and into the main administration office. As she marched to the stairs, Pat heard music coming from Arthur's office. *Those damn Walkmans*, thought Pat. *As soon as I get to the bottom of this nonsense downstairs, I'll demand Cheryl stop listening to music. I don't want mistakes with the stocktake.*

The stair landing was dark, so she flicked the light switch once, then twice. Nothing.

Pat jumped in fright as Ingrid loomed from behind, swallowed in the shadows.

'You were quick.'

'I got straight through.'

Ingrid started to close the door.

'Don't. We have no light.'

'I've brought a pocket flashlight,' Ingrid said, taking one from her jean pocket, envisaging this exact scenario. Ingrid closed the door and trained the light on the steps.

'This light is an OHS issue,' said Pat.

'I will write it down.'

Pat looked at Ingrid and thought of Toby and their discussion before Christmas.

'Please go down, Pat.'

Pat eyed Ingrid closely.

'Please hurry Pat, I beg you.'

Ingrid shivered.

Pat turned and made her way down slowly in the semi-darkness. Ingrid's torch cut out as she started her descent. Three steps down, something cut into Pat's leg and she stumbled, throwing a hand against the wall to arrest her fall.

'No ...' Pat started to say just as a hand pushed hard into her back and she flew forward. Before she could scream out, her head bounced once, twice, thrice upon the cold, hard steel stairs.

In the office, Cheryl continued to type up the stocktake results to the beat of 'Dirty deeds done dirt cheap'. Through her headphones, she thought she heard the rumble of distant thunder. Taking off her headphones, she strained her ears. Nothing. *They did say the possibility of a thunderstorm this evening.* She shrugged her shoulders, put her headphones back on, and continued with her task.

Ingrid walked down to the fishing line and cut it off with a Swiss blade knife, which she took from her pocket, leaving no trace of the line. She walked slowly down to Pat, who was sprawled unconscious and bloody on the stairs. Ingrid kneeled, carefully avoiding a pool of blood beginning to trickle down the steps.

Pat's eyelids flickered, then opened, her pupils dilating in recognition as Ingrid brought her face close to hers.

Pat tried to mouth something. No sound came out, but Ingrid guessed it to be a plea for mercy. But as she bent closer, she heard Pat gasp, 'Toby. Toby. Wolf.'

Ingrid grabbed a fistful of Pat's hair and, biting her bottom lip, pounded Pat's head into the edge of the step with all her might, once, twice, thrice. Pat's eyes rolled into the back of her head as Ingrid pinched Pat's nostrils closed and covered her mouth.

While she waited for Pat to die, Ingrid amused herself by watching Pat's blood oozing down the steps. She wondered whether by the time Cheryl found her, Pat's body would be a shrivelled prune.

Finally, Ingrid took away her hands and, careful not to step in any puddles of blood, descended the steps, sauntered to the back entrance, and left the building.

At home she sat with her uncle watching the New Year Eve's celebrations from Sydney on TV before going upstairs to sit by her bedroom window and watch the fireworks over Lighthouse Point. The sound of exploding fireworks, and a brewing thunderstorm on the western horizon, intermingled with distant sirens coming closer and closer.

Downstairs the phone rang urgently.

Ingrid smiled.

PART 2

THE ROBBERY

CHAPTER ONE

THE BEQUEATH

Pat's family held her funeral on the following Friday at St Michael's. The coroner gave a verdict of an accidental fall. Rumours swirled through Symes about Pat abusing Rohypnol before her death. Most agreed she came back too soon from her illness.

Symes closed at midday so staff could attend the funeral.

Arthur, guided by his niece, shuffled to a second-row pew in the church. For the first time, he met Pat's elderly parents and her partner, a short, nondescript woman of fifty-five.

'Partner?' he said, bewildered. 'Pat had a business?'

'No,' whispered Ingrid, squeezing his arm. 'A life partner.'

Pat lived with a woman? thought Arthur as his niece led him to his seat. *Pat lived with a woman!*

Arthur gave a short eulogy at the service. He had known her close on thirty years, yet he realised he did not know one thing about her life. It took him all night to compose a short three-minute speech. He had spent half the night staring at a blank page. What did he know of Pat the person? Little, he realised now.

Pat had worked for him for more than thirty years, yet he did not know what she liked or disliked. He had never thought to ask whether she had children, or even a husband. Now he knew. *Pat lived with a woman!*

Pat came to work and did her work methodically and diligently. So, at the funeral, that is what he spoke about. Her punctuality, her diligence in following orders, her brisk businesslike walk through the office; how in all the years he knew her, she had not failed him once. He stopped there, determined not to think about Pat, or her funeral, one more second. He took his notes, frowned, and gruffly limped from the pulpit, helped down by his niece.

It rained so hard through the service that the organ struggled to be heard above the hiss of water hitting the roof. At the cemetery, Arthur huddled beneath an umbrella, which his tall and attractive niece held for them both. He breathed in her perfume, held her hand tightly, and pressed her close as the coffin was lowered and the minister recited the last rites.

Arthur looked miserably out the car window at the windswept and soaked landscape as he, Dr Harris, Ingrid and Doug drove home from the funeral. Arthur felt the irresistible urge to shout, 'Take me back to Pat's grave! I want to give her a piece of my mind! How dare she slip and crack open her skull.' He wanted to command her to rise from the ground like Lazarus and return to her post.

How dare she go and die on me! How dare she do it, just as I was about to expand my business interests. I needed her to look after Symes: dutifully keep the store running while I doubled, tripled, quadrupled my wealth. I needed all my mental energy for the complex series of real estate and business transactions to bring the marina development to fruition, not for the petty running of the store, with all its stupid human complexity and emotions. I had promoted Pat to deal with that. Yet, what does she do as soon as she's given extra responsibility? She goes and dies on me! I should have stressed the importance of her role. How dare she fall down the stairs! How dare she! Such insubordination! A sackable offence. If she was in the car, I would have struck her with my open hand.

Instead, he slapped his thigh so hard the others stopped talking and looked at him. Arthur, not wishing to talk, turned his head sharply and looked out at the mist-shrouded landscape and imagined hurling abuse at Pat as she sat behind her desk.

The car halted suddenly in the middle of the street a few metres from Symes. The chatter in the car also stopped.

Roused from his introspection, Arthur barked at Doug, 'Why have you stopped?'

'A fallen tree Mr Symes.'

The wheeze of the windscreen wiper trying to keep up with the deluge echoed in the car. The flashing lights of a police car and an SES van blocked their progress in front of Symes. Through the haze and rain, Arthur spied an uprooted jacaranda tree fallen across the road. Its purple flowers were strewn across the wet asphalt like confetti at a wedding.

'That jacaranda has been there a while. I wondered when it might come down,' said Doug.

'It was a lovely tree,' added Ingrid. 'I noticed it on my first day.'

As they waited for the signal to pass, Arthur tried to recall the jacaranda tree outside his property. He couldn't visualise it, or any tree on the street. *Who thinks to look at a tree?* he thought. *I never had the time. Yet here it lay strewn across the road. A great tree once dominating the landscape, felled by wind, rain and time. Dead. Why had I never noticed it?*

They finally received the signal to pass and Doug eased the car into the garage.

As Arthur unsteadily made his way back up the back steps into his house, he felt a surge of anger towards his niece, the doctor and Doug.

I'm old, he thought as he collapsed into an armchair and stared at the carpet, *and with age I will be dependent on these people for my survival.*

'Would you like a drink, Uncle?' asked Ingrid, placing a hand on his shoulder. Arthur waved her away and stared out into space. Pat was dead and he felt old and helpless.

Who could I trust to look after Symes while I attended to the property deals? He looked up and saw Ingrid behind the bar pouring a whiskey for Jack Harris and a bourbon for Doug. *Could I trust her with the business? She was smart and gutsy. I liked how she stood up to me. It showed spine, and she knew what she wanted and how to get it. But could she help me with my business? No,* he mused, watching her pour herself a chardonnay with soda.

She was too young and the wrong sex. The men would not listen to her or take her seriously.

Doug downed his bourbon and plonked the empty glass on the bar. *Doug running Symes?* The thought of Doug placing his scuffed steel cap boots under any desk of consequence at Symes sent a shudder down his spine. *I would sooner see Cheryl in charge.*

Where were the leaders? The next generation? All the team leaders at Symes were nothing but a bunch of yobbos, with nothing on their mind except sport and petty domestic interests. Why did Pat have to die?

He sighed, slapping the arm of his armchair. *How selfish of her leaving me alone to look after Symes.* Arthur no longer felt despondent, but angry at Pat again. *How could she leave as I was about to strike big in the property market?*

He looked at the three at the bar talking and drinking his alcohol: Dr Harris, his best whiskey, Doug his best bourbon. *They were eating and drinking Arthur Symes into the poor house. Was that their game? To see me thrown onto the street for the second time in my life?*

Doug's scuffed steel cap boots, muddy from the rain, dangled like idiotic puppets on a string. *He hadn't wiped his shoes before coming into the house!* Arthur noticed muddy tracks on the carpet. *To think I would be dependent on these people for so many basic functions. I couldn't allow this. The chardonnay cost ten dollars a bottle, and the whiskey twenty dollars a bottle. It was like Ingrid had opened a window and my money was scattered with the wind.*

Outside, the rain came down harder. The sky rumbled. The room lit up with a flash of lightning.

'Did Pat have any children?' asked Dr Harris.

'Only a Labrador,' said Doug.

'So, Ella her partner will inherit the lot,' Ingrid said.

'I heard she's leaving half of it to her niece and nephew and the other half to Ella,' said Doug.

'Pat's a fool!' cried Arthur. His piercing words brought a silence to the room, even the rain stopped, as if the vehemence of Arthur's words had shocked nature into momentary silence. 'A person should never bequeath money to a relative. NEVER!'

Arthur glared at Ingrid and pointed at her. 'If you're expecting once cent out of me, missy, you have another thing coming. Let me make this plain. You will not inherit a single cent from my estate. Not a cent! Why should I give a little upstart like you one penny? You haven't done anything to earn it. Why should you, after a few short years, inherit money you didn't do anything to deserve? Squander it no doubt. A person should learn to make their own way in life without help from anyone. I would rather see my money thrown on a bonfire than see another person inherit it. If you want to be rich, roll up your sleeves and start working. All my money is going to the Salvos when I die. Every cent! Do you hear?!'

'You're joking, right?' Ingrid said, slivers of ice running through her veins.

'I don't joke about money,' cried Arthur.

Doug put down his glass and made a motion to leave.

'As for you!' Arthur said, pointing to Doug. 'How many times do I have to tell you to wipe your shoes before coming into my house? You're nothing but a shit kicker who can't do the basics right. Why, if it wasn't for your father begging me to take you in, you would be on the dole. Now get out of my sight.'

Doug stormed from the room, his face bright red.

Arthur rose to his feet, drained and weak. He shuffled up the main stairs to his room and fell onto his bed.

'I'm sure he wasn't serious,' Ingrid said.

'Unfortunately, he was,' said Jack, moving his bar stool closer to Ingrid.

'I was a witness to his current will. Every cent he owns will go to the Salvos. Your uncle has strong views on bequeathing. He believes each person must make their own fortune without the aid of their parents.'

'I admire his strict and noble ideals,' she said, forcing a smile onto her face.

'I know what a difficult man your uncle is to live with,' sighed the doctor, placing a hand on hers, 'and I want you to know, if ever you need anything from me ... anything ... let me know. I know how mean and selfish your uncle can be.'

'Thank you, Jack,' Ingrid said, placing her free hand on his. 'You're such a kind man.'

Oh my god! thought Ingrid as she sat on the end of her bed later that night, *I have wasted my time here. I won't inherit a thing! Not one cent.*

She walked to the window and stared out at Symes' large neon sign. *If I can't inherit the money, I need to take what I can now and be done with the place. But how?*

The rain had stopped, and the night was filled with the drone of cicadas and the dripping water from Symes' corrugated iron building. As the clouds parted and the waning moon winked down at her, a half-formed plan merged in the recess of her mind. One so ambitious and so tantalising that she felt dizzy with its audacity.

Yes. Yes. I will do it. Everything is there for the taking.

CHAPTER TWO

AUSTRALIA DAY

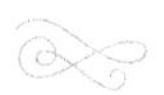

As a mark of respect to Pat, Symes did not open until the following Tuesday. Business was slow. Disbelief and grief hung in the air like the summer humidity. The shock of Pat's death echoed in the hearts of the staff rostered on. Pat had been at Symes from the start. She was like a foundation stone, which without warning had been smashed out.

Arthur decided to return to his old position and run Symes. He couldn't trust anyone else but Pat to run his business. He built-up cash in the strong room. He cancelled the extra security provisions Pat had put in train before Christmas as money he could ill afford to spend, especially with his big investments on the go.

Ingrid assisted Arthur during this time. She cleaned out Pat's office when Arthur couldn't bring himself to do the task. She comforted the cashiers when they burst into tears in the changerooms. She organised a beer and pool night for the boys on the following Thursday night at her uncle's house. 'A way to cheer them up,' she told a less-than-impressed Arthur.

Arthur tried out a few finance officers from an agency. Many didn't last a day, falling sick, usually after lunch. Barb resigned after Pat's death.

'The younger generation don't want to work,' he growled.

Arthur came to rely on Ingrid to take over their duties.

As staff returned from their summer holidays, Ingrid was the first to break the news of Pat's death and offer them her support.

For Australia Day, she organised a barbeque in the carpark for customers and friends of Symes. In the evening, she planned a bicentennial party for the staff at Lighthouse Point to watch the fireworks.

If Pat was the stone on which Symes was built, Ingrid was now the heart that kept Symes beating at this difficult time.

It was only fitting that on the last Friday in January, with all the staff back on deck from their summer Christmas holidays, Arthur Symes announced to the thunderous applause of the packed administration area, that Ingrid Symes had passed her probation and was now a full-time member of Symes.

Ingrid smiled and blushed as each staff member came and congratulated her on passing probation and again thanked her for the thoughtful gifts that she had given them at Christmas. But one would expect that generosity from the niece of a rich uncle.

With Pat gone, Ingrid considered her position secure, her plans unfolding in the right direction as she cleaned up the deserted office after the last person had taken his pay.

She was singing the chorus of 'I think We're Alone Now' by Tiffany when a voice startled her.

'What happened to Pat?'

She swung around to face a tanned and serious-looking Toby.

'I thought you had resigned?'

She turned back and continued cleaning up.

'I've merely been on a long holiday.'

Ingrid furtively looked at the entrance before turning and saying, 'It might be better for all concerned if you did resign.'

'A threat?'

'No one likes you,' she hissed. 'I would leave before you're pushed.'

'Down the stairs?' asked Toby.

'Forced out,' Ingrid said, inhaling sharply.

'Was that the deal you gave Pat?'

Ingrid came close to Toby, and digging her pointed nail in his chest, said, 'If I catch you making up tales behind my back, I will sue you for every cent you own. I will hurt you and everyone you love.'

'Ingrid!' shouted Arthur, emerging from the strong room. 'It's time to leave.' He locked the strong room.

'Still here, Toby?' he said, putting his keys in his pocket

'Yes Mr Symes. I was just talking to your niece.'

Toby smiled, his eyes not leaving Ingrid's.

'Yes, yes,' Arthur said. 'Now no more idle chit chat. I want to find out what that miserable Mrs Sarsovy is making for dinner, and you better go home, Toby. I want you in bright and early to help me open up.'

At the office door, Toby stopped and kept the door open for Arthur and Ingrid. Arthur walked down the stairs, stopping halfway and turning. Both Ingrid and Toby stood on the landing looking at each other.

'Why are you two still on the landing?'

'I was being a gentleman and offering your niece the chance to go first, Mr Symes,' Toby said.

'I don't believe in tradition,' Ingrid said.

'Ingrid! Come down now. I haven't got all night.'

Ingrid reluctantly complied, but she gripped the railing tightly, her back stiffening with Toby inches behind her, their footfall echoing along the wall.

Outside in the dusk, Toby turned to Arthur. 'I'm struck by how alike you and your niece are, Mr Symes. God has obviously brought you together for a reason.'

Before Arthur could reply, Toby turned, and was swallowed by the gloom and a swarm of butterflies.

'That is one strange boy,' Arthur said.

Ingrid watched Toby go, shivering a little as her uncle cursed the humidity.

How could Toby know about Pat? A guess? A lucky guess? Toby had many of these, she thought. *He's a threat that has to be dealt with.*

'What are you doing still standing there? We need to be getting home,' Arthur said.

'Sorry, what?' Ingrid shook herself free of her private musings.

'We will be late.'

As she walked with her uncle cursing his Hungarian cook, a new dimension to her plan took shape in the darkest corner of her mind.

What was the saying? Killing two birds with one stone?

CHAPTER THREE

RESIGNATION

Doug slammed the driver's door of his Sandman panel van and made his way up the driveway to the kitchen door of Arthur's house. Sticking out of his top pocket was the resignation letter his mum had typed out for him the previous night. He intended to give it to the old man on Monday morning, but when Arthur called him before dinner on Friday saying he wanted to see him first thing Saturday morning, he thought, *What the hell!* He decided to give the old boy his resignation before storming off.

After the funeral, Doug had taken a weeklong sickie. He was done with Symes. He was done with the lot of them. He had discussed packing in his job at Symes and leaving Old Town for good with his mum and sister. When he finally returned to work, he skulked down on the shop floor, refusing to go up into the main office to see Arthur when ordered.

To his surprise, his boss made it down the stairs on his first day back and tried to engage him in small talk. *He would need to do more than that to make up for all the years of abuse.* Ingrid was also super friendly, coming downstairs to speak with him. *Was she flirting with me? Nah, she was mocking the shit-kicking storeman.*

Doug took another week off. He and his sister only settled the plan via phone on the Thursday night after Australia Day. He would hand in his resignation on Monday, then, after seeing out four weeks, he would move up to Brisbane to live with his sister until he found a job and a place of his own.

All Friday night at the Railway Hotel he fantasised about how he would deliver the news to the old man. After his second beer he visualised marching into the entertainment room with muddy shoes to deliver the letter. After several more beers he determined to throw the letter at the old boy's feet, spit out what he really thought of him before storming out the door. After downing a few bourbons, he added a backhander to the scene. *Fuck the holiday pay and my other entitlements. My dignity is more important than money.*

Yet as he stood in the kitchen watching the old man shuffle towards him, all the bravado of the night before vanished, replaced by the old habit of fear as he stooped to a servile posture.

'I hope your mother is well Doug?'

'Eh yeah, not bad,' said Doug, taken by surprise. Arthur Symes never asked questions about his family.

'Look I need you to take my niece shopping,' Arthur said, dangling the car keys in front of him. 'And here is a dollar for your trouble. Why don't you take the car down the coast?'

Doug wanted to laugh. A dollar and a spin in his car. That is how much he thought the years of abuse was worth. *A measly dollar and a spin in his car!*

He was about to take out his letter and throw it at the old man's feet when Ingrid appeared in the kitchen and he gulped, forgetting everything.

Doug felt confused and self-conscious as he eased the car onto the street and drove down to Old Town Road.

Ingrid, dressed in a red dress with matching stilettos, looked as if she was going to a party. *And why was she staring at me?* He swerved to miss a stationary car.

'I was disgusted with the way my uncle spoke to you after the funeral,' she said after a time, her eyes never leaving him.

Doug said nothing as his bottom lip quivered.

'You're twice the man he is.'

The dashboard hummed as Doug slowed the car.

'I've always said, you're the man running the show at Symes.'

'Your uncle doesn't think so,' said Doug.

'Well, he's a fool,' Ingrid said. 'You should be running Symes.'

'I would run things differently,' said Doug after a time.

'Yeah, you wouldn't put up with any of the bullshit.'

Doug blushed as they slowed for one of the few traffic lights in Old Town.

'Now whereabouts do you want to go?' asked Doug.

Ingrid placed her hand on his on the gear stick and squeezed.

'I want you to drive me to the beach.'

CHAPTER FOUR

DOUG IN LOVE

'I don't know why we need to sneak around,' said Doug as they lay in the back of his panel van a week later.

'I don't want anyone finding out about us,' she said.

'But why?' said Doug.

'Because I don't want people to know.'

'Can I at least tell me mum and sister.'

'You can tell no one, especially your mum and sister.'

Ingrid sat up and searched Doug's face. 'You haven't told them about us?'

'Relax,' he said, trying to pull her back down. 'I haven't told anyone, especially me mum and sister.'

'What did you tell them about not resigning?'

'I told 'em I changed my mind. They know better than to question my decisions.'

It wasn't quite what he said. He had told his mum and sister he didn't feel ready to pack it in. Wanted to earn some extra cash before making the decisive move to Queensland. Also, the old man had said he was sorry. A lie, but it made his change of heart look less weak.

'You must promise me Doug Haywood, not to tell anyone about us. If I find out you have told one person, I will never speak to you as long as you continue to breathe.'

'Relax I don't know why you're so edgy. I promise,' he said, sitting up and kissing her on the mouth.

Ingrid sighed, laying back down with her head on his chest.

'We need to make another scene at the office tomorrow,' she said. 'Make it look like we don't like each other.'

'Isn't this all a bit over the top?'

Ingrid sat up again. 'As I've told you, the only way to strike back at the old man is by forming a secret partnership. Tomorrow I want you to have a go at me. I want you to do it in the tearoom at lunchtime.'

Doug Haywood did not realise until now how much he loved Ingrid Symes.

He'd had other women before. Not as many as he liked to boast about at the Railway Hotel. There was a stumpy woman with two kids from a previous relationship. She was about six years older than him. He had lived with her for two months, while his mum renovated. She provided a feed and a fuck, but nothing more. He came and went as he pleased. When she demanded more, he packed his stuff and moved into the Railway Hotel.

There was also a brief fling with a cashier from Symes. It fizzled out when she moved to Sydney for netball.

For Doug Haywood, soon to turn thirty, Ingrid Symes represented something different in his life. She was self-assured, glamourous, the boss's niece, and so beautiful. He couldn't keep his eyes off her.

She had also seen his potential. He wasn't just Doug Haywood, a nobody; a foreman in a hardware store in a small provisional town a hundred kilometres from the big city, but Douglas Haywood, a man who could go places, if he wanted. One day he could be the big boss in the strong room, doling out the money. He could be hosting Friday night dinners with the town bigwigs.

Ever since they first made love at the beach, he walked on cloud nine, whistling wherever he went. Nothing could upset or irritate him. He even gave Toby a good-natured slap on the back after work.

Although buoyed by the favour shown by the hottest girl in Old Town, Ingrid's coldness in public stabbed at his heart. *Why couldn't they declare their love to the whole town?* Yet he played along with the charade. He gave an academy-award performance in the tearoom in front of a crowd.

'Christ, why didn't you pass on the message?' spat Doug. He pointed his finger in Ingrid's face for good measure.

Everyone in the tearoom stopped talking and turned to look.

'Don't point your finger in my face, and if you have a problem, take it up with my uncle,' snapped Ingrid, jumping to her feet.

'I will, I will,' he shouted as she stormed from the room.

'God, I hate her,' he said. He looked around the tearoom, which was a sea of frowning female faces, except for Toby, who sat with book in hand.

'Bloody women,' he said to Toby.

Toby said nothing, but Doug felt Toby staring at him a long time after he turned to finish his lunch.

*   *   *

Over the following week, they put on several more scenes.

'When can we drop all this nonsense?' whined Doug.

'When we have my uncle's money.'

'All you want to talk about is your uncle and his money. Why don't we talk about something else for a change?' sighed Doug.

'We can't make a life together without money,' Ingrid said, putting on her bra.

'Why steal from your uncle? Why not wait till you inherit the lot?'

God you're so stupid! She wanted to say, *Remember at the funeral?*

Instead, she said, 'I don't inherit a single thing. Nothing. The only way I'm going to get it is by taking it.'

'It's a bit risky though.'

Ingrid stopped dressing and glared. 'Where's your ambition, Douglas Haywood? Where's your drive? Or are you afraid? Want to spend the rest of your life vacuuming his carpet?'

'No bloody way,' said Doug, rising to his haunches. 'I'm up for anything.'

A car engine interrupted their conversation. Headlights shone through the curtain of the back window. Ingrid froze as the car stopped.

'It's only ...' Doug started.

'Shhhhh,' interrupted Ingrid.

The car engine started again. Ingrid sighed with relief as the headlights dipped and the car turned, the engine roaring away.

'I thought no one comes down this road,' Ingrid said.

'Relax. Someone took a wrong turn.'

'I don't like it. We can't meet like this.'

'Relax, Ingrid,' he said, putting his hand on her shoulder. Ingrid immediately brushed it off.

'We can't meet again. It's too dangerous.'

'Look if you want a place to meet where no one will ever find us, I have the perfect spot.'

'Where?'

CHAPTER FIVE

THE SHACK

Ingrid silently left the house just after midnight. Her uncle's snoring followed her down the stairs and out the back door. It was a clear night, with a full moon following her across the lawn and out the back gate. She skirted around the far side of the store, walking the short path between the fence line and carpark to the rendezvous point.

'A man of mystery,' she whispered as she gave Doug a hurried peck on the cheek. Ingrid felt alive: in her element. She always liked the subterfuge of the night. The witching hour when people and reason slept, and the whisper of conspiracy held the world in a secret embrace. The only observer, the moon in its celestial orbit, remained mute but sympathetic.

Earlier, in the centre of Old Town she was drawn to a knee-length hooded Gothic velvet coat in a shop window. She had to have it. As soon as she put it on, she felt a connection with it. And now in the carpark she felt as dark and mysterious as the night.

'Okay you better spray yourself with this,' whispered Doug, taking out a can of Aeroguard.

'Where are you taking me?'

Doug smiled as he fiddled with the carpark wire fence, peeling away part of it to reveal an opening.

'You want me to go into the mangrove swamp?'

'Well, you wanted a place where no one can spy on us.'

Ingrid felt the glamour of the night quickly evaporate as she left the order of the carpark for an unknown wall of darkness. She cursed Doug as her coat caught on a branch. *What was I thinking in trusting a dumb shit like Doug to find a secure place for us to meet?*

As she followed Doug into the darkness, she noted they followed a well-worn groove through the knots of trees. Here and there tell-tale markers showed the path they must take: a torn sheet wrapped around a branch, or a dab of paint smeared on a rock at their feet. Doug's torchlight locked onto these as they continued through the mangrove. The only sound was the hum of cicadas and the swish and crunch of their footsteps. Ingrid was conscious of many inquisitive non-human eyes watching them descend.

The further they walked, the more distinct the sound of the ocean breaking onto land became. The air becoming stiller, the smell more rancid. The path was now wooden boards traversing many dank pools at their feet.

'Here it is,' said Doug, stopping to shine his light ahead. Ingrid could see nothing but a wall of mangrove, but as her eyes adjusted, she saw a wooden frame of a wall and a door.

Doug debated for a long time during the day whether he should take Ingrid to the shack.

As a boy, Doug's old man took his sister Jules and himself on access weekends via the runabout into the small inlet, anchoring the boat in the shallow water, and setting to work on the shack in the mangrove.

When Julie refused to go with her father after a while, claiming her father's temper and unbearable mosquitoes, Doug found himself riding alone in his father's panel van from his mum's place to the Symes carpark. He helped carry the wood that his father had scrounged from his job in the local timber mill down to the water's edge. Over a six-month period, through heat, wind, rain and mosquito bites, father and son constructed the shack from the ground up.

The shack was reachable by boat, though so well disguised that Doug and his old man needed to create clear landmarks to guide them to the spot. One could also reach it from Symes carpark, or by a longer, rugged walk from Whalers Point.

'Well, what do you think?' said Doug when they entered.

The shack was one large room with nothing in it except an old battered chair, a table, and a mattress in the corner. There was a small opening for a window with a red cloth acting as a curtain.

'Here's something neat,' said Doug.

He moved aside the table and lifted a half-metre-by-half-metre floorboard, exposing a metre-deep wooden cavity filled with fishing gear.

'I use it for storage.'

Ingrid continued to gaze about the shack. Closing her eyes, she scanned for human sounds but heard nothing but the sea.

'Well, what do you think?' he asked.

She turned and smiled. 'It's perfect.'

* * *

'Why don't we pack it in and go to Queensland? We can stay with my sister. You would like Jules,' said Doug, kissing the top of Ingrid's head. He loved the smell of her conditioner.

'My uncle has already accumulated two hundred thousand in the safe,' Ingrid said, playing with Doug's chest hairs.

'Good for him,' said Doug. 'Now, what do you think about the Queensland idea?'

'After we take the money.'

Doug looked up into the darkness of the shack.

'You still on about stealing the old man's money?'

'He's sick. I'm not sure how much longer he will live, and once he dies all his money goes to the Salvos.'

'You don't need money to be happy,' said Doug.

Ingrid sat upright and stared down at Doug. 'How can we start a new life without it?'

'We have each other.'

'You're too sentimental, Doug.' Ingrid sat up and put on her top.

'But Babe,' said Doug, 'all you need is a little cash to be happy.'

'You're a fool, Douglas Haywood,' Ingrid said, rising from the mattress and pulling on her jeans. Doug stood and put on his pants.

'Stealing money is serious,' said Doug. 'It's breaking the law.'

'We're not doing anything wrong,' Ingrid said. 'All his wealth is stolen. He bribes the police and politicians. He rips off his customers and his employees.'

'Stealing is still serious business.'

'How long have you worked at Symes?' she asked, crossing her arms.

'About fourteen years,' said Doug.

'I bet he's underpaid you for most of those years.'

Doug nodded. In his first years the old man had him working from 6am to 5pm for money he knew now to be below award wages.

'You're the unsung hero of Symes, Douglas Haywood. It's your hard work that is the foundation of Arthur's success. Why, you're the man running Symes. Yet he underpays you. How many times has he said a good word about you?'

Doug looked down at the floor.

'You can't remember a time when the old man hasn't been gruff or downright rude, can you?'

Doug shook his head.

'He has you vacuuming and doing basic household chores like some domestic servant.'

Doug grimaced.

'He treats you like a housewife! Yes, he will have you wearing a frilly little apron soon.'

Doug clenched his fists and looked at Ingrid, eyes blazing. He wanted to strike out. If the old man had been in easy reach, he would have punched him, but instead he looked into the chocolate-coloured eyes of Ingrid. She was a woman. A man shouldn't hit a woman.

Doug hung his head and took one deep breath after another trying to calm his galloping mind as two seagulls outside argued over a scrap of bread.

'It's dangerous, though. We take a big risk,' he said after a moment of silence.

'Crossing the road is dangerous!' shouted Ingrid.

She enjoyed the remoteness of the shack. She could vent, say what she wanted to say without being overheard.

Doug didn't like this hard, ruthless edge to Ingrid. It frightened him.

'Don't you want to make something of your life?' she cried, pacing the shack. 'Go places? See things? Do great things? Be someone? Or do you want to be stuck in Old Town for the rest of your life, working at Symes, working as a ...'

Ingrid stopped before she said shit kicker. She needed to keep her anger in check. He may be a moron, but she needed him. Instead, she smiled and ran into his arms.

'Oh Doug, I only want the money so we can be together.' She wrapped her arms tightly round his neck as she brought her lips close to his ear and whispered, 'Once we have the money and a suitable time elapses we can show our love. Yes. We can say how we fell in love because of the robbery. The shock and violation of trust brought us together. I was unnerved and you comforted me. And when more time passes, we can quit our jobs and the town and head north to Queensland to see your sister.'

She kissed his check. 'You can buy a car like my uncle's and we can drive up and down the Pacific Highway forever. We can be free. Free of my uncle, of Symes, of this stupid town.'

Doug sighed and kissed her head, inhaling her scent. He squeezed her tightly. 'Oh Ingrid Symes, I love you. I would do anything for you.'

With her face hidden in his chest, she smiled. 'I know Douglas Haywood. I know.'

The cicadas droned as the water licked the pylons beneath.

'I've decided we should take the money the week leading to Easter,' she said after a time.

'How?' asked Doug, looking down at her.

'I have a plan, but it involves adding another member to our group. You don't mind splitting the money three ways?'

THE WOLF OF OLD TOWN

By 9am on the last Friday in February, the mercury hit 35C. The air throbbed with humidity and the cicadas droned incessantly.

Even as the sun disappeared behind the ranges, the heat did not dissipate. Instead, the humidity intensified, the air wrapping tighter around the guests like a suffocating warm coat as they walked listlessly up the hill to Arthur Symes' house.

Ingrid stood on the porch, cool and erect in her red dress and matching high heels, greeting each guest with a vivacious smile as they arrived.

She loved the heat. Winter always left Ingrid lifeless and wanting to hibernate. In the fading light of this oppressive evening, she glowed with vitality, with beauty, with purpose.

When the detective arrived solo, Ingrid smiled and took his hand, holding it a long time before she whispered, 'I'm so glad you came. After dinner I would like you to teach me billiards.'

'The old boys might want to play.' He smiled, catching his reflection in her eyes.

'Well, we can sit in a corner and talk.'

Rob bent down close to her face, drinking in her large dark eyes and the smoothness of her cheeks.

'I would love that,' he said, breathing in her perfume.

'So would I,' she said, squeezing his hand before darting around him as the mayor and mayoress came up the path to the porch.

Rob walked inside, his head held high, a grin on his face, and his shoulders thrown back. He admired his form in the reflection of the hallway mirror. It had been a tough couple of months. But he consoled himself with the thought that he hadn't lost his touch with women as he swaggered to the bar.

It was also on this sticky Friday that Jack Harris finally brought his sister Beata to dinner.

Ingrid eyed Beata closely as Doctor Harris, wearing a dark suit and red silk tie, led her up the pebbled path. She had curly dark hair and wore a multi-coloured caftan with numerous beads slung around her neck, jangling and clinking as she walked.

'Ingrid, this is my sister Beata. Beata, this is Arthur Symes' niece, Ingrid.'

Both women smiled. Ingrid was immediately struck by the disorder and chaos in the other woman's appearance. How her green eyes darted one way then the other like a startled rabbit.

Jack lingered at the door, expecting a minute of chit chat with Ingrid, but Ingrid smiled absently at him and said, 'Please go in, dinner is about to start. I've marked your place at the table.'

Ingrid moved to greet the federal member and his wife coming up the path.

Surprised, Jack found his seat marker at the other end of the table next to Arthur, Beata seated opposite him. He looked down the table as Mrs Sarsovy wheeled out the meal and saw Ingrid whispering to the detective in the seat he usually occupied.

Mrs Sarsovy served the dinner: a range of cold meats and salads, which she placed in the middle of the table. The guests pounced on the free food, filling their plates to the brim, except for Jack Harris, who held back and eyed this gluttony with disdain. He frowned as he saw Ingrid smile at some whispered joke from Rob Charles. The doctor undid his top button and loosened his tie.

For the next ten minutes, the sound of food being devoured, the ding of cutlery on china, the glug glug of pouring wine, and the whoosh of beer heads rising, dominated the table. Two pedestal fans rotating at high speed, tried valiantly to keep the humidity at bay. But alas, it pressed close, as if squeezing the night slowly to a boiling point.

The men valiantly downed one beer after another, the women drinking iced water. Yet it wasn't enough to relieve the oppressive heat. Arthur finally put down his utensils and said, 'This blasted heat. When is the change coming?'

As if in answer, the room lit up with lightning, and several seconds later the earth rumbled.

'It looks like nature has answered you, Uncle,' Ingrid said, glad of the chance to rise from her seat and peer out the window. Rob's shoe was beginning to cut into her leg.

'So, Beata,' said Sinead after another lapse in conversation, 'your brother tells me you have been living in Byron Bay these last few years.'

'Yes, but I've come back to Old Town to help Jack with his practice.'

'What did you do in Byron?' Deidre asked.

'I was a psychic healer.'

Her brother crossed his arms. Arthur rolled his eyes. The men fidgeted in their chairs.

'How fascinating,' said Doris. 'Do you intend to practice in Old Town?'

'No, she will not,' said Jack. The sudden vehemence in his voice stiffened the table. His eyes followed Ingrid as she sat back down and took a sip of her wine.

'I've told you before,' said Beata, turning to her older brother. 'I will not have you dictating to me how I should live or what I should believe in.'

The table froze. The whirling of the two pedestal fans was like the roar of jet engines.

'I don't want any hocus pocus associated with my practice.'.

Ingrid took the opportunity, with all eyes on Beata and her brother, to smile at Rob and rub her own leg across his beneath the table.

Beata scoffed at Jack. 'I won't be using your practice to advertise my services.'

The table fell silent again as Arthur regretted inviting his doctor's sister.

'I'm sorry,' said Beata, addressing the table after a time. 'My brother is a sweet man and a good doctor, but he's not a believer in my work.'

The women smiled to themselves. They took an instant liking to Beata. The way she stood up to her pompous and imperious brother.

'How long have you had the gift?' Sinead asked.

'Ever since I can remember,' said Beata. 'From an early age I could recognise people's auras. I could sense spirits around people.'

'This weather is dreadful,' Arthur said loudly, pulling on his shirt collar.

As if in tune with Arthur's irritable voice, the room lit up again. The house shook seconds later.

'Uncle Arthur, your voice commands nature,' smiled Ingrid. Several at the table laughed. She noticed Beata eyeing her closely.

'Looks like a change is coming,' said the mayor.

'I would be most eager to sit for you, Beata,' said Doris. 'Do you have a card?'

'I'm having flyers made.'

Arthur rose to his feet. *How could anyone believe in that nonsense?*

The men also rose, many hoping to grab their bribes and have a few decent drinks at the bar. The detective reluctantly stood too. He wanted his money but was also enjoying the attention from Ingrid. He would hold off on the booze.

The doctor rose too, seemingly unsure what to do. As he did not play billiards or drink heavily, he slunk into one of the armchairs.

The room lit up again and the house rumbled as the men moved over to the billiard table.

'How do you see people's auras?' asked Janine.

'It's hard to say,' said Beata. 'I can see ...' She cast her eyes on each woman at the table before her gaze locked on Ingrid. 'I see ...'

'See what? asked Doris.

'I see colours,' said Beata, turning to Doris, 'and have these feelings about people.' Her gaze returned to Ingrid. 'I can also see the future.'

Beata spoke, not so much to the women at the table, but as if to the ephemeral ghosts pressing all around.

Ingrid smiled at Beata, but Beata did not return her smile. Instead, Beata frowned before shaking her head and turning her attention to the other women.

Ingrid saw her chance. She rose from the table and walked quietly into the other room. The men were setting up for a game of snooker. Arthur was standing in his usual spot behind the bar, while Rob, as she expected, sat by himself on the lounge, waiting.

Jack watched Ingrid pass him by and sit with Rob. He rose and, loosening his tie more, went to the bar.

Ingrid sat close to Rob. Not too close though. It was a room with many eyes. Lightning, like the flash of a camera, illuminated the room, making everything pronounced for Ingrid, every face sharp and distinct, embedding into her memory like a snapshot in time. Strangely, she saw the room three hundred and sixty degrees.

Arthur bent conspiratorially over the bar, his miserly mouth in the act of whispering to the mayor. The men were all arms and legs and protruding bellies, like a band of cocksure roosters holding their cue sticks, mouths open in the act of laughing at a whispered dirty joke. Dr Harris, at one corner of the bar, his perfectly manicured hair now in disorder, downed a scotch. The women at the table, all hands and animated faces, were in the act of gossiping.

But it was Beata's face that drew Ingrid. She sat amid the women, not engaged in the conversation, but staring at Ingrid, a look of fear and bewilderment etched on her facial features.

Crazy woman, thought Ingrid, as the world rumbled and the room unfroze, time beginning to move forward once more.

Ingrid felt Rob's arm creep around the back of the couch towards her shoulders. She was glad when the phone rang.

'I better answer that,' she said, rising.

'Why don't you stay and talk?' he implored, grinning. The phone stopped.

'See, someone has answered it.'

Ingrid sat down on the couch again, but this time a little away from the detective.

Mrs Sarsovy entered the room.

'Doctor Harris, a call for you.'

The doctor stood and left the room.

The room lit up again, followed by thunder.

Jack re-entered the room and strode across to Arthur at the bar.

'I'm sorry Arthur, but I must leave. A child has fallen ill, and I must make a house call straight away.'

'In this weather?'

'Luckily, it's only down the road. I will be straight back.'

Ingrid used the distraction to lean closer to Rob, and in a low voice, whispered in his ear, 'We must be discreet. Call this house at midnight.'

Jack strode over to his sister. 'I have to go and see a patient, Beata.'

'I will come with you,' she said, rising.

'No stay here, I won't be long. Besides it's about to rain.'

'But I want to come with you,' she said. 'I want to leave this house.'

'Nonsense, you will be happier here.'

'I'm not feeling well. I need to leave this room. I need fresh air.'

The room lit up and shook.

'I insist you stay here. The rain is coming, and I will not see you soaked,' he said imperiously, not brooking any more argument.

'I will only be half-an-hour at most,' said Jack, in a softer, more tender voice.

Beata wilted as her brother left the room. She did not engage with the women around her.

The thunder rumbled again, the lightning lighting up the room like a camera flash.

Several gasps and muffled cries came from ladies at the table. Even the men stopped their pool game and stood alert.

The room lit up once more, followed instantaneously by thunder. At the window, the curtains billowed out. The venetians rat-tat-tatted as a gust of cold air blew stray napkins from the table, knocked over unlit candles, and toppled the fans with a thud. Arthur scurried to the window. An almighty crack, then a boom, shook the house. He jumped back as the ceiling lights popped and the room fell into darkness.

The women squealed. Even the men jumped, the mayor dropping his wine glass, which shattered at his feet.

The room lit up again, the earth rumbled louder, and Beata sobbed hysterically. Deidre went over to comfort her. But Beata looked up with teary and bloodshot eyes and cried, 'The wolf is here! The wolf is here!'

The wind abated as everything grew silent, except for Beata bawling hysterically.

'The wolf is here! Oh my god! The wolf has transformed.' Beata's bloodshot crazy eyes locked on Ingrid.

'Repent. The wolf is hunting. Hunting!'

'Get her out of here!' shouted Arthur. 'Get her out of here!'

The sudden whoosh of the rain, which now fell in a torrent, drowned out his words.

In the confusion, Ingrid sprang to her feet and motioned to Rob.

The women crowded around a sobbing Beata.

'I can't be in this room. I need to leave! I need to leave!'

'Wait for your brother, Beata,' Janine said. 'It's raining hard.'

'It's okay,' Ingrid said. 'Rob will take her home and I will find her brother.'

Ingrid took Beata by the hand and, with the detective trailing behind, led her to the door.

'I'm glad to see her gone,' Arthur said quietly to the mayor. 'One thing I cannot stand is hysterical women. Now let me fix the power!'

The lightning and thunder had quickly passed towards the ocean, leaving a hard and steady rain. Rob brought his car up the driveway and Ingrid, taking Beata by the arm, ran with her and into the back seat of the car.

Ingrid had no intention of searching for Dr Harris. Instead, they drove to Beata's brother's surgery.

Beata did not want to communicate, keeping her face looking out the window.

Fine by me, thought Ingrid, though she kept up the caring pretence by placing a hand on Beata's shoulder, rubbing it while smiling at Rob, who was viewing her in the rear-vision mirror.

By the time they reached the surgery, the rain and humidity had moved offshore, leaving the air cooler as Ingrid led Beata to the front steps of her house.

Beata, eager to be alone, disappeared behind the front door, locking it as she did so. Ingrid, glad to be done with her, walked back to the car and got into the front passenger seat. She placed her hand on Rob's, which was gripping the gear stick. She leant closer to him, whispering, 'Drive me to Lighthouse Point!'

CHAPTER SEVEN

THE PLAN

Rob dropped anchor and waded through the shallow water to the shack. While Doug with his arms crossed, eyed the tall newcomer with suspicion, Ingrid began her brief.

'The old man keeps anywhere from three fifty to five hundred K in the safe at any one time.'

'How do you know?' asked Rob.

'Because I've taken over the banking. Last week, armed guards delivered two hundred K to Symes. Also, I saw the insurance premium he paid. The memo my uncle signed said he held three hundred thousand in the strong room at any one time.'

'Crazy. What's the security like?'

'The money is stored in a vault. The only two people who know the combination is the old man and the bank. The vault is in a strong room.'

'What about security cameras and alarms?'

'The store is alarmed. As for security cameras, they're pointed on the office, the strong room, the safe door, and on all entry points of the warehouse.'

'What about patrols?'

'They patrol only twice a night, once at 9pm, the other at 3am, and they only review the cameras once an hour.'

'Where are the controls for the alarms?'

'Downstairs near the back entrance in a locked cabinet. You have ten minutes after unlocking the doors before triggering the alarm.'

'You've done your homework, but I can't see how you can steal the money,' said Rob. 'You have the alarms, the locks, the security cameras, even the fucken combination on the safe. If you pull it off, everyone will know it's an inside job. Look, I know two guys in Sydney who can come down and hold-up your uncle in the strong room. They will take a cut of the action ...'

'I don't want any outsiders,' interrupted Ingrid.

'Scared of guns?' jeered Rob.

'Guns?' scoffed Ingrid. 'Guns don't scare me. What I don't want, though, is to share with a few stick-up men. Besides, it's too messy.'

'What's your plan then?'

'Doug and I will steal the old man's keys, disable the alarms, open the safe, and take all the money.'

The distant waves lapping the shoreline filled the silence.

'Wow! You think big,' laughed Rob. 'Real big.'

'We split the money three ways.'

'Where do I fit in?'

'We need you to swing the investigation away from Doug and me.'

'Not an issue, but like I said, a robbery of this nature, and suspicion is bound to fall on someone on the inside.'

'I've thought of that too,' Ingrid said. 'I have the perfect fall guy.'

Doug, who had been looking between the detective and Ingrid as they talked, dropped his head and rubbed the back of his neck.

'A guy called Toby Zachariah,' Ingrid said. 'He works as a storeman.'

'Throwing an innocent man under the bus. That's serious.'

'You will approve of our choice. He's a drug dealer. Remember the story at the last Friday night dinner before Christmas? About the guy who got wasted and made a scene at the church?'

Rob lifted his eyes to the ceiling of the shack before dropping them and saying, 'Oh yeah.'

Doug looked up sharply at Ingrid. She did not see his surprised look. She had only eyes for the tall detective.

'It's settled,' said Rob. 'We take the money, and the drug dealer will get what he deserves.'

'Toby a drug dealer?' said Doug. It was the first word he had spoken.

Ingrid finally saw his look of surprise and reacted.

'You hate him, I hate him. Everyone in Symes knows what he's like. Get with the program!'

Doug blushed and cowered. *It's the first time she's looked at me since this detective dropped anchor and came inside the shack.*

'We must strike on the Wednesday evening before Easter,' Ingrid said, returning exclusively to Rob. 'The safe will be flush with cash. The old man has organised all the money from his key businesses to be put in the strong room on the Wednesday. He will do the pays on Thursday and dole out his bribes for a special Thursday evening dinner. He has organised security to pick up the money and deliver it to the bank on Thursday.'

'How are you going to pull it off?' asked Rob.

'Easy. There are three sets of keys. The master key kept by my uncle has four keys on it. One to open the strong room, a key for the office, a key to open the doors downstairs, and another for the alarm cabinet. He never lets it out of his sight for a moment. That leaves the other two sets. One set is with Doug with only two keys on it. One key for all the doors downstairs and the other for the office door.'

'The third set is with me.' She took a set of keys from her jean pocket. 'It has the key for the alarm cabinet and the strong room. My uncle has two people open up each day.'

'He never uses the main key set if he can help it,' said Doug, wanting to redeem himself and show them he wasn't a bit player in this plan.

Rob and Ingrid looked at him briefly before turning their attention to one another.

Ingrid continued. 'What we do is use the old man's master keys to open the strong room, but make the robbery look like a person using my set was the only one used. I'm telling my uncle I no longer want to open and close the store. Doug will promote Toby and give him my set. We make it look like someone forced entry through the men's toilet window downstairs, disabled the alarm, threw a cover over all the cameras, then smashed in the glass pane of the office door before using the key to open the strong room door. Both the strong room door and the alarm cabinet keys are on Toby's key ring.'

'But how do you open the safe?' queried Rob. 'It has a combination. You can't smash your way in there.'

'Easy. It doesn't close. After lunch, my uncle will find himself sick and unable to go on. I will give him a little poison. Nothing too strong, just enough to make him ill. Doug and Toby will finish the closing. Doug will ensure the safe door isn't locked properly. We will blame this on Toby the next day.'

'Shit, a lot of things can go wrong,' said Rob. 'The closing of the safe door is important. If it fails, there can be no robbery.'

'We don't need to worry,' Ingrid said. 'I've also worked out the combination. The old man changes the numbers every Monday. I've found the notebook where he works out the sequence. He follows the same pattern. In his system the last number becomes the first and the first becomes the second every week and so on. The numbers continually rotate through the same cycle. The old man is nothing but predictable.'

'Okay, so it doesn't matter if it closes,' said Rob. 'But where do I come in?'

'We need you to swing the investigation to Toby. Plant as much evidence as possible linking him to the robbery. Arrest him and throw away the keys.'

Ingrid stopped and searched the detective's face. 'Do you think you can do it?'

Rob looked down at the floor as waves crashed to shore and the red rag of a curtain fluttering with a sudden gust of wind filled the silence.

'I want to add another element to our plan,' said Rob, lifting his eyes.

'What element?' Ingrid crossed her arms.

'I've been trying to nail a drug dealer for a while. A low life by the name of Dimitri Lvodic. I want to use him as the fall guy.'

'I want Toby as the fall guy and no one else,' Ingrid said, shaking her head.

'No, hear me out,' said Rob. 'We include both.'

'How?' Ingrid said, frowning.

'I will have two officers staking out Dimitri's house on the night of the robbery as well as the week leading up. What type of car does Toby drive?'

'He rides a yellow bike all over town,' said Ingrid.

'Perfect,' said Rob. 'We get Doug here to ride past the stakeout on a yellow bike and turn into the laneway next to Dimitri's house. The idea is to make it seem like Toby had delivered the money to Dimitri. Here is the thing. I will lift the stakeout in the early hours of the morning of Easter Thursday. I know Dimitri holds a stash of drugs in his house. On the day after the robbery, not only do we raid Toby's address, we also use the robbery as a pretence to raid Dimitri's house looking for the money. Yet instead of the money, we uncover a stash of drugs. We can make it seem as if Dimitri used the money to buy drugs. It's a win-win. We have the answer as to what happened to the money. Your uncle can claim the insurance and I get my man in the slammer.'

Ingrid lifted her head and looked at the ceiling. Outside, the sea continued to rhythmically break onto land.

'But promise me you can pin the thing on Toby?' Ingrid said. 'Promise me you can?'

'Pin it on him?' laughed Rob, puffing out his chest, 'I can make Mother Teresa out to be a whore if I wanted. By the time I'm through interrogating this Toby character, he will admit to the whole damn thing. Mate, he will be happy to go to prison.'

'Toby will rue the day he ever came to Old Town,' smirked Ingrid, her eyes fixed on the detective.

Rob puffed out his chest while Doug frowned at Ingrid then the detective.

* * *

'Why should I be the one who impersonates Toby?' muttered Doug after the detective left by boat. 'I'm doing all the work befriending Toby. Now you want me to impersonate him.'

'Can't you see it's necessary?' sighed Ingrid.

'I don't know why you're involving the detective.'

'The detective is crucial to our plans. With him running the investigation, we're protected. Without him, suspicion immediately falls onto us.'

'I can organise everything,' said Doug. 'I can work around the issues.'

'How Doug?' Ingrid was tiring of the conversation and wanting nothing more than to go home to bed.

'I have a lot of power at Symes. I'm the bloody foreman. I can make things happen,' said Doug, clenching his fists. He wanted to put his fist through the wall of the shack. Better still, the face of the detective.

Doug watched Ingrid putting on her jacket and organising her hair.

'Also, I don't like the way this detective looks at you. And I didn't like it the way you looked at him.'

Ingrid looked sharply at Doug. *I should have anticipated jealousy. Doug was like all men. An imbecile.* She took a deep breath and slid into the role.

'Oh Doug, you're a sweet, sweet man,' she said, taking his hand and squeezing it gently.

'Can't you see that with the detective we're protected? Oh Doug, I would much prefer to do this job with only the two of us.'

She kissed him softly on the lips. 'I love you, Doug.'

Doug sighed and held her tight. His eyes moistened, his heart softening. Looking at her chocolate-coloured eyes and soft cheeks left him weak-kneed, defenceless. *My god she's so beautiful*, he thought. *So, so gorgeous.*

He was carried away with the thought of their life together. Travelling along the freeway, two free spirits going from place to place in Arthur Symes' car. He saw the open road, the radio on loud, the windows wound down, the smell of eucalypt and sea, the tyres eating white lines. Then the thought of Toby interrupted the reverie.

'Toby's a little shit I agree, but he's no drug dealer.'

'Oh Doug,' she said, tightening her grip. 'I love you so much. Don't you see this? All I want is for us to be together and we can't have a life until we take the money. The story about Toby was a little white lie, but think of our life together.'

She pressed herself closer to him, and closing her eyes began describing the mental images popping into her mind.

'I see us on the open road with the radio blaring going from town to town. Once a month you can drive us into Sydney to see a band. Wouldn't that be nice? On Sunday we could watch your team play. I could cook you a roast and bring you a beer as you sat watching the TV.'

Such a strange thing to say, she thought. *Cooking a roast! Where had it come from?* But she saw the image as clear in her mind as a still reel from a 1950s ad. Doug the man slouched on the couch with a beer in his hand, and her the woman in the kitchen, like a domesticated drudge.

She knew she had hit the mark for he squeezed her tight.

'Oh Ingrid, there isn't anything I wouldn't do for you.'

'I know Doug, I know.'

She patted his back and turned her developing yawn into a sigh of love.

TOBY PROMOTED

'Toby mate, up here.'

It was Monday morning, and Doug, leaning on the landing of the stairs outside the main office, finally spied his quarry emerging from one of the aisles carrying a packaged hose reel.

Doug drained the last mouthful of his instant coffee, and crushing the foam cup in his fist, threw it in the bin at his feet. Toby stopped, looked up and squinted.

'Toby, up here.'

Christ, thought Doug, *the stupid boy is looking at me open-mouthed. Doesn't he understand bloody English?*

'Up here Toby!' He waved again.

Doug didn't want to talk to him, but he remembered Saturday night's promise to Ingrid as they lay naked on the floor of the shack. He waved Toby to come up the stairs with a forced smile, his attempted civility not helped by a raging hangover from half a bottle of bourbon he'd consumed the night before.

'I've been looking for you all morning,' said Doug as Toby came wearily up the stairs, like a tiny mammal approaching a large and unpredictable predator.

'I told you on Friday I would be late as I had a medical appointment.'

Doug felt a spasm of anger rising with the words *I told you,* but he managed to catch himself in time and smiled.

'Yeah, no worries pal,' he said, dimly remembering a conversation with

Toby regarding a doctor's appointment.

'I need to speak to you. Ingrid is no longer doing the lock ups, and well, I thought you would like to become my right-hand man.'

'Why don't you ask one of the twins or Tiny or Tom?'

Doug inhaled sharply and mentally counted to three.

'I'm asking you,' said Doug, 'because all the twins care about is fishing, Tiny is caught up with his church group, and Tom ... well, Tom isn't the most reliable bloke going around.'

'Besides,' said Doug, placing a big meaty hand on Toby's shoulder, 'you're the smartest of my crew.'

Toby looked at him dubiously.

'How long have we known each other, Toby? Two years? I reckon you and I started off on the wrong foot. How about you and me go out for a drink next Friday night? Get to know each other better. You're a Crow Eater, right? You can tell me all about who you barrack for in the SANFL. You look like a Glenelg fan to me.'

'I don't follow football or sport,' frowned Toby.

Doug giggled nervously. All the study on aerial ping pong and the guy doesn't even like sport.

'Why are you asking me to be your right-hand man?' Toby asked.

Doug inhaled sharply. 'Okay. It's not me who wants you. It's the old boy. He wants to promote you. He's taken a shine to you over the last few months, sees you're a bright type of guy and wants to promote you. I'm trying to get on your good side. I reckon one day I will be reporting to you.'

Toby said nothing. He nodded his head and studied Doug's face.

'Tonight I'll show you how to lock up.'

'I finish at three. As I told you on Friday, I'm moving.'

Doug inhaled sharply, then, poking Toby in the chest said, 'We will do it tomorrow. Remember, I need you to be doing the lock up with me Easter Wednesday. Are you in?'

Doug noticed an arch in Toby's eyebrow, a flicker in his eyes.

'Are you in?' repeated Doug.

'If that is what you want, then okay,' Toby said.

'Great,' said Doug, slapping him on the back. 'Now remember, you're not to be sick on the Wednesday before Easter. Real important.'

'Of course,' said Toby.

'Now, on with your work,' said Doug. 'Looks like someone wants their hose reel.'

Doug was glad to see Toby walk back down the stairs. Something about Toby's last look troubled him. *It was as if… as if…* Doug shook the thought away.

* * *

The next day after locking the store, Doug led a reluctant Toby to Arthur Symes' house.

As planned, Ingrid stood on the stool cleaning the top shelves of the bookcase of her uncle's office as Doug and Toby entered.

'Ah, the new assistant foreman,' Arthur said, rising from his desk.

'I would prefer not to have this job,' Toby said.

'Nonsense. What young man doesn't want a promotion? When Ingrid suggested you be the assistant foreman, I thought it a wise choice.'

'It's nice of her to consider me,' Toby said, looking up at Ingrid.

'Oh Uncle,' Ingrid said, not returning Toby's gaze, 'I wish you would find a better place for the keys for your filing cabinet.'

'It's a good enough spot. Besides, who would steal from me.'

'You should listen to your niece,' Toby said. 'It's not a good idea to leave your valuables out. One should not give ideas to those closest to you.'

Ingrid took a pen knife from the top shelf and stepped off the stool.

'I will make us tea, shall I?' she suggested. As she passed Toby in the narrow study, she had the irresistible urge to plunge the pen knife into his heart and twist.

* * *

After Toby left, Doug eased the old man's car up the driveway close to the front door and, leaving the keys in the ignition, headed for his assignment.

Ingrid, taking her uncle by the hand, led him slowly up the path and helped him into the passenger side. She reached the driver's side then stopped and said out loud, 'I left my purse, Uncle. Wait one second.'

Ingrid ran inside the house, and grabbing the gloves she had placed on an armchair, darted to the kitchen and unlocked the back door. Taking the hammer planted near the back step, she smashed the windowpane of the door, ensuring glass shards fell inwards.

Leaving the door to swing open with the breeze, she ran into the study, overturning the contents of the shelves as she reached up and took the keys for the filing cabinet. She opened the drawers and emptied the files on the floor. Next, taking the exercise book, she left it open on the page with the combination on the desk.

Quickly, taking the jar of money, she stuffed all the crisp fifty- and one-hundred-dollar bills into her purse planted behind the study rubbish bin.

She let the empty jar shatter at her feet before running back to the front door, throwing the dishwashing gloves over the bar counter as she ran out. She locked the front door, and taking a deep breath, calmly walked across the lawn to the driver's seat.

* * *

'So, what time did you leave to go to the restaurant, Miss Symes,' said Detective Sergeant Rob Charles, standing in Arthur Symes' kitchen.

'A little after six o'clock.'

'And when did you return?' he asked.

'Around nine.'

'Do you know what has been taken?'

'Four thousand dollars in hundred-dollar bills,' Arthur said, surveying the glass strewn across his kitchen floor. 'It was my emergency funds.'

'Where was that held?'

'In a glass jar in the locked filing cabinet.'

Rob continued to write.

'Was anything else disturbed?' asked the detective sergeant.

'Yes, my notebook with the combination for the safe. I should change the code?'

'I wouldn't yet Mr Symes. This is probably the work of kids. I wouldn't change things unnecessarily.'

'I want you to find the people responsible for this.'

'I will put everyone on the case, Mr Symes. Can I ask whether you had any visitors today?'

Arthur dropped his head and looked at the shards of glass on the kitchen floor.

Ingrid also pretended to think it through before saying, 'We didn't have any visitors, except Toby Zachariah. He came into the study.'

'Toby Zachariah,' repeated Rob, committing the name to his notebook before snapping it shut.

'It wouldn't be Toby,' Arthur said.

'At this stage it's most likely kids,' said Rob. 'Forensic will be finished soon. I have several patrols in this area. I will see what they bring up.'

'I will see the detective to the door,' Ingrid said.

'When can I see you again?' asked Rob under the moonlight on the pebbled path. He tried to come close, but she backed away.

'Not until the robbery is over,' she whispered, glancing back to the house.

'You're ready for Thursday morning?'

'I'm on the morning shift. I will be the first officer on the scene. Let's go to the beach tonight,' he whispered.

'No,' she said. 'We can't meet until well after the robbery.'

'Remember the deal, princess. After the robbery we play by my rules. Do you understand? By my rules.'

Ingrid watched an angry Rob walk up the path to his car.

* * *

Ingrid found her uncle in the kitchen sweeping up the broken glass.

'I will organise a glazier tomorrow,' she said. 'I'll make us a cuppa.'

Arthur nodded and continued to sweep. Ingrid shivered with the sea breeze coming through the shattered door.

Arthur took off his jacket and placed it around her shoulders as she turned on the kettle.

'What's this for?'

'You're cold.'

Ingrid eyed him curiously. 'I thought you would be upset about the money.'

'I was. But now,' Arthur looked at the door, then back to his niece, 'I'm glad we weren't home when it happened. You could have been hurt.'

He came close and hugged her. Ingrid, unsure what to do, scrunched her face and patted his back.

CHAPTER NINE

THE BIG DAY

Doug ate his breakfast moodily on the morning of the robbery before pecking his mother's cheek.

'What is it with you, Doug?' she asked. 'Ever since returning to work after Christmas you've been so moody.'

'I'm fine,' he snapped as he snatched his keys and stomped out to the car.

All morning Doug walked about the packed store without any purpose until he remembered his job.

'Where the fuck is Toby?' he yelled at Tom in aisle eleven, not caring he swore in the presence of two old ladies searching for picture frames.

'I don't know,' said Tom.

'What a stupid fuck you are.'

Doug stormed off and searched for Toby down the aisles, brushing aside customers requesting directions.

'Where's Toby? Have you seen Toby?' he asked one cashier after another.

Finally, he found him in the change rooms putting on his uniform.

'Where the fuck have you been?'

'I start at 9am today. Remember? You organised the roster.'

'Oh yeah,' said Doug, recalling. 'Yeah. Yeah, well I want you to restock aisle twelve.'

'You look tense Doug. Anything the matter?'

Doug had the urge to grab Toby by the throat and push him against the locker. *I'd like to smash the little bastard into a bloody pulp.* But he took a deep breath and walked out onto the shop floor.

Doug continued to walk aimlessly through the Easter crowd, his ears pricking with every announcement on the store's intercom, barely audible with the hiss and rattle of the rain on the corrugated iron roof.

Around 4:30pm, the intercom announced, 'Doug Haywood, you're wanted in the main office. Doug Haywood, you're wanted in the main office immediately.'

Doug bounded up the stairs two at a time and found Arthur Symes slumped over his desk and Ingrid standing over him

'My uncle isn't feeling well. He needs you to lock up tonight.'

'I'm fine,' Arthur said, straightening in his chair before clutching his stomach and keeling over again

'Uncle, you're not in a fit state. You must go home. '

'I'm fine.'

'You must come home. I will call for Doctor Harris.'

'I will go home, but no doctors. I'm perfectly fine.'

Arthur rose to his feet unsteadily and Ingrid led him to the door.

Doug found himself alone in Arthur's office for the first time in his life. He sat down in his chair, took the master keys which the boss had left in the in-tray and put his feet on the desk. *I'm numero uno of Symes multipurpose store*, thought Doug. He picked up the phone and called Cheryl.

'Any calls for Mr Symes, put them through to me, Cheryl. I'm in charge this afternoon. Oh, and get me a coffee.'

'Get your own,' said Cheryl, slamming the receiver down.

I'll make the bitch pay later, he thought. Then he realised what he was about to do and froze. *Fuck!*

He looked up and jumped in his chair.

'Toby! How the fuck did you get in here without knocking?'

'I knocked but you looked distracted,' Toby said.

'You should have waited until I called you in.'

'I was looking for Mr Symes, but Cheryl says he has gone home sick and you're in charge.'

'That's right, I'm the main man.'

Doug leaned back in the chair and put his feet back on the desk.

'I need you to sign these forms for me,' Toby said, handing over two sheets of paper.

'What are they?' asked Doug, scanning the forms without looking at the detail. He hated paperwork.

'One's a petty cash form. I bought a lock and set of keys. It's only for a dollar.'

Doug took a pen and signed it before throwing the form back at Toby.

'The other is a leave form.'

'When for?'

'The date is on the form.'

Doug looked closely and saw 31/8/88 written in pencil.'

'Bloody long time away.'

Toby said nothing.

Doug took the pen and signed it, throwing the form back to Toby.

As soon as Toby left, Doug noticed the clock.

'Shit,' he said, swinging his feet off the desk and jumping to his feet. 'The plan!'

He hurried into a crowded main office. Cashiers milled about the strong room with Toby handing Cheryl his forms for processing.

'Toby, mate,' said Doug. 'I want you to clean up the men's toilets downstairs pronto, then start locking up.'

Doug's attention turned to the cashiers. *Shit*, he thought, *the old man manages the drawers at the end of the night.*

He opened the strong room. The safe door was ajar. He motioned to the girls to come in one at a time.

Doug took their cash drawers and put them into the safe. None of the girls came all the way into the safe with him. He placed his hand on the younger girls' shoulders, winked, and said to each one, 'Have a good night, darl.'

To the older women, he wished them the best.

Delores, the head cashier, came in last and together they totalled the drawers, which was close to ten thousand dollars.

Doug made a performance of pretending to shut the safe and turning the combination. Delores left and Doug, leaving the door ajar, sat down in the strong room and waited for Toby.

My god, it's pay day tomorrow, he thought.

'Doug,' said Cheryl, appearing at the door, 'a call for you line one.'

'Put it through in here.'

The phone rang.

'Doug, Ingrid here. Have you locked up?'

'I have Toby doing it now,' he whispered, rising from his seat and locking the strong room door.

'Did you order Toby to clean up the toilets in front of everyone.'

'Yes, but there's a problem.'

'What?'

'Tomorrow's pay day. We need to leave some for the staff.'

'What?' she hissed.

'We can't take all the money.'

'Jesus Christ, Doug. Why are you thinking about that, at a time like this?'

'The staff are innocent. They shouldn't be forgotten.'

'The staff will be fine. The bank will send emergency funds for the pays.'

'I'm sorry, Ingrid. I'm sorry. It's ...'

'Listen Doug, the money will soon be ours. Ours! We can do whatever we want then. Go wherever we want. Won't that be great?'

'Ingrid,' Doug closed his eyes and leant his forehead against the locked door.

'Do you love me?'

Silence.

'Do I love you?' she answered. 'You're the only one I love. Now remember to bring Toby to the house after you lock up.'

'Ingrid.'

'Yes.'

'I love you.'

'I know Doug. I know. Now remember you're driving Toby home tonight.'

'I really love you.'

'I have to go. My uncle is calling.'

The line fell dead.

Doug put the receiver down when a knock came from the other side of the door.

'Delores and I have locked up the store,' said Toby as soon as Doug opened the door.

Doug wanted to take his frustrations out on Toby, but he inhaled a deep breath and sighed. Toby peered past him to the safe.

'I should check the safe is closed?'

'No need.'

'But part of the procedures ...'

'I said there's no need.'

Doug pushed him back into the empty office and locked the strong room door. They continued the lock up, then, after turning on the alarms and closing the back staff door, Doug turned to Toby. 'The old boy wants to see you at the house.'

'I want to go straight home.'

'Relax,' said Doug. 'I'll drive you home. Grab your bike. I'll shove it in the back of the panel van.'

'I would rather ride.'

'I said I will drive you,' said Doug, grabbing the bike as Toby unlocked the chain. Wheeling it to his panel van, Doug threw it in the back.

They started walking the short distance to the house.

'Remember Toby, when all you wanted to do was find any excuse to go to the old man's house?' reminded Doug, restless and nervous, unable to handle the silence.

'And I remember all the fights we had over it.'

'You used to fire up. You hated my guts,' smiled Doug.

'I did, but I always respected you, Doug. For all your faults you put your job first.'

Doug stopped walking and so did Toby. Doug leant on the wire mesh fence and looked back at the neon Symes sign, taking one deep breath after another.

'I preferred the old Toby,' said Doug, trying to keep his voice from cracking. 'The one before your sickness. At least I knew where I stood. These days I don't know what to make of you.'

'Doug, there's something I should tell you about my time in hospital. I have a warning. A warning about Ingrid. Don't go ahead ...'

Doug grabbed Toby by the collar and pushed him against the wire mesh fence. He wanted to pummel his face. *If I hadn't a job to do, I may have done it.*

'Listen here,' seethed Doug. 'I don't know what you're going to say, but don't say it.'

Doug shook him again for good measure, unable to formulate into words all the conflicting emotions he felt.

'Don't talk to me again. You hear?'

'Is this what you want?' asked Toby, raising his palms.

Doug let him go without answering.

'It's your choice,' Toby said.

* * *

The old man sat at the kitchen table in his dressing gown when Doug and Toby entered.

'Here's the master keys,' said Doug. He also took out his own keys, which cut into his skin through his pocket, and placed them on the table.

'I hope you're feeling better Mr Symes.' asked Toby.

'Much better thank you. I don't know what came over me before.'

'It might have been something you ate Mr Symes. Or drank,' suggested Toby as the kettle boiled to a crescendo then died. Ingrid poured out two cups of tea.

Ingrid noticed Toby eyeing her closely as she brought her uncle his drink.

'Yes, well whatever it was,' Arthur said, 'I'm feeling much better now.'

'Doug, here is a beer, and Toby, here is a cup of tea for you,' Ingrid said, bringing over a tea.

'So, the takings for the day?' asked Arthur, rubbing his hands together.

Doug handed over the slip of paper.

'Good figures,' Arthur said. 'Did you lock up?'

'Everything is secure.'

'I cannot be sure of the safe,' Toby said. 'Doug didn't let me check it.'

'What?'

'It was closed. I checked it,' said Doug.

Ingrid, not expecting this turn in the conversation, interceded. 'You shouldn't be thinking about work. You should be relaxing, Uncle. Doug has done the lock up countless times before.'

She came behind her uncle and placed a hand on his shoulder, stroking her uncle's hair with her other hand as she watched Toby lift his cup to his lips.

Arthur reached up and patted her hand resting on his shoulder.

'My niece likes to bully me, Toby.'

Toby lowered his cup without sipping and looked at Ingrid then Arthur before smiling. 'I must comment on how well you look Mr Symes, even with today's sudden sickness. One could say you look almost ten years younger.'

'Apart from today, I do feel different,' Arthur said, surprised by his own words.

'I think your niece has had a lot to do with it,' Toby said.

Ingrid smiled through gritted teeth.

They all fell silent. Doug nervously took a swig of his beer. Ingrid eyed Toby closely.

Toby looked down at his tea and started whistling.

'What are you whistling?' asked Arthur, knitting his brow.

Toby stopped and looked at Arthur. 'It was a song I heard on the radio this morning. It was an old song from the 1930s. The announcer said it was What is ... What is ...' Toby clicked his fingers.

'What is This Thing Called Love,' Arthur said, completing Toby's sentence.

'I think you're right,' Toby said.

Toby brought the teacup to his lips as the doorbell rang urgently: once, twice, thrice.

'Who could it be at this time?' asked Ingrid.

The doorbell rang more urgently. Once, twice, thrice.

'Answer that, dear,' Arthur said to Ingrid.

The doorbell continued ringing until Ingrid placed her hand on the doorknob.

She opened the door to an empty porch. Stepping out onto the porch, she looked around.

'Who is it?' called out Doug, coming up behind her.

'It's odd,' she said. 'No one.'

'Let me see.'

Doug walked out onto the lawn and looked around.

'Probably kids,' said Doug, shrugging his shoulders and stomping back into the house.

Ingrid returned to the kitchen as Toby took his cup away from his lips and placed it back on his saucer.

'Who was at the door?' asked Arthur.

'No one,' Ingrid said.

'I want everything locked up tonight,' Arthur said. 'Maybe the robbers from earlier this week wanted to see if we're still home. Ingrid, I want you to take the car and park it in the driveway. Make it look like we're home.'

'Well Mr Symes, I better leave,' Toby said, rising to his feet and yawning.

Ingrid looked down at his empty teacup on the table.

* * *

Toby continued to yawn as Doug drove him down the hill and into town.

'Go straight to bed, Toby,' said Doug. 'You've had a long day.'

'Even though you've been a bastard to me, I respect you,' Toby said.

'Fuck. Don't go all sentimental on me Toby. I'm a big shit,' said Doug, swerving to remain on the road.

'You're not a shit.'

'Yes I am, and you hate my guts and I hate yours. Okay?'

'I once did hate you, but that was before going into hospital. I seethed with anger. But I see things more clearly now. Each of us have a plan, Doug.'

'Listen here,' said Doug, swerving into Legerdemain Street and pulling up opposite the gym. 'Don't give me anymore of your God bullshit.'

'I want you to think before it's too late.'

Doug jumped out of the car and took Toby's bike from the back of the van.

'Here you go Toby. You better get inside.'

'There's still time,' Toby said.

'What?'

'Doug! Oh Doug!'

Doug turned momentarily from Toby to see Frankie crossing the street.

'Great I caught you. I need to cancel your Saturday session. I'm driving my wife to Sydney for a conference, and I thought we would spend the long weekend there.'

'Sure. No worries Frankie.'

Doug turned back to Toby, but he had gone.

'Where did Toby go? Where did he go?' said Doug, turning side to side.

'Isn't his bike hanging up on the hook of that house?' asked Frankie.

Doug turned and saw a yellow bike swinging on a hook outside the door of the blue house. He ran onto the road and froze as a black Commodore turning into Legerdemain Street braked and skidded to a halt in front of him. As Doug's hands fell on the bonnet, his eyes locked onto the detective's eyes in the driver's seat.

Doug continued his dash across the street and bounded up the stairs three steps at a time, passing the gym and taking the fire exit onto the roof. He peered down at Toby's building across the street.

Darkness, except for a few streetlights, enveloped Toby's house. Doug squinted. He could see the bedroom. As he peered closely, he made out a lump on the bed.

'Good boy. Sleep tight Toby,' muttered Doug.

'Fuck! Why did you make such a scene?' demanded Rob, bursting onto the roof of the gym, their designated meeting spot. 'The old guy thought you were mad.'

'I thought I lost Toby,' said Doug, turning back to look at Toby's window.

'His yellow bike is on the hook,' said Rob. 'What's happening inside?'

'Looks like he's gone to bed,' said Doug.

'Alright give me your keys.'

Doug handed Rob the keys to his panel van.

'Be careful with her. She has a sticky clutch.'

'Here are the keys for the black Commodore. Remember, go to the Railway Hotel and have a beer. Stay there for a time. Talk to as many people as you can.'

'Yeah, I know.'

'You better be off.'

'Fuck. Don't tell me what to do. I'm already doing everything.'

'Every detail is important,' said Rob.

'What are you going to do if Toby comes out?' asked Doug.

'Don't know. Knock him unconscious. But I better go to the car. If he does make a move, I want to be on him.'

They went down the stairs and Doug jumped into the black Commodore and turned right onto Old Town Road. He was glad to be away from the detective. *Everything about the bloke disgusts me. His swagger. His flashy suits, and the aftershave. Did he bath in it? I'll be glad when the robbery's over, and I've the money and can finally take Ingrid away from this corrupt town.*

He parked in the Coles carpark and entered the Railway Hotel. He made a big scene ordering his drink.

'Nifty, a bourbon mate,' he said, banging the bar with his fists.

Doug saw several regular customers from Symes. He chatted with them for a long time about Symes, the new footy season, the cricket season just ended, and life in general.

A train whistle punctuated the strains of Hunters & Collectors' 'Do You See What I See' on the jukebox, and Doug perfunctorily saw from the corner of his eye the 7:05pm train leave for Sydney.

Alan Marshall, the station master, entered the bar and Doug broke off from his current conversation to buy him a drink.

'Nifty, a drink for my friend. What do you have Alan?'

'You don't have to Doug,' said Alan Marshall, taking a stool.

'Least I can do. Busy day?'

'Yeah. Yeah.' Alan Marshall's eyes glazed over.

'What's up? Looks like you've seen a ghost.'

'I was thinking about Judy.'

'Who?'

'Judy my wife. She died two years ago. Car swerved and hit her.'

Doug looked at the clock then leapt from his stool. He was late.

'I don't normally think about her death,' said Alan. 'Except, I had a strange conversation on the platform, you see ...'

'Look Alan, I would love to speak longer with you, but me mate has come into the bar. Here is some money for a couple of rounds. Try to forget your troubles.'

Doug slapped ten dollars on the counter then went around to the other side of the bar. Following a waitress, he slipped through a service door. Before he could be challenged, he passed through a back entrance and into the carpark.

'Where have you been?' hissed Ingrid, as Doug pulled in at the bottom carpark of Symes away from the security cameras.

'Gee, some way to greet a guy,' said Doug.

'Where are the keys?' she said, pecking him on the cheek.

'What are you all dressed up for?' said Doug, looking down at Ingrid, who was dressed in her black dress and taking off her high heels.

'I went to the cocktail bar to establish an alibi.'

She slipped off her dress and put on overalls, placing her dress in the boot of the Commodore.

'Did the policeman drive you back?'

'We don't have time for this,' Ingrid said. 'Let's get going.'

Doug reluctantly put on his gloves and black balaclava, and taking the yellow raincoat skirted the perimeter of the building to the back door. Ingrid, wheeling a yellow bike she had hidden in the bushes, and careful not to fall into the security cameras' view, placed the bike in view of one of the two cameras at the back entrance. With a stepladder she'd hidden behind a skip bin, she climbed the ladder and threw a hessian bag over the other security camera.

'Okay, go Doug.'

Doug hesitated.

'What are you waiting for? Go!' cried Ingrid.

Doug stumbled up the steps and put the key into the lock.

'What's taking you so long?' she hissed.

'I don't know how to turn it.'

With trembling fingers, Doug managed to open the door as a car roared past. Doug jumped inside and shivered uncontrollably. The car roared away, replaced by the droning of the cicadas. Doug took a deep breath before continuing to the alarm and security camera cabinet, stumbling in the torchlight as he reached it, and gashing his head on the brick wall. He checked his head. There was a smudge of blood on his fingers.

His hand shook as he unlocked the cabinet. 'What button do I press? What button do I press?' he whispered.

'Have you killed the alarm and cut the power?' hissed Ingrid from the back door.

'I'm having trouble remembering the code.'

With step ladder in hand, Ingrid marched over to Doug, and pushing him aside, killed the alarm and the power to the security cameras. Picking up the stepladder, she marched into the men's change rooms toilets. The *crack* of breaking glass soon followed.

Ignoring instructions, Doug went to Toby's locker. He moved it away from the wall and slid the panel up. During the week, he had found which locker belonged to Toby, then set about loosening the back one night. He fished his hands inside and plucked out Toby's steel cap boots. Doug had come up with an idea of leaving Toby's boot prints in key spots. He would show Ingrid he knew how to organise evidence; he didn't just take orders.

He sat on the bench and put on the boots, and for a few seconds he looked at them, marvelling at how well they fit, a better fit than his own boots.

'What the hell are you doing?' cried out Ingrid, coming into the main change rooms.

'I never knew a little guy like Toby could have such big feet.'

'We don't have time to compare feet. Get upstairs and start filling the bags,' she said, throwing him two large *Puma* sports bags.

'Remember to bash in the door with the hammer,' she said taking a hammer from a plastic bag. 'This has Toby's prints. Remember to leave it at the safe.'

Doug went to the back door and stomped in a puddle near the entrance.

His head was throbbing but blood had stopped flowing. He then walked inside and up the stairs, slipping several times and hitting his gash.

He was conscious of every sound: the pigeons cooing in the rafters, his own laboured breathing, and the noise of Ingrid breaking glass and moving objects.

He fiddled with the office lock. A simple task that he had done countless times. Yet tonight he couldn't master it. Finally, the door opened, and he went to the strong room and opened it with a shaking hand. He pulled open the safe door then stood mesmerised in front of the money.

'What are you doing standing there?' shouted Ingrid, rushing in. 'Start filling the bags.'

Ingrid grabbed handfuls of money from the shelves and shoved them into the bags. She stopped and turned to Doug, who was standing inert, stupefied. 'Grab the hammer and bash in the windowpane of the office door like I told you.'

Doug tried twice to break the windowpane, but the hammer merely vibrated on it. He couldn't bring himself to use the necessary force.

Ingrid, groaning under the weight of one bag, dropped it and ran up to Doug. She grabbed the hammer from his grasp, and turning her head, smashed the window in, glass shattering on the floor of the office. She set to work on smashing all the glass out.

'Put the hammer on the floor of the safe and grab the other bag, and let's get out of here.'

Doug went inside the safe, dropped the hammer, and picked up the other Puma bag. He dropped it twice in the strong room before heaving it onto his back.

They marched down the stairs. Ingrid walked lightly with her bag. Doug was bent over under the weight of his, stumbling on the last step.

Doug went to the men's change rooms.

'What are you doing?' Ingrid hissed. 'Let's get going.'

'I need to change my shoes.'

Before she could answer, he walked into the toilets and made footprints on the broken glass.

He frowned at the carnage at his feet. Among the shattered shards of glass, he noted one solitary glass Jalousie slat not smashed by Ingrid. He picked it up, and looking up at the exposed window placed the change room bench beneath it, and standing on it placed it back in.

In the change room, Doug took off Toby's boots and placed them back in Toby's locker. Taking a screwdriver and three screws he had strategically placed above his locker, he reapplied the back. Doug took his boots and put them back on. Then, slinging the bag of money on his shoulder, he walked around the edges and passed the smashed change room door to the back entrance, careful not to touch any of the muddy prints. His gash now throbbed like a bass drum.

'What the fuck were you doing?'

'I changed my boots,' he said, handing her the bag of money, which she stuffed into the boot of the Commodore now parked at the back entrance.

'Have you put the power back on for the security cameras and set the alarm?'

Doug blushed. Covering his face, he went back inside and turned on the switches.

When he returned, Ingrid was shutting the boot.

'Right, you need to wait until I leave, then at eight fifty-five take off the hessian bags from the security cameras. Make sure they see the bike and you in the raincoat. Then pedal out.'

'I don't know why you and the detective need to take it by boat to the shack. I can walk it down and be back in time for the patrol.'

'There's not enough time for that,' snapped Ingrid, taking a Puma bag stuffed with pillows from the boot of the car, and handing it to Doug. 'I told you he's dropping me off at the shack. We will all meet there tonight.'

Doug put on the yellow raincoat and placed his arms through the handles of the Puma bag before taking the bike.

'Remember, dump the bike and pillows at the creek. When you throw the bag over, put this money in.' She handed him a wad of money from the robbery. 'Rob will pick you up on Anderson Street.'

'Ingrid?'

'Yes.'

'I love you!'

Ingrid inhaled sharply and shoved the money in his side pocket.

'Get behind the dumpster.'

She pecked him on the cheek before getting in the car and driving away.

Doug sat shivering in the shadows behind the dumpster, looking at his watch every thirty seconds. He wanted so much to be in the car with her.

Finally, the time came. He moved over to the two cameras and in quick succession pulled the hessian bag off, then, in sight of the camera with his face turned, he hopped on the bike and pedalled.

Doug rode out into the street, his heart beating fast, his gash a dull throb. He saw the headlights of an approaching car and knew it would be security. He pushed the hoodie of the yellow raincoat as far down his face as possible and pedalled fast, picking up speed as the car passed him and turning into the top carpark of Symes.

The hood of the yellow raincoat lifted off his head as he flew down the hill. The fishing boats on the Pacific winked in the distance. He wondered whether the twins were on the sea. *How simple life was for them. How simple life had been for me once.*

At the intersection he braked, then turned left. He pedalled hard, not wanting security to catch him. He turned left at the next street, and groaning, started the journey uphill again.

Thirty minutes later, he cycled into Dimitri's street with the hood pulled low. He passed the unmarked police car and turned into the laneway. He took the Puma bag off his back, and taking out the pillows, placed the money in the bag and flung it over the fence. He continued to the creek, dismounted, and threw the pillows into the darkness of the creek. He wheeled the bike along the creek for another ten minutes. Finding a spot thick with bracken, he pushed the bike into the creek and continued walking.

Doug walked for another twenty minutes until the creek met up with Anderson Street. He threw the raincoat into the creek then waited at the end of the street until his feet were sore. The black Commodore finally came into view, flashing its headlights twice.

'Did you throw the bag with money over the fence?' asked Rob.

'Yes! Fuck yes. I'm not stupid. And did you call off the surveillance?'

'Yes, and they saw you.'

'Did they see my face?'

'Relax. They saw some guy on a yellow bike wearing a yellow raincoat.'

They drove to the Railway Hotel in silence. Rob dropped him in the carpark. Doug made his way through the staff entrance into a crowded inebriated bar, the smell of cigarette and stale beer heavy in the air.

'Dougy boy,' said Tom, propped up at the bar corner.

He wouldn't remember a thing, he thought. Doug slapped him on the back and continued moving through the crowd. The noise of the music and the inebriated laughter was ear-splitting. He found several more people he knew and chatted to them for a time.

'Nifty, I'll have a bourbon.'

As he continued along the bar, he stopped every so often to have a quick chat with any person or group he knew. In this way, he made it to the front entrance where he noted Alan Marshall sitting on the same stool where he had left him only a few hours before, staring into space.

'Still here, Alan.'

Alan turned and looked at Doug.

'I've been thinking about my wife's death.'

'Shit Alan, that is one way to make yourself miserable.'

'The world is changing, Doug. It's changing. The wolf has come.'

'What?'

Alan's eyes looked glazed.

'Have you been smoking the wacky tobacco?'

'I had a conversation before I came here tonight and ...'

Doug slapped Alan on the back. 'You better get some rest. I'm off home,' said Doug, noticing the time. He opened the front door of the bar and made his way outside to the Commodore parked on the street.

'Did people see you in the bar?' asked Rob.

'Yes.'

They drove in silence to the boat moored at the bottom of Symes and Old Town roads and made the short boat journey into the mangroves.

When they entered, Ingrid was counting the last of the money and placing it into a large steel box.

'We have four hundred and ninety-four thousand K exactly,' Ingrid said, rising to her feet to stand with her conspirators and stare at their ill-gotten gain.

Outside, the breeze that blew all night slackened, the chorus of insects hushed. Only the rhythmic lapping of water on the pylons beneath their feet broke the silence.

The three spent a long time saying nothing as they looked down at the money.

Rob thought about paying off his house.

I can move to LA and begin auditioning, thought Ingrid.

Doug saw the money and his new life with Ingrid, riding the highway in the old man's car.

'I have three large padlocks and keys,' Ingrid said, taking them from her overalls. She dropped to her knees, shut the case, and put the three padlocks with a snap on the handles. She passed one key to Doug, and the other to Rob, and pocketed hers.

As they lowered the case into the cavity and closed the trap door, silence fell once more. Doug felt as if an unknowable presence watched them from the ceiling. He even lifted his head, then winced as he touched the throbbing wound on his head with his fingers.

'Here is the one thousand to plant on Toby, Rob,' said Ingrid, breaking the silence.

Rob took the money without taking his eyes off the trapdoor.

'We've done our part, Rob. It's up to you now. Tell me you can do it!'

'Do it?' exclaimed Rob, turning to smile at Ingrid. 'By this time tomorrow, both Dimitri and your boy Toby will be under arrest for robbery.'

Ingrid returned his smile.

PART 3

KATE TRENGOVE

KATE TRENGOVE

Detective Sergeant Rob Charles opened the bottom drawer of his desk and poured himself two shots of whiskey, which he downed in rapid succession before taking two peppermint drops to hide the taste. He took a mirror from the drawer and combed his hair, then looked at his watch.

Although knowing the initial phase had gone to plan, he couldn't help feeling a little nervous and apprehensive.

Unable to concentrate on his report, Rob went to the kitchen to make a coffee. As he passed the inspector's office, he noted his boss in conversation with a woman.

'Ah Rob,' said the inspector, catching sight of him. 'If you could come in a minute?'

'Rob, I would like to introduce you to Kate Trengove. She's the trainee detective I told you about.'

'Oh,' said Rob, furrowing his brow and dimly recalling a conversation around the subject. 'I thought it wasn't for a few weeks, and we were getting Banksy.'

'We were, but there was a mix up in Sydney. A post came available in Tweed Heads, so they sent Banksy there. That left this post, and well, Kate was available, and we thought, why not now and not after Easter?'

Kate rose to her feet and shook Rob's hand. Rob eyed her absent-mindedly. Late twenties, crisp business suit, hazel eyes, short-cropped hair. *Rather attractive*, he thought, *but not my cup of tea.*

'Kate's father worked at this station with me back in the 1970s. I'm sorry for your loss, Kate. Glen was a fine man, and even finer officer.'

'Thank you,' Kate said.

'I talked to your mother, Kate,' added the inspector. 'I don't know any case particular to the one she described relating to a boy and a girl, or an abandoned house.'

'I thought it might have something to do with a particular cold case he worked on at homicide.'

'It doesn't match,' said the inspector.

'Thank you for checking anyway,' said Kate.

The inspector turned to Rob. 'I want you to take Kate under your wing. Show her how we do things in Old Town.'

'Train her?' asked Rob. 'But now isn't a good time. Maybe Jacko could show her the ropes.'

'I want you to train her.'

The inspector turned to Kate. 'Rob is one of our best detectives. Always getting results.'

'But I can't train her. You see ...'

Constable Parks entered the inspector's office without knocking.

'Inspector, there has been a robbery at Symes.'

'Well Kate, it seems you have your first case,' said the inspector.

*　*　*

'I didn't understand the conversation in the inspector's office,' Rob said to Kate as he drove them towards Symes, wanting to keep his mind from the task ahead. 'Something about an old case?'

'My father was obsessed with a cold case. A robbery gone wrong he worked on twelve years ago. Dad didn't talk about many cases with the family, but this one he did. It hit him hard.'

'What happened?'

'A man, one Ron Moon, was found murdered in his bed, bludgeoned to death with a hammer. His wife discovered his body in the early hours of the morning. She worked as a nurse on nightshift. The only witness to the crime, his eight-year-old adopted daughter, was found cowering and shaking in her bedroom cupboard. He always said the girl's look troubled him.'

'Did they ever find the bastard?'

'One man. The girl gave a detailed description of the attacker. But he was acquitted for a lack of corroborating evidence.'

'It's bloody typical. We spend the time catching the bastards, then the bleeding hearts let them go. It's always those cases where you know the suspect's guilty but can't prove it, which eats you up as a detective.'

The new detective turned away from Rob and looked out the window as they came to a halt outside Symes.

They arrived to a chaotic scene. Customers lined the entrance demanding to be let in. Staff milled about the back entrance dazed and uncertain. Rob picked his way through the confusion and up the stairs, careful not to step on the muddy footprints, leaping over the shattered glass into the office.

As soon as Arthur Symes saw the detectives he jumped to his feet and out of his niece's embrace.

'Someone has stolen all my money! Find those responsible. Lock them up!'

'Uncle, you must take it easy,' Ingrid said, putting a hand on his shoulder and trying to make him sit again. But he would have none of it.

'You must find my money!'

'Okay, what has happened?' asked Rob, taking out his notebook.

'Doug and Arthur opened up this morning and found the glass pane of the office door smashed in, the strong room open and all the money gone,' Ingrid said.

Rob turned to Kate. 'I want you to get everyone out of the building except for Arthur Symes, his niece and the foreman, and secure the crime scene. Make sure forensics also get here quick smart.'

Rob stepped into the strong room. Arthur tried to follow him, but Ingrid stopped him.

'Okay, everyone out of the office and assemble in the car park,' said Kate.

They began to leave.

'Sir, you will need to leave too,' Kate told a man with a large bag.

'I'm Doctor Harris, Mr. Symes' personal physician. And you are?'

'Detective Constable Trengove. Now, you need to leave.'

* * *

Alone in the strong room, Rob pocketed several coin bags and note straps. Next, he carefully followed the muddy trail past the doctor and Kate arguing, down the stairs and into the toilet. Here he studied the scene for several minutes before picking up several shards of glass. He turned and jumped with fright. The trainee detective stood behind him.

'Is forensic coming?'

'They're five minutes away,' Kate said.

'Get them to look at this scene, looks like our man came through the window,' he said, rising to his feet. He noted Kate's folded arms and followed her gaze to the window.

'Problem, Constable?'

'It seems strange after crawling out, to put back one window slat don't you think?'

Rob looked up and frowned.

'Possibly whoever did it wanted to make it look from the outside as if the window was still secure. Now come on, let's do the witness statements.'

* * *

'Let me get this straight. You and Doug opened up,' said Rob, taking down Arthur's statement, Ingrid and Doug standing on either side of him.

'Yes,' Arthur said.

'And what about the night before. Did you lock up?'

'I wasn't feeling well so Doug and Toby locked up.'

'Toby?'

'Toby Zacharia,' added Ingrid. 'He has a set of keys.'

'To the whole building?'

'Only to the strong room and the box that controls the alarms and the cameras,' Ingrid said. 'The other set, the one with Doug, opens the doors leading into the building and this office.'

'Are there any other keys?'

'I have a master set,' Arthur said, 'but I've kept it locked in my bedside drawer since the break in.'

'Break in?' interrupted Kate.

'There was a break in early this week at Mr Symes' house?' asked Rob.

'Someone stole all the money in the jar and opened my notebook with the combination to the safe.'

'It's too early to say whether the two robberies are linked, Mr Symes. Let's not jump to conclusions just yet.'

'Toby was supposed to be here,' Arthur said. 'Where is Toby?'

'He took today off,' said Cheryl, who managed to remain in the office. 'I have the leave form signed by Doug here.'

Doug blushed as the eyes of the room fell on him. He sensed them lingering on the band-aid covering the gash on his forehead.

'I have the security guard on patrol last night,' said Detective Constable Adam (Irish) Bailey, entering the office followed by the security guard, 'This is Mohammed Malik.'

Mohammed was a tall, well-built youth. After prompting, he gave his account of the night in a thick accent.

'I visited the building twice last night.'

'Did you leave your car?'

'Of course. I checked the perimeters and the doors as per contract.'

'What about the toilet window near the staff entrance on the north side?' asked Kate.

Mohammed gave a puzzled look.

'It's around two metres from the ground,' she added.

'I don't remember any window.'

'What about strange or suspicious vehicles in the area,' continued Rob.

Mohammed scratched his cheek.

'Motor bikes, a person walking, or maybe a push bike?'

Mohammed's eyes widened. 'I saw a person on a yellow bike pedalling around 9pm. He had a heavy Puma bag slung over his shoulder.'

Rob smiled briefly before resuming his questioning.

'Did you get a good look at him?'

'Only that he had a yellow raincoat on. One with a hood.

'Toby!' gasped Ingrid.

'Pardon Miss Symes?' said Rob.

'Toby Zachariah rides a yellow bike and wears a yellow raincoat.'

'You called for me Detective Sergeant?' asked a blurry-eyed Detective Constable Tim (TJ) Jackson entering the office.

'Did you see anything suspicious at your stakeout at Dimitri's house last night, Constable?'

"Yes, we did. Someone in a yellow raincoat on a yellow bike with a Puma bag turned down the laneway backing on Dimitri's property. We've seen that rider every night for the last week.'

'Toby is consorting with criminals,' shouted Arthur, jumping to his feet. 'I want Toby arrested! I want this Dimitri arrested.'

Ingrid made a show of trying to restrain her uncle, but he broke free of her feeble grasp.

'What are you waiting for? Arrest them!'

'Don't worry Mr Symes. We will find your money,' said Rob. 'But one question. Are the men's change rooms downstairs locked?'

'Yes,' said Doug. 'Every night.'

'What about yesterday?'

Doug hesitated. He could feel beads of sweat begin to accumulate at his receding hairline. His head throbbed. *All these people are waiting for an answer.*

'It was Toby's responsibility to lock it. I had him clean up the toilets down there yesterday.'

'Oh my god?' cried Arthur, clutching his chest and breaking into hoarse, rapid inhalations.

'Uncle, you must calm yourself,' cried Ingrid, trying to guide her uncle back to his seat.'

'Where does this Toby Zachariah live?' asked Rob.

'Cheryl, take out the employee register,' Ingrid said.

'Mohammed, you can go. Bailey, stay behind,' snapped Rob, strutting over to Cheryl's desk as she took out a red book from a locked filing cabinet. Rob snatched it from her hands and opened the entry to Z. Without looking, he pretended to write down the address. Snapping shut his notebook, he turned to his crew assembled at the door.

'Bailey, I want you to stay here and take statements and coordinate forensics. The rest, let's make some house calls.'

In the carpark, Rob divided his troops.

'TJ, I want you to grab a couple of constables and bring in Dimitri. Watto and Danno, you follow me and Trengove in the car. I want to bring this Toby Zachariah in.'

'What about warrants?' asked Kate.

Senior Constable Anthony Tones Daicos sniggered.

'Let's nab our boys first,' Rob said. 'We can worry about the paperwork later.'

Rob wanted to whistle as they zoomed down the hill towards the gym. Everything had gone to script. All the actors, even those not in the know, playing their parts beautifully. *Soon I'll have Dimitri where he belonged behind bars, and the dealer boy under arrest. With a bit of massaging, I'll have both arrested on charges of robbery tonight.*

'Do you want me to look up the address?' asked Kate.

'No need, we're here,' said Rob, turning right into the street. He slowed and parked two doors down from Toby's place on the corner.

'You wait here. I'll check out the house,' said Rob as he jumped out of the car.

'Watto, you and the boys wait in the car,' instructed Rob as Sergeant Tom Watkins parked the police car behind his. 'I will check out the place before giving you the call. Don't want you uniformed boys causing a commotion.'

From the side mirror, Kate saw Rob disappearing behind a fence; her eyes were drawn to the name of the street, Legerdemain. She thought on the street name for a long time.

Out of sight, Rob quickly put on his gloves. Taking from his pocket the coin bags and note bands, he placed them in a rubbish bin. Behind a brick near the wheelie bin, he took the small parcel of heroin he placed there the night before and put it in his suit pocket.

He returned to the cars and motioned for the trainee detective to alight. At Watto's car, Rob laid out the plan.

'Okay, I have staked out the place. There's only one entrance in and out. We knock once, announce ourselves, then go in. I will go up the stairs. Watto, Tones and Trengove, you cover me at the bottom, then follow me after ten seconds. Parksie, you check the bins and surrounds.'

At the gate, Rob drew out his service pistol.

The yellow bike was swinging gently on the hook with the breeze. Senior Sergeant Tom Watkins called out, 'Police! Open up!'

Rob banged on the door, and to his surprise the door, already ajar, creaked open. Rob looked at Watto before pushing open the door and plunging upstairs.

'Police! Police!' Rob shouted.

He plunged blindly into the main living area, the adrenalin flowing through his veins. He took a sharp step to the right, saw no one in the room, and taking the package of heroin deftly from his pocket, threw it on the couch.

The trainee detective appeared at the head of stairs with her gun drawn as Rob passed the red curtain, which had been parted by a cord. Ingrid had already briefed him on the layout of the building, and he plunged in expecting to find the other rooms, the kitchen, bathroom and bedroom, and his quarry, stirring with the commotion. But he charged into an empty room with only a single white sheet covering a rolled-up blanket on a bare single mattress.

Rob put down his gun. He came out of the room and found Kate with her gun down, checking the kitchen without a fridge. She turned on the sink and no water came out. She clicked on a light switch and no light came on. She moved back into the living room and noted the heroin. She put on her gloves and put it in an evidence bag.

'Okay, this is strange,' said Constable Danny Parks at the head of the stairs holding the yellow bike in hand. 'I checked downstairs and found note straps and coin bags in the bin.'

'What's strange about that, Constable?' asked Rob.

'It's this bike,' said Constable Parks, lifting the front wheel off the ground. 'Do you notice anything odd about it?'

Rob shook his head.

'It has no pedals or chain,' said the trainee detective.

'It doesn't have brakes either, and both tyres don't have an inner tube,' added the constable. 'It's not even put together properly.' He dropped it and the front tyre came loose from the frame.

'No one rode this thing last night. I doubt it has ever been ridden. The wheels are the wrong size for the frame.'

'It was put together for show,' mused Constable Trengove.

Before Rob could snort his disagreement, a man in his thirties with a name badge announcing Richard Jones on the lapel of his snappy business suit stood at the head of the stairs.

'This is a crime scene. Leave!' snapped Rob.

'I'm the real estate agent,' said the man. 'I've come to put up the 'for sale' sign on the front.'

'Ah,' said Rob, turning his attention to Richard. 'We're looking for a tenant who lives here. A Toby Zachariah. Where is he?'

'Who?' asked Richard, looking from one police officer to the next.

'Toby Zachariah. The man who lives here?'

'This property has been vacant for a year. A family dispute over the will prevented it being sold earlier.'

'A squatter then?' snapped Rob.

'Not possible ... you see ...'

Rob lost track of what the real estate agent said. From the corner of his eye, he noticed Kate Trengove near a battered armchair leaning down and picking up a decorative scarf and placing it in a plastic bag.

'.... we have security patrol every night,' continued the real estate agent.

'Security aren't doing their job,' said Rob. 'We found a parcel of heroin on the lounge and note straps and coin bags from a robbery in the bin. Whoever did the robbery used this place as their base.'

'We would like your security to provide us with a report for the last few nights,' said Kate.

Richard left and Rob, dumbfounded, pretended to scour the room for evidence, but madly tried to think how he could play it.

Where the fuck is Toby? he thought.

'Is the address right?' asked Kate.

* * *

Rob tried to call Symes from the gym. He called Ingrid's extension first, then the main number, finally the house, but he kept getting an engaged signal. Leaving Sergeant Watkins to organise forensic for the house, he sped back to Symes with the trainee detective. Rob jumped out of the car as soon as they screeched to a halt in front of the building. He bolted inside, rushed upstairs, and pushing Doug aside, stormed up to Cheryl, 'Do you know what the offence is for obstructing justice?' he screamed in her face. 'I could have you thrown in jail for giving me the wrong address. Now show me the real employee files.'

'I don't know what you mean?' muttered Cheryl, on the verge of tears.

'Get me the file. Now!' he screamed.

Cheryl unlocked the filing cabinet with trembling hands. Rob snatched it out of her grasp and opened on Z.

Toby Zachariah was the only entry. The address: 6 Smith Street Old Town. Rob jotted it down in his notebook. He marched passed a perplexed Ingrid and Doug.

Twenty minutes later, they arrived at 6 Smith Street, a vacant lot in a quiet suburban street in the hills of Old Town. Rob marched to the houses either side of the vacant lot and asked their occupants if they knew a Toby Zachariah. The occupants of both houses shook their heads.

Rob, in a feverish burst of activity, doorknocked on one side of the street while Kate doorknocked the other, without any luck. No one knew a Toby Zachariah.

Finally, exhausted, Rob called through to the station. 'I want a bulletin to all stations in NSW for a Toby Zachariah.'

After cursing loudly, he spied Constable Trengove standing on the footpath staring at the fence of the vacant lot.

'What are you looking at?'

'What? Sorry. Oh nothing, just this graffiti.'

Rob read the clear writing in white paint on the wooden fence.

Dear K

The H is Silent

D

'We don't have time to waste on stupid graffiti. We have to find out where this 'Toby Zachariah is.'

Dimitri

'For the hundredth fucken time, I don't know any bloke called Toby Zachariah, or any kid riding a yellow bike.'

'Explain to me why he was seen at your house last night?'

'I don't know what you're taking about,' said Dimitri, shaking his head.

'Then explain why this bag used in the robbery was found on your property,' said Rob, throwing the Puma bag on the interview table.

'I've never seen it before,' said Dimitri, slumped in his chair.

'This was used in the robbery!' shouted Rob, slamming both hands on the table.

'So, some bloke throws a Puma bag over the fence. Doesn't mean I'm your man,' said Dimitri.

Rob pushed his chair back, rose, and walking up to the wall, began rubbing the back of his neck. He had been interviewing Dimitri for an hour and was exhausted with the charade.

'Can you explain where you were last night between 6pm and 10pm?' asked Kate.

'For the hundredth time, I was watching tele.'

'What programs did you watch?' asked Kate.

'Why don't you ask one of your mob parked across the street. They could probably see me tele through their binoculars.'

'It's a simple question Mr Lvodic. What were you watching?'

'Why would I commit a robbery when I know I have the cops watching my every move?' said Dimitri, appealing to the female detective. 'Tell me love, why I would steal from that crook Arthur Symes? He has everyone on the payroll. The council, politicians, and the police. I'd be dead in ten seconds if I stole from him.'

Dimitri stopped speaking. His eyes widened, and leaning towards Kate, said, 'How much did he pay you to firebomb the new hardware store opening on the edge of town? Funny how a major competitor to Arthur Symes is put out of business. Or is that your boyfriend's role?'

'Enough!' yelled Rob. He opened the door and motioned for the constables on the other side of the doorway to take Dimitri away.

'Wouldn't surprise me if the old man did the robbery himself for the insurance. It's the type of thing he would do,' said Dimitri as he was led from the room. 'You can't detain me forever. I have rights,' he called out as Rob slammed the door on him.

Rob really wanted to drag Dimitri back and beat a confession from him. He would have done it if he wasn't being shadowed by the trainee detective. Rob went back to rubbing the back of his neck until it burned.

He looked at his watch. He needed a drink.

'I found Toby Zachariah and his bike,' said TJ, bounding into the interview room clutching a pile of video tapes.

'Where?' cried Rob, spinning around.

'I don't have him exactly, but I know where his bike is, and where he was on the night of the robbery,' said TJ, putting the tapes on the table.

'Get to the point. Where is he?'

'His bike is at the train station and he's in Sydney.'

'Sydney?'.

'Look,' said TJ, putting a tape in the video machine.

Rob and Kate stood behind TJ as a grainy image of a person on a bike came to a halt below the security camera; the figure got off the bike and chained it to the fence.

'This was taken at Old Town railway station yesterday evening at 6:30pm.'

Rob noted the familiar pick-up zone of Old Town Station in the background of the shot. The man on the bike lingered below the camera in clear view, putting on a jacket.

'It's Toby Zachariah. I checked with Alan Marshall and he confirms he was at the station at 6:35pm and boarded the 7:05pm train for Sydney. Mr Marshall and Toby chatted for thirty minutes.'

'Very convenient of him to do so.'

'Well, we traced Toby to Central Station. He alighted there before catching a Bondi Junction train and getting out at Kings Cross.'

TJ placed another video in the machine and paused it on the image of a young man coming out of the station.

'Toby Zachariah again. I have confirmed it with Alan Marshall.'

'The time?' asked Kate, straining to read the date and time stamp on the video.

'We have him at Central Station at 8:45pm. At the Cross 8:55pm.'

'So, our man is in the Cross.'

'No, I have him on camera walking out of the Cross and down William Street towards Hyde Park. I lose him around Palmer Street.'

'Great. He could be anywhere in Sydney,' said Rob.

'But don't you see?' said TJ. 'He couldn't have committed the robbery. He wasn't anywhere near Symes at the time it was committed.'

Rob collapsed onto the nearest seat and stared up at the still image of Toby walking out of Kings Cross Station. Even with the grainy image, he could see a mocking smile on Toby's face.

Rob made an excuse for dinner and took three shots of whiskey, trying to think how he could possibly swing the investigation. He needed to speak to Ingrid. Nothing was going to plan.

When he returned to the interview room, he found Kate Trengove and TJ discussing the robbery before a whiteboard. On one side of the board was a list of tasks:

Go over interviews,

Develop timeline.

List of Suspects. Arthur Symes, Ingrid Symes.

'I thought it would be good practice to begin structuring the evidence,' Kate said. 'We should begin reinterviewing key people at Symes with Toby Zachariah now ruled out.'

'I wouldn't rub him out,' said Rob, taking the whiteboard marker from Kate's hand and scrawling Toby's name in big black letters before rubbing out Arthur's and Ingrid's names.

'I can't see how he fits into the picture now we can place him in Sydney at the times the security cameras were switched off,' Kate said.

'He's in this up to his neck.'

Kate crossed her arms and frowned.

'Toby broke into Arthur Symes house earlier in the week and stole the combination for the safe, then slipped this to Dimitri, or one of his associates, along with his keys, jumped on the first train to Sydney, making sure he was picked up by closed circuit TV,' said Rob, looking at a frowning trainee detective and TJ.

'If so, why the elaborate charade with the yellow bike?' Kate said. 'Or the bag thrown over the fence. It makes no sense.'

'It ties Dimitri to the robber and one of his cohorts chucked the money over the fence,' said Rob.

'But look at it this way,' Kate said. 'The bag was found in the backyard with a thousand dollars inside. Well, if you have a bag of money thrown over the fence, why not take it inside before taking the money out? Also, why leave money in the bag? As for the toilet window, if you're using it to make your escape, why place one of the window slats back in after climbing out? If you're robbing a place you want to get out of there quick smart.'

'They wanted to make it look like everything was still normal,' countered Rob. He had hoped this piece of detail could have been swept up in the usual detective practices of Old Town, but this new trainee detective was too keen. Too willing to question.

'So, what do you think happened?' TJ asked Kate.

Kate looked at the whiteboard. She took a deep breath before turning and saying, 'It's an inside job. Whoever did the robbery had access to the keys and knew the combination or left the safe open. Maybe Arthur Symes made it look like a robbery for the insurance. Or maybe someone close to him undertook the robbery, making the crime scene look like Toby Zachariah was the culprit.'

Kate took a red whiteboard marker from the table and wrote Arthur's and Ingrid's names in big bold letters above Toby Zachariah's.

'We should learn more about her,' Kate said. 'Hasn't she recently joined Symes?'

'She's not capable,' said Rob, crossing his arms. 'Not the type ... as for Toby ...'

There was knock on the interview room door. They turned to see an excited Constable David Woody Williams.

'We did an initial search of Dimitri's house.'

'Did you find any drugs?'

Woody shook his head.

'What about any money?'

Woody shook his head.

'What are you smiling about?'

'I found something else dumped in the creek.'

'What?'

Woody disappeared from the doorway, returning a minute later wheeling a yellow bike.

'I found it in the creek about a hundred metres from Dimitri's.'

The room fell silent as they all looked at the bike in disbelief. Rob wanted to burst into hysterical laughter as Woody rang the bell and Kate took her red marker and wrote at the top of the whiteboard:

Three Yellow Bikes????

Chapter Three

A Secret Rendezvous

'You were supposed to make sure he went into his house!'

'I did.'

'Yeah, to the wrong fucken house.'

'Hey, I was told he lived there!' cried Doug, jumping to his feet and squaring up to the detective. 'I saw him to the door.'

'But did you see him go in?'

'His bike was on the hook outside the front door. What was I supposed to think?'

'It was the wrong fucken bike. As for signing holiday leave for the Thursday, what were you thinking?'

'He tricked me into signing it. It said the thirty-first of August on the form when I signed it.'

'As for the window slat, what the fuck were you thinking?'

'Fuck, I'm the one putting his neck on the line in this group,' said Doug, glaring at Rob and looking imploringly at Ingrid. 'I did my job. Besides, I thought you could make Mother Teresa look like a whore?'

'I can't run the investigation without anything to go with.'

'I thought you guys were the best police force money could buy?'

'Hey, you don't know what it's like being a copper,' said Rob, pointing his finger at Doug's face. 'Every day I put my life on the line and what thanks do I get?'

"Stop it!' shouted Ingrid, who all this time sat cross-legged on the floor of the shack staring out into the shadows.

'Toby has played us all for fools,' she said, rising to her feet. 'But can't you see this is perfect. It shows his guilt. There's a robbery and the next day he takes an annual leave day via a holiday form he put in only the day before; then vanishes from the earth.'

'We have proof he wasn't at Symes when the robbery was committed,' said Rob.

'You're running the investigation, change the evidence.'

'Shit, it's not that simple, princess. I have people watching me.'

They fell silent, each looking down at the floor.

'By the way, did you lose a scarf?' asked Rob.

Ingrid looked at the detective blankly.

'We found one in the house.'

'Shit,' Ingrid said. 'I left it there the day I had coffee with Toby.'

'Yeah, well the trainee detective found it near the armchair.'

'Was she the one who asked questions about the toilet window?'

Rob nodded.

'I thought you worked alone?'

'I usually do, but my boss hit me with her only today. He wants me to train her.'

'Well, she's your responsibility,' Ingrid said. 'See she doesn't get too nosey.'

The conspirators fell silent. Outside, the waves lapped the shore, the insects droned.

'Okay, this is the new narrative,' said Rob 'I will redo the interviews after Easter, so we need to get our stories straight.'

Rob turned to Ingrid. 'Ingrid, you need to play the devoted and loving niece. You have your alibi for Wednesday night?'

'I was having cocktails at the Lagoon bar,' Ingrid said.

'Great. I will call the bar over Easter and confirm you arrived around 6pm and left around ten o'clock. Doug, you were where?'

'At the Railway Hotel drinking in the corner,' Doug said, crossing his arms.

'Great. I'll call Nifty and obtain a statement tomorrow. I will draft it to place you there from 6:30pm to 11pm. Meanwhile, I will look to reangle the investigation to an associate of Dimitri. I've broken into Dimitri's house and left a floor plan of Symes with markers for alarms and an address book we seized from an earlier raid. I've put an entry in about Toby. Make it look like he was the inside man. I will do another search of Dimitri's property and stumble upon it, along with an extra stash of drugs I have from a previous drug bust. I can say the money was used to pay for the drugs and they used the back fence near the creek to make the transaction. I will make out Toby gave one of Dimitri's associates the keys, making his way to Sydney to avoid being implicated.'

'Okay, it sounds good, but I don't like the idea of the interviews,' said Ingrid.

'Don't worry, I will manage them.'

They fell silent again. The gurgling water underneath their feet lulled them into a meditative contemplation.

"We better go, Ingrid,' said Doug.

'I would like to stay a little while longer.'

'Then I'm staying too,' said Doug.

Ingrid gave Rob a furtive glance. After several discreet minutes, she dusted herself down and let Doug lead her back up to the carpark.

'I don't like the plan,' said Doug as they walked by flashlight. 'He was supposed to have it all settled by now.'

'Give him time,' Ingrid said.

'From now on you leave things to me,' said Doug. 'I don't like this detective.'

'Okay.' Ingrid pretended to yawn.

'I don't like the way he looks at you.'

'Look Doug,' Ingrid said, stopping. 'I'm tired. I want to go to bed.'

At the bottom of the empty carpark, Ingrid gave Doug a peck on the cheek before walking up to the house. She sensed Doug following her.

She went upstairs, and seeing her uncle still sleeping from the sleeping tablets, went to her room. She made an elaborate show of fiddling by the window before switching off the light.

She could hear the hum of Doug's panel van in the carpark. She waited half an hour. Finally, the panel van revved, then purred onto the road and slipped away.

She silently went downstairs and sat in the kitchen near the phone and chain smoked. It gave one ring and she it picked up.

'I need to see you again tonight. There are things we need to discuss.'

'I will meet you in the shack in half an hour,' she whispered.

She made her way swiftly back down to the shack and into the arms of the detective.

Ingrid made their lovemaking passionate and intense. She wanted it over quickly. When he was done, she rolled off him and began her questioning.

'What's the matter?' she said, putting her jeans back on.

'I didn't want to say it before in front of Doug, but this is serious. I don't have enough evidence to pin it on Toby.'

'I thought you were going to turn it, so Toby was the one who gave his keys to one of Dimitri's men.'

'And if it's proven in some way, he never passed the keys, what then?'

'It's your job to make it look that way.'

'I thought you knew this guy?' said Rob.

'What do you mean?'

'I've had three officers looking all over town for information on this bloke. No one knows anything about him. He doesn't seem to have any friends in this town or acquaintances, or anyone with any interest to know where he lives or what he does outside of work. As for the drug dealing, none of the regular junkies have ever heard of him.'

'What about the library?'

'The library had Symes as his main address. If it wasn't for that and the incomplete employee file, you would swear the bloke never existed.'

The drone of cicadas filled the shack. Rob rubbed the back of his neck then exhaled loudly.

'What's the real problem Rob?' asked Ingrid, looking at him closely, sensing something more.

'The investigation is proving to be problematic.'

'You can work around that. You said you're a top-notch detective.'

'You don't understand,' said Rob. 'This trainee detective is watching my every move.'

'Get rid of her.'

'I can't. She's the daughter of another copper who worked with my boss.'

'I thought you knew how to organise things,' Ingrid said, putting on her top and jumping to her feet.

'I want you to find Toby and put him in jail,' she said, pacing before Rob. 'I want this case closed with no niggling loose ends. I want him tried and convicted and never released.'

'It's pointing to an inside job,' said Rob. 'Someone other than Toby, with access to the keys, who did the job and tried to frame Toby.'

Ingrid stopped pacing. She looked down at Rob slumped in the corner.

'What are you saying?'

'I'm not saying anything.'

Each looked away from the other. Rob down on the wooden floor at his feet, Ingrid towards the trap door. Outside, the cicadas continued droning and a seagull hovering above, crowed. The shack was dark and cold.

'We can't throw Doug under a bus,' Ingrid said slowly and quietly, not bringing herself to look at the policeman. 'If it comes to that, other steps need to be taken.'

The waves lapped and licked the pylons beneath their feet.

'He's keen on you,' said Rob, looking up at Ingrid.

Ingrid made a face and scoffed. 'He means nothing to me. Nothing.'

For the first time, Rob recognised the cold gleam in her eye. Her rigid cheeks. Ingrid looked down at him and noticed his look.

'It's you I love, Rob,' she beamed, falling to the floor and ruffling his hair. She planted a kiss on his forehead, then kissed him slowly and passionately. She enveloped him in her arms.

Rob leant back and let Ingrid kiss him. Her kisses reached his ear and she whispered, 'I love you so much Rob. I want us to be together, and if anything threatens that then you must take action.'

Rob grabbed her by the hair and yanked her head back, exposing the smooth whiteness of her neck.

'I don't believe you, princess. You're nothing but a liar.'

'You have me wrong. I love you, Rob.'

'Listen here, princess, I expect a bigger split. Also, you will do what I tell you from now on. Do you understand?'

He shook her head. 'You need me more than I need you.'

'Of course,' she said. 'Take what you want, I'm all yours.'

Pulling her hair harder, he rolled on top of her and took her once more.

CHAPTER FOUR

THE INTERVIEWS

On Easter Tuesday, Rob, with Kate shadowing, descended on Symes. Ingrid gave them Pat's old office as an interview room.

'I would like to start with your uncle, Miss Symes.'

'My uncle is at home sick,' Ingrid said, with a trembling bottom lip. 'Ever since the robbery he hasn't eaten or slept. He's so lethargic. I've had Doctor Harris out twice to look at him. I'm so worried about him. I don't know what I'm going to do.'

Rob, forgetting for a moment it was all a performance, passed across the tissue box as tears ran down her cheeks.

'I would like to ask you a few questions also Miss Symes,' said Rob, as Ingrid wiped her eyes. 'If you believe you're up to it.'

Ingrid nodded, and sighing, sat down. 'I'm willing to do whatever it takes to bring those responsible to justice.'

'Miss Symes, where were you between 3pm and midnight last Wednesday the thirtieth of March?' asked Rob.

'I knocked off at 3:30pm, went home, and had something to eat. From 6pm until 11pm I was at the Lagoon cocktail bar.'

'The one in town?'

'Yes, I caught a taxi back around 11pm.'

'Can anyone verify your statement?' asked Rob.

'The barman. His name is Brad.'

Rob wrote down the details.

'Your uncle was ill on the day. What was the matter with him?' asked Kate.

'I don't know. He didn't say, and I didn't want to pry.'

'Unusual your uncle falls sick in the afternoon, and that night there's a robbery,' said Kate.

'I don't know what you mean. I didn't pay much attention to my uncle on Wednesday. I was looking forward to a night out.'

'Thank you, Miss Symes. That will be all for now,' said Rob. 'If you could call Doug Haywood in, I would like to speak to him next.'

As Ingrid rose, Kate leant forward and peered closely at Ingrid's watch.

'Excuse me for staring,' she said. 'It's a pretty watch.'

Ingrid smiled then stiffened. 'My uncle gave it to me for Christmas,' she said, unable to read this female detective.

'Very nice.'

'You could have it if you like, it has stopped working. I only wear it for show. I've never had any success with watches.'

Ingrid left hurriedly.

Doug came in and sat with his arms crossed and a sour, defiant expression stamped across his face.

'Mr Haywood, this is a follow up from the interview you gave last Thursday,' said Rob looking down at his notes. 'I would like to know where you were between 3pm and midnight last Wednesday?'

'Well after I sent Toby Zachariah to clean up the toilets, I saw to the cashiers and counted the takings for the day. After that I locked up with Toby, then went across to Mr Symes house before going home. I spent the rest of the night at the Railway Hotel playing the pokies and talking to people.'

'Who closed the safe?' asked Rob.

'Toby did.'

'Did you see him close it?'

'I had turned my back on him.' Doug blushed, his gash throbbing.

'What was the matter with Arthur Symes?' asked Kate.

'How should I know?' said Doug, shrugging his shoulders. 'He was sick, that's all I know.'

'That's all for now,' said Rob. 'We have your details. We will call you later.'

Doug rose to go.

'By the way Mr. Haywood. That is a mighty gash on your forehead,' Kate said. 'I hope you're alright?'

'Yeah, I tripped at home. Hit my head on the brickwork of the house,' said Doug, placing his fingers on the band-aid.

Kate winced as Doug turned and left the office.

'I will do the checks on Mr Haywood's and Miss Symes' alibi, also check the video on the safe closing,' said Rob. 'I want you to follow through on the forensics.'

'Don't you think we should have asked more questions of the foreman and the locking up? Also, we could have asked more questions of the niece. She ...'

'I will be asking the questions,' snapped Rob. 'I want you to watch and learn.'

I want this woman gone from my investigation. I'll speak to the inspector this afternoon.

'I'm getting a coffee,' said Rob, springing to his feet and walking out into the crowded and noisy main office area.

Rob made it as far as the kitchenette door when a wheezing Arthur Symes pushed his way past the two workmen fixing the new office door.

'What's happening with the investigation?' he cried out, clasping his eyes on Rob.

'Uncle Arthur,' Ingrid said, running over to her uncle. 'You should be in bed resting.'

'How can I rest when my money is missing?'

'We're doing everything we can, Mr Symes,' said Rob. 'Everything we possibly can.'

'I thought you had leads. I thought you had your suspects at hand.'

'We're working as best we can,' said Rob, conscious that the room had hushed and they were being watched.

'Why haven't you found the people responsible and punished them? Where is Toby? I want to know where he is!'

'I'm here, Mr Symes.'

These words, so clear and distinct, rang out in the office like the *ding* of a Tibetan bell in a hushed meditation hall.

The room shifted attention to Toby standing in middle of the room, as if risen from the dead, as if he had materialised out of thin air.

'You wish to interview me, Detective?' asked Toby.

A long silence followed.

* * *

'It's 10:50am on the fifth of April 1988. This is an official interview Mr Zachariah. Do you understand this?'

'Yes.'

'Can you give me your full name and address?'

'My name is Toby Zachariah. I live at 6 Smit Street, Old Town.'

'Can you clarify why your payroll details have 6 Smith Street, Old Town?'

'No. All I can say is that it was written into the payroll register incorrectly. I live at 6 Smit Street.'

'Can you spell that?' asked Constable Trengove, her face drained of colour.

'S.M.I.T.'

'Without a H.'

'Yes.'

'Show your driver's licence,' said Rob.

'I don't have one.'

'Birth certificate.'

'I don't have it on me.'

'Tell me where you were on the night of Wednesday thirtieth of March, between the hours of 5pm and midnight?' asked Rob.

'Doug had signed a leave form for the Thursday, so I took the train into Sydney on the Wednesday night.'

'Where did you stay in Sydney?' asked Kate.

'At the Woolloomooloo Hotel. Here is the business card for the place.' Toby took a card from his pocket and passed it across the table. 'They can confirm details of my stay.'

'How long were you in Sydney?' asked Kate, taking the card.

'I stayed all the Easter long weekend and came back today by car. Frankie and his wife gave me a lift home. Frankie is the owner of the gym I go to.'

'In Doug Haywood's statement to us, he claimed you closed the safe.'

'That's not true. I locked up downstairs and Doug locked the strong room. He wouldn't let me check whether the safe was locked.'

'That's a lie,' said Rob.

'It's the truth. Check the cameras. I'm sure they will show who locked the safe. There are cameras on the strong room door.'

'In his statement to us, Doug Haywood said he drove you home from work on Wednesday evening,' said Rob.

'No,' Toby said. 'He drove me to the gym.'

'Can you explain the discrepancy in the stories?'

'No, I can't explain it at all. Doug was insistent on driving me home after we visited Arthur Symes' house.'

'How long were you at Arthur Symes' house?' asked Rob.

'Not long, fifteen minutes. Ingrid made us tea. Then Doug drove me home. He said I was tired.'

'And were you?'

'No, not in the least. He kept telling me to go to bed and sleep. He kept talking in the car about taking it easy and not leaving my house. Yet he drove me to the gym. I didn't understand why he did that, and not being particularly fond of Doug, I took my chance to cycle to the station.'

'You didn't go into the vacant house?' asked Rob.

'Sorry, I don't follow,' Toby said, a look of puzzlement etched across his face. 'What vacant house?'

'There's a house across the street from the gym. On the corner of Old Town Road and Legerdemain Street,' said Kate.

Toby shut his eyes, as if mentally trying to find the house with his mind's eye.

'The old house across the street from the gym? Right opposite it?' asked Toby. 'The one with the faded blue paint job?'

'Yes. Have you ever been inside?' asked Kate.

Toby took a deep breath and leant forward.

'How long have you known Dimitri Lvodic?' interrupted Rob impatiently, wanting to get to the heart of his investigation.

'Dimitri who?' asked Toby.

'Dimitri Lvodic. Don't play games with me. You're a small-time user and dealer.'

'A dealer of what?' Toby looked shocked.

'Heroin, speed, dope.'

'I don't do drugs.'

'Never? Not even a little dope?'

'No.'

'You're a pretty good liar!' shouted Rob. 'You and Dimitri planned the robbery.'

'I don't know any person called Dimitri.'

'How do you explain this?' asked Rob, pushing a drawing across the table.

'What is it?'

'It's the floorplan for this office with the combination instructions on the bottom right-hand side.'

'I know nothing about it.'

'How then, do you explain your name being in his address book?'

He passed it to Toby who read the Z entry before turning to another page.

'If you note the handwriting with my name, it's different from the other entries.'

Kate took the address book and examined it carefully. 'What about the hammer used to break into the office here? It has your fingerprints on it. Also, the same fingerprints are on the hammer used to break into Arthur Symes' house earlier in the week.'

'Look, I pick up a lot of hammers in my job at Symes, and I don't know who this Dimitri is,' Toby said. 'I don't know why my name is in this address book. I don't do drugs. I don't consort with criminals. I was in Sydney all Easter. I don't know what else to tell you.'

Rob crossed his arms and stared at Toby. *This is futile*, thought Rob. *Toby isn't intimidated and I've got no solid evidence to go on.*

'That will do for now,' sighed Rob before leaning over the table. 'But remember, we will check everything you have said and will be wanting to ask more questions.'

'Anytime,' Toby said, rising to his feet.

'By the way, Toby,' Kate said, looking up from the address book. 'Why did you go to Sydney?'

'What relevance does it have to this case?' Toby asked.

'Nothing. Just curious,' Kate said.

'I was ... I was at a conference.'

'What conference?' asked Kate.

'It was an IANDS conference.'

'IANDS?'

'International Association for Near-Death Studies.'

The photocopier wheezed into life, breaking the silence. Rob scratched his head.

'Why the interest in near death?' asked Kate.

'It's ... Well ...' Toby looked at Kate. 'I fell sick a year ago and ... I died for several minutes in hospital.'

The humming photocopier stopped. The room fell silent again.

'Did you have an ... *experience?*' Kate asked.

Toby gulped and opened his mouth to speak.

'That's enough for today,' interrupted Rob, rising to his feet. 'We will be asking further questions. Do you have a home telephone number?'

Toby wrote out a number on a slip of paper and passed it to Kate before leaving the office.

'My god, he's up to his neck in this business,' said Rob, sitting and leaning back in his chair. 'Notice how calm he was? Not fazed by any of the questions? He's one smart boy. He planned the robbery, there's no doubt about it.'

'He's smart,' Kate said, 'but he's not involved.'

'I want you to keep your mouth shut in the interviews,' said Rob. 'I don't want you interfering in my investigation.'

'I didn't interfere with your interview. I merely asked Toby a question about his time in Sydney. I was curious.'

'It's irrelevant to the case.'

Rob crossed his arms and frowned. He was about to say something when they heard a commotion outside the office. The raised and agitated voice of Doug was followed by the slower, quieter, more reasonable voice of Toby.

Rob charged out into the main office to find Doug pointing his finger in Toby's face.

'He tricked me into signing the form and I can prove it was Toby who stole the money,' Doug said to the those gathered in the office.

'Don't Doug. Don't.'

'Why? Have you something to hide, Toby?'

'No. You need to think things through, Doug.'

'See?' Doug pointed at Toby. 'He has something to hide. I bet any money the boot treads in Toby's locker match the muddy prints left at the robbery scene.'

Rob tried to grab his arm, but Doug wrenched it away. 'Mr Haywood, I want you to step into the interview room.'

'I can break this case wide open,' said Doug, pointing at Toby.

'I think we should test Mr Haywood's theory,' said Kate. 'That is, if Mr Zachariah consents to opening his locker?'

Rob scratched his head. He didn't know what to do. *Didn't the stupid fool realise Toby wasn't anywhere near Symes at the time of the robbery?*

Ingrid, too, was caught off guard, unable to formulate a strategy, and left to watch the scene unfold in silence.

They all walked down the stairs and crowded around the men's change room lockers. Arthur Symes, Rob, Kate, Ingrid, Toby, Doug, Tiny, the twins, Dean and Daryl.

'I want everyone to open their lockers for police inspection,' called out Arthur. 'If anyone refuses, they're sacked.'

'Okay Toby, open your locker,' said Doug, crossing his arms.

'Do you want this, Doug?' Toby asked.

'What do you think?' snapped Doug.

'Okay then.' Toby walked over to locker number seven, took out his key, and snapped open the lock.

Doug's mouth fell open as Toby took out a pair of boots and placed them on the floor at the feet of Kate.

'That's not your locker,' said Doug.

'This one is your locker,' said Doug, pointing to number eight, the locker he had fixed the back for.

'I've never used that one,' Toby said.

Doug grabbed Toby's keys and tried to insert the key into the lock. It went in but wouldn't turn. He tried another key without success.

'I want all these lockers opened,' demanded Arthur.

Each of Doug's work crew opened their lockers and showed their shoes. Those on shift who had their shoes on already, took them off and passed them to Kate, who compared their tread.

Doug even opened his locker, number six, and showed his boots. Wrong tread but right size.

All the lockers were open except for number eight.

'Whose locker is number eight?' demanded Arthur. 'Who owns it?'

'Toby does!' cried Doug.

'Your keys?' Kate asked Toby. Toby gave his keys, and she tried the lock but to no avail. Next, she tried Tom's keys, then Daryl's.

Finally, Kate turned to Doug. 'Are you sure about this, Doug.'

'Yes!' said Doug, folding his arms even tighter and feeling all eyes on him.

'Well, pass us your keys,' Kate said to Doug.

Doug looked at Kate. He fished in his pocket and gave her his keys.

She tried his locker key, but it failed. To his surprise, Doug noticed her take another key on the chain. One like his locker key. One he had not noticed before. She put it in, and the lock snapped open in the silence.

Doug blushed bright red as she took from the bottom of the locker the pair of boots muddy from the robbery.

Kate turned them over and checked the tread against the photo.

She placed the boots on the ground.

'Mr Zachariah, will you put the boots on?'

Toby slipped the right boot on. Lifting the boot off the ground, it slid off his foot.

'Mr Haywood?' Kate said.

Doug looked wide-eyed at Kate, then the others.

'It wasn't me! It wasn't me!' he cried out before bursting from the change rooms, swinging open the back door, and marching down the steps to his panel van.

He could hear his name being yelled out as he sped away, gravel flying in his wake.

'Fuck! Fuck!' he screamed, bringing his hands onto the car horn once, twice, three times. Every day for a week leading up the robbery he had watched Toby open and close the locker. Now he realised he had been stooged. Doug screamed.

After driving aimlessly for an hour, Doug parked outside the Railway Hotel and bought himself a double bourbon, which he consumed in two gulps before ordering another.

'So, have they fingered anyone for the robbery at Symes?' said Sammy, one of the regular patrons in the empty bar.

'How the fuck should I know?'

'I thought you were in the know.'

'Mind your own fucken business,' said Doug, taking his third drink and walking to a window seat.

He sat on a stool staring out at the railway station. He sensed people coming and going from the bar, and people whispering about him behind his back.

Finally, the full force of what had happened that morning hit him. He kicked the wall. *What went wrong? Toby had pretended number eight was his locker. How did the key get on his key ring?'*

'Give me another double bourbon,' he called out to Nifty, 'and change for the phone.'

Doug sculled his drink then left the empty glass at his window seat and headed to the phone booth outside the pub. He rang through to Symes.

'Ingrid, it's me.'

'Doug.'

'I need to see you,' he said, bursting into tears. 'I need to see you.'

'You shouldn't be calling me like this,' she whispered.

'I need to see you alone. I can put things straight.'

Silence.

'Do you love me?' he sobbed.

Silence.

'Do you love me?' he sobbed louder.

'Where are you? Everyone is looking for you.'

'Tell me you love me. Please tell me. Please tell me.'

'Tell me where you are,' Ingrid said, her voice cool and calm.

Doug sobbed silently. Wiping his eyes, he stuttered, 'The Railway Hotel. Now tell me you love me.'

'I love you,' she said in a flat whisper.

'No, tell me you love me.'

'I have to go.'

'No, no, no,' he cried, but the phone went dead. He took another coin and rang but her number was engaged. He rang again and it was still engaged.

He slammed down the receiver. He was about to call again, when from the corner of his eye he saw a taxi pull up outside the station and Toby exit. Toby unchained his bike from the wire fence and in one motion jumped onto it and peddled away.

Doug dropped the receiver and clenched his fist as he burst from the telephone box.

He could still just see Toby in the distance. *I know where the little prick is going.*

Doug banged into several people on his way down the street, but didn't stop to apologise.

CHAPTER FIVE

THE FIGHT

Toby was sparring with Frankie when the gym receptionist called from the stairs, 'Hey Frankie, important call for you on line one.'

'Take five Toby. I need to attend to a call,' said Frankie. 'When I come back why don't I teach you to counterattack. You have perfected the rope-a-dope.'

'I still want to practise it.'

'In real life, Toby, you won't have ropes to absorb the punches.'

'I'm training the mind, not the body, Frankie.'

As soon as Frankie left the ring, Doug heaved himself up and through the ropes.

'You set me up, you dog!' said Doug.

Toby's eyes widened.

'You were supposed to be sleeping!' Doug screamed.

The *slap* of leather gloves slapping leather bags stopped. Frankie's boxing gym falling silent.

'I never said I was tired.'

'I drove you home. I told you to go to bed.'

Doug, unsteady on his feet, stepped towards Toby. 'But you didn't listen. You never listen.'

'Doug, you need to stop and think. You're drunk.'

'No, you listen, you little prick. You set me up!'

Doug threw a punch with his ungloved hand, Toby ducking. Doug, stupefied by bourbon, tottered into the ropes. Staggering to his feet, Doug swung around to face his nemesis.

'Everything was organised, and you go and fuck things up as usual.'

'Listen Doug,' Toby said, stepping back. 'I don't want to fight you.'

'Bullshit. Lift up your fists, you little prick,' slurred Doug, lifting up his. 'I know you've wanted a piece of me ever since we met. Go on take a swing. Give me your best shot.'

'Doug I've changed. I'm not the same person I was.'

'You set me up with the boots and planting the locker key on my keyring. You tricked me with the leave form and the locker.'

'You set yourself up,' Toby said.

Against all his training, Doug lunged at Toby, swinging his right fist. Toby fell back onto the ropes and bounced away, Doug tripping, his head banging on the padded pole, his fist skinning the ropes, a chunk of flesh coming away.

Enraged and bleeding, Doug staggered around and lunged at Toby, grabbing him by the throat and shoulders, and pinning him to the ropes.

'You're being used, Doug.'

'Fuck you!' screamed Doug.

Doug threw Toby onto the canvas and jumped on top of him. He threw a wild punch aimed at Toby's face, but his fist smashed into the canvas instead. Doug heard a crack, and a searing pain flowed from his knuckles up his arm. He didn't care, he wanted to kill Toby. He wanted to gouge his eyes out if necessary. With his bung hand, he grabbed Toby by the throat and cocked his left fist, eyeing Toby as lay supine on the canvas.

Doug froze. Toby looked up at him, still and serene.

'I'm not afraid to die, Doug.' Toby said calmly. 'I've died once and am ready to die again. If it makes you happy, do it. But remember, two's company three's a crowd.'

'Fight me you prick! Fight me like a man!' Doug sobbed.

He cocked his fist back further and through the tears aimed for Toby's nose, but felt his arm held back. Soon he felt others pulling him off, lifting him to his feet.

'Calm down, Doug,' whispered Rob, with his arms wrapped around Doug's shoulders and neck.

Doug didn't lash out. The fight had left him. His right knuckles throbbed. With the ropes loosened and lowered by Frankie, Rob dragged Doug off the canvas, down the fire stairs, and kicking open the back door, threw Doug against the tin fence of the back alleyway.

'What the fuck are you doing, Doug?'

A pedestrian momentarily appeared at the corner of the alleyway before passing. Rob grabbed hold of Doug and dragged him further down the alleyway where he pushed him against the fence again, which squeaked and groaned with his weight.

'What the fuck are you trying to do?' yelled Rob as he shook Doug.

'Killing the little prick.'

'Get your act together. You're fucking everything up.'

'What's up between you and Ingrid?'

'There's nothing between us,' said Rob, grabbing Doug's mouth and looking to both ends of the alleyway. Luckily no one had followed them out. 'Keep your voice down.'

'You're setting me up. You want to put the blame on me.'

Rob heard the fire door opening.

'You're going to do me over, take the money and ...'

Rob punched Doug in the stomach. Doug clutched his abdomen and keeled over groaning.

'Keep to the script,' whispered Rob, dropping to his knees with Doug.

Kate appeared at the fire exit. 'Everything okay?'

'Everything's fine,' said Rob. 'I'm going to take Doug back to his home so he can cool off.'

'Do you think that's wise?' queried Kate. 'He tried to kill someone.'

'I know what I'm doing. Go in and make sure the other guy's okay.'

'Toby's gone.'

'Then take the car and go to the station. I'll meet you there.'

'Frankie, I need to borrow your car,' said Rob.

'Doug should go to the station,' advised Kate.

But Rob, holding Doug tightly, kept walking. He didn't want Doug anywhere near a police station.

* * *

Rob called through to Symes on the pay phone outside Doug's house. Ingrid had left for the day. As per protocol, he left the appropriate number of rings one minute apart. With his last coin, he made another call. It answered immediately.

'It's Rob.'

'Where's Doug?'

'At home sleeping.'

Ingrid sighed.

'All the evidence now points to Doug,' said Rob. 'I can't twist it any other way.'

'There's only one thing left to,' Ingrid said. 'Doug Haywood cannot see another sunrise.'

Rob closed his eyes and placed his forehead on the glass pane of the booth.

'It doesn't need to be like this,' he said, clutching hard the telephone receiver.

'In his state, he will give us both up. You can see that Rob, can't you?'

Rob pressed his forehead harder into the glass.

'Rob, I don't like it any more than you do, but we can't let him give us both away. We have a future together, darling. You and me together at last.'

'Were you and Doug ever ...?'

'Ever what?'

'You know.'

'Never,' Ingrid said. 'Doug only wanted the money. Ever since that night in the car with you I have only loved one person and that is you.'

'I don't believe you, princess. I don't believe you.'

'It's true. I love you, Rob Charles.'

Rob pinched the bridge of his nose with his fingers and sighed. 'Okay,' he said after a time, 'but I want a bigger split than fifty-fifty. Do you understand?'

Ingrid inhaled, after a moment's pause said, 'Of course, darling, now this is the plan.'

Chapter Six

The Meeting at the Quarry Gates

Doug killed the headlights at the end of the dirt road outside the gates of the abandoned quarry.

'What do you want?' he said to Rob, who appeared from out of the shadows.

'We need to discuss today and work out a plan for the investigation,' said Rob.

'Can't it wait? I want to go home and sleep.'

'Look, it's important to straighten out your story tonight.'

'Okay, jump in,' sighed Doug.

Rob moved around to the passenger side and slid in with a knapsack.

'Look Doug, I know we haven't started off on the right foot, but I want to help you. I hear you like bourbon.' Rob opened the knapsack and took out a bottle of Maker's Mark bourbon.

'Who told you that?'

'Ingrid.'

'She told you I liked bourbon? When?'

'The first time she floated the idea of the robbery. She talks about you all the time.'

Rob unscrewed the top and passed the bottle to Doug.

'I don't feel like drinking. Not after today.'

'It will do you good. Have a swig.'

'I'm hungover still.'

'It will help with the hand,' said Rob, looking down at Doug's swollen and bandaged knuckles.

'You did some real damage to it today.' Rob took Doug's hand and examined it in the moonlight.

'I'm not proud of what I did or said. I wish I could take it back. I wish I could take back the year and start again. I wish ...'

Doug took back his bandaged hand. 'I wish I never became involved in the robbery.'

'You nearly killed the guy,' said Rob.

Doug winced as he recalled Toby's serene look as he cocked his arm back. He wondered what would have happened if he had let his fist fall.

'Look, don't worry about today. We won't be pressing charges. You're in the clear. I'm going to load everything onto Dimitri. You just gotta hang in there though and let me run things from now on.'

Doug nodded.

'Sure you don't want a drink?' asked Rob, offering the bottle of Maker's Mark.

Doug shook his head.

'You don't mind if I have this,' said Rob, taking a bottle of Glenfiddich from his knapsack.

Doug shook his head.

'If you're not going to drink, at least take some water. I hate drinking by myself.' Rob took out a bottle of water, unscrewed the cap, and passed it to Doug.

'Look Doug,' said Rob, 'you and I need to straighten out your story. I want to finalise this case. I want my share of the money so I can take my family out of this town.'

Doug put the water bottle to his lips. It hovered there before he lowered it without drinking.

'You're not interested in Ingrid?'

'Ingrid?' laughed Rob. 'What did you say that for?'

'I thought you and her.' Doug stopped. 'I thought you liked her.'

'Ingrid? You gotta be kidding me,' said Rob. 'She's not my taste.'

'You swear?' quizzed Doug, taking a sip of the water.

'I only want the fucken money. I have a wife and kids to support. Why would I chase after a stupid bimbo like Ingrid?'

'I had my suspicions,' said Doug.

'Look, I know she likes you. But she's upset with you.'

'I've done nothing wrong. I did everything I was supposed to. How was I to know he didn't live there? Or the boots. Or the glass slat.'

"With women, it isn't about being right or wrong, it's about feelings.'

'I want to take her away from here,' said Doug. 'Away from all the corruption and bad influences. Stealing the money was a mistake.'

'Look, I have an idea how you can convince her.'

'How?' Doug took another sip of water.

'Write her a note. Tell her you're sorry.'

'About what?'

'At being a fucken male. Girls like to hear how men are idiots and how they're always right. If you apologise, even though you've done nothing wrong, she will love you for it.'

Rob took a pen and piece of paper from his pocket and handed it to Doug.

'What do I write?' asked Doug.

'Say I'm sorry.'

Doug took the pen and looked at the detective. His eyes wanted to close. He felt lightheaded. He wrote 'I'm sorry', the y falling away on the page. Rob snatched the pen and paper from him. Doug yawned. He tried to keep his eyes open, but his head drooped. He closed his eyes and put his head on the steering wheel.

* * *

Doug woke to a *hissing*. He tried to open the car door, but his confused mind couldn't grip the handle. He turned to Rob for help, but the passenger seat was empty. The sudden thought, *I've been stitched*, cut through the fog of his addled brain. He unbuckled his seat belt and tried to open the door, but something or someone had jammed it shut from the outside. He tried to wind down the window, but the winder was gone. He bashed on the window, gasping and coughing uncontrollably. His head hit the steering wheel and the horn groaned. He tried to scream, but wheezed and grabbed his neck, coughing uncontrollably.

Doug no longer sat in the seat, but floated high over the car. He saw the detective close by. He moved from here and saw Ingrid at dinner with several ladies. The phone was ringing. Ingrid answered. 'Is it done? You took his keys from his body?... I love you ...'

Doug saw this, but felt detached from it. He thought of his mother and instantly saw her pacing her room.

'I'm sorry,' he cried out, but she did not look up from her pacing. *What has happened?*

He found himself on the ceiling of a small room. One wall was dominated by books and a person in a chair reading.

'Toby.'

Toby shot to his feet, and dropping his book, looked up at him on the ceiling.

'Toby, beware.'

'I know,' Toby said.

Doug saw into the essence of Toby. In this state, Doug knew all at once every event in Toby's life, he knew every thought Toby had ever had. He knew the truth. The truth about Toby and his part in it.

Doug saw in the corner of the room, a pin prick of light growing in brilliance. Soon Doug forgot about Toby, Ingrid, his mother, and the world.

CHAPTER SEVEN

THE SERMON ON THE MOUNT

Doug's death sent a shock wave through Old Town. First, the robbery and now Doug's suicide. Two events so close together and seemingly linked.

It was all people could talk about on Wednesday.

Symes did not open, the staff too shocked to work. They milled about the carpark in whispering groups trying to piece together the events of the last week. Make sense of it all.

Ingrid rose to the occasion. She personally visited Mrs Haywood to comfort her on the loss of her only son. She put Symes and her uncle's business at her disposal.

Ingrid, although supportive to the Haywoods, hinted to several town dignitaries, the inspector, the mayor's wife, and a reporter, about Doug's strange behaviour before the robbery. How he had hung around the office longer than usual asking her unusual questions about her uncle's movements.

To several Friday night women, she confided privately how uncomfortable she felt in Doug's presence. They marvelled at her strength at this time — the robbery, dealing with her uncle's despondency, and finally the suicide of the foreman.

To Doug's friends from his school and the Stingray footy club, none could understand how a bloke like Doug Haywood could be a thief. He was too trusting, they said. Too loyal. Ingrid took time to visit and console them one by one. Soon the story of Doug's confrontation with Toby in the gym circulated through the town, and it was hinted by one or two of Doug's mates that Toby and Doug had fallen out over the money. How security saw Toby's bike pedalling away from Symes the night of the robbery. The police were only waiting for the coroner's determination and the funeral before making their final move.

After a report from Detective Sergeant Rob Charles, the coroner ruled Doug's death a suicide and released the body for burial.

By the morning of the funeral, most of Doug's faults had been forgotten. He was a top bloke with a heart of gold. A great mate. To the press, he was a budding Rugby League and boxing champion. A hard worker who treated everyone well. In short, a saint!

The entire town packed St Michael's to pay their respects. The Haywoods crammed into the front pew along with Ingrid, taking a break from nursing her uncle to sit with Mrs Haywood and hold her hand.

Detective Sergeant Rob Charles and Detective Constable Kate Trengove sat in the pew behind the Haywoods. With all the pews filled, it was standing room only from there.

On the wall behind the altar, images of Doug flashed: Doug as an infant in his mother's arms; Doug as a small boy, sunscreen over his nose holding a large fish; Doug as a teenager with several mates playing cricket; Doug in the Old Town Stingray jumper holding aloft the championship trophy; Doug in a Parramatta Eel's jumper; Doug dressed in high vis in a staff photo; Doug with a bourbon in his hand, smiling, surrounded by his mates at a barbeque.

'The Lord be with you,' said the minister, John Smith.

'And also with you,' replied the congregation.

'I am the resurrection and the life, says the Lord. Those who believe in me, even though they die, yet will they live.'

The organ played 'The Lord is my Shepherd', the monotone voices of the congregation listlessly and languidly following tunelessly behind.

Greg Bowie, Doug's best mate, gave the first eulogy. A pithy five-sentence homily: 'There was no better mate than Doug Haywood. You could always count on him in a fight. He could make you laugh too. We miss you mate. I bet you're giving 'em hell in Heaven.'

Doug's sister recited Psalm 23.

The congregation then sang 'When I survey the Wondrous Cross'.

Reverend John Smith rose into the pulpit as the organ groaned out the last chord. He opened a manilla folder to the notes he had placed there that morning on his kitchen table, and pushing his glasses up his nose, began reading, 'Jesus told them another parable: "Ask and it will be given to you; seek and you will find; knock and the door will be opened to you."' He stopped speaking. He turned the pages over. This wasn't the sermon he had prepared. He intended to recite John 11:1–44, Lazarus rising from the dead. Yet a typed verse from Mathew 7:7 stared back at him. *How on earth?* He had never typed these notes before.

He looked up at the silent, expectant congregation, perplexed. Shocked. He had put the sermon for Lazarus in this folder. In the rafters above pigeons cooed.

In this silence, the church door creaked open. Several heads turned to spy the new arrival. Muffled gasps issued from the back rows. More heads turned. Soon the whispering intensified and cascaded through the congregation to the front pews.

Toby Zachariah, dressed in suit and tie, stood at the entrance. The doors thundered shut behind him.

As the whispering intensified, Ingrid Symes turned, and eyeing Toby, squeezed Mrs Haywood's hand tightly. Toby's footfall echoed through the church as he took the only free spot against the wall near the church doors.

Reverend John Smith spied the newcomer. His eyes narrowed with dim recognition before he dropped his head to the alien notes. *I can't change them*, he thought, so continued in a clear voice:

'For everyone who asks receives; the one who seeks finds; and to the one who knocks, the door will be opened. Which of you, if your son asks for bread, will give him a stone? Or if he asks for a fish, will give him a snake? If you, then, though you are evil, know how to give good gifts to your children, how much more will your Father in Heaven give good gifts to those who ask him! So, in everything, do to others what you would have them do to you, for this sums up the law and the prophets. Enter through the narrow gate. For wide is the gate and broad is the road that leads to destruction, and many enter through it. But small is the gate and narrow the road that leads to life, and only a few find it. Watch out for false prophets. They come to you in sheep's clothing, but inwardly they are ferocious wolves.'

The reverend stopped there and looked up at the young man who had recently entered the church. He remembered him now. He was the one who made the scene in this church a year ago to the day. He dropped his head and hoped he would not make another scene.

'By their fruit you will recognise them. Do people pick grapes from thornbushes, or figs from thistles? Likewise, every good tree bears good fruit, but a bad tree bears bad fruit. A good tree cannot bear bad fruit, and a bad tree cannot bear good fruit. Every tree that does not bear good fruit is cut down and thrown into the fire. Thus, by their fruit you will recognise them.'

Reverend John Smith stopped speaking, for the typed notes stopped there. Usually, he would continue with a sermon on the passage, elucidate a meaning. He opened his mouth and as he did so, his eyes fixed on the young man at the back of the church who had lifted his eyes to the ceiling. *Is he going to make a scene like last time? Please let it not be. Please let it not be.* Disconcerted, the reverend dropped his head and said, stuttering, 'I call on Ingrid Symes to provide the last eulogy.'

Ingrid, wearing her Dior black velvet dress, stood, and with her pointed-toe black high heels clicking in the silence, took the reverend's place in the pulpit.

She smoothed out her notes and lifted her eyes to the packed congregation. A look of sadness and grief was etched across her beautiful countenance. She examined the faces below, feeling the room. Firstly, Doug's distraught relatives and friends in the front pews. She saw Rob frowning before dropping his head. She scanned the faces to the back pews. Her eyes fell on Toby. For a brief second, a feeling of rage and terror rose in her chest as their eyes locked. *I must not,* she thought. *I'm on a stage and have an audience to please.* She took a deep breath, and not looking down at her notes, let her voice carry to the back of the church:

'I only knew Doug Haywood for a short time … excuse me,' she sniffled as she battled to keep the tears away. 'But I came to know him as a sweet and beautiful human being. When I first arrived in this wonderful town, I knew no one. I had lost my mother and father only recently. Yet I found the kindness of my uncle,' she looked at her uncle in the second pew, who was hunched over, head bent, looking at her with one eye, the other closed. 'I found another home in this town. Doug was so kind to me in those first few days, showing me this beautiful town, introducing me to so many wonderful people. In Matthew it says: "for I was hungry, and you gave me food, I was thirsty, and you gave me drink, I was a stranger, and you welcomed me." Doug, like a Christian, showed me charity and kindness and I considered him like a big brother I never had. Although in the last months we drifted apart, and I cannot profess a close bond with Doug like his family and friends, I can understand what they saw in this beautiful man. Excuse me.'

She momentarily hid her teary eyes in her handkerchief. 'Like many, I'm reeling from his passing.' Her voice cracked once more as she stopped and put her handkerchief to her mouth.

After a few well-timed seconds she continued, 'If his death is to have any meaning, let it be as a warning. A warning that we should be our brother's keeper. We should be vigilant to signs of distress of our neighbour. We should go out of our way to care for our family, our friend, our neighbours.'

Ingrid stopped. A muffled sob followed as she turned her head slightly. The church was silent, except for a solitary dove cooing from the rafters.

'Thank you,' she sobbed. Taking her notes, she descended slowly from the pulpit.

She stopped at the coffin, closed her eyes, and with her right hand outstretched, touched the lid, giving out a faint sob before mouthing audibly, 'Goodbye Doug.'

She moved back to her seat. From the corner of her eye, she noted the effect of her speech. Tears were streaming down the faces of the Haywoods, there were nods of approval from the Friday night ladies in the third and fourth rows, Doug's friends stoically tried to keep from bawling, and she could see the sad, drawn faces of the congregation. Momentarily, a smile flittered across her face.

She caught sight of the trainee detective eyeing her. Ingrid did not like the look. Toby was frowning at the back of the church with his arms crossed. She threw him a withering glare before realising she was on stage and reapplied her mournful countenance.

To the strains of 'Stairway to Heaven' by Led Zeppelin, Doug's mates carried Doug's coffin from the church.

As Ingrid watched Doug's mother and sister sobbing as the coffin was lifted into the hearse, Ingrid no longer looked at this scene through temporal eyes, but hovered above, looking down at the congregation spilling out onto the steps of the church. She saw them no longer as an audience, but her people. She was their Ingrid the Great, shaping and leading them, some dying and suffering, but always for a noble purpose, her purpose.

As she hovered, surveying her people, she sensed another entity close by watching her intently, and she tumbled back into her temporal body.

The trainee detective stood next to her.

'It was a touching speech you gave,' said Kate.

'Thank you.'

'It's sad what has happened.'

'Yes. Yes, it is. Detective?'

'Detective Constable Kate Trengove.'

Ingrid smiled and moved to stand next to Mrs Haywood. *I don't like this woman. I don't like her at all.*

CHAPTER EIGHT

THE RECEPTION

'Remember Mrs Haywood, my uncle and I are at your disposal. If you need anything, remember I'm here for you.'

'Thank you, Ingrid,' said Mrs Haywood, dabbing her eyes dry. 'Your words at the funeral were so kind. And what you have done for my family, I cannot thank you enough.'

'It is the least we could do. Isn't that right, Uncle?'

Arthur Symes had not heard a word. He had followed his niece about the room dazed and confused, a shuffling heap of skin and bone; stunned by the loss of Pat, of his money, and the death of his foreman; trying to fathom the changes in the room. All these people eating and drinking, and it wasn't a Friday evening. He felt so fatigued and disorientated these days.

'Yes,' he said, looking at his niece and not knowing what he said yes to, but feeling as if he should say it.

With the partition peeled away, Arthur's living room overflowed with funeral guests. The billiard table and furniture were pushed to one side and replaced with a long trestle table piled high with plates of cakes, sausage rolls, hors d'oeuvres, boiling urns, coffee cups, wine and beer; attended to by solemn bow-tied waiters. The reception, as well as the funeral, all paid for by Arthur Symes, but brought into existence by Ingrid.

On one side of the room near the beers, Doug's friends gathered. Bowie, Doug's best mate, and Lock from the Old Town Stingrays towered in the centre of the group, downing beers and eyeing moodily the blow-ins come to mourn their mate.

On the other side, the extended Haywood clan congregated, while dotted about the room, small pockets of people ate and talked in low reverential tones.

'If only Doug had found a nice girl to settle down with,' said Mrs Haywood. 'None of this would have happened.'

'Of course,' Ingrid said, rubbing Mrs Haywood's hand.

'Ingrid!'

Councillor Fiona Townsend took Ingrid's arm and led her away from Mrs Haywood.

'Let me say how impressed I was by your eulogy. I don't think I have heard a finer speech. The council is putting together a seminar later this year on youth suicide. This is a big issue in regional Australia, and I thought you could give a speech.'

'I would love to,' Ingrid said. 'My uncle and I want to establish a foundation to tackle this very issue.'

'Council would be interested in helping you,' said Councillor Townsend. 'Have you ever thought of running for council? Or state parliament? Politics in Australia is always crying out for strong and compassionate female voices.'

'Well, I have thought about it ...'

Ingrid stopped.

A recognisable and dangerous voice had started up behind her.

'Mrs Haywood, I'm sorry for your loss.'

Ingrid spun round. The entire room quietened.

'Although I cannot say your son and I were close, and we had our differences, I always admired his devotion to his family, his friends and Symes.'

'Thank you. Thank you. What is your name?'

'Toby. Toby Zachariah.'

'Toby, thank you.'

'I'm shocked by his passing,' continued Toby. 'Until only six months ago he was so happy.'

Ingrid's eyes darted about the hushed room, listening intently to Toby's words. She instantly recognised the danger in this conversation. She needed to end it. She looked at Doug's friends, catching Bowie's boozy bloodshot eyes.

Bowie understood immediately what should happen. He plonked down his glass and stormed over to Toby, pushing him away from Mrs Haywood.

'You have some hide coming here,' he said. Toby staggered back before collecting his balance. Bowie grabbed him again by his suit and shook him. The room took a collective breath.

'You're not welcome here.'

'I don't know why you're having a go at me,' Toby said. 'I had nothing to do with his death or the robbery.'

What had been alluded to in whispered conversations all week was now in the open.

'Oh yeah?' scoffed Bowie. 'What did you say to him at the gym?'

'I said two's company, three's a crowd.'

The meaning of these words passed by Bowie, but not Ingrid.

Rob saw the danger from the other side of the room. He threw down his coffee cup and pushed his way through the knot of people to Bowie.

Bowie cocked back his fist. The room erupted into screams and muffled cries.

'Go on hit me Bowie,' Toby said, not blinking. 'Hit me. If it helps you.'

'You're trying to be funny,' said Bowie.

Ingrid pushed forward, lips parched, eyes widened, breath held, waiting, willing the punch. She wanted to see blood stream down Toby's face. She wanted to see his nose smashed in, bone and skin ruptured like pus, his teeth smashed in his mouth. She wanted to see him shattered, beaten to a pulp, whimpering for mercy.

'Off him,' said Rob, pushing Bowie towards his friends, who gathered around him and gave him back slaps.

Rob turned to Toby and, grabbing him by the collar, marched him out the door into the kitchen.

'Now fuck off, or I will have you arrested.' Rob flung open the door with his free hand.

'I hope you know what you got yourself into,' Toby said, eyeing the detective closely.

Rob tightening his grip on Toby. 'What did you say?'

'Detective Sergeant.'

Rob turned.

'Everything okay?' Kate asked, standing at the entrance.

'I was showing Toby the door.'

Rob pushed Toby out into the backyard, locking the door behind him.

The main room returned to normal, but with subdued intense whispering.

Ingrid could sense the guests in their little groups discussing what Toby meant by 'two's company, three's a crowd'.

This led Ingrid to wonder, *What did he know?* Or, and this made her inhale sharply, *Does he know?*

Ingrid circulated. To the Haywoods, she said, 'Toby upsets everyone, even nice guys like Bowie.' She shook her head. 'He has always had a way of sending people over the edge.'

To Doug's remaining friends at the wake, Bowie unfortunately not one of them, she repeated the story of the gym and Toby. How the police knew; how Toby had been leading Doug astray in the days before the robbery.

To the non-Haywoods, she lowered her voice and whispered, 'I shouldn't say anything, but I heard from the police that the third person Toby alluded to is a man called Dimitri, a small-town drug dealer. Doug, Toby and this Dimitri were seen together a day before the robbery.'

To several of the prominent Friday night women, she told a mixture of these stories, and how Toby sexually harassed her in the tearoom.

The room thinned. An hour after the incident with Toby, Ingrid saw the last guest to the door.

Ingrid sent the waiting staff home. She asked them to come back the next day to clean up. She needed time to be alone and think.

She returned to the big room, lit a cigarette, and walked aimlessly through the empty space. She had always been careful with both men. Always quick to distance herself from Doug and the detective. As for her private meetings with each of them, they were private. She had kept all correspondences to a minimum. She knew she had not been followed or that anyone knew about the shack. *Doug wouldn't tell Toby. No, it was a guess. A guess.*

'Doug never liked Toby.'

Ingrid gasped in fright, dropping her cigarette as she spun around to her uncle, who was slumped in one of the armchairs pushed into the corner.

'They always fought like cat and dog,' Arthur said.

'You've have had a long day, Uncle, it's time for a nap.'

Ingrid went to the kitchen and made him a brandy with a triple dose of sleeping tablets. She stood over him while he drank it before leading him to the couch tucked in a corner where she made him lie down and close his eyes.

'You've been such a godsend to me over these last few days,' slurred Arthur. 'I don't know what I would have done without you.'

'I know. I know,' Ingrid said, tapping her foot.

Once certain he was asleep, Ingrid took his keys, crossed the front lawn, and entered the closed Symes warehouse. She lit a cigarette, throwing the match beneath a shelf. The immense empty warehouse, with its high tin roof, doves cooing from the rafters and cool cement floor, gave her the feeling of solitude and space to walk aimlessly and plan.

She took a pocket torch from a shelf and stuffed it into a pocket, then opening the door to a small storeroom and lighting another cigarette, entered.

'You have some hide giving the eulogy!'

Ingrid swung round. On a pallet of cement mix bags sat Toby.

'And you have some hide coming to the reception,' she said, recovering her breath.

'It was a rather good speech you gave though,' he said. 'How he was like an older brother to you. How we should all be our brother's keeper. And touching the coffin ... what a deft touch.'

Toby stopped and eyed her closely. 'You have so much talent, but all you want to do is destroy.'

'I don't know what you mean.'

'Come now. You used Doug to commit the robbery. When he threatened to blow your scheme, you had him murdered.'

'Rubbish. How could I force Doug into his car and pump it full of carbon monoxide? Besides, I was entertaining that night.'

Somewhere a dove cooed. Ingrid smiled. 'Where were you on that night, Toby? I'm sure the police will be asking that question soon.'

'You can't go on killing. You need to stop and think,' he said. 'It's only a matter of time before you're caught.'

'Caught?' scoffed Ingrid. 'I've done nothing wrong! In fact, I'm the victim in all of this. I'm dealing with a sick uncle. I've had a robber break into the house I was sleeping in.' Ingrid's voice began to crack with emotion. 'I've carried Symes since the death of Pat, and what thanks do I receive? None. None whatsoever.'

Ingrid started to sob, tears falling down her cheeks. 'In all these months no one has asked me, how I am doing. Whether I'm doing okay. It's so unfair how I'm treated.'

'Drop your act. It doesn't work with me.'

Ingrid's tears stopped instantly, replaced with a glare.

'I won't let you go on destroying,' Toby said.

'What a lovely sentiment,' Ingrid responded. 'Playing the hero are we Toby? How virtuous of you. Also, how bloody boring. Where's the fun in that?'

'This isn't make-believe Ingrid. This is real life. You're playing with people's lives.'

'What do you care about real life? Why don't you leave this town to me?

You can go and bother your god to your heart's content.'

'I came back to stop you.'

'Oh, who is pretending now?' Ingrid laughed then scowled. 'You're right Toby, this isn't make-believe, and you're not the hero, and I'm no evil harlot leading men astray for her own benefit.'

'You said it, not me.'

'Oh, I see what this is all about,' said Ingrid. 'It's all about the narrative. How sexist men like you keep strong independent women like me in line. Portray our strength, our daring, our independence as evil. So, this is how I'm to be portrayed? As a villainous seductress? An Eve tempting men with the forbidden fruit?'

'I don't think you're evil. I don't think you're strong either. You're hurt! Damaged!'

'Shut up.' She slapped him.

Until this moment, Ingrid had enjoyed their repartee. But not anymore. Inflamed, she came close and pushed her finger into his chest as she hissed, 'You've accused me of robbery and killing Doug, all with no proof. If you accuse me in public of the robbery, or the death of Pat or Doug, I will sue you. I have a lot of friends in this town. A lot of friends in the *right* places.'

Ingrid smiled, and keeping her finger pointed at his heart, came a little closer. With her face inches from him, she whispered, 'This is a small town, and you need to be careful. Very careful.'

'You're threatening me? How classy of you, Ingrid.'

'No,' smiled Ingrid, removing fluff from his shirt before grabbing his tie and dusting it down. 'I worry about you, that's all. This is a tough town, and you're on the bottom of the pecking order. You're hated. You don't have any connections like I do, and I would hate to see you hurt.'

'Your threats would work if I feared death. But I don't. I welcome it.'

Toby took a long knife used to slash open pallet wrappings. Holding the blade, he offered Ingrid the handle.

'Instead of ordering one of your goons to do it. Why don't you do it yourself?'

Ingrid took the wooden handle, marvelling at its smooth feel in her grip, mesmerised by the twinkle of light on the polished silver surface of the blade, *How sharp the edges look. How it could cut through skin and bone, sever arteries.*

Toby slid off the pallet and lifted his shirt to reveal his smooth abdomen with a tuft of blonde chest hairs quivering and several ribs visible with his rising and falling breath.

'What are you waiting for? Kill me! But on the condition that you leave this town.'

She felt a quiver of excitement run down her spine at the thought. She took a firm grip of the knife as she placed her left hand on his shoulder, digging her nails through his shirt into his skin. She extended back her other hand holding the knife. With a guttural cry, she brought it with all her strength towards Toby's stomach.

She screamed with rage as she let the knife drop on the concrete floor. The skin on Toby's abdomen was untouched.

She pushed off him, breathing rapidly. Blood oozed through his shirt from where she had dug in her nails.

'You're not worth the effort,' she said.

'You don't have the guts to do it,' he said, dropping his shirt.

'I have the guts, but also have the brains. A kill needs to be planned, not done out of blind emotion.'

She looked at him, and nodding her head, smiled. 'I must congratulate you.'

'Why?'

'On being so brave and in making everyone think you lived in the house. Your alibi was outstanding. As for the boots, clever. You're a worthy adversary, Toby.'

'I'm going to stop you,' he said.

'How?' Ingrid laughed. 'You don't have any friends or people to rely on. This is a corrupt town and I have all the main pawns on my side. You're in checkers.'

'It's checkmate and I'm far from it. Remember when we met in the vacant house and you said I should try being a good citizen? Well, thank you for your advice. I understand what I must do now.'

'How did you get in?' she snapped, the smile disappearing from her face.

'These days no one locks up or turns on the alarms. I came in through one of the doors.'

'Well, you can see yourself out.'

Ingrid turned and opened the door of the main warehouse. She took a step before stopping and looking back.

'I was magnificent in church today, don't you think?' Her eyes glazed over as she sighed, a radiant smile breaking across her face. 'I had them hanging on my every word. I look forward to doing the eulogy at your funeral, Toby.'

Ingrid scrunched her face and, putting emotion into her voice, lifted her eyes and said, 'Toby may have been an outcast, a recluse, but not to me. He was so much more. I saw glimpses of the beautiful soul he was.'

She looked at Toby, her theatrical mournful expression turning into a glare.

'Pity it would be to an empty church,' she added before slamming the door shut in his face.

BOWIE

The phone gave two rings once every hour before cutting off, but Ingrid ignored them all. Instead, she put on her cloak and left the house.

She parked Arthur's car in the carpark and made her way down the pathway to the main beach at Lighthouse Point.

Ingrid readjusted her cloak against the steady sea breeze. Over the rhythmic crash and whoosh of waves, she heard the waft of heavy metal music. A little way off, she saw the flames of a campfire flicker and dance with the breeze, illuminating a group of people crashed around it.

She crunched her way unevenly along the beach, cursing the sand lodging in her sneakers. The subdued voices and music became more distinct.

'Hi,' she said to a guy with bloodshot eyes, who was sprawled on the sand near the fire: 'Do you know where Bowie is?'

'Bowie. Bowie,' he said, not comprehending her words.

Ingrid stepped past him and found another young man sprawled on the ground. 'Do you know where Bowie is?'

'He's here somewhere,' he slurred, a little more conscious of his surroundings. 'He might be at the bonfire.'

'You're looking for me?' came a clear voice in the shadows to Ingrid's left.

Bowie sat alone with a bottle of Jim Beam in his hand, away from the bonfire in the shadows where the beachgrass meets the sand.

Smiling, Ingrid walked over and sat down next to him. 'I came to see how you were doing.'

Bowie did not look at her. He took a swig of the bottle and looked out to the sea buried in the darkness.

'You spoke well today,' she said.

'You spoke real nice too,' he said, taking another swig and not taking his eyes off the darkened horizon. Above, a lone gull hovered and crowed.

Ingrid motioned for the bottle, and taking it from Bowie's grasp, took a long swig. It tasted foul, her mouth and throat on fire, but she thought it better to imitate than irritate.

'I don't blame you for what happened at the reception today,' she said, handing back the bottle.

'Why?' Bowie took another swig.

Ingrid felt cold with the constant sea breeze cutting through her thin clothes.

'The way Toby treated Doug,' she said. 'How he manipulated him. It was well known at Symes. Toby was getting in Doug's ear.'

The bourbon made her feel light-headed. She corrected her posture in the sand, drawing closer to Bowie. She wondered whether she should place her head on his shoulder. *No, maybe he has a girlfriend, and she's at the campfire. Better wait a little.*

Bowie remained silent. He was harder work than she anticipated.

'If I had been you, I would have beaten Toby into a pulp. No one would have blamed you if you had. It was common knowledge Toby and Doug met in secret.'

She took the bottle from his hand and sculled. She didn't like spirits, but she was cold and wanted to warm herself.

'I'm so sorry for what Toby did to Doug. What he did to you,' she said, handing back the bottle, this time ensuring her hand touched his. 'Bowie, I want you to know I'm here for you.'

Ingrid smiled at him.

'Toby did nothing to me,' said Bowie, putting the screw top on the bottle and throwing it into the shadows.

'Did nothing?' Ingrid stiffened. 'He has as good as killed your best mate.'

'You can't force a man to commit suicide. No, Doug is to blame for his own death.'

Bowie, turning to look at Ingrid for the first time, frowned and said, 'Yeah, I got hot under the collar today and made a fool of myself. But thinking about it later, I don't believe Toby had anything to do with it.'

'Well, you would be one of the few people in town who does,' she said.

''I don't care what other people think,' said Bowie. 'I was angry, but more with Doug for doing himself in, than anyone else. I took it out on Toby. Anyway, Toby came and saw me earlier tonight. We had a long chat. He told me he didn't have anything to do with Doug's death and I believe him.'

'You believe Toby?' cried out Ingrid, wishing she had never come to the beach.

'Yeah! I'm a pretty good judge of character.'

Ingrid shot to her feet and dusted herself down.

Fuck you! Fuck you! she wanted to spit out. *You small-minded working-class dickhead with your flannelette shirts and heavy metal music. Men like you don't think beyond your dick. I hope you marry some equally dim-witted, constipated, bottle-blonde bimbo, who turns into a fat, ugly whore, pushing out one fucking screaming turd of a child after another. I hope you die of cancer and your fucken football side the Stingrays is decimated.*

She didn't say any of this, instead, she smiled. 'I better leave.' She turned to go.

Bowie shook his head and sniggered.

'What's funny?' she said, stopping and glaring.

'Toby said you would come and try to speak to me. Try and butter me up.'

'Yeah well ...' For the first time since coming to Old Town, Ingrid was lost for words ... out-played. 'I only came to see how you were doing.'

She turned and began walking away.

'Going so soon?' called out Bowie. 'What did the reverend say about a wolf? A wolf in sheep's clothing?'

Sniggers came from the bonfire.

She quickened her pace, realising she had confirmed Toby's prediction. All the way up to the car, she took one deep breath after another, trying to compose herself. *Why didn't I kill him when he gave me the chance? Why?*

CHAPTER TEN

A Loose End

'Where were you last night?' demanded Rob.

'I was out walking.'

'All fucken night?'

'I needed time to think.'

'I spent all night trying to call you.'

'I told you I would call you, not the other way round.'

'Listen here, missy, I put my neck on the line for you. I will call you when I want, and you will answer.'

'Toby's a problem.'

'Everything's fine. Doug is dead. He will take the rap. I will link him to Dimitri. All you need to do is spread stories about Doug acting suspiciously. We wait several months and the money is as good as ours.'

'What about the two's company, three's a crowd quip? Toby knows more than he's letting on.'

'So, what? If he had any suspicions, he would have passed them on by now. Besides, like you said to people at the reception, we can say the quip was about Dimitri ... thieves falling out.'

'I don't like it. He's up to something. I know it.'

Rob grabbed Ingrid by the shoulders and gently shook her.

'Relax! Everything is fine. I'm in charge of the investigation. You have your uncle under your thumb, so there's nothing to worry about. All we do now is play it safe for a time. I will wrap up the investigation. You just keep spreading stories about Doug and everything will work out fine.'

'He's smarter than I realised. And he knows, Rob. He knows.'

'Knows what?'

'He knows about us and our plans for the robbery.'

'He knows nothing.'

'If he knows nothing, how did he avoid our trap?'

'Luck.'

'What about the house not being his? The address in payroll being incorrect? Tell me that isn't deliberate!'

'Simple. He didn't want people to know where he lived, so he pretended it was his.'

'He knew we were setting him up.'

'How could he know?'

'I don't know, but he has some sixth sense. Some way of knowing things. He accused me of murdering Doug.'

'What? When?'

'After the reception. I went into the warehouse to think and I found him waiting for me in one of the storerooms. He accused me of the robbery and murdering Doug.' Tears welled in her eyes. She fell into the detective's arms.

'Please hold me, Rob. I'm so scared.'

'What is it with you and this Toby bloke? Maybe he has a sixth sense like you say. He still needs to pass his suspicions to the police. That's me. Then the courts need evidence, not hunches, before they will convict.'

Rob stroked her hair.

'I know, Rob. I know I shouldn't worry,' she sobbed.

'Then don't,' said Rob, planting a kiss on her forehead. 'I will protect you.'

'I know you will. I know now I should listen to you and follow your lead. I shouldn't worry, knowing you will look after it all. But I can't help it. He's a loose end we need to tidy up.'

'What are you saying?' said Rob, pushing her away

'He needs to have an unfortunate accident.'

'You can't go around whacking every person you don't like.'

'I thought that's how detectives like you worked.'

'This isn't El Salvador, honey,' protested Rob. 'We don't go around whacking every person who gets in our way. Killing someone is serious business. Once you kill someone, you multiply the number of people involved in the investigation, and you don't know where it may end up. Look at the robbery. Fuck! It nearly went off the rails.'

'What if he starts blabbing all over town about his suspicions?'

'We'll deal with that when it comes up.'

'I know,' Ingrid said, falling back into his arms. 'I know I'm being overanxious. I know you're in charge now and everything will be fine, but I'm not thinking of myself. I'm thinking of us. I want us to be together. I love you, Rob Charles.'

Ingrid squeezed him tighter. 'I've loved you since the first time I laid eyes on you.'

'Bullshit.'

It was her turn to push him away.

'You didn't read me well. I was in love with you, Rob, from the beginning. I didn't realise it until the night in your car.'

She hugged him again, kissing his cheeks, his forehead. Then she whispered in his ear, 'Let's go away sooner rather than later. What the hell with the case. We can take your boat and head up the coast to Queensland.'

She squeezed him tight. 'What could be better than stopping in some small coastal town? You could launch your boat and fish. I could sit on the beach or in a small café and read. When you come back, I can cook the fish on the beach. We can make love under the stars. Imagine it, nothing but the open road and miles of ocean, sand and beach passing us by in the car window. We can start again in another state. Buy a little house somewhere by the beach. You can find a job as a policeman or in security. Or we could start our own business together. With all the money from the robbery there's nothing to worry about. You can fish all weekend and when you come home, I will have a meal ready for you. We can make it happen. All we need to do is eliminate one tiny problem.'

Rob looked down at Ingrid. He did not push her away this time.

'You owe me, princess. You owe me big time.'

CHAPTER ELEVEN

TOBY INTERVIEWED

Six Smit Street was a nondescript corner house in the hills of Old Town. Rob parked several doors down, and with Kate by his side, walked slowly to the house, noting the side fence. *Easy to scale*, he thought, although he had no way of seeing the backyard. He made a mental note to ask for the toilet, using it as an excuse to scan the surroundings. Once that was done, he would make the interview as short as possible. *No need to prolong it*, he thought, *now that Doug was the main and only suspect*. As Kate knocked on the door, Rob checked for security cameras. None.

The door opened and Rob stepped back in surprise. The sergeant at his first posting as a cadet straight out of the academy stood before him. Sergeant Alan Mills, or Snapper as they called him, stood in the doorway, silver-haired and hunched over.

'Good God! Is it Razzle?' exclaimed Alan.

'Sergeant!'

'I'm retired now. Call me Alan, or Snapper if you like.'

'Snapper, good to see you after all these years,' said Rob.

'This is Kate Trengove. She works with me.'

'Ah! You must be Alan's daughter. I worked with him for many years at Parramatta. A fine policeman. I suppose you're here to see Toby.'

'Correct.'

'He rents the bungalow out the back.'

'How long has he lived with you, Sarge?' asked Rob, falling into a familiar role of probationary constable.

'Ever since he left the hospital in February last year. My wife is a nurse's aide there. She took him in to keep watch over him. He was quite fragile after his stay there. He has only just moved out of the spare room and into the bungalow.'

They stopped briefly to speak to Edith, Alan's wife, who offered to send them tea or coffee before they passed into the backyard and over to a single-room bungalow.

After a few knocks, they entered a room with a kitchenette, a bench, and a single bed. In the small living space next to the bed, Toby sat in an armchair reading a book. All around him on the floor were books, and behind him, a bookcase dominated the wall. A small cassette player at his feet was playing a slow classical piece.

While Alan assembled chairs out of the chaos of books, Rob moved to the window and, parting a blind, looked out at the backyard to the fence line.

It wouldn't be too difficult to jump and approach the bungalow undetected, he thought. He was looking at the locking mechanism on the window when Toby's voice startled him.

'I keep the window unlocked and open at night. However, a sensor turns on a light if anything bigger than a cat jumps the fence.'

Toby sat eyeing Rob intently. Rob, as if woken from a dream, noticed the others staring at him from their seats.

Rob moved nervously to the remaining empty seat.

'It must be force of habit,' Toby said, not taking his eyes off the detective, 'to check out every room you enter for entry and exit points.'

Rob frowned and tried to read Toby's expression. He understood why Ingrid hated him. It was as if Toby saw straight through him, and could read his innermost thoughts.

'Yeah, force of habit,' grinned Rob, clenching his fists.

'Lovely piece of music,' Kate said. 'I've heard it before.'

'Beethoven's 'Moonlight Sonata',' Toby said, casting his eyes on Kate. 'I like to play it at night. If I was to die, or an assassin was to jump the fence, it would be the music I would like to listen to before the end.' His eyes moved to Rob.

Rob was thankful Kate continued with the small talk.

'I see you read philosophy … Nietzsche, in particular.'

'Not anymore. I don't subscribe to his philosophy. I'm giving away all my old books as they no longer resonate with my new thinking.'

'Wasn't your favourite book *The Count of Monte Cristo*?' said Alan, picking up a battered and well-thumbed book at his feet, like a proud father not understanding the contents, but equating its weight with an intelligence beyond his own.

'You said you were obsessed with it,' he continued. 'What was it about again?'

'A man thrown in prison for a crime he did not commit,' Toby said, staring at Rob. 'In prison, he learns of a great hoard of treasure hidden on the Isle of Monte Cristo. He escapes, unearths the treasure, and uses it to plot the destruction of the three men responsible for his incarceration.'

Rob bit his bottom lip and shifted in his seat as Toby's eyes moved to Alan then Kate. 'It's a tale of vengeance and redemption. Of a man who wheedles his way into the lives of his enemies to seek revenge. I realised after my time in hospital that the things I thought were true and relevant weren't important. I'm not the same person as the one who came to Old Town. The old Toby died on the operating table. The books I once read, I no longer find interesting.'

'What are you reading now?' Kate asked.

Toby showed the cover of his book: Swedenborg's *Heaven and Hell*.

'Who was Swedenborg again, Toby?' asked Alan. 'I know you explained him to me once.'

'He was an eighteenth-century Swedish scientist, polymath and genius, who began having mystical experiences in his fifties.'

'Toby started reading Swedenborg after coming out of hospital. He was in at the same time as your father,' Alan explained to Kate.

'Your father was in hospital?' Toby looked surprised.

'Yes, he passed away last year,' Kate said.

'I don't understand what a smart bloke like you is doing in Old Town, Toby.' Rob was tiring of the small talk and wanted to get this interview over as quickly as possible. He also wanted to unsettle Toby. Give him some of his own medicine.

Toby took his eyes off the trainee detective, reluctantly it seemed to Rob, and fixed his gaze on Rob. 'I like it here.'

'I find it odd, a smart bloke like you, coming and living in a town like this.'

'I don't see anything wrong with it.'

'I mean, you're smart. Why not go to Sydney and make something of your life, instead of working at Symes?'

'We're all different,' Toby said. 'I'm not ambitious. I have other priorities.'

"Was stealing five hundred thousand K one of your priorities?'

Rob didn't care what his old sergeant thought. He wanted shake Toby up. Get under that smooth exterior.

'Money is of no importance to me,' Toby said. 'I have everything I need.'

'We have several questions about the statement you gave us,' Rob said, taking out his notebook and pen.

Toby smiled at Rob. 'I don't think I will be of any use to you in solving the robbery.'

'On the day of the robbery, you and Doug locked up,' said Rob.

'Yes.'

'Who shut the safe?' asked Rob.

'Doug did. He didn't let me check it. He seemed agitated.'

'And what time did you lock up?'

'Around five o'clock. Give or take.'

'How long did it take you to lock up?'

'Hard to say.'

'Well try!' snapped Rob.

'Thirty minutes. Then we went to Arthur Symes' home. I wanted to go to the railway station, but Doug was insistent I should go to Arthur's house. He threw my bike in the back of the panel van without asking me.'

'Doug drove you home?' asked Kate.

'He drove me to the gym.'

'Why would we believe he drove you home?'

'I don't know.'

'But you went into the vacant house?'

'I didn't live there.'

'You didn't answer the question!' said Rob.

'Doug had acted strangely all day,' continued Toby. 'He had acted strangely for the last few weeks. One minute trying to be my friend, the next putting me against the wall. Ever since Ingrid came to town, he started acting like Dr Jekyll and Mr Hyde.'

'Have you ever been in the vacant house?' Rob asked.

Toby crossed his legs. He looked at Alan then Kate. 'I've been in there once.'

'When?'

'To stop Ingrid from finding out where I lived.'

'What do you mean?' Kate asked, leaning forward in her seat.

'Ingrid started following me about before Christmas. When I caught her spying on me, I pretended I lived at the vacant house, hoping I could throw her off the trail.'

'Why do you think she wanted to follow you?' questioned Kate.

'I don't know, you better ask her. All I know is, she was a bad influence on Doug.'

'You've changed your story from our last interview,' said Rob, hoping to take the direction of the interview away from the topic of Ingrid.

'I should have said something.' Toby sighed and looked at Kate. 'Look, I can't help you. I have no reason to steal Arthur Symes' money. I no longer value money or wealth.'

'What do you value now?' asked Kate

Toby stared up into the corner of the ceiling before lowering his eyes.

'Have you ever woken from a dream, Detective? One you have forgotten, except for the overwhelming feeling you need to complete a mission, but didn't know what that mission was? It had been erased from your mind. Yet the feeling of urgency remained?'

Toby's eyes were fixated on Kate as he continued, 'I no longer fear death. It's the one thing I take away from my stay in hospital. I know we don't die.'

Toby turned his gaze onto Rob. 'And there's no more dangerous person in all the world, than one who doesn't fear death.'

Rob clenched his notebook tightly. He felt Toby's eyes drilling into his very soul. He felt as if a voice in his ear whispered, *He's mocking you, Rob. He's mocking you.*

'You're behind this robbery,' proclaimed Rob.

'Why would I commit the robbery?' Toby asked. 'Why would I throw it all away for the sake of money? Betray my friends, my colleagues, my reputation, my good name, the institution I serve? Kill someone in cold blood?'

Rob sprang from his seat and fell on Toby. The room erupted into gasps and cries of, 'Razzle!' 'Detective Sergeant!'

Rob grabbed Toby by the collar and threw him against the bookcase, which rattled. Books plonked onto the floor, one clonking Rob on the head, enraging him further.

'What are you implying, you little shit? Come on. Spit it out.'

Rob shook him against the bookcase again, more books falling to the ground.

'Detective Sergeant!' Kate cried out.

'I imply nothing. Your actions however, Detective, speak of guilt.'

Rob grabbed Toby's neck with one hand and squeezed. As he cocked back his other fist ready to strike, he locked eyes with Toby. *How serene he looks. As if not only expecting to be hit but welcoming it.*

'I'm sorry for you. Truly I am,' Toby said.

Rob inhaled sharply and let Toby go. He looked around at the others. His old sergeant and Kate were staring at him, shocked.

He looked back at Toby, who eyed him with a laser-like intensity. Rob felt as if he stood naked, and those in the room saw his soul, shrunken and darkened by booze, sin and corruption.

'I need fresh air,' Rob said, marching from the room, eyes downcast.

Unable to face his old sergeant's wife, he left by the side gate. He felt as if he could have crawled beneath it.

In the driver's seat, he considered his reflection in the side mirror: bloodshot eyes, matted unkempt hair, blotchy skin. He tried to remember a day over the last few months without a drink. He couldn't.

His reverie was broken by Trengove at the driver's side window.

'I will drive. You need to take it easy.'

'I'm fine.'

Rob followed her gaze to his hands, twitching uncontrollably on the steering wheel. He alighted from the car and walked around to the passenger door. Toby ran from the house towards them.

'Detective! Detective Trengove! You said your father passed away only recently?'

'Yes.'

'Which hospital?'

'John Hunter.'

'When?'

'Why do you want to know?'

'When?'

'Fourth of February last year.'

'Detective, do you have a red box?'

'Pardon?'

'Do you have a red box?'

'I don't know what you mean?'

'Did your father give you a red box?'

'I don't …' Kate looked down at the road before lifting her eyes. 'I have no red box.'

Toby deflated before Rob's eyes.

'What is this about?' asked Kate.

'It's complicated,' Toby said. 'It must be another person. You see. I thought it might be you. You see I met a …'

Toby hesitated. 'I met a man on a journey. He had a message for his daughter. The answer she seeks is in the red box.'

Rob blurted out, 'Who the fuck are you?' yelled Rob. 'How the fuck do you … '

'There are no secrets in this world, Detective. No secrets, Detective.' Toby turned and walked back to the house.

* * *

'The little shit is lying. Fuck. I know he's up to his neck in this robbery, but I can't put my finger on how,' said Rob as Kate drove them back to the station. 'That's why I put him against the bookcase. I know he's behind it, but he's too smart to leave any evidence. The guy manipulated Doug. He's working with Dimitri. He's only waiting until things settle down before moving out of Old Town with the cash.'

He glanced at Kate for her reaction, but she stared at the road ahead. The dashboard hummed. He sighed, realising he no longer believed in his own lies, terrified at how Toby saw straight through him. *Toby saw my dark secrets. My god, how could be know?*

'You went a bit far,' she said finally, in a calm, level voice.

'Fuck, you're too green. You don't know what it's like seeing little shits like Toby get away with murder. Sometimes you need to shake things up, bend a few rules. Once you have been a detective for a while, you will get a second sense as to what people are about. He's the mastermind. Bright and cool under pressure. He didn't flinch, not once.'

'Toby isn't involved in the robbery,' Kate said, shaking her head as they came to a stop at an intersection. 'But he's holding something back. Something important. But we should also check out Ingrid Symes.'

'You're not buying his crap on the niece?'

'Why not? It's more obvious. She lives with her uncle, has access to the keys. Also, a Doug and Toby combination does not sound likely. Everyone I spoke to said they hated one another, but Doug falling under the spell of Ingrid Symes ... that is more likely.'

'We have our suspects–Doug and Dimitri. Doug is dead, Dimitri is in custody. Once I have Toby and his fake name Zachariah checked out, we will have him as well.'

'You may find something interesting about Toby, but it won't be about the robbery.'

'What about the red box?'

'I don't know what it means,' Kate said.

They drove in silence for a time.

The image of Toby's serene and laser-like expression came to Rob's mind. *It was as if Toby had seen what I'd done. As if he had looked right into my soul and seen all my secrets.*

'Oh my god! Oh my god! What have I done?' he cried, cupping his head in his hands and bawling.

Kate pulled the car to the side of the road.

'Shit what have I done? What have I done?'

'You got a little hot under the collar,' Kate said. 'It can happen to any of us.'

Rob shook his head, tears falling down his cheeks.

'You don't understand. I've done things. Things I'm not proud of. I've ... I've ...' Rob inhaled sharply. Outside, a flock of lorikeets squabbled.

'Do you want to discuss it?' Kate asked after a time.

'I can't Kate. It's complicated. I wish I never came here.'

'Came where?'

'This bloody town.'

A lone magpie swooped the lorikeets perched on a cypress tree.

'The little shit got under my skin,' said Rob. 'You leave the academy all idealistic, ready to make a difference, then you see how the world really works. Crooks walking free to enjoy their ill-gotten gain while you're working fifteen-hour days, weekends, and for what? Shit money, four weeks holiday, a gold watch at retirement, and you never stop thinking about the cases you couldn't solve. I bet your father took that all the way to his death bed.'

Outside the car, the squabbling from the lorikeets reached a crescendo.

Kate's eyes moved away from Rob and out of the car, tears beginning to well.

'I know how hard it is to lose a dad. Not a day I don't think about my old man's death,' said Rob.

'Every day I think about the night my dad died,' Kate said. 'And what he said to me before he passed away.'

'What did he say?' said Rob.

'I was stationed at Tamworth when my mum called to tell me Dad had a stroke with not much time left to live. He was in and out of a coma and each time he woke he kept calling for me. When I finally arrived at the hospital, I sat by his bed and held his hand. When he woke and saw me, he said: "Go to the abandoned house and save the boy. Promise me you will save the boy. You can't save the girl." Then he closed his eyes and never woke. I never worked out what he meant by that. I thought it had something to do with case of the girl in the cupboard, that is why I asked the inspector about the case on my first day. I knew they worked on it together.'

'Shit, they are some last words,' said Rob, glad to forget his problems for a while. 'Though I wouldn't read too much into it. My old man said some crazy stuff before he died too. Mind you, he had dementia and didn't speak towards the end. Yet in the last week of his life, every time he saw me, he would shout: "Rob don't let her get on your back! Don't let her get on your back!" When he fell into his final coma, he would rave about a dead pelican and a lighthouse. I wouldn't think too much about it. The random thoughts of a dying and misfiring brain.'

'Look Rob, why don't you take some time off. This case has gotten to you.'

'I can't. I need to see this case to the end. Once it's over, I can leave this god-forsaken town for good. I suggest you also leave as soon as possible. And also Constable, don't breathe a word of what I said to you. You hear?'

Rob turned to look at Kate, but she looked passed him to the footpath, her face ashen.

'What's up?'

'What? Sorry,' said Kate as if waking from the dream. 'Sorry, I was looking at the graffiti on the fence.

Rob squinted and read the writing on the wall:

Dear K

Every detail tells a bigger story

D

He shook his head at the disorder of the public streets.

'Constable, we better return to the station.'

Chapter Twelve

The Order

'You wanted to see me, Inspector?'

'Yes, Detective Sergeant. At ease. I've just got off the phone with Alan Mills. You know him, I believe.'

'Snapper!'

'He says you pushed his boarder Toby Zachariah against a bookcase and physically threatened him.'

'I have good reason to believe he was connected with Dimitri Lvodic, a small-town drug dealer involved in the robbery at Symes. I believe he was the mastermind.'

'Detective Sergeant, I am taking you off the case.'

'Sorry?' said Rob.

'I'm taking you off the case.'

'Why? What have I done?'

'I'm concerned about you. Ever since Christmas you have not been yourself.'

'I'm fine. In fact, I've never felt better.'

'What's going on Rob?'

'Nothing, everything is fine.'

'I can see things aren't right. If it's about the promotion, it's a small set back all police officers face ...'

'I said I'm fine.'

The inspector sighed and leant back in his seat.

'You're to take two weeks holiday effective immediately. Take Sally and the kids on a road trip up the coast.'

'I need to stay on this case. I'm close to wrapping it up. If I can only put pressure on Toby, I can crack this case further open.'

'I thought the head storeman Doug Haywood was the man?'

'He was in a conspiracy with Toby Zachariah and Dimitri Lvodic.'

'I can't let you continue with the case and intimidate witnesses. I've been speaking to Constable Trengove ....'

'I want her off the case,' said Rob. 'All she has done is undermine the investigation. I don't care what she's said.'

'It doesn't change my mind, Detective Sergeant. You're off the case.'

Rob straightened and took a deep breath.

'Who's going to run it?'

'I've called in two members of the armed hold-up squad from Sydney. They will be here tomorrow. Kate will brief them. That is all.'

The inspector dropped his head to his paperwork. Rob stood staring down at his boss. Finally, he left the inspector's office. In the hallway, he saw Trengove coming the other way.

'I hope you're happy. I'm off the case.' He came close to her and pointed his finger in her face. 'You talked to the inspector. I'm going to fuck your life.'

Rob stormed out of the station and walked to the nearest pay phone.

* * *

'You have news?' Ingrid asked, tiring of Rob marching back and forth in the shack like a caged lion.

'You're on your own, princess,' said Rob finally.

'Sorry?' Ingrid was sitting sideways on the lone seat.

'I'm off the case.'

'What?'

'I'm off the fucken case!' repeated Rob. 'Don't you understand fucken English?'

'Why?' Ingrid gripped the back of her chair tightly.

'I interviewed Toby today and I ... I ...'

Ingrid lent forward. Rob turned his face to the wall and rubbed the back of his neck. 'And I stepped over the line.'

'I don't follow.'

'I lost my temper with him and shoved him against a bookcase.'

'Why?'

'The prick got under my skin,' said Rob, turning to face Ingrid. 'It was as if he could see straight through me. Knew what buttons to press. It was as if he was reading my mind. Anyway, I nearly killed him.'

'Why didn't you?' snapped Ingrid. 'The little prick deserves it.'

'Because there were witnesses. The trainee detective and Snapper.'

'Snapper?'

'Toby boards with a retired police sergeant. Alan Snapper Mills. Snapper was the sergeant at my first posting. He rang the inspector and I'm off the case.'

Ingrid jumped to her feet. 'Why didn't you arrest him? You're the law in this town. You can do whatever you want!'

'Fuck,' said Rob, coming up to Ingrid. 'I can't go around arresting people I don't like. I need solid evidence.'

'It never stopped you in the past.'

'I don't put people in prison, the courts do. Snapper will see right through the evidence. Fuck. He thinks the sun shines of out Toby's arse.'

'What's going to happen now?'

'We split the money, eighty-twenty, then I'm going on holidays.'

'What about me?' demanded Ingrid. 'Your job was to swing the investigation away from me.'

'You're fine. You have your alibi with Doug's death, having tea and cake with all those two-faced bitches from Friday nights. As for the robbery, I've forged a statement placing you at the Lagoon bar until midnight.'

'Who's taking over the case?'

'Some detectives from Sydney.'

'I need a guarantee they won't investigate me,' Ingrid said. 'That trainee detective won't come after me.'

'She might. She reckons you're a piece of work.'

'This isn't what you signed up to do,' shouted Ingrid.

Rob turned his back on Ingrid, and looking at the wall, said, 'You gave some performance at the funeral. What a fucken act. I wonder whether you love anyone but yourself. You're the wolf in sheep's clothing the minister spoke about.'

He turned and eyed Ingrid. She looked beautiful in the moonlight streaming through the window, but also dangerous.

'That's not true. I have only ever loved you, Rob.'

'Did you ever tell Doug you loved him? Told him what he wanted to hear so he would do what you wanted?'

'No never.'

'He told me he wanted the money so he could take you out of Old Town.'

Rob grabbed Ingrid by the shoulders and shook her. 'Maybe Toby's right and you're a bad influence. Maybe that's your game? You find men who will do your bidding, seduce them, then once they stop being of any use, you kill them.'

'No never,' Ingrid said, placing a hand on his cheek and rubbing it.

'I only humoured Doug. God! How could I love him after I knew a man like you?'

'I don't believe you,' said Rob.

'You must believe me. All I care about is you,' Ingrid said, searching his eyes and face.

Rob grabbed her wrist and with his other hand pulled her hair back.

'I've risked everything for you. Everything!'

He screamed these words at her face before pushing her away. She staggered back before collecting her balance.

'Toby's right. I've thrown everything away, my job, my career, my family.

I've killed someone because of you. I've risked it all for you.'

He pointed at her. 'And I don't believe you anymore.'

He turned and placed his forehead on the wall and sobbed until he grimaced and began punching the wall with his fist.

'What have I done with my life?' cried Rob. 'Chased after the bad guys but in doing so I've become one of them.'

Ingrid retreated into the shadows of the shack.

'Fuck! Fuck! Fuck!' he repeated, beating the wall with his fist. The mangrove fell silent as Rob sank to his haunches, buried his head in his fists, and sobbed.

Ingrid, creeping close, bent down and enveloped Rob.

'Poor baby. Poor baby.' She stroked his hair. 'You need a holiday. You need to go down the coast. Take your boat and cruise along the coast. Fish then sleep beneath the stars and forget everything. You're right,' she said, stroking his hair like a newborn infant. 'I love you, Rob. But I know I have asked too much of you. We will split the money and go our separate ways.'

CHAPTER THIRTEEN

CHECKMATE

Ingrid returned home around 10pm in a state of shock. Arthur called out from the front room as she opened the kitchen door. 'Is that you Ingrid?'

'Yes,' she said, wondering why he was still up.

'Put on the kettle, love,' he called out. 'We have a visitor.'

Ingrid sighed.

'The usual for me,' Arthur added. 'Toby what will you have?'

'Nothing for me,' Toby called out.

The teaspoon Ingrid held, clattered on the floor. She stood rigid in front of the kettle for some time before marching into the living room.

Arthur Symes sat in an armchair chuckling, while opposite him on another armchair sat Toby. A chess game was in progress between them.

'We've been playing for two hours,' Arthur said. 'I've already lost one of my knights and my king is running out of options.'

'You can still survive,' Toby said, glancing up at Arthur. 'But you need to make a decision.'

'Toby is an excellent player, Ingrid. Probably the best I've come across. Better than Jack Harris, that's for sure. When I took his queen, I thought I would have him in checkmate in no time, but since then he has played a brilliant defence. So much so, I'm the one in check.'

'You can still win Mr Symes,' Toby said.

'But only if I sacrifice my knight.'

'Or queen,' Toby said, glancing at Ingrid.

Ingrid frowned, looking dubiously at the chess board, trying to fathom the rules.

'Toby was saying so many nice things about you.'

'That's nice of him,' Ingrid said, forcing a smile.

'He was saying how lucky I am to have you.'

Toby looked up from the game and smiled at Ingrid.

'I was saying to your uncle how important family is. Not money nor power, but family and love.'

'It's so nice to see you keeping my uncle company,' Ingrid said, placing a hand on Arthur's shoulder and bending over to kiss his bald head.

'Now be a good girl and make a cuppa,' Arthur said.

Ingrid marched back into the kitchen and made her uncle's tea with a lot of banging of china on china. She wanted to scream at the top of her lungs, run into the living room and begin tearing Toby's eyes out. Instead, she put a quadruple dose of Rohypnol in her uncle's tea and dutifully took it out.

'Are you sure you don't want a drink Toby?' asked Arthur.

'No, I don't like how your niece makes my tea.' He smiled at Ingrid, who poked her tongue out at him behind her uncle's back.

'You should learn chess, Ingrid,' Arthur said.

'Thanks, but no thanks.'

'I've always said chess is the perfect training for business. It teaches you to strategise.'

'They say grandmasters can think upwards of fifteen moves ahead,' Toby said. 'Though I believe it's a myth.'

'It's incredible that the mind is capable of computing so many variables,' Arthur said, shaking his head.

'As I said, it's probably a myth,' Toby said, looking up from the board and smiling at Ingrid. 'Though grandmasters have the ability to anticipate all their opponent's possible moves well in advance.'

Ingrid frowned, then looked at her uncle's untouched tea sitting by the board.

'I don't see the point in chess,' she said. 'It is a stupid game, with stupid rules.'

She took a large black piece from the board.

'What does this piece do?' Ingrid asked, admiring its shape.

'You've taken my queen,' Arthur said. 'Give it back.'

'The queen you say?' Ingrid snatched it away from Arthur's outstretched reach.

'The queen is the most powerful piece in the game of chess,' Toby said. 'Able to move any number of squares vertically, horizontally or diagonally.'

'But the king is the key piece,' Arthur said. 'The idea of chess is to have your opponent's king in a position in which any move it makes will mean it will be taken by one of your pieces.'

'It is called checkmate!' added Toby.

'Where is your king, Toby?' asked Ingrid.

Toby did not look up, but continued to study the board.

'I said, where is your king?'

Toby pointed to his king.

Ingrid placed the black queen in the square occupied by the white king, scooping the king into her fist.'

'There. You lose.'

'You can't make that move. It's against the rules,' Arthur said. 'The queen needs to guard against Toby's pawn. If it makes it to the end, he can swap it for a queen endangering my king.

'When have you ever worried about the rules?' Ingrid said. 'You break them all the time and here you're faithfully following them in this stupid game.'

With the back of her hand, she swept the pieces from the board. They scattered across the floor.

'There. No one has won.'

'That was uncalled for Ingrid,' Arthur said, dropping to his knees to pick up the pieces.

'Why don't you drink your tea,' Ingrid said. 'You wanted me to make it, and now you're letting it grow cold.'

'I want it to cool down,' Arthur said, but obediently he took a sip, winced, then drained half the cup.

'There. Happy? You will excuse me Toby, but my niece bullies me terribly.'

Arthur leant back in his armchair. He felt soporific so he closed his eyes to rest. Toby hunted for the scattered chess pieces on the floor, placing several he found on the board. Ingrid watching moodily as Toby arranged the black queen, the two kings, a black knight and several pawns.

She took an armchair and pulled it up to the game.

'What are you doing here?' she asked.

'Playing chess with your uncle.'

'Don't play me for a fool. What are you doing here?' she demanded, glancing briefly at her uncle, his eyes closed, his chest rising and falling with unconsciousness.

'I came to see your uncle about the robbery,' Toby said, not looking up at Ingrid. He continued to arrange the pieces on the board. 'He had the impression I was somehow involved in it. I wanted to assure him I had nothing to do with it.'

Toby looked up at Ingrid, and smiling, added, 'As you can see by his amicable disposition at chess, he believes me.'

Ingrid fumbled for a cigarette and lighter from her jean pocket, dropping the packet before lighting one into life with a trembling hand.

'I had an interesting visit today, but I suppose he's already told you,' Toby said, continuing his arrangement of the board.

'I don't know what you mean?' Ingrid leant back in her armchair and took a long drag of her cigarette.

'The detective assigned to the robbery came to visit me today. He's a rather interesting fellow.'

Ingrid bit her right thumb nail and glared at Toby.

'I was in the middle of giving my evidence when he lost his cool with me.

I don't know what I said to upset him. Do you have any theories, Ingrid?'

'I don't know what you're talking about.'

'It was inconsiderate of you knocking all the pieces from the board,' Toby said. 'I was only three moves from winning the game before you swept them away and drugged my opponent. But you never had any respect for the rules.'

'Chess is a stupid game,' Ingrid said.

'There,' Toby said, arranging the last piece on the board and reclining back in his armchair. 'This was exactly how the game was positioned before you swept the pieces from the board. Shall I show you how I would have ended it?'

She did not answer, but took a drag on her cigarette.

'Your uncle plays black. We're down to our last pieces.'

'He still has his queen, one knight and a rook, but his king is trapped. He has one last option. Sacrifice his last remaining knight, or his queen.'

Ingrid looked at the board and bit her lip.

'When put in this position, the conventional wisdom is to sacrifice the knight. But if you do that, my pawn takes this position and checkmates his king. So, you see it comes down to sacrificing the queen.'

Ingrid exhaled and butted out her cigarette.

'You can see yourself out,' she said, jumping to her feet.

She ran upstairs, slamming the bedroom door behind her and placing her weight against it, taking one deep breath after another.

She listened as the front door opened then closed. Walking to the window, she looked out at the neon Symes sign glowing across the fence line.

I need to stop thinking about Toby and his silly chess metaphors. I've other things to worry about, like a detective with wavering loyalties. A weeping detective, liable to confess at any time. Rob was only useful to me while he ran the case, guarding me from suspicion. But the idiot has blown it. He's a threat.

She went downstairs and checked her uncle sleeping in the armchair.

Looking down at the chess board, she noted the black queen and knight. One needed to go, and she knew which it should be. *Rules be damned.*

She went into the kitchen, and taking out her slip of paper, called the number.

A woman's voice answered. She hung up and called again. A woman's voice again. *Only two more moves and I'll win. I'll defy Toby if it's the last thing I do.*

CHAPTER FOURTEEN

THE BOAT

Rob dropped anchor outside the shack. Ingrid waded out in the shallow waters to his Silverton 37c boat in nothing more than a bikini and a jumper. A black knapsack was slung over her shoulder.

'Aren't you cold?' he asked, helping her in.

'I thought you could warm me up first,' she said as she wrapped her arms around his shoulders, kissing him passionately.

He pushed her away. 'I only came tonight for my cut.'

'Sure, I understand. Let's discuss?'

She sat on the floor of the boat near the motor.

'There's nothing to discuss,' he said, taking a seat at the helm. 'I've come for my money.'

'Sure, but I need some assurances.'

'Like what?'

'I won't be investigated.'

'Look, blind Freddy can see it was Doug. As long as you play the dutiful niece everything is fine.'

'I'm sorry it came to this.' Ingrid sighed. 'I liked you, Rob. I really did.'

'Don't play me for a fool. This is what you do. You manipulate people. Use them.'

'No Rob, you have me all wrong. All I wanted was the money rightly owed me. I did what was best for all of us.'

'You used me as you used Doug.'

'I was never in love with Doug.' Ingrid said. 'He wanted the money. He was the one who suggested the robbery. The only reason I agreed to it was because I feared him. You saw him in the gym. He could have killed Toby. Oh God! I haven't told anyone this, you can't repeat it. He tried the same on me. For some reason, he thought I was in love with him. He pushed me against the wall and threatened he would tell my uncle I slept with him. Lies, but how could I tell what my uncle thought. He's a strict, conservative man. I feared him Rob, feared him deeply.'

'What about the eulogy?'

'I only did it under sufferance, Rob. I felt sorry for his family, especially his mother. Look I don't have to explain myself to you. You want this as a simple business transaction, then let's split the money eighty-twenty and go our separate ways.'

Rob eyed her closely. Ingrid took off her jumper, and coming close to him, she placed her hand on his. 'No strings attached.'

She took off her bikini top, and taking his hand, led it to her breast.

'Take me, then take your cut. No strings attached.'

He grabbed and kissed her. She broke away and diving into the knapsack took out a bottle of scotch. Unscrewing it, she poured it down her neck and over her breasts.

Greedily Rob descended on her and they fell on the floor of the boat as he licked her neck and breasts dry. Ingrid continued to pour the scotch on her body, letting the bottle drop. She threw her head back and moaned as he tore off her bikini bottom and had his way with her.

After a few thrusts Rob fell off her and lay looking up at the stars, panting. He managed to grab the bottle and put on the screw top before the precious liquid drained out.

Ingrid cuddled up close to him and began rubbing his chest then shoulders.

'My you're tense.'

'I haven't had a drink in two days, that is until now,' he said.

'Roll on your stomach,' she said.

'What?'

'Roll on your stomach,' she said. 'I will rub some oil on you.'

She took from her backpack a bottle of body oil.

'I thought it might come in handy.'

Rob yawned and rolled compliantly onto his stomach.

Ingrid mounted his back. Rob flinched as Ingrid poured out a dob of oil onto his skin. With both hands she rubbed the oil into his shoulders momentarily removing one hand to take the rope from the bag and place it in closer reach.

She continued rubbing the oil into his shoulders. She leaned close and whispered, 'I will be sad to see you go, Rob. We had a lot of fun together. But you want your freedom and I respect that. It would be lovely going down the coast with you. Stopping along the way to fish and camp on a deserted beach. Wouldn't it be lovely camping under the stars? Making love. You could go out and catch dinner and I could cook it on a campfire. We could fall asleep listening to the waves lapping the shore. Hear it?'

Rob, exhausted and soporific, lifted his head slightly and heard the waves rolling and breaking rhythmically to shore.

'How peaceful. How relaxing it would be. Nothing to worry about, only the rhythmic whoosh of waves.'

Rob felt the boat beneath him rise and fall with the motion of the water. He closed his eyes, his mind dissolving into slumber.

Ingrid waited until she heard the first snore. Then she took the noose end, and still rubbing his back, gently with one hand, fed the rope end underneath the small space between the boat and the detective's head, grabbing his hair by the roots, she gently lifted his skull slightly off the floor to ease the rope to his neck.

'Please don't wake. Please don't wake,' she muttered, her heart racing with fear, anticipation, and animal excitement.

She brought the knot of the noose close to his neck without restricting his breath. 'Ten, nine, eight,' she counted, her heart beating faster, 'seven, six, five, four.' Her eyes dilated, 'three, two, one,' the excitement reaching a crescendo. 'Zero,' exploded in her head.

On the towel she had placed in the middle of his back, she jammed her knee in hard, and with as much force as she could muster, yanked the noose tight around his neck.

Rob ripped out of sleep; his head was yanked back and he clutched at his neck. He tried to breathe but only gurgled. He felt an intense pain in the middle of his back. A great weight on it. He flayed about trying to grab her off him.

His mind was exploding with, 'Bitch! Bitch!' He thrashed about and kicked.

Ingrid held on for dear life. A shiver of excitement rose from the base of her spine and exploded in her brain as he thrashed and trembled beneath her, his hands grabbing at her hair. She tightened the noose as his thrashing turned to spasms. He grabbed her hair tighter and yanked. She screamed, and through the pain, tightened the noose more and yanked with all her might.

The terror gave way to calm. Rob felt lighter and more alive than he had ever felt before as he rose high into the air. Hovering five metres above the boat, he saw a woman on top of a man's back with a rope around his neck, yanking. The man's body convulsed beneath her. He felt repulsed by the vulgar scene, then curious. He came down and looked at the purple figure. *That's me*, he thought. *If that's me, I must be ... be ...?*

He hovered on the ceiling looking down at his children and Sally in the big bed. Sally was tossing and turning in a light sleep. He called down to them. Sally opened her eyes. 'I'm so sorry,' he said. 'I'm so sorry Sally.'

Next, he floated on another ceiling looking down at Toby.

Toby opened his eyes.

'Toby.'

'I know,' he said.

Then the room flooded with an intense white light, and Rob was pulled towards it. He forgot everything, Toby, his wife, the earth.

Ingrid let go of the rope, and unclasping Rob's rigid fingers from her hair, collapsed onto his rapidly cooling body and stroked his hair.

At least he lasted long enough this time, she thought. She giggled uncontrollably.

As the euphoria subsided, a strong wind rose up. Ingrid shivered. She had work to do. She put on her bikini and took off the chain with the two suitcase keys from his neck. Taking her own key, she added it to the chain before putting it around her neck.

She fed the rope end through the railing above the cabin entrance, and with a strength that surprised her, she yanked Rob's body to its feet. Keeping the line as taut as possible, she wound the rope around a handrail, tying a knot just like the twins had taught her. Rob's bloated and blue face was scowling at her. She took his left hand and placed it on his penis, letting the body swing with the breeze.

From her backpack she took gloves and a towel. She cleaned the detective's back of oil, then wiped every surface she may have touched. She placed the typed note in the cabin.

Finally, she took up the anchor and starting the motor headed through the mangroves to the open sea. She jumped with fright as a pelican glided into the boat collapsing at the feet of the detective swinging idiotically with the motion of the boat.

'Get away stupid bird,' she cried. She kicked at it with her foot, but it moved to the stern and collapsed, exhausted. She didn't have time to waste on it.

She stuffed the gloves and towel into the backpack and flung it overboard. It sank immediately. She pointed the boat for the open sea, then dived overboard, swimming back to the mangrove swamp.

She reached the shack frozen and exhausted, drying herself down with a towel from another bag she had placed there earlier in the day. She changed into jeans, sneakers and a thick jumper, then opened the trap door, and taking the keys, unlocked the box. The money was still there. It was hers. All hers.

* * *

Ingrid made it as far as entering the back door when the kitchen light snapped on and Arthur Symes, dressed in the robe she bought him for Christmas, stood looking at her.

'It's two o'clock. Where have you been?'

"I couldn't sleep so I went for a walk.'

'Who are you seeing?'

'No one,' she said. 'I only have one person in my life now. You.'

She sneezed.

'My god,' he said. 'Your hair is matted, and what are those scratch marks on your neck?'

He came up to her and tried to touch her neck. She backed away.

'And you're wet. Have you been swimming?'

'I like to go for a swim at night.' She sneezed again.

You're shivering too,' he said. 'Let me make you a cuppa.'

She sat on the kitchen stool as Arthur made her tea with a slice of lemon.

'I want to thank you, Ingrid,' he said as she took a sip of tea.

'Thank me for what?'

'For making me realise there's more to life than money.'

'What?' frowned Ingrid.

'I've spent a life in pursuit of wealth. But since you've arrived, I've realised it's better to enjoy the simple pleasures in life, like well-cooked food and good company. You've been a bright spot in an otherwise dull and tawdry life.'

He leant forward and hugged her. She scanned the wall over his shoulder as she patted his back frigidly.

Out of nowhere she felt a surge of anger, like ripples of waves from a passing boat crashing onto the shore of her consciousness. She hugged him tightly. She wanted to squeeze the life out of him. Take a knife and stab his eyes, his neck. She wasn't sure if she loathed his genuine affection or his weakness.

THE LIGHTHOUSE AND THE PELICAN

'Auto-erotism,' declared the forensic medical examiner, Tom Crouch. 'He must have slipped and lost consciousness.'

'Any word on how long he's been dead?' asked the inspector, standing on the sand and fixing his eyes on the medical examiner. He didn't want to look at the naked body of a fallen comrade in such a compromising position.

'I would say twelve hours.'

'Any signs of foul play?'

'None. My initial thought is misadventure.'

'Can you provide a preliminary report by tonight?' asked the inspector.

'No problem.'

'I know you're not a marine vet, Tom,' said the inspector, moving closer to the boat. 'But what is the story with the pelican?'

'Pelican?' Kate lowered her gaze from the lighthouse on the cliffs above, to the inspector and the medical examiner.

'There's a dead pelican in the boat.'

Kate moved to the edge of the boat as two police officers pushed it further onto the sand. She kept her eyes off Rob's bloated blue face scowling angrily. When she first arrived and saw Rob's body dangling, she had blurted out, 'My god!', before vomiting on the sand.

'He must have flown in last night and died,' suggested Tom.

'Something to it?' asked the inspector.

Kate answered thoughtfully. 'This beach, the lighthouse, and the dead pelican. Before he died, Rob told me a story of what his dying father said on his deathbed.' Kate stopped speaking. She turned pale before continuing. 'His dying father warned him about a lighthouse and a dead pelican, and woman on his ...'

With one leap, Kate jumped into the boat. She joined the crime scene investigators and before anyone could stop her, she was looking at Rob's back.

'Tom, do you think you could have someone look at this?' asked Kate.

'Why?' he asked.

'It looks like someone smeared cream on his back,' she said. 'Also, what about this bruising?'

'The dead body banging against the frame of the cabin door?'

'Or someone straddling him. Or a knee,' proposed Kate.

'There seems to be only minute traces of cream. Maybe from the day before.'

'Or someone towelled him down.'

'I found this note down in the cabin,' said Constable David Williams, appearing above deck with a note in his gloved hand.

The inspector put on his gloves before opening the typed note.

'Dear Sally,
I'm sorry for what I have done to you and the boys.
Your darling husband Rob.'

'I should be the one to break the news to her,' offered Kate.

'Agree,' said the inspector. 'And Kate ...'

'Yes.'

'I know Rob's death has been a shock, but I want you to remember that the words of a dying man about future events does not constitute evidence.'

Kate nodded then left the beach.

CHAPTER SIXTEEN

MRS. CHARLES

Kate ambled up the stone path to the front porch of a cottage set in the hills of Old Town. Two garden gnomes stood guard in a small flower bed below a window. There was a swing couch on the porch with a small sign next to the door: *Home Sweet Home.* The laughter of children bouncing on a trampoline came to Kate as she reached the front door.

Kate took a deep breath then knocked, waiting stony faced as she heard approaching footsteps. The door opened and through a flyscreen a woman's voice said, 'Yes.'

'Mrs Charles, my name is Kate Trengove. I'm from Old Town CIB.'

Kate showed her badge. 'Can we please talk? This is important.'

* * *

Sally did not cry when Kate gave her the news. She looked out into space, the squeaking from her two boys bouncing on the trampoline filling the silence.

'Is there someone I can call for you, Sally?'

'I knew I would have to tell the boys that their father was leaving,' said Sally after a time, as if speaking to another presence in the room. 'I never thought it would be forever.'

'What was your husband's mood over the last few days?' asked Kate.

'I don't know,' said Sally. 'We were for all purposes separated. Rob was sleeping in the spare room and came and went as he pleased.'

'I'm sorry,' Kate said.

'What's there to be sorry about? That's what policing does to you. Rob thought he was so strong. Thought he could go into the force to make a difference. We were high school sweethearts, you know. Rob wanted to be an electrician then. In his last year in high school, Ricky, his kid brother, overdosed at the Cross. After his death, Rob was determined to join the police force and catch every drug dealer he could. We married soon after he graduated from the Academy. The first few years were good, though we never had much money. Rob was always so fun-loving, so generous, always telling me about the things he had seen when he was in uniform: the funny stuff, and the not-so-funny incidents. But Rob was always so ambitious. Always looking to get ahead. After becoming a detective, he changed. He became secretive, aloof. He also started drinking too much. I was happy when he was sent to Old Town. I thought it would be good for him to get away from Sydney, away from all the bad influences. I know he had an affair with a woman at his last post. She used to call late at night. Every time I picked it up, she would hang up.'

Sally took a deep breath and sighed. 'For a time, things improved. He stopped drinking. He seemed happier and like his old self. Then he started going to Friday night dinners at Arthur Symes'. The first night, he came home drunk. It was soon after that he bought his boat. He never said how he made the money, but it became his pride and joy. He spent more time with it then with me or the kids. His secretive nature returned. I know he was seeing another woman in the last few months. I could always recognise the signs. The new clothes, the excessive aftershave, the calls late at night. Last week I told him I wanted a divorce.'

'Do you know who the woman was?'

'No, but I know she called him last night. Rob had come home late and was having a shower when the phone rang twice. Each time I picked it up, the person on the other end hung up. I know she was involved in his death. I know it.'

Sally stopped and looked down at her tea.

'I would like to obtain phone records for your house. Also, I would like to look through your husband's things,' said Kate.

'I saw him after he died,' said Sally, tears falling down her cheeks as she looked down at the kitchen table.

'His spirit came to me as I slept. I opened my eyes and I saw him floating on the ceiling. He communicated with me telepathically. He was sorry.'

Sally sobbed. She placed her hands to her heart and bawled. Kate extended her hand to comfort her, but Sally pushed it away and bawled uncontrollably.

The laughter and bouncing on the trampoline stopped and the back door opened. Rob's two boys bounded into the kitchen.

Kate excused herself from the room.

In the spare room, she looked through his closet and the bedside cabinet. In the top drawer she found an address book and scanned the entries. She looked under S: Arthur 4948 4562. She looked under I and found the following entry:

Ingrid. Two rings two minutes apart, pick up phone. Three rings twenty seconds apart, end of Whalers Point pier.

Kate shut the notebook and stared at the wall.

In the kitchen, she found Sally surrounded by two uncomprehending boys.

'I would like to take this book of your husband's.'

Sally, teary eyed, looked up dumbly at Kate and nodded.

*　*　*

Kate drove towards the station, the little black book perched on the passenger seat. She turned on the left indicator as she came to the intersection with Old Town Road. The road was clear in either direction,

yet she did not turn; instead, she stared at the big billboard across the street:
Turn Right for Answers

Below this:
A Message from your father in Heaven

Kate took one deep breath after another. An Australian flag fluttering in the breeze, subsided to reveal the remaining words: New Hope Church, 292 Old Town Road, Old Town.

Kate stared at the two lines on the billboard.

A car came up behind her and beeped. Kate, woken from a dream, flipped the indicator and turned right.

* * *

'My uncle cannot see anyone at present, Detective Trengove. He's sleeping,' Ingrid said with a nasally twang.

'I haven't come to speak your uncle. I have come to speak to you, Miss Symes.'

Ingrid's eyes narrowed. 'Come in,' she said, then sneezed.

Ingrid led the detective into the kitchen.

After the formalities of a beverage offered and declined, Detective Constable Kate Trengove started. 'This morning, Detective Sergeant Robert Charles was found dead in his boat. It had washed ashore at Lighthouse Point.'

Ingrid placed a hand to her chest and gasped audibly. 'Oh my. Oh my. How did he ...? I mean, how terrible!'

Ingrid's eyes moistened. Kate stared back at her coolly. 'You knew the detective well?'

Outside, a lawnmower spluttered then roared into life. Ingrid tilted her head and gazed hard at Kate. 'I'm not sure what you mean?'

'The detective sergeant was a regular visitor to this house before the robbery.'

'Yes, but I didn't know him. He was my uncle's guest.'

'That's a lie.'

The noise of the lawn mower faded; the fridge hummed into the void.

'I don't know what you mean?'

'I mean, you knew the detective intimately.'

'Sorry?'

'You had an affair with him. You used him to rob your uncle then had him murdered.'

The noise of the lawn mower returned as Martin the gardener rounded the lemon tree and made his way towards the house.

The two women eyed each other as the noise of the mower built to a crescendo, then, with a turn, slowly ebbed to a whisper. Ingrid threw her head back and laughed and laughed before dropping her head and hissing, 'Oh, stunning! And your evidence?'

'This is the detective sergeant's address book,' Kate said, taking out the black notebook and opening it. 'Under the entries for I is your name and the method of communication.'

Kate laid out the entry for Ingrid to look at, but Ingrid refused to look down. 'You can ask any of the ladies from Friday night. I found the detective abhorrent.'

'Then how do you explain this entry in his address book?'

Ingrid sneezed. 'I don't know what it is, or what it means. All I know is, he was a sleaze, and I wouldn't have anything to do with him.'

'Where were you between six last night and five this morning?'

'I don't see why I should answer.'

'I'll repeat. Where were you between six last night and five this morning?'

'She was with me all night,' Arthur said, shuffling into the kitchen in his dressing gown with his walking stick leading the way.

'I had trouble sleeping, so my niece stayed up with me,' he placed a protective hand on her shoulder. 'We played chess until five in the morning.'

'Yes, I was up all night with my uncle playing chess.' Ingrid smiled, placing her hand on her uncle's hand resting on her shoulder.

'I don't appreciate the Old Town police force questioning my niece. I want you out finding real criminals.'

'Mr Symes, I have reason to believe your niece may be involved in the robbery, and last night murdered Detective Sergeant Charles. I believe her cold is from being out on the water last night, and those marks on her neck …'

'Didn't you hear what I said? She was with me all night. As for the robbery, I will not hear you besmirch a member of my family. Now leave my house immediately. I will be speaking to the inspector on this matter this afternoon.'

Kate looked at Arthur, then Ingrid's smiling face. The constable took the black address book, and without looking further at either person, quit the house.

Ingrid sneezed. 'How long have you been standing there?' she asked, turning to look at her uncle.

'Long enough.'

'Everything she said is lies. Vicious and unsubstantiated lies.'

'Ingrid. Whatever trouble you're in, I can help you.'

'I don't know what you mean,' she said, rising to her feet. 'It's all lies.'

He shuffled towards her, and resting his cane on the table, took both her hands. 'Today is a new start. Let's forget everything that has happened in the past and begin again.'

Ingrid wanted to take back her hands and shrink away, her body becoming cold and numb with every touch of his kindness.

'I can help you, Ingrid. Truly, I can help you. I've thought about it. Toby is right. Money isn't important. Family is. Tomorrow I'm changing my will. I'm going to leave everything to my closest living relative.'

Ingrid's mouth fell open.

'I do it with one condition, Ingrid.'

'What?'

'You never leave me.'

Ingrid fell into Arthur Symes' arms and hugged him tightly. 'Till death do us part,' she said.

CASE CLOSED

'I will make this short, Detective Constable,' said the inspector. 'I've just gotten off the phone with Arthur Symes. He says you accused his niece of murdering Rob.'

'Correct.'

'What evidence do you have?'

'Sir, Rob's death wasn't a suicide. I have reason to believe Ingrid Symes was with him last night and she had a hand in his death.'

'Arthur Symes has assured me he can vouch for his niece's whereabouts.'

'He's lying, sir. I know he is. She killed Rob and was involved in the robbery.'

'What evidence do you have?'

Kate took out Rob's address book and passed it to the inspector.

'This is Rob's address book. Look at the entries under I. Look at 'Ingrid'. It has the code used between Ingrid Symes and Detective Sergeant Charles. I've checked the phone records for Detective Sergeant Charles' house on the night of his death. Three phone calls no more than five seconds in length and two minutes apart were made.'

'Arthur Symes said he called the detective last night and the 'I' was his code.'

'He's covering for her.'

'For what end?'

'I don't know. It doesn't make sense. Maybe the uncle and the niece are in it together.'

'Again, what evidence do you have?'

'Inspector, I know in my bones that Ingrid Symes is at the bottom of this. Give me time and I can bring you evidence to show she conspired with Doug Haywood and Rob Charles to rob Symes, and frame Toby Zachariah and Dimitri Lvodic. When Doug Haywood threatened to psychologically break, she had him killed. When Rob threatened to break, she had him killed too.'

The inspector jumped to his feet, shaking with anger.

'I won't hear you, or anyone else, defame Rob, or accuse any officer under my charge of corruption.'

'I don't like to do this either, Inspector, but I don't know how else to explain the things I have seen.'

'I won't hear you speak ill of Rob or any of my officers. Rob's death was not suicide, or a murder, but a tragic accident. Doug Haywood's death was a suicide. Besides, it's all academic. Arthur Symes wants us to drop the investigation into the robbery.'

'You can't let this go. This is no longer about a simple robbery. This is about Ingrid Symes. She's a danger to everyone around her. I fear she's a psychopath.'

'You're no longer on the case. You cannot prove anything. Besides, I have another job for you to work on.'

'I can't let this go.'

'Detective Constable, you will follow orders. You're off the case.'

Kate stiffened and sighed, 'Yes sir.'

The inspector took from his top drawer a plastic sleeve with a piece of paper inside, which he handed to Kate.

'As you may know, Roofies or Rohypnol abuse is a big issue in this town. A sixteen-year-old girl was raped last month after having her drink spiked with the drug. A chemist at Whalers Point sent this to us after filling it for the customer. He became suspicious after reviewing it a second time. The address of the recipient, Judy Smith, lives in Old Town, but the prescription was filled in Whalers Point. I want you to see what you can make of it. I want you to talk to the prescribing doctor. A Doctor —'

The inspector squinted at the piece of paper. 'Doctor Jack Harris.'

He looked up at Kate. 'Detective Constable, you looked troubled.'

'Not at all, Inspector. I will call the chemist straight away, but first I would like forensics to look over the prescription.'

Chapter Eighteen

A Change in Will and Testament

'Now, if you can sign here, it will be legal,' said the solicitor to Jack Harris.

Jack took the pen and signed the witness signature block.

'Well Mr Symes, that changes your will. All your assets will pass to your closest living relative upon your death as you specified in your instructions. Now, if you will excuse me, I need to head back into town,' said the solicitor, putting a copy in his briefcase and rising to his feet.

'I will see you to the door, Andrew. I need to speak to you privately about the mangrove deal,' Arthur said.

Ingrid took a sip of her tea as Arthur, walking stick in hand, led Andrew Solomon to the front door.

Jack rose and sat close to Ingrid. 'I must compliment you, Ingrid. You've made such a difference to your uncle's personality since coming to live with him.' He put a hand on hers and patted it.

'No, he has changed me,' she said, smiling dreamily. 'He took me in and cared for me when I had no one.'

She wondered whether she should begin sobbing, but thought better of it. She didn't want the doctor to comfort her. She wanted him to let go of her hand and leave. She wanted to be alone, to brood and strategise.

'You will be a wealthy woman on the death of your uncle.'

'It's not the money I think about. I'm only glad I have someone to love and who loves me.'

'There are many people in this town who care deeply for you, Ingrid.

Many people.' He squeezed her hand tightly. She wanted to slap him, but smiled instead.

The doctor's pager beeped. He sighed as he looked at it.

'Damn. Damn. It's an urgent call from surgery.'

Jack rose slowly to his feet and took her hand again. 'If only I wasn't a doctor. If only I was thirty years younger.'

Good God! What is it with the doctor and my hand? she thought.

'Ingrid, there's something I must ...' He took a deep breath. 'Ingrid. You see. I ... I ...' He looked at her intently. She noted how bloodshot his eyes were and the unevenness of his morning shave.

Jack sighed, letting her hand drop. 'I must go.' He turned and quit the room. His voice and Arthur's mingled on the porch before the door slammed and silence returned.

Ingrid smiled. *I've won. I've won!*

CHAPTER NINETEEN

BEATA'S TALE

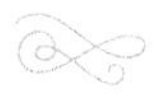

'I was hoping to speak to Doctor Harris,' Kate said, showing her badge to an odd-looking woman at the surgery reception desk.

'I'm sorry, I don't know where he is,' said Beata. 'Do you want to speak to Doctor Faci? He's also rostered on.'

'No, I would like to see Doctor Harris.'

'I will page him,' said Beata. She put through the call.

'Why don't you take a seat? He should call back soon.'

'Who manages his prescription and appointment book?'

'I do. I'm his sister, Beata. Beata Harris.'

Beata took out both books and Kate read through them.

'This entry for the seventh of December 1987, an appointment from four to five o'clock for Ingrid Symes is in blue. Dinner with Arthur Symes in another hand for five to eight pm is in black.'

'The entry for dinner is mine. My brother rang me up after his appointment with Miss Symes. Miss Symes had invited him to stay for dinner and play chess with her uncle.'

'You don't sound happy about it.'

'I never liked that house or the people in it. I never liked it after the death of Pat.'

'Pat?'

'Yes Pat. She fell down the office stairs at Symes on New Year's Eve.'

'Who was Pat?'

'She worked for Arthur Symes. She had worked for him ever since he

289

opened the business and had only just been promoted to manager. Arthur Symes looked up to her. I knew her quite well before I went to live in Byron Bay. The coroner classed her death as an accident, but I always thought there was something more to it. I warned my brother about the place, about the family, but he said I imagined things.'

'What was it about the family that troubled you?'

'Arthur Symes is a dreadful human being, and I know his niece is a bad egg too. I wouldn't be surprised if the detective's death I heard about on the local radio had something to do with those two. The night I saw him in at Arthur Symes' house, I had a bad premonition about him.'

'Tell me more?' asked Kate, taking a chair and pulling it close to the reception desk.

'Arthur Symes holds dinner parties every Friday night. All the important people in town go. They say Arthur uses the dinners to hand out his bribes and do his corrupt deals. My brother said your detective was a frequent Friday night guest. I remember going and feeling a bad energy in the room.'

'What do you mean by bad energy?' queried Kate, leaning forward.

'I went on the night of the powerful storm in February. The one that cut power to half the town. The room was humid and oppressive. I was seated at the dinner table and ... and I must tell you Detective, I'm psychic. I can sense things around people, in places, and I sensed a malevolence, an evil in the room. It was the girl ... Ingrid. I know she was up to no good with the now-dead detective. They were whispering in the corner when I felt it.'

'Felt what?'

'The wolf.'

'Sorry? What?' Kate frowned.

'I don't understand it myself, but I felt an overwhelming presence of a wolf.'

'A wolf in the room?'

'No. Not in the room,' said Beata, closing her eyes, 'outside in the rain and thunder, circling, hunting, coming closer, growing stronger, becoming more aware, more powerful, ready to make its move. I've never felt anything so pervasive in all my years of psychic practice. It grew so intense it popped out the lights and I screamed: *The wolf is here. The wolf is here.'*

Beata opened her eyes, a look of terror etched into her face.

'I must say I made a fool of myself. I lost connection with the wolf when the lights went out. Ingrid and the detective drove me home.'

'They drove you home?'

'Yes, and I note they didn't drive back to the house, but continued down the hill towards the town.'

Beata looked deeply into the young detective's eyes. 'You don't know whether to believe,' Beata said, 'all these signs around you, yet your police training tells you to ignore them. Don't.'

'I would like to return to the dinner party.'

Beata's eyes locked on Kate's. 'Someone close to you has recently passed on, I believe.'

'I was called.'

Kate jumped as she turned see to a frowning Jack Harris.

CHAPTER TWENTY

DOCTOR PATIENT CONFIDENTIALITY

'Doctor Harris, can you tell me whether in the last six months you have prescribed the drug Flunitrazepam, commonly known as Rohypnol?' asked Kate, seated in the consulting room.

'No never. I don't ever prescribe Flunitrazepam.'

'Doctor Harris, can you tell me if you have a patient by the name of Judy Smith?'

'No. I have no patient by that name.'

'Are you certain?'

'Detective, I know all my patients' names.'

'Is this your handwriting?' asked Kate, passing across the table one of the prescriptions in a plastic sleeve.

'No. This isn't my handwriting.'

'It looks like your handwriting.'

'Detective, I know my own handwriting when I see it.'

'How do you account for three prescriptions being made out for a total of one hundred and fifty tablets and presented to three separate chemists over a two-month period?'

'I can't. I don't know how this would be. I would never prescribe Flunitrazepam, especially with its many abuses in this town, and I never let my prescription pad out of my sight.'

'On the seventh of December last year you had a consultation with Ingrid Symes before staying for dinner.'

Jack Harris' face turned white. 'Surely you don't suspect her of stealing my prescription pad?'

'I haven't implied anything Doctor Harris.'

'I must warn you, Detective, I refuse to discuss my patients -'

'I do not intend to ask anything about your consultation with Miss Symes. I merely want to know where you placed your consultation bag.'

'Well Ingrid ...you see ... I believe ... it was placed in Arthur's study.'

'You started by saying Ingrid. Could I put it to you: she placed your bag in the study for you?'

'No, I mean, I ... I ... Yes.' He exhaled.

'Thank you, Doctor Harris,' Kate said, snapping shut her notebook and rising to her feet. 'You have been most helpful.'

'It was me, Detective Trengove.'

'Sorry? I don't follow.'

'I wrote out the prescription.'

'You said it wasn't your handwriting.'

Jack reddened. 'I wasn't being truthful.'

'Why?'

'The prescription was for ... was for ... was for my sister Beata. She has trouble sleeping.'

'Why the assumed name?'

'Because I didn't want people knowing.'

'Why not make it out to your sister? Why the fake name? Why the change in handwriting?'

'Because —'

'Doctor Harris. I should warn you, perverting the course of justice is an indictable offence.'

'I will swear in court.'

'I suggest you consider the evidence you give carefully. I will give you a day.'

Kate left the surgery.

TO KILL OR NOT TO KILL

After Jack Harris left, Ingrid rose, and walking a few metres across the room, fell into an armchair.

'Why don't we go out to dinner tonight?' Arthur said as he hobbled into the main room. 'Just the two of us.'

'If you don't mind Uncle, I would much rather stay at home.'

'The dinner is on me.'

'I would rather stay home. Maybe tomorrow we can go out,' Ingrid said, patting his hand.

Arthur hobbled away grumbling.

Ingrid lost track of time after her uncle went to bed. The room darkened around her as she brooded. Her gaze fell on the chess board, the pieces still arranged on the squares as Toby left them.

She gasped. The single black knight had gone from the board. She looked for it all over the table and in the box, but couldn't find it.

The white pieces were fewer in number than the black pieces, but she guessed well positioned. For the first time, she wished she understood the game. Wished she understood what he was up to.

She bit her nails and lit a cigarette. *What am I missing? Why is Arthur covering for me? Does he think I killed Rob?* She inhaled sharply. *Does he suspect I had a part in the robbery? If yes, why is he covering for me? Is he that infatuated with me, that he would lie? As for the female detective, she guessed everything, but does she have enough proof yet? Rob and his little black book. Christ! Never trust men. No attention to detail.*

Ingrid's mind methodically worked backwards over every event, every word, every kill. The death of Rob Charles, her uncle giving her an alibi. The calls to and from the house, her uncle saying he made the calls. *Tomorrow I'll ensure his statement is taken. As for the death of Doug, over ten witnesses could place me in this room on the very night of his passing. As for the robbery, hadn't Doug incriminated himself in front of all the staff? What was to link me to the crime? But to make sure, I'll get Arthur to vouch for me on that night too. He could provide a sworn statement he picked me up from the cocktail bar. I have him wrapped around my little finger and he would repeat anything I told him to say to the police. I know how to deploy him across the board to counter the detective's move.*

As for Pat's death: ancient history. The coroner ruled it an accident. Besides, I was home watching TV with Arthur. The old biddy came back to work too soon. But still, the little black book troubles me. I'll sleep on it and come up with a good strategy to counter it in the morning.

She yawned and stretched. It was close to midnight.

She ambled upstairs to her bedroom. Already her uncle's snoring reached her through the thin walls. She threw open the window to the mild autumn evening and let the sea breeze wash over her face, play with her hair, and fill her nostrils.

Somewhere a party swayed to the rhythm of Sade, 'Hang on to Your Love'. Her mind relaxed and softened. The image of Toby floated to her on the breeze and she stepped back and fell on her bed looking at the ceiling.

'Toby. Toby.' She sat bolt upright. 'What are you up too? Coming to the house to see my uncle. Why that move?' She hated this. She hated how she couldn't discern his motives, understand his moves.

She bit her bottom lip as Sade's song faded, and the guitar riffs from AC/DC's 'Highway to Hell' started. Her uncle's snoring grew louder and louder, in sync with the drumbeat.

She rose and closed the window, and without thinking, grabbed her pillow in both hands, feeling its softness and malleability.

Her uncle's snoring continued its dreadful melodic scale. The sound reminded her of the oboe that the nuns taught her to play. How she wanted to block the racket out with the pillow; smother her uncle, the nuns, the foul stench of men, the face of God.

To kill now, or kill later, that was the only question on her mind. If she walked into his room and placed the pillow over his face and smothered him, the house, the business, all his earthly riches, would be hers. She would be rich enough never to work again; rich enough to do exactly as she pleased. She would sell the house and the business and move away from Old Town; the town where she had seen so much grief, so much tragedy. She would move to Los Angeles and begin pursuing her acting career — her dream to walk upon the stage, and appear in television and films.

Ingrid saw her dreams reflected in the jolly face of the waxing moon winking down at her, goading her to act. Do it! Do it now! Take from life what so many have taken from you, Ingrid. Only one more kill, Ingrid. Only one more kill Ingrid and you will be free. Free from ever having to work again. Free like a bird to soar on the wind, to go anywhere, be anything.

She bit her bottom lip and placed the pillow on the windowpane, and as if smothering the moon, pushed hard until she heard a crack. She had the mongrel to do anything. She lowered the pillow. The moon had lost its smooth translucence and was now fragmented and distorted.

The opportunity beckoned, but what of the risk? Another death would bring suspicion on to her. There had been too many deaths, so close to each other, and all closely related to her. Pat's accident, Doug's suicide, the misadventure of the detective sergeant. The sudden death of her uncle would arouse suspicion. Especially within twenty-four hours of him bequeathing his fortune to her. Also, she needed his written statements about the night of the robbery.

Oh, how she wanted to kill him, even if it was only to end the snoring that continued louder than ever. How tired she felt at the pretence of being the loving and dutiful niece. *It was like a stupid part in a well-paying sitcom. Professing love for a person I can't stand. I recoiled every time he placed his arms around my shoulders or left a wet kiss on my cheeks. His noxious odour, his foul breath in my hair.*

She wanted to do it now and blow the consequences. No canned laughter or soft focused lighting could mask this tawdry drama.

As for the doctor always touching my hand, I would kill him also to be done with his touch. She shook her head at the arrogance and presumption of all men. *Yet to kill now was too risky. Better to wait. Other opportunities would come.*

She felt a weariness, but also pride. *Unlike a man, I can control my impulses, delay gratification. How base and stupid all men are.*

The snoring stopped and the house fell quiet. Too quiet. As if the cracked and barren moon winked down at her with a new energy, a new supernatural force.

She sighed, and realising she was tired, put down the pillow, undressed and got into bed.

* * *

Even though it was a cool night she had trouble drifting to sleep. She had the strange feeling someone on the ceiling looked down at her, looking through her, recognising her nature, seeing her plans, and yet still loving her. She hated the feeling. She rose and closed the blind on the cracked moon. Shivering, she jumped back into bed.

Still the feeling of being coolly observed from above continued. She placed the blanket over her head and finally drifted off to sleep.

* * *

Ingrid woke the next morning to the *purr* of a lawn mower, the rat-tat-tat-tat of the sprinkler and the clipping of the gardener's trimmer at work on the hedges. It was after 10am when she opened the blind. Brilliant sunshine filled the room through the cracked glass, and birds chirped and argued. She dressed and made her way down into the kitchen. The house was quiet, eerily quiet.

She made herself a coffee and noted that her uncle's unwashed porridge bowl and coffee cup were not in the sink. He usually left this for her to clean up. She went to his pokey office, but it was empty, with no sign of him having been there.

There was a knock at the back door.

'Hi Ingrid, is your uncle in?'

'I haven't seen him this morning, Martin.'

'Well, it's like this, Ingrid,' said Martin, sheepishly scratching his ear. 'You see Mr Symes gives me my pay every Saturday for the week's gardening. If he's not about, he leaves it under the mat here.'

He pointed to the mat at his feet. 'But there's nothing. I need me money or me missus will be upset.'

Ingrid walked past Martin to the garage. It wouldn't surprise her if he had shot through to avoid paying Martin. *That was Arthur Symes through and through: strategic with the big end of town debts, miserly with the rest.*

His car remained under its cover.

'I can come back in an hour or so if you like, but I need me money today.'

She no longer took any heed of Martin. A strange feeling crept over her as she quickened her pace back up the path to the backdoor, doubling her pace through the house, Martin on her heels.

'If you could give me fifty dollars now, I can come back tomorrow to grab the rest.'

She ran up the stairs and knocked on her uncle's door.

'Uncle Arthur.'

No answer. She knocked again.

'Uncle Arthur!'

She walked in, Martin following. Her uncle was in bed. She went over to him, her heart sinking as she saw his cold lifeless body. She shook him. 'Uncle Arthur. Uncle Arthur. Martin, quick! Call an ambulance!'

CHAPTER TWENTY-TWO

ALL CIRCUMSTANTIAL

'I told Arthur to slow down. Sooner or later his heart would give out. This is natural causes, Detective. Natural causes.'

'I understand Doctor Harris, but the coroner will want to run tests, toxicology and so on.'

'I'm telling you, his heart was going to give out the way he lived.'

'Your approximate time of death?'

'It's hard to say ...'

'It was just after midnight,' Ingrid said, not lifting her eyes from the imaginary spot on the floor.

Kate and Doctor Harris, who had been whispering at the dining table, turned to look at Ingrid slumped in an armchair, her cigarette burnt, unsmoked, to the butt end, a long trail of ash ready to fall.

After finding her uncle's body, Ingrid, dazed and shocked, had retreated to the main room, and collapsed into an armchair to chain smoke, while others saw to her uncle.

'I couldn't go to sleep with his snoring last night. It abruptly stopped around midnight,' Ingrid said.

She did not tell them how, before it stopped, she had debated whether to smother him to death. Or about the unearthly presence she felt in her room around that time.

Ingrid lit another cigarette and returned to staring at the floor.

'Thank you, Doctor,' Kate said. 'I would like to talk to you later this evening about your statement from yesterday. Now, if you could leave us, I would like to talk to Miss Symes alone.'

'I'm not leaving. Miss Symes is in shock and in no position to give evidence to the police.'

'I assure you, this is a routine matter, Doctor Harris.'

'I cannot allow you to interview her.'

'I will be fine Jack,' Ingrid said, turning to face the doctor.

'Ingrid,' said Jack. 'You're in no state to be interviewed. I must insist I stay and call a solicitor.'

'Go along Jack. I'm fine.' Ingrid smiled before turning back to stare at her spot on the floor.

Ingrid sensed the doctor looking at her, debating whether to stay or go. His pager went off and she heard the front door being opened then closed. Ingrid let out an audible sigh. The feeling of being examined closely returned. But unlike the night just gone, this wasn't an unearthly presence, instead, it was a corporeal one watching from the dining room table.

Ingrid heard the detective rise from her seat and the scuff of a chair being dragged across the room. Kate Trengove loomed into her vision, drowning out the vacant space and capturing her attention.

'Miss Symes, I would like to ask you a few questions about last night.'

Ingrid nodded. She understood the protocols. She took a deep breath ready to give a performance, but thought, with irony, there was no performance to give. No lies to tell, no scene to rearrange into a convincing narrative. Her uncle had died, but not by her hand, but natural causes.

'When did you see your uncle last?'

'It was around six last night. He had gone to bed early. I stayed up before going to bed around eleven-thirty. His snoring kept me up, suddenly stopping around midnight. I fell asleep after that and woke around ten and discovered him dead in his room.'

She shrugged her shoulders.

How boring is the truth? she thought. *I wish I'd gone in and done the job as originally planned. Then I could have built a narrative worth listening to.*

'You're certain of the time of death. Why?'

She shrugged her shoulders and wondered whether it was such a good idea to have made this point. 'A feeling.'

'Or maybe that is the time you went into his room, put a pillow over his face, and ended his life.'

Outside, a solitary crow laughed.

'How can you say such a sick thing?' Ingrid said, expressing shock, outrage and indignation. Her bottom lip quivering, she was glad for the chance to perform.

'Easily,' said Kate. 'He changes his will to bequeath all his fortune to you and within twenty-four hours he's dead.'

'How dare you say that! I didn't want his fortune. I am a simple person. I don't even like money.'

'What about the Prada handbag at your feet, or the Christian Louboutin black high heels shoes you wore at the funeral?'

'So, I like to buy a few expensive things. It doesn't make me a money-hungry murderer. I loved my uncle. He was my world. He took me in when I had no one. He gave me a roof over my head, food to eat, company. Why I would do anything to have him here alive and by my side.'

The tears flowed down her cheeks. *Is this what it felt like to lose someone precious, to mourn?* Except instead of her uncle, she imagined losing the five hundred thousand dollars. *What would it feel like to have it taken from me? Not being able to look at it, feel it, spend it.*

For a second, Ingrid imagined this cool and enigmatic woman opposite her trying to take the money. Ingrid wanted to lean across and scratch out her eyes. Bite. Scream. Punch. She quickly stopped thinking of the money and the tears stopped too. She took several deep breaths, and taking from her pocket a handkerchief, blew her nose.

'You killed your uncle.'

Ingrid felt like throwing back her head and laughing at the absurdity of it all. How she wanted to jump to her feet and scream: *For fuck sake, you stupid bitch! Yes. Yes, I organised the robbery. I ordered Rob to murder Doug, and as for your beloved detective, I strangled him on the boat, loving every second of it. I even pushed a slag called Pat Martin down the stairs, but I repeat, I didn't murder Arthur Symes. He died of natural causes.*

'No. I did not.'

'Miss Symes, do you recognise this?'

Kate took a scarf from a plastic bag at her feet. Ingrid inhaled sharply. She remembered Rob's warning about the scarf.

'Yes, I do know that scarf. It was mine, but I gave it to Cheryl Donaldson when I first came to Old Town. Did you know she and Toby are seeing each other secretly?'

'You gave it to Cheryl? That's surprising, for there is only one set of fingerprints on the scarf and they match the prints you provided us the day after the robbery. Any reason why?'

'Maybe Cheryl wore gloves,' Ingrid said, not wishing to concede the point.

'In Toby Zachariah's statement to police, he said he met with you in the vacant house before Christmas. You followed him and he pretended to live at that address.'

'He's lying. Cheryl and Toby are lovers. It's common knowledge at work. Besides, she's a thief. She stole my scarf and placed it at the house opposite the gym to make it look like I was connected to it.'

'You said you *gave* the scarf to Miss Donaldson.'

Ingrid took a drag of her cigarette, then exhaling, said, 'Gave, stole, what's the difference? Cheryl had access to the HR records. Maybe it was she who changed Toby's address to the house opposite the gym to throw the police off.'

'How do you know the house is opposite the gym?'

'It's common knowledge. People do gossip.'

'Where were you on the night of the robbery, Miss Symes?'

'I've already given a statement about this.'

'I ask again: Where were you on the night of the robbery?'

'At the Lagoon bar.'

'Who were you with?'

'I've already given a statement to police on this matter.'

'Who were you with?'

'I went alone. People can testify I was there.'

'You went alone? A girl like you went alone and sat in a bar?'

Ingrid lifted her eyes to the ceiling before dropping them to the detective.

'I went to see Brad.'

'Brad who?'

'Brad the barman. You see … well, I don't know how to say this.'

'Say it.'

'Well, Cheryl and Brad are an item. But you see, Cheryl has been seeing Toby on the side. Anyway, I always fancied Brad, so I went to see if I had a chance. He can vouch for me being there the whole night.'

'Yes, he did see you, but only for ten minutes from six o'clock.'

'I didn't speak to him the whole time. Besides, the statement …'

'The statement what?'

'Brad's statement cannot be true,' Ingrid said. 'I was there most of the night. You see, I talked to another man.'

'And his name?'

'I don't know. It escapes me at present.'

'You don't know his name?'

'He was from Melbourne if I recall. A builder.'

'What company did he work for in Melbourne.'

'I don't know.'

Silence returned to the room as Kate wrote this all down.

'Miss Symes, do you recognise this?'

She took from the bag at her feet a prescription slip in a plastic sleeve and passed it to Ingrid.

'What is it?'

'It's a prescription for Rohypnol. It was filled at Whalers Point chemist on the twenty-second of December last year.'

'So?'

'Three of these have been presented to chemists in several towns near Old Town.'

'So?'

'The prescribing doctor for all three is Doctor Jack Harris.'

'I can't see how this has anything to do with me,' Ingrid said, butting out her cigarette before lighting another.

'All of the prescriptions have your fingerprints on them. Why Miss Symes?'

Ingrid took a drag of her new cigarette and blew it above the detective's head.

'Don't know.'

'You used these drugs to help murder your victims. Rohypnol was found in Mr Haywood's system and in Detective Sergeant Rob Charles' blood stream. The coroner also found traces of it in the bloodstream of Pat Martin.'

Outside, a hovering seagull gave out a plaintive cry.

Ingrid took another drag of her cigarette and this time blew the smoke close to the detective's face.

'Are you accusing me of the death of Pat Martin?'

'I spoke to the coroner regarding Pat Martin's death. He found heavy bruising around the head and neck area consistent with falling downstairs. But do you know how she died Miss Symes?'

Ingrid took another drag.

Kate continued. 'She died of suffocation due to blood in the mouth and nostrils restricting air flow. The coroner also noticed bruising on the nose. On re-examination it could have been caused by someone pinching closed the nostrils.'

Ingrid took another long drag. Butting out the cigarette, she lit another.

'The night of the stocktake, you took over the duties of the finance officer when she fell sick suddenly.'

'I left before eight. I left Pat with Cheryl.'

'Miss Donaldson has given a statement saying you made the teas.'

'She's a liar. She made the teas and she had the motive to kill Pat. Cheryl hated her.'

'I put to you Miss Symes, that you put Rohypnol in Ms Martin's tea, then lured her onto the stairs, where you pushed her to her death. You did it because she wanted to fire you. I've spoken to Miss Martin's partner, who gave a statement that before Christmas last year, Pat had a meeting with you, where it was explained she wasn't going to extend your employment beyond probation.'

'So? The best thing she could have done was fire me. I hate working there.'

'I also contend you're responsible for the death of Doug Haywood.'

'Doug committed suicide. If you're accusing me of forcing someone to run a hose from his exhaust pipe then you're mad.'

'How did you know about that?'

'As I told you last time, do you think the police are the only ones who know what goes on in this town? Besides I was here on that night. There were over ten witnesses, including the mayor's wife.'

'And Detective Sergeant Charles?'

Ingrid's eye widened. This time, she channelled anger.

'I told you, I had nothing to do with his death.'

'You were having an affair with Detective Sergeant Charles. You conspired with him and Doug Haywood to rob your uncle. You made it look like Toby Zachariah was the robber. When the plan unravelled and Doug threatened to give you away, you ordered the detective to kill Doug, and when Rob threatened to crack, you lured him to a rendezvous on his boat, where you drugged and strangled him.'

The room fell silent. The daylight was beginning to recede from the room, the approaching gloom weaving long shadows across Ingrid's face.

'My god, listen to you,' Ingrid said, breaking into giggles. 'You paint me like some monster killing and robbing people at will. It's absurd. Your detective was a drunken womaniser. Ask any of the women who came to Friday night dinners, and they will tell you how much I hated the man. He was a creep. He would be the last person I would have an affair with.'

'We have records of phone calls between this house and Detective Sergeant Charles' house on the night of his death,' Kate said. 'Also, many odd calls over the last few weeks from phone booths across Old Town. One in particular on the night of Doug Haywood's death to this house from a phone booth in town.'

'My uncle has already stated, he called Rob on the night of his death. He has already provided evidence to your inspector that he and I stayed up the night playing chess. As for other phone calls on the night of Doug's death, I don't know anything about them.'

Kate gave out an audible sigh. She put down her pen and notebook, and leaning forward, said softly, 'Ingrid, I'm giving you the opportunity to confess. I know you killed the detective and ordered the death of Doug Haywood. I know you committed the robbery. I'm certain you killed Pat Martin and your uncle. It's only a matter of time before you're caught and convicted. I'm giving you a chance to come clean. To consider the people you have killed. You have the death of four people on your conscience.'

'I have nothing to confess. I'm innocent. How dare you even suggest such a thing. Besides, we have the presumption of innocence in this country. You need more evidence before you can arrest me.'

Ingrid butted out her cigarette and lit a new one, revelling at the idea of giving evidence in court. *My god! I would give the public a performance they would never forget.*

Ingrid could sense that Kate was trying to contain her anger as she consulted her notebook. Ingrid took a drag of her cigarette and considered her interrogator closely, looking for a chink in the armour, something she could wound her with; let this woman with her crisp suit know she was messing with the wrong woman. And that she was dealing with the wolf of Old Town.

A series of images appeared in Ingrid's mind's eye. They came in rapid succession, as clear and crisp as short videos. She saw this detective standing before an older male officer. He was shouting: 'I won't hear you speak ill of Rob or any of my officers. Rob's death was not suicide, or a murder, but a tragic accident....You're no longer on the case. You cannot prove anything. *This detective had come on her own volition. This wasn't an official investigation. She was one woman in a force desperately trying not to investigate one of its own.*

More images came. A bloodied and battered baby on a country road surrounded by glass. A little way off in a mangled wreck of a car, a mother screams: 'Where's my baby? Where's my baby?'

This image gives to way to a man wielding a knife. The young detective standing before him as a uniformed constable with her gun drawn: 'Drop the knife! Drop the knife!,' she yells, Ingrid could feel the detective's uncertainty and fear as a visceral and involuntary shiver running down her spine. The detective now a raw constable takes a step back, and stumbling, falls over, the attacker on her, before a shot rings out and the man wielding the knife falls dead before her. Her partner, lowering his smoking gun, says: 'Are you okay Kate? You can't hesitate.'

This image is replaced by the bloated and scowling face of the detective swinging with the breeze, the detective vomiting on the sand.

She saw the young detective as a constable on routine patrols, the late nights called out to domestics, writing reports. She saw her in the crowded bars on Friday night, surrounded by the boozy boys' police club, swapping stories and perceived her nagging persistent question. Is this the career for me? Have I made the right choice? Is there something else to life?

She saw also the images of babies and children, casually seen in shopping centres, out on patrol, or jogging. The detective looking longingly at her expectant friends.

She saw the detective seated next to an old man in a hospital bed connected to tubes and monitors. The rhythmic laboured breathing changed gear as the old man's eyes fluttered open and his glassy bloodshot eyes fixed on her. His pupils dilated as he stretched out his hand: 'Kate, you must save the boy. You must save the boy. Whatever you do, you must save the boy. The girl can't be saved.'

'What boy, Dad?'

'You must promise Kate that you will save the boy.'

'What boy, Dad? Dad, what boy? What boy? Dad? Dad? Wake up. Dad!' The monitor flatlined.

She saw the detective alone in a tiny cramped flat crying herself to sleep.

The image of a young man speaking appeared: 'I'm leaving Kate. I can't handle you fixating on your father's death. I can't stay. Kate, I'm leaving. I'm leaving. I'm leaving.' His words echoed in the empty flat.

Ingrid saw all of this in only an instant, as quick as it takes to blink one's eye, yet she saw the opportunity.

'I must congratulate you on your work, Detective,' Ingrid said, her mouth curling into a smirk. 'It's a pity nothing will come of it. All your so-called evidence is circumstantial and easily accounted for by a good barrister. Also, this is a corrupt town ... a very corrupt town, and you don't have the backing of your superiors or your colleagues. They would rather sweep your work under the carpet than investigate one of their own.'

'I came here hoping you would do the right thing by the families of Pat Martin, Doug Haywood and Rob Charles, and confess,' Kate said. 'Recognise the pain you have caused them ...'

'Pain? Pain? You know nothing about pain. Do you know what it was like being raised by nuns?' shouted Ingrid, trembling with hatred for this woman before her. She took a drag of her cigarette, exhaling onto Kate's face.

'You must hate your life,' Ingrid said. 'All those late nights and weekend shifts, writing reports, the tedious footslog along abandoned streets, dealing with lowlife scum, surrounded by male chauvinist pigs with their Friday night dirty jokes, and all this time wondering what he meant about saving the boy. You may never know, but it will nag on the edges of your mind for the rest of your life. Maybe he rebuked you for not saving the baby girl thrown from the car. Yes. A rebuke. You made a big mistake following your daddy into the police force.'

Kate turned white, her mouth opening, her bottom lip quivering. Ingrid smiled.

Kate trembled, tears ready to fall.

Out of the silence, the cuckoo clock chimed the hour.

'I believe that clock is ticking for you, Detective. With no man, you don't have long now.'

The slap caught Ingrid by surprise, her right cheek reddening and throbbing as she looked up at the young detective rising to her feet and breathing rapidly.

'I don't know who you are or what powers you possess, but I'm going to stop you, if it's the last thing I do. You may fool half this town, but you don't fool me. You're a murderer and a whore.'

'Wait till your inspector hears about this. An officer must follow the rules.'

'Oh yeah?' scoffed Kate. 'Don't count on it.'

Kate turned to leave.

'Detective,' said Ingrid. Kate stopped. 'You don't have the guts to be a police officer.'

CHAPTER TWENTY-THREE

THE DREAMS OF INGRID SYMES

Ingrid remained in the armchair and continued chain smoking, not noticing the growing darkness enveloping the room, or the cold pinching her skin, or the throbbing cheek from the slap.

I should have worn gloves when writing the prescriptions. Damn! she thought. *I need to think of a way to counter this loose end. As for the scarf, so what if I met Toby in the house? Is that a crime? They are small circumstantial pieces of evidence.*

She knew she needed to be careful. No more schemes. No more killings. She had the money. She could do whatever she wanted, as long as she kept her head down the police would not investigate. *They want to sweep this under the first rug they found. I'll invite the inspector tomorrow. Get to know him better. Yes. I wonder what he likes to drink.*

She would lay low for the next six months, then sell everything, and move to Hollywood. But not before throwing a party, and through sobs, declare how she couldn't stay. There were too many bad memories in Old Town. How they would feel sorry for her. Understand her circumstance. Wish her the best. *Yes, I'll put as much distance between myself and the female detective as possible.*

In Hollywood, she imagined being the greatest actress the world had ever known. She saw the petty actresses playing their pathetic roles badly. *I'm much better than all of them combined. Hadn't I played the role of dutiful niece, supportive workmate, and lover, flawlessly? No role is beyond me.*

But why a movie actress? Isn't life the greatest stage of all? And isn't this town, with its simple people, and the big house, the best stage to strut my stuff?

Why not stay and take over Arthur Symes' life? Why should I run away from the detective? Why should I be the one to leave Old Town? The detective needed to leave. Maybe have an unfortunate accident, she thought.

Yes. Yes. She imagined running Arthur Symes' business, continuing with the Friday night dinners and even include a Saturday dinner party. *I'll turn these into elegant events: themed, masquerade balls, Halloween, Friday the thirteenth affairs. I could invite a younger, more eclectic crowd.* She saw the town elite continuing to enjoy the free food and drinks the Symes household always offered.

But already she saw problems. *Would the town elite prefer my hospitality over Arthur Symes'?* She was no fool. She knew the men were not likely to respect a twenty-two-year-old woman. *Take the bribes, sure, but include me in their schemes?*

No. She would play them differently. She could play the vulnerable daughter in need of 'Daddy's help'. She could let them help her run the business, run the town, playing one off against the other.

But she saw problems with this strategy too. Their wives and partners. *They would see through the act. Women were more discerning in these matters.* She couldn't court gossip so soon after recent events.

Instead, she would stop the bribes. Arthur's game, not hers. Instead, she would hire an experienced management firm to help her run Symes. *Yes, that's the most mature and sensible course of action.* She would hire a shrewd firm with a brief to teach her everything about business and investment.

She could no longer rely on the bribes to council officials and the police to insulate Symes from its antiquated business practices. *Soon competition would come, and I'll need to be prepared.*

I'll install myself in Arthur's office as of Monday. Call a meeting of all staff for 9:00am. I'll close the business for this event. I'll make the staff assemble at the bottom of the office stairs. Then at 9:10 I'll open the office door and descend the steps wearing my Dior black dress, Christian Louboutin high heels, adding elbow-length ivory gloves to the ensemble. With my hair styled, every eye would be on me. The girls envious and admiring, the boys lustful and desirous, eyeing the curve of my body as I descended. The chink, chink of my high heels on metal ringing out as I made my way to the bottom. The assembled mass would part to reveal Toby, seated, his hands tied to the chair, tears falling from his eyes.

'Please forgive me Ingrid. I love you. I've loved you ever since I first cast eyes upon you.'

Ingrid would run her hand through his hair. With a delicate caress of her gloved fingers, she would wipe the tears from his cheeks.

'You had your chance Toby Zachariah, but now you must die.'

Tiny would appear carrying a black velvet pillow with a diamond-encrusted button. On top of the pillow is a pallet knife. She would take it in her hand. The wooden handle is smooth, the blade polished, winking in the store lights.

She grips it tightly and brings it close to his face. He looks at the blade and shakes. 'Please, let me worship you, Ingrid.'

She brings her lips to his and kisses him gently as she thrusts the knife into his abdomen and twists.

'I love you too, but you defied me and must now pay the price as the sacrifice of my ambition.'

His lovely blue eyes widen in shock before flaming out into a cold lifeless stare. She would rip out his heart and, with the assembled staff cheering, spread his blood all through the building to appease the spirit of life. *Isn't that what we all do every day? Sacrificing life so others may live?*

The scene changes.

She turns one way then the other, admiring her two-piece strapless ivory lace wedding gown with long tail in a full-length mirror.

Arthur Symes stands at the door in top hat and tails.

'You look wonderful,' he says.

She takes his arm lovingly as he leads her through the high wooden door into a stone church, her body trembling with anticipation. Arthur Symes leads her up the aisle, people packed on either side. In the distance she sees the groom. Her heart begins to flutter as she smiles at individuals she knows in the congregation.

At the altar, Arthur Symes gives her hand to the groom: Toby Zachariah.

Next, she sits in a rocking chair in a dressing gown. In her arms lies a sleeping baby. How she marvels at the tiny fingers tucked beneath its chin in prayer, the delicate lashes, the plump cheeks as she rocks the baby gently. She sings softly to it as she feels an arm across her shoulder and a warm body squeezing next to her in the rocking chair. It's Toby.

The melody of Smokey Robinson's 'Being with You' floats on the breeze.

'It was so much easier to think of you, Toby, as I made love to Rob and Doug. It made it so much easier to play the part of the enthusiastic lover. You realise now why I killed them, Toby. Why they had to die. I killed them for you, Toby. Yes, I killed them so we could be together. I killed them because … because … I love … I love you. Toby Zachariah, I love you.'

Her heart beat so loud she thought it might explode. It beat so loud she heard its discordant rhythm in her ears. Bang. Bang. Bang.

* * *

Ingrid woke with a start and sat upright in her seat, shivering. A loud knocking came from the kitchen. She had dozed in the armchair. The room was dark and cold, and a full moon hung like a pearl, smiling.

'Oh my god! I'm in love with Toby Zachariah,' she whispered to the moon. Bang. Bang. Bang.

As reality reassembled around her, she realised someone was knocking on the kitchen door. She rose stiffly, and disorientated, staggered into the kitchen and opened the backdoor.

'I came back to see how you are, Ingrid,' said Jack Harris, his few remaining hairs uncombed, his eyes bloodshot.

'I'm fine,' she said, wiping away the sleep.

'Good.' he said, breathing rapidly and taking both her hands. 'I know about the prescription pad and the drugs. The detective interviewed me. I promise on my life to say it was me who filled out the prescription. I would sooner go to prison than see you accused.'

Ingrid stiffened, then smiled.

'I can help you with your addiction, Ingrid. I will do whatever it takes to see you get the best treatment.'

'Jack, Jack,' she repeated, not knowing what to say.

'Ingrid, I know this isn't a good time.' He squeezed her hands. 'I feel as if I am crossing a line as your doctor, and your uncle only just passing, but I cannot contain my feelings any longer. I feel as if I might burst if I don't say something Ingrid.'

He breathed rapidly, and stuttering said, 'I love you. There, I've said it. I know it's highly inappropriate. I know I'm old enough to be your father, but I don't know what else I can do. I can't sleep. I can't eat. I can't do anything but think of you. I can't even tell my sister. I'm a wreck, Ingrid. I'm a wreck. You know there is nothing I wouldn't do for you.'

'Oh Jack.' Ingrid smiled and squeezed his hands back.

The phone rang.

'I should answer it,' Ingrid said, glad of the interruption.

In her uncle's poky office, she picked up the phone. 'Hello, is Arthur Symes there?'

'I'm sorry, he isn't.'

'This is McKenzie's Land Clearing. Can you tell Mr Symes we will begin removing the scrub between Symes and the sea tomorrow? But we need to store our equipment in the bottom carpark at Symes.'

'You're clearing the mangrove swamp?'

'Yeah, for the proposed marina. My boys will begin survey work in there tomorrow.'

'The shack!'

'Excuse me, love?'

'Yes. Yes. Arthur Symes gives his permission for you to put your equipment there.'

'Great. Thanks.'

She hung up.

'Are you okay?' said Jack at the office door.

'I'm fine but I need to be alone right now Jack.'

'I understand, but I need to know where I stand,' he said. 'Am I being an old fool?'

'I think I love you too, Jack. I know I need you now more than ever. But I … if you love me, you must give me time and space to think things through. It has been a trying day and I need to rest.'

'Of course,' he said, shaking his head, his eyes moistening. 'I'm a stupid man for discussing my feelings at this time. You're grieving. I will come back tomorrow.'

'Yes,' she said. 'And we can discuss your statement to the police.'

She ruffled the few remaining hairs on his bald head affectionately.

'You're a special person, Ingrid.'

'I know. Now go!' she said firmly, but good-naturedly.

Jack turned and left. She listened as the kitchen door opened then closed. She made her way to the front door, and opening it slightly, watched as the doctor drove away.

She slammed the door shut, and leaning against it, closed her eyes. She took one deep breath after another, trying to slow her beating heart.

I've won! I've won! The infatuated doctor would provide a cover for the prescriptions. Ingrid smiled. *What a stupid fool he is. What stupid fools all men are.*

Her eyes sprung open. *No time to think of the doctor now*, she thought. She had to move the money out of the shack immediately.

CHAPTER TWENTY-FOUR

THE COLD CASE FILE

Tears streamed down Kate's eyes as she drove into the empty carpark beneath the police station. She burst into uncontrollabe sobbing as soon as she parked.

'Please tell me what you mean! Please tell me what you meant!' she repeated. 'Please give me a sign. I beg you!'

Kate heard a car door slam and she quickly dried her eyes and checked her face in the mirror.

As Kate locked her car, a voice called out, 'Excuse me, are you Kate Trengove? Glen Trengove's daughter?'

Kate turned to see a rather burly, tall man with a thick moustache.

'Yes.'

'I heard you were working in Old Town. My name is John Davis. Detective Sergeant John Davis. I used to work with your father in homicide before he fell ill. He was a good man. I'm sorry for your loss.'

'Thank you.'

'Are you okay? You look like you've seen a ghost.'

'I've had a ... I've had a ... a tiring day.'

'Yeah, policing can be draining some days. However, I have something for you. You see, I've been carrying around your father's belongings for the last twelve months in the boot of my car in this box. I'm not sure why I never gave it to your mother Dulcie. Anyway, I only found out today that you worked here, and I thought you might want it. I was going to put it on your workstation. I only came to see the inspector. I'm off to Coffs

Harbour tonight.'

John Davis stopped speaking and peered closely at Glen Trengove's daughter. 'Are you really okay?'

'Oh my god,' Kate said, stumbling back to her car.

'There's nothing confidential in the box really. A few trinkets, trophies, several photos of you and your mother. Also, clippings from the newspaper on the cold case he worked on several years back about the girl in the upstairs closet. I also added to the collection a recent clipping from the local paper about a girl they found in a ravine in Austria. She went out hiking, slipped and fell. Her body remained buried under two metres of snow all winter. It was the girl from the cupboard. I hope you don't mind me adding to it. Your father was always obsessed with the case. Always said he could never shake the little girl's look from his mind.'

'Yes, he told me the same,' Kate said.

'Well, I better go. Your father was a fine detective. One of the best I ever worked with.'

John Davis stopped and peered closely at Kate. 'Are you sure you're okay? Can I call someone?'

'I'm fine. Truly I am, and thank you,' Kate said as she took hold of the red box in her trembling hands.

* * *

Kate rode the elevator to the main level, her eyes fixated on the red box.

'Ah! Detective Constable, where have you been? Interview room one. Now. We have the detectives from Sydney,' said the inspector as the elevator pinged open.

The inspector took a step towards the room then stopped and turned. 'Are you okay Kate?'

'I'm fine,' Kate said, taking a deep breath.

Kate entered the interview room and sat near the door without introducing herself to the two detectives from Sydney.

'It seems we have got you up here for no reason. Detective Constable Trengove can give a summary of the case. Detective Constable? Detective Constable. Kate. Kate.'

'Sorry. What?' Kate looked up from the red box.

The door burst open and Detective Tim Jackson entered. 'You won't believe what I have found from all the background checks I've been doing.'

'Ingrid Symes? What did you find about Ingrid Symes?' Kate asked, jumping to her feet.

'Nothing at all,' Tim said, waving the question away with his hand. 'Except she went overseas. Both her parents are dead. She went to Ladies Methodist College in Sydney.'

'Methodist Ladies College,' corrected Kate, putting down the box and snatching the manilla file marked Ingrid Symes. She began looking over the notes inside.

'It's Toby Zachariah,' said Tim. 'Or that's not his real name. It's an alias. The name he went by in South Australia was Toby Woolf.'

Kate looked up.

Tim continued. 'Yet even that isn't his real name. In 1985 he changed his name by deed poll from Toby Symes to Toby Woolf. Toby is the grandson of Arthur Symes.'

Tim grinned at Kate then the inspector.

'I've been looking at this all wrong,' Kate said, turning to address the new detectives, who both looked at her with furrowed brows.

'I've been looking at everything back to front.' Kate took the manilla folder and the red box, and turned.

'Detective Constable, where are you going?' said the inspector.

With her red box tucked under her arm, she said, 'I'm off to see the wolf of Old Town.'

Kate marched from the room, from the inspector shouting commands for her to return, from the police force, forever. She threw her badge in the wastepaper bin then travelled two steps at a time down the fire stairs and into her car.

CHAPTER TWENTY-FIVE

THE MONEY

Ingrid ran upstairs and grabbed her dark coat and an empty backpack she found in one of the cupboards. Grabbing her keys and a flashlight, she headed out the backdoor and down to the carpark, ensuring she kept to the shadows.

I'll bring the money home and hide it in the garage. No, better still I'll place it on the top shelf of Arthur's cupboard. I'll ask someone to help me clean out his things. They would stumble upon the money. I could claim he had stolen it for the insurance. Yes! I could lay the seeds before the find. I would tell several of the ladies from Friday night how my uncle wasn't concerned in private about the theft of the money. How in public he put on an act. But alone with me, he smiled and whistled. How he confided to me he wanted to make an example of Toby and Doug. How he nursed an irrational dislike of both men. With the money found, what was the point of the investigation into the robbery?

A full moon hung low in the sky as she passed through the hole in the wire fence and into the mangrove. She didn't need the torch. After so many clandestine trips she knew the twists and turns of the route by rote, the power of her sight magnified by all the nocturnal visits to the shack allowing her to see every branch, every stone, every stray twig in her path. She stepped easily around every obstacle, every dank puddle. The smell of the sea, of mangrove and wet earth, was intoxicating.

Her eyes and perceptions were sharpened; she sensed the many nonhuman eyes watching her passage. She felt at one with this mangrove, with the insects, reptiles, birds and predators. Especially the predators.

She reached the shack and for a moment she looked at it ruefully. It would be the last time she ever laid eyes on it. *What a sentimental fool I am.*

Tomorrow I'll invite Toby for afternoon tea and announce my victory. Maybe I could make him see we were meant to be together.

She moved the chair away and shone the torch down on the trap door. *With the money there was nothing stopping us from being together. I could pay for his medical degree. Yes, he would see reason. He would learn to love me. Worship me.*

She pulled up the trap door, and removing the hessian sacks, stared at the steel box. With a heave, she lifted it out of the cavity, and taking the three keys, began unclicking the locks.

Outside, a currawong perched on a tree and gave a soft plaintive cry, which cut through the droning cicadas.

She undid the last lock before taking off her backpack and placing it close by. *It would take several trips,* she thought, *to move all the money.*

She opened the box and looked down dumbfounded.

Instead of the cash, she looked down at white plastic bags. She tore at one. It was filled with sand. She put her hand into another. Sand.

Her eyes widened in disbelief as she stabbed at one bag then another with her fingers. She rose to her feet and ran about the room looking for another box, another reason for her loss. Her feet hit against something sharp. She fell.

She placed her hands to her head, and breathing rapidly, tried to fathom what had happened. She heaved the steel box onto its narrow end and ran her torch along its back. Black industrial tape held the back in. Someone had cut through and taken the money, replacing it with sand. *But who?*

Outside, a solitary crow laughed. Ingrid, on her knees, screamed. Her cry of anguish pierced the subdued quiet of the mangrove. All around, birds took flight, snakes turned and slithered away.

Ingrid beat her head on the floor. She wanted to tear her hair from her head. Instead, she screamed until she sobbed and rocked on her haunches.

'Who stole from me? Who? Who?'

She took the torch and swung it around the room looking for evidence, disturbance, the perpetrator. Her torch fell on a large pallet knife and a texta pen on the floor. She now noticed the subtle waft of methylated spirits in the shack. She threw the texta pen as hard as she could. It bounced against the wall. She picked up the knife and gripped it tightly. She swung the torch on the walls and noticed some writing.

She concentrated the light on the words scrawled in a big cursive hand:

'I have the money. If you want it come and get it.
The Wolf of Old Town.'

Ingrid stood looking at the letters for a long time, dumbly, stupidly. Her mouth was open as she breathed rapidly and shallowly.

Finally, she threw the torch at the words and screamed. The torch shattered into a hundred pieces. Birds and insects that had only begun to settle and chatter now took flight and scurried away for good. *The mangrove's cursed.*

Ingrid screamed again until she started to convulse. 'I've been double-crossed. I've been doubled-crossed.'

'Oh my god! Oh my god! Get it together. Get it together,' she told herself. She took several deep breaths then stood rigid like a Buckingham Palace guard, white and numb, every thought and emotion, like the birds of the mangrove, taken flight.

She stood staring at the wall blankly, as one word began to drum on the edges of her consciousness. Softly, then louder and louder with each passing heartbeat. One word, one name, beating rhythmically in time to her heartbeat, growing quicker and louder until it burst into her conscious mind, 'Toby! Toby! Toby! That son of a bitch Toby.'

She didn't love him. She loathed him and she knew where he was. The vacant house by the gym.

Ingrid made it through the mangrove swamp to the carpark without the torch. The dead face of the moon illuminated her path.

She made it back to Arthur Symes' garage and tried turning the ignition of the Monaro. It clicked rapidly, but impotently. She turned the key again. The motor clicked rapidly and noisily before dying.

She tried again. The engine groaned then died. She beat her fists against the steering wheel and screamed, then yanked on the steering wheel until it cracked.

Jumping out of the car, she slammed the door shut, the side mirror coming loose. She took a deep breath and began the walk into Old Town. In her coat pocket she clutched the pallet knife. She kept to the shadows, crossing the street if she saw another person coming towards her.

She walked through the deserted suburban streets, zigzagging down towards the gym. When she came to a house party, she diverted down another side street. After an hour and a half, she finally limped onto the main street of Old Town.

Outside the gym, she encountered three drunken males, no older than nineteen, turning from a side street.

'Hey honey, how about a kiss?' one of the boys slurred.

His friends sniggered.

Ingrid whipped out the knife. 'If you come near me, I will cut it off.'

The boys took a step back as Ingrid crossed the road blindly, pointing her knife at a driver who skidded to a halt in front of her and blared his horn.

Ingrid put the knife back in her coat as she reached the vacant house. The door was ajar and she entered. A soft light was on the stairs as she climbed them.

She found Toby seated in the armchair, eyes closed in the posture of meditation. Before him on the glass-paned coffee table lay the money stacked in an open suitcase.

'Who are you?' she cried out. The light bulb popped in the lamp on the table beside Toby, the room falling into darkness.

Ingrid momentarily shivered. Toby opened his eyes, looked at the lamp then Ingrid without blinking.

'Who are you?' she cried again. Everything in the room jumped except Toby. Outside, a streetlamp blew, a car horn blared into life then died.

'To understand who I am,' Toby began, 'we must first know who you are.'

Chapter Twenty-Six

Waking Alan Snapper Mills

Alan Mills was catapulted out of his nap by an incessant pounding on the front door.

'Okay I'm coming. I'm coming,' he shouted, rising stiffly from his chair.

'Who's there?' asked Edith from the kitchen.

'I don't know,' grumbled Alan as he shuffled into the hall, the incessant knocking starting again.

An agitated Kate Trengove holding a red box stood on the porch.

'I need to speak to Toby urgently, Mr Mills.'

'I'm sorry he went out after dinner, Kate.'

'Do you know where he is?'

'He didn't say.'

'I have the red box. It was me all along. I have the red box.'

Alan, disorientated from being woken abruptly, looked dumbly at the red box thrust close to his face as Kate pushed past him into the house.

Kate placed the red box on the living room table.

'I don't understand,' said Alan. 'What do you mean about a red box?'

'Alan, everything I'm about to say might sound crazy to you. I can hardly believe it myself, but after I interviewed Toby, he asked me whether I owned a red box. He told me an old man instructed him to tell his daughter to look in the red box. Well today I was handed this box by a policeman who knew my father at homicide. Strange incidences, graffiti on fences, signs on billboards, and I don't know what to make of it all.'

'Well, you can start by looking in the box, dear,' said Edith, who had come into the living room to stand next to her husband. 'That was the instruction, wasn't it?'

Kate tore off the lid and took out the contents. The typical office mementos filled the box: a golf trophy, pictures of her mother, of her graduating from the police academy, and as a young girl. A family photo from ten years ago. She took out a fat manilla folder filled with newspaper clippings.

'These are articles from the case twelve years ago. Of the man found stabbed to death in his bed. A robbery gone wrong,' Kate said.

'I remember that case,' said Alan. 'Your father was obsessed with it. He found a terrified young girl in a cupboard in her room. She gave a detailed description of the robber.'

'Here is the portrait of the robber, as given by the girl,' said Alan, taking a pencilled drawing from the folder.

Kate snatched the picture from Alan's grasp. 'It's too detailed. Too elaborate.'

Alan took the picture and looked at the drawing of a sharp-eyed man with wavy black hair and jet-black eyes.

'What do you mean?' said Alan after a time.

Kate did not answer. She collapsed into a seat, a look of shock and disbelief etched across her face.

'What is it?' he said.

She handed him a newspaper clipping from the Old Town Standard with the headline, 'Girl Falls to her Death in Austria'.

They read the article, which was about a young Australian girl found buried in the snow of a ravine. They found her in October. She had slipped and fallen from a great height and remained lost for over six months. Authorities identified her as Jenny Pistoria.

'It's the girl from the cupboard!' exclaimed Alan.

'Read the date they believed she died,' said Kate.

Alan read: 'Authorities estimate her date of death as being 4th February 1987 as it was the last entry in the pocket diary found on her body.'

'What's significant about the date?' said Alan.

'My father died on the fourth.'

Kate rose to her feet and looked at Edith. 'When did Toby die?'

'It was the fourth of February too.'

'Oh my god! All these messages. The graffiti, the billboards ... they're all messages from my father. He's been trying to contact me all this time.'

'Graffiti, billboards? I don't follow,' said Alan.

'Toby Zachariah is not his real name. His name is Toby Symes. He's the grandson of Arthur Symes.'

'What?'

'What if Toby came to Old Town to confront his grandfather? No.'

Kate paced.

'He came to worm his way into his grandfather's business. Seeks his revenge, but he dies, and on the other side he sees something else. He sees the future. He meets my father who wants me to look in the red box. Why? What has it to do with the robbery?'

Alan did not interrupt. He could see Kate was mentally a long way away, piecing together a strange puzzle, one beyond normal policing procedures.

'On his death bed, my father implored me to what? The boy will try to save the girl. He can't save the girl. He told me I had to save the boy.'

Kate looked at the red box, breathing rapidly, her mind spinning.

'Oh my god, he didn't mean children. The boy is Toby, and the girl is Ingrid. Toby is confronting her.'

'About what?' probed Alan, not following the logic.

'About Jenny. He knows Ingrid is ... Jenny.'

'I don't follow,' said Edith.

'Ingrid Symes went to a Methodist Ladies College. Jenny Pistoria, an orphan girl, was raised by the nuns.'

'I still don't follow, dear,' said Edith.

'My father was troubled by the young girl's look. Why? Why?' Kate straightened, her eyes wide.

'Oh my god! My father didn't look into the eyes of an innocent young victim, but into the eyes of a murderer. It's why the case obsessed my father. His instincts told him the girl killed her adopted father, but he couldn't bring himself to this proposition. Ingrid is the girl in the cupboard. No. No. Oh God, she's going to kill Toby. And she's going to kill him tonight and it's my job to stop her. Where is he?'

Kate shouted this at the red box. She shook it.

'Maybe he has gone for a walk, or to a friend's house,' suggested Edith.

Kate turned to Alan.

'Oh my god, he's gone to the vacant house opposite the gym! It's the abandoned house.'

Kate strode to the door.

'Wait,' said Alan.

'You can't stop me, sir.'

'I'm not going to, love. I'm coming with you. But let me grab a coat first. It's chilly out.'

CHAPTER TWENTY-SEVEN

REVELATIONS

'Ingrid Symes is not your real name,' said Toby. 'What is it? Cara, Carly, Karen, Katie, Jenny? Jenny Pistoria? But what is a name to you but a façade, a pretence to hide who you really are? An orphan who moved from one foster home to the next. Taught by nuns to love the Church, despise spirituality, but fear God.'

Toby sighed before continuing. 'You left school early and took one menial hospitality job after another, none satisfying your grandiose image of yourself. With the money you stole from your last foster home, you escaped overseas for an Australian rite of passage. A backpacking adventure through Europe.

'Was it in one of the youth hostels you first met Ingrid Symes? How remarkable it was to meet someone so like you, in height and looks. Why many people passed you off as sisters. Twins almost.

'Was it in the youth hostel you heard Ingrid Symes' story? How she too had no relatives in the world except for a miserly rich uncle. When did you decide to kill her and take her identity? It wasn't till you ascended high up into the Austrian Alps that you executed your plan. You took a hire car together. At the highest point you took over the driving duties. Did you lace her coffee with drugs? It was when you reached the top of the mountain, at a deserted lookout, that you stopped. With no cars on the road, you bashed Ingrid's skull with a steering lock. Then, dragging her from the car, you slung a backpack over her shoulder and pushed her off the edge, but not before swapping passports and identities.'

Toby stopped and considered Ingrid, who was staring at him open-mouthed, gasping like a fish out of water.

'How do I know?' Toby said, as if guessing her thoughts. 'At the very moment you pushed Ingrid over the edge and to her death, I died in hospital and hovered overhead, watching a scene I did not comprehend. I drove with you through the mist to the next town. Thoughts of gaining the rich uncle's money, uppermost in your mind, as well as your past.'

Toby stopped and closed his eyes. 'I can see that drive through the mountains more clearly than this room I sit in. I see the lucky dice hung over the rear-vision mirror. I see a stuffed koala with a broken nose lolling about on the back seat. That was Ingrid's toy as a girl. She told you its significance.'

Ingrid inhaled sharply and collapsed into the armchair.

'When the money ran out, you returned to Australia. How brave of you to pass through customs on another person's passport and travel to Old Town to face Arthur Symes. How you must have trembled when you stood before him for the first time, wondering whether he recognised you as the imposter you were.

'That's why I nearly fainted when I saw you for the first time. I recognised you from my near-death experience. I recognised the truth of what you had done, and what you were about to do.

'On the other side, I was shown not only what had happened, but what was yet to happen. I saw you planning with the detective and Doug in the shack. I saw the plot against me. I was shown so many alternative possibilities. I saw one, where your killing destroyed half the state. I saw also a young girl. A girl no more than eight years old, naked on a bed. Her expression was blank as a man, her adopted father, rolled off her.

'Is that when you learnt to leave your body and astral project? Have you ever wondered why you can read people's thoughts? Why the two of us have heightened psychic abilities? Don't you realise? You and I are forerunners of a new spiritual age dawning across the planet.'

Toby paused for a moment while Ingrid sat in the chair, white-faced and stunned.

Toby continued. 'Which comes to who I am. You guessed correctly the first time we spoke in this house before Christmas. I did not come to Old Town on a whim. I came to Old Town for a purpose. Not for any reason of greed, but revenge. You see, Arthur Symes had driven my father to despair and an early death.

'I came to Old Town to seek my vengeance on him. I wanted him to suffer like he made my father suffer. I wanted to destroy the things he loved. I would meet his cruelty with even greater cruelty. I would meet his remorselessness with more remorselessness.

'I joined Symes and bided my time. After work I followed him everywhere, plotting and planning. I wanted to worm my way into his life, then bring his world crashing down around him.

'What type of world rewards a man like Arthur Symes? What god allows a man like him to prosper, while great men like my father die alone and poor? What type of god allows it? I soon discovered Arthur Symes only loved the money in his safe. So, I decided I would steal it. I had no desire to keep it. Instead, I had fantasies of tying him to a chair and burning all his ill-gotten gain before him. So, consumed with hatred and thoughts of retribution, I failed to heed the nagging pain in my stomach, the nausea, the weight loss. Finally, a trip to the doctor, followed by a specialist, confirmed the first stage of pancreatic cancer. An aggressive strain.

'I was rushed to hospital but deteriorated quickly. On the operating table, I died and went to another realm.'

Toby stopped. His eyes became misty and he looked above Ingrid to the ceiling. 'There are no words in the dictionary capable of describing the beauty and love in that other realm,' he continued. 'Also, time does not exist as it does here. The events, if one can call them that, happened all at once, yet in no particular order.

'I woke in a beautiful garden where every blade of grass pulsated with life.

Everything sang praise to God, radiating out waves of love. The entire garden filled with the most celestial music. I was given a life review surrounded by beings of light. I was shown how my preconceptions, values and beliefs led to my sickness. I relived my life again and saw every action of mine, from not only my perspective, but of the person I interacted with, and the persons they interacted with. How even a simple smile can have such a profound effect. How every thought and action ripples through eternity.

'I was shown people like Doug and Arthur Symes as spiritual beings making elementary mistakes, mere children in the cosmic scheme. I saw the life of a young orphan girl. Moved from one home to the next, dreaming of escape and becoming a great actress. Abused and neglected, and who found comfort in daydreams. A girl who even killed with a hammer.

'At the edge of a pond, I met Jesus and we talked for decades about life and how I should live it. He threw stones into the still pond and I watched the water rippling to the opposite bank. The love He felt for me was so intense it was physical. There is no judgement there, Jenny. None whatsoever. You are loved Jenny Pistoria, no matter what you do here.

'I met a man imploring me to tell his daughter to look in a red box. I did not understand why, when I would never return to my old life. I wanted to remain in the light forever, but the beings of light, which remained with me all through my NDE, told me I had to return. I had a mission. Before I could protest, I found myself cast back to earth. They are the barest of outlines of my near-death experience.

'For two weeks I lay in hospital staring at the ceiling crying with pure joy. I had seen a world of beauty beyond comprehension. Mortal words cannot begin to describe the joy, the love there. But I found myself in my cold, heavy body, racked with pain, but also cured of all cancer.

'I had a mission, but what was it? As soon as I felt able, I started to speak about my experience. Firstly, to the doctor. But he said I was deluded and committed me to a mental asylum. I went to church to pour out my testament, but no one wanted to hear. The more I tried to explain myself, the more people ignored me. I returned to work but with new eyes, a new sensibility.

'As soon as I saw you, I knew you were not Ingrid Symes. I realised you to be the orphan girl from my NDE. But in the twenty-four hours you had been at Symes, you had wormed your way so effectively into Arthur Symes' world, into the affections of many at Symes, that I didn't know what to do or say. When I tried to broach the subject with Arthur Symes on your first Friday, he nearly threw me out of the strong room.

'At first, I thought I could ignore you. I feared that by associating with you I would fall into old dark habits. I was determined to forget this world. Retreat into the monastery of the mind. Occasionally, I tried to warn people about you. Yet every time I spoke the truth, no one wanted to listen. I tried to warn Arthur, and Doug, but they were so far under your spell that they became enraged when I told the truth. The more I tried to force people to listen and understand, the more they refused to listen.

'After Pat failed to heed my warning before Christmas, I left Old Town for good. I went to Alice Springs with the intention of never returning. While staying at a friend's house I had the most terrifying dream. I walked through the charred remains of Old Town, dead bodies everywhere. I walked up the hill to Symes, now a grotesque palace, with dark entities laying waste to the surrounding countryside.

'At Symes I found you sitting on a blood-stained throne, all around you the rotting stench of flesh. I woke troubled, but did nothing. I was determined to ignore it, yet the next night, a being of light showed me again the pond where I met Jesus and where we cast stones. I saw Jesus casting the smallest pebble into the pond, and I saw it ripple out across the still water and lap against the far side. I saw it push a stranded mouse struggling to stay afloat to the safety of the bank.

'I realised my mistake and what I needed to do. Jesus had been teaching me by casting stones into the still pond. For too long I had tried to force people to understand. I veered towards displays of grand gestures. Instead,

I needed to attend to the smallest events. It's not the major works, the grand gestures, or decisive actions of great humans that changes the course of history, but the accumulation of small incidental acts people perform daily: opening and closing doors for others, smiling at a stranger, passing a compliment. Life is the accumulation of little acts.'

Toby stopped speaking and closing his eyes recited. 'I speak to you through the dew of the morning. God. I speak to you through the waves of the sea. Be still, know I am God.'

Toby opened his eyes.

'I realised what I needed to do. I needed to attend to the smallest gesture, words, and acts. Be mindful of every small event and thought. Be present in the moment and God would speak through me. It was when I let go and listened, everything fell into place. I stilled and God spoke. He said, 'Go here', and I went there. 'Speak to this person', and I spoke to that person. I let God lead me. The proverb says: trust in the Lord with all your heart and lean not on your own understanding; in all your ways submit to him, and He will make your paths straight.

'Over our game of chess, I told Arthur Symes the truth about who I was and who you were. This time he listened and nodded. He wasn't surprised. In the beginning, he saw you as free labour to exploit. Yet over time he came to admire your boldness, cunning, ambition and bravery. Before you arrived, Arthur Symes was a joyless miser with a heart of flint. Yet through your attempt to manipulate him, you opened him to love. It was why I felt conflicted regarding you. I saw God working through you. I realised God works even through those most misguided and bent on evil, to bring hope and peace to the world.'

Toby smiled.

'Consider the book on public speaking you gave Tiny. I've seen the positive ripple effect of that present on Tiny's future in my silent meditations. You even awakened a new sensibility in Doug and the detective. You're like Faust's Mephistopheles, trying to do evil, but always ending up doing good, because God has ordered it so.'

Toby stopped speaking and looked down at the money.

'You may be wondering what Arthur Symes did to my father. You see, my father was the son of Arthur Symes; the one he threw onto the street as a teenager. My father never recovered from this blow. It did not make him stronger, only weaker.'

Toby looked at Ingrid. 'You're possibly too stunned to understand all of this, but there's one thing you need to know. Arthur Symes is my grandfather and the will stipulated the money is to go to his closest living relative. He wrote it like that knowing I was his closest relative and you were an imposter. He wanted to right his wrong.'

Toby looked down at the money again. 'As his grandson I'm his heir. All this, and all his property is mine.'

Ingrid's eyes widened. She shook.

'Arthur Symes' condition was, I was to look after you. Be your guardian angel. Ingrid ... Jenny, we need to put this money to good use,' Toby said, wide-eyed and intent on the young woman in front of him.

'Can't you see you have played the wrong game? The world isn't a world made up of matter, but an infinite and eternal world made up of spirit. You and I are forerunners of the new age dawning. Can't you see it, Jenny Pistoria? Can't you sense it in the wind? With your extra-sensory perception, your telepathy, you must sense it. Jenny. Humanity is beginning to wake up. This money could be used to help speed up the transition.'

A car screeched to a halt outside.

Ingrid shot to her feet and clutched the knife in her pocket. 'My name isn't Jenny. My name is Ingrid Symes. Ingrid Symes.'

Outside, two car doors slammed.

'The money isn't yours. It's mine,' said Toby. 'But I want to help you.'

The door downstairs opened, and the room echoed with hurrying footsteps on the stairs.

Ingrid did not hear it at all. She took out the knife.

'Ingrid Symes! Drop the weapon or I'll shoot.'

Ingrid turned to face Kate. The gun pointed at her face.

'You don't have the guts.' She turned and lunged at Toby with the knife drawn high.

'I said drop it!'

Ingrid charged towards the unblinking, serene eyes of Toby. *I will stab at his eyes until they can no longer see.*

Time slowed. Ingrid could see everything from 360 degrees: the open window and the fluttering curtain; the young detective at the head of the stairs, gun drawn, pointed first at her head, then the subtle drop of the gun's barrel to her chest; the bullet sailing across the room; an old man with white whiskers peering from behind the shadow of the young detective; a cockroach with its antennas twitching by the ledge. Her view narrowed on Toby, so calm and unflinching as if welcoming her knife attack.

She let out a guttural cry, ready to sink the knife in, when the bullet ripped through her chest. An explosion of blood, skin and bone. A loud ding echoed in the room as one bullet then another passed through her and ricocheted against the wall.

Her grip on the knife loosened against her will. The knife fell and clattered onto the ground as another bullet pierced her back. Spasms ran through her body as her knees buckled and her useless body crashed onto the money, then rolled with a thud onto the floor.

A piercing, unearthly shriek echoed through the room. Kate dropped to her knees and cupped her ears to muffle the shriek.

The lights in the room started turning on and off dementedly before the light bulb in the ceiling popped, showering Kate in glass splinters. Outside, all the streetlights popped. Sparks issued from the electricity wires. Kate trembled uncontrollably as something as cold and as sharp as a sword blade ran through her.

'Who's that?' cried Kate jumping to her feet. 'Stop, Stop!' She spun round, gun drawn and trembling as she heard a voice say, 'Shoot! Shoot!'

The room was darker than the dark side of the moon. Darker than the deepest cave.

'Go on shoot! Shoot!' The words echoed in her mind as if someone was whispering in her left ear. She swung around to face the voice, the gun twitching uncontrollably in her hand.

'Shoot! Go on, do it, you coward. Your father would shoot,' the voice said. A surge of anger welled inside Kate. *The bitch*, she thought. She wanted to shoot her into her hundred pieces, tear skin from her body. She tensed her trigger finger, but halted. 'What are you waiting for? Shoot!'

A voice inside Kate cried out, 'Daddy would.'

'No Kate. No,' Toby shouted.

Trembling, Kate lowered the gun. A gun only seconds before aimed at Alan cowering in the corner.

Another unearthly cry pierced the room.

Like an icy lance, it ran through Kate, knocking her off her feet. She felt something cold claw at her face, her eyes. She put her hands to her neck. She couldn't breathe. She gasped for air.

Somewhere in the dark a light shone. Toby's voice, clear and calm, called out, 'Ingrid Symes, in the name of Jesus Christ, I command you to leave.'

In an instant, Kate felt the presence besieging her dissipating, a smoke-like form rushing to the open window. A great whoosh filled the room as the windowpane shattered into a hundred pieces. Kate's view was obscured by Toby jumping in front of the window. A thousand shards penetrated his back.

Outside, dogs howled, car horns blared, terrified people ran onto the street seeking answers.

'What happened?' called out Alan, huddled in the corner. 'What just happened?' he repeated louder, trembling uncontrollably.

Toby looked down at Kate, and addressing her, and her alone, said, 'Ingrid Symes has left the house. She can't hurt anyone anymore.'

THE END

Thankyou for reading the first novel by Henry Larsen.

Please leave an appraisal of this novel on Amazon or at:
www.writecreativepress.com/contact

All comments good, bad and indifferent go a long way in helping the author.

You can contact the author directly leaving a comment via:
henrytlarsen@ outlook.com

For more details on upcoming books by this author please visit:
www.writecreativepress.com